I0780341

ONLY FOR LOVE

LEXI

HE TOLD ME HE LOVED ME AFTER A DAY.
I SHOULD HAVE SEEN THE RED FLAGS, BUT I DIDN'T.
IF YOU WOULD HAVE TOLD ME I WOULD FALL FOR A MAN WHO WOULD
SLOWLY TAKE ME AWAY FROM EVERYTHING I LOVED,
I WOULD HAVE TOLD YOU THAT YOU DIDN'T KNOW ME.
HE WAS WHAT NIGHTMARES WERE MADE OF.
I JUST DIDN'T KNOW I WAS LIVING IN THE NIGHTMARE.
UNTIL MY EYES WERE OPENED AND I MADE MY ESCAPE.
I WAS READY TO FIND MYSELF AGAIN.

KIRBY

FIRST TIME I MET HER I WAS STRUCK BY HOW BEAUTIFUL SHE WAS.
THEN I SAW THE FEAR IN HER EYES.
FEAR I'VE SEEN BEFORE, BUT WASN'T SURE IT WAS MY PLACE.
ONE CHANCE ENCOUNTER TURNED INTO TWO.
I DIDN'T WANT ANYTHING FROM HER, EXCEPT TO GET HER THE HELP SHE NEEDED.
WHAT I DIDN'T EXPECT WAS I WOULD LOSE MY HEART TO HER.

BOOKS BY NATASHA MADISON

Only For Series
Only For Tonight
Only for Love
Only for Her
Only for Him
Dream Series
Shattered Dreams
Forbidden Dreams
Buried Dreams
Stolen Dreams
Forgotten Dreams
Meant For Series
Meant For Stone
Meant For Her
Meant For Love
Meant For Gabriel
Made For Series
Made For Me
Made For You
Made For Us
Made for Romeo
Southern Wedding Series
Mine To Kiss
Mine To Have
Mine To Hold
Mine To Cherish
Mine To Love
Mine To Take
Mine To Promise
Mine to Honor
Mine to Keep
The Only One Series
Only One Kiss
Only One Chance
Only One Night
Only One Touch
Only One Regret
Only One Mistake
Only One Love
Only One Forever

This Is
This Is Crazy
This Is Wild
This Is Love
This Is Forever
Southern Series
Southern Chance
Southern Comfort
Southern Storm
Southern Sunrise
Southern Heart
Southern Heat
Southern Secrets
Southern Sunshine
Hollywood Royalty
Hollywood Playboy
Hollywood Princess
Hollywood Prince
Something Series
Something So Right
Something So Perfect
Something So Irresistible
Something So Unscripted
Something So BOX SET
Tempt Series
Tempt The Boss
Tempt The Playboy
Tempt The Hookup
Tempt The Ex
Heaven & Hell Series
Hell and Back
Pieces of Heaven
Heaven & Hell Box Set
Love Series
Perfect Love Story
Unexpected Love Story
Broken Love Story
Mixed Up Love
Faux Pas

Only for LOVE

ONLY FOR SERIES

NATASHA MADISON

One

Lexi

"GOOD CLASS," THE Pilates instructor, Chelsea, says as she claps her hands. "You guys did great!"

I smile at her and get off my Pilates reformer, walking over to grab the spray bottle; my legs buckling a bit after the workout I just did. I spray the disinfectant on my machine before wiping it down.

"Thank you again, Chelsea," I say, picking up my water and returning the spray bottle near the front of the room.

Snatching my keys and phone from one of the wooden cubbies at the front door, I head out into the Arizona heat. The sun is already scorching even though it's just a little before 7:00 a.m. I press the unlock button and slide into my champagne-colored Bentley, a birthday gift two months ago.

I start the car and pull out of the parking lot to head home. The soft music plays in the background, a classical number, something I never thought I would come to like, but with time it grew on me. The mountains in the distance fill up my view as I make my way into the gated community my husband and I live in.

Driving past the golf course, I pull in front of my black garage door and turn the car off, grabbing my stuff before walking past the four other garage doors, which are all closed with no cars parked in front of them. The first garage door holds Trent's everyday Land Rover. The second one holds his BMW, which he drives on occasion. The third has the golf cart he takes when he's going to play golf, and the fourth is the Rolls-Royce he bought himself as a gift. That one he only uses when he wants to show off. Walking past the windows I know are in my dining room, I see the shades are still drawn. I look down at my running shoes as I turn and walk down the white bricked walkway toward the front door.

I open the front door and put my keys on the glass table by the door next to a green-colored vase with fresh white roses. Something that is replaced every couple of days. I untie my shoes before kicking them off and placing them in the sliding door closet on my right and slip on my indoor slippers before walking toward the kitchen.

I pass the formal dining room on my left, where we entertain all of Trent's friends. The brown table with ten chairs looks more like it's a conference room than someplace where you would have your meals and enjoy time with friends.

The whole house has a museum-like feeling to it, something I've come to live with. I've grown used to the lack of warmth from both the house and our marriage. I turn left when I get to the big open space, going toward the kitchen and stopping in my tracks when I see Trent sitting on one of the stools. My pulse speeds up a bit not expecting him to be up at this time, let alone dressed and sitting at the island. The long marble island off to the left holds six stools. Two chandeliers hang over it with gold wiring. It's a dream kitchen. Beautiful, opulent, a façade...

"Morning," I greet him softly. "I didn't know you would be up so early." I walk over and kiss his cheek. He's already dressed in black dress pants and a white button-up shirt, the smell of his aftershave lingers. His black hair is cut perfectly since he goes every two weeks to have it trimmed. It's also styled perfectly without a hair out of place.

"Is that why you snuck out of the house?" he asks, picking up his cup of coffee from beside him as he scrolls on his massive iPad, reading the news.

"I didn't sneak out of the house." My hand moves over the top of the granite island counter gently, feeling the coolness of it, before I pull open one of the fridge doors. I grab the fresh pineapple and strawberries before walking to the butler's pantry behind the wall of the kitchen. I make my protein shake, adding in half a banana, before walking back out and taking a sip of it.

"Where did you go?" he asks me, not taking his eyes off the iPad.

"I went to the six a.m. Pilates class," I tell him and his eyes look up at me, before giving the top half of me a look up and down. The frown on his face telling me what I already know. The outfit is going in the donate pile as soon as I wash it.

"Dressed like that?" he asks me. I look down at the white workout T-shirt I have on that shows my black sports bra underneath it and matching black tights. "You're just giving it away for free now." He shakes his head.

"It's a class full of women." I take a sip, looking down at the outfit I bought two weeks ago, thinking it would look nice with my skin tone.

"I thought I told you to do the private classes here." His voice is calm. "You have that whole workout room. I bought you the reformer and everything. Wouldn't it be so much easier for you if you just did them here? You wouldn't need to leave the house. It's better to have one-on-one classes anyway, isn't it?"

"She couldn't get me in this week," I reply.

"Then find someone else," he states, not leaving room for a response, and I just nod my head. "Besides, I don't think what she is doing is helping you. You seem a bit pudgy these days." The lump forms in my throat. "You shouldn't even be drinking that shake, it's full of sugar." He sighs. "I thought we discussed this already, and you said you would be going back on the diet that works for you."

"I weigh the same thing I do every single day," I inform him, knowing it'll just piss him off.

"Well, your scale must be broken." He pushes away from the island and comes over to me, grabbing the protein shake and dumping it into the sink. "No sugar, no carbs," he orders. "It's not good for you and makes you puffy."

"Okay," I reply, not willing to argue with him. Instead, I walk over to the fridge and grab the eggs out of it. "Why are you up so early?"

"I have to go to work so you can afford to not go to work," he snaps at me. "I have surgery at eight."

"That's earlier than usual," I respond, grabbing a pot. "I have a meeting with Cheryl this morning at ten." I mention the head of the fundraising committee for the hospital where he's the head of neurosurgery. "We are doing the final touches on the charity auction we are doing next month." He sits back down on his stool. "It's a bachelor auction," I tell him, as if he's listening to me. "I was thinking of reaching out to some of my cousins to see if they would…" I trail off when he looks up at me.

"You will not." He shakes his head. "I have an image to uphold and having your scrappy hockey player relatives coming to my place of work isn't a good look. Some of them don't even have teeth."

I shake my head. "That's not true," I mumble.

"Why don't you leave the bachelor part to Cheryl and you take care of the rest? If you are coming to the hospital today, don't forget what I said." I nod at him. "When you are there, you are representing me."

"I know." I put water into the pot and then rinse out the protein shake he tossed into the sink. "Do you think you'll have time for lunch?"

"Not sure. Depends on if anyone else is around that

I need to talk to." He pushes away from the island, meaning if someone else is more important than you, you can fend for yourself. "I'm not sure if I'm coming home tonight or not."

"Okay. Maybe I can come stay with you in the city, then."

"No." He shakes his head. "I have an early flight to New York in the morning, and we both know you disturb my sleep with all the noise you make."

"How long will you be in New York?" I ask him, again ignoring another dig he throws my way.

"Why? You going to take off again and not be here when I come home?" he snaps. He reminds me of the time he said he was going to be gone for two days, so I snuck out and went to my best friend's baby shower. Only for him to call me in the middle of it and tell me to get my ass back home because we had dinner plans he never told me about.

"I have too much to do with the auction to take off, so I'll be here."

He seems satisfied with my answer as he stops beside me. "Poached eggs are a perfect breakfast for you," he says cheerfully. "Do you need me to pick out your outfit for today, or can you do it yourself?"

"I was going to wear my white summer dress with the blue flowers on it."

"Isn't that one sleeveless?" He tilts his head to the side. "Your arms are not the best part of you." He smiles. "How about you wear something to cover those flappy arms. Besides, you aren't going for tea; it's a meeting, you dress accordingly."

"Okay, I'll wear the green pencil skirt with the white wraparound cotton shirt," I tell him and he smiles.

"That sounds beautiful." He nods. "Now, don't forget to put your best foot forward." He kisses me. "Have a good day."

I nod at him as he grabs his iPad and walks out the front door. The pot of water is boiling on the stove now, and I think about making the poached egg but opt to not eat anything and grab a cup of coffee instead.

Settling in with my cup of coffee, I make my round of texts to my family members.

I text my father first.

Me: Hey, Dad, just touching base. Hope you and Mom are well.

I press send before I tell him how much I miss him some days, and pull up the text thread with Ariella, my best friend. I speak to her more than anyone because she is the one who asks me the least questions, and I don't have to lie to her constantly.

Me: How is baby Jagger? Send me some cute pictures.

I smile before pulling up the text thread with my sister, Zara, and the last time she messaged me was two weeks ago. She sent me pictures of the twins, and I had a small breakdown at how big they have gotten and then hated myself for not being around more.

My last message to her was me telling her I hoped I could visit soon. Trent won't approve, but I should still try.

Grabbing my cup of coffee, I walk up the stairs and toward my bedroom. Trent and I have had separate bedrooms for the last three years. He just couldn't sleep properly with me in the bed. Apparently, I tossed and turned too much and woke him each time. So we have bedrooms at the opposite ends of the house.

Walking in, I see the bed already made since I make it as soon as I get up. I start the shower and take off my gym clothes, putting them in the donate pile that I make once a month, before stepping into the shower. It's always full of the clothes Trent doesn't like me to wear.

I take my time doing my hair, parting it in the middle and then smoothing it down. I got my black hair from my mother, who has the same color. I tuck it behind my ears before doing my soft, everyday makeup. My crystal-blue eyes pop even more when I apply the black mascara.

Stepping into my walk-in closet, I see all my clothes tucked away neatly behind see-through cupboard doors to keep the dust off them. All my clothing is sorted by type and then by color. I walk over to the middle of the room and grab a matching white-bra-and-panty set before I slip the green skirt on. I zip up the side zipper before grabbing the white shirt and tying it in a bow on the side. I then go to grab the pair of sky-high nude pumps I usually wear, with a peep toe since it's summer outside.

By the time I switch my things into a matching-colored Hermes bag, I'm right on schedule. My car is still outside and it's even more ridiculously hot out, so I start the car and leave the door open for a second before getting in.

My stomach rumbles as I make my way over to the hospital and I think about stopping and quickly grabbing some egg whites from the local coffee shop, but then I might be late and I will never, ever risk being late. I pull up to the hospital and scan the visitor card I use.

Holding my purse in my hand, I walk into the hospital, the cool air hitting me right away. The atrium is filled with plants and the ceiling is all windows, making it extra bright and cheery. I make my way toward the elevator, but stop when I see Cheryl standing laughing with someone. His back is to me, but he's wearing jeans and a white T-shirt. I can see he has tattoos on his arms. Cheryl spots me over the stranger's shoulder, and I can hear her softly say, "There she is."

I put on the smile I have to have on. The smile I'm trained to have when I'm in the hospital or anywhere around Trent or his friends. It happens in slow motion, or maybe that's the way I think it happens in my head. Everything around me stops, feeling like even the people stop in their tracks. The sound of my own heartbeat thumps in my ears when I see his side profile and the smile on my face almost falters, but I quickly recover it.

"Kirby, I'd like for you to meet my co-chair," Cheryl says with glee. "Lexi Yoder."

Two

KIRBY

I TURN MY head and I'm having an out-of-body experience when I see her. I feel like I'm being kicked in the stomach as I watch her walk across the room. She looks just as perfect as the first time I saw her at my best friend's baby shower. Her green skirt sways side to side just past her knees, and her white top is tied around her tiny waist. I swear, the only things I can hear are the clicking from her sky-high heels and the shallow breathing coming from my chest.

"I'd like for you to meet my co-chair," Cheryl says with her head high. "Lexi Yoder."

"Lexi," I say her name and stare into her eyes, and just like the first time, I feel like everything has left my body. The nerves hit me right away. My heartbeat picks up, feeling like I'm on the treadmill going a million miles a minute. My palms get a bit sweaty while the back of my neck feels like the sun is burning into it. I shake my head. "This is a surprise." I extend my hand to her instead of kissing her cheek, which is what I would like to do.

"Kirby," she says, reaching out her hand, a smile plastered on her face, and her eyes shield any emotion she might have.

"What are you doing here?" she asks and then she shakes her head. "I'm sorry, that question is rude."

"Not rude at all." I put my hands in my pockets before I do something stupid like try to touch her. "I'm from Phoenix. You?"

"My husband works in this hospital. He is the head of neurosurgery," she replies, mentioning her husband and his title. "Nice to see you again."

"Wait, you two know each other?" Cheryl asks, looking from me to Lexi, who stands with both her hands holding her together in front of her.

"We share a two-month-old nephew. My best friend is married to her best friend," I reply, mentioning Jaxon and Ariella.

She smiles at Cheryl, avoiding looking back at me. "Well then, this is fantastic news. I've just strong-armed Kirby to join the list of bachelors," she states. I can see the look in Lexi's eye flinch, but she quickly covers it up.

"Strong-arm is a bit of a stretch." I nod. "It's a good cause and I'm always happy to help."

"He's a very generous donor for the children's ward as well as—" I hold up my hand, making Cheryl stop talking.

"I don't think we need to bore Lexi with that." I quickly stop her from saying the rest. "I'm surprised you didn't get any of your cousins to come and join the auction. How am I the only hockey player?"

"It's summer vacation and I know how much they like their downtime, so I didn't want to bother them." The excuse flows out so easily, but I know she's lying straight through her teeth. Her family is the most generous family I've ever met in my life. Her uncle even runs one of the biggest foundations in the hockey world, and she has a couple of cousins who run hockey camps in the summer for young underprivileged players.

"Well, I guess I can make a couple of phone calls and see if any of my friends are in town." I look at both of them.

"I don't think we could ask that of you," Lexi quickly speaks up, and I can feel the tremor in her voice. "I think we have nine bachelors already." She looks at Cheryl. "Ten with Kirby."

"More bachelors equal more money." Cheryl raises her eyebrows.

"This is very true," Lexi tries to cover up. "We will take whoever we can."

"I'll make a couple of calls," I tell them, "and I'll let you both know."

"I can't wait!" Cheryl squeals. "You have my number." I nod. "And I gave you Jimmy's number too. He's the head bachelor in charge." She laughs. "He will let you know everything you need to know."

"I'll call him when I leave here," I assure her. "Ladies, have a great day." I look back at Lexi. "It's good to see you again, Lexi."

"It's nice to see you," she answers out of respect

before I turn and make my way over to the elevators. I press the button going up and then shake my hands to get rid of the tingling that started when she walked up.

As Cheryl and Lexi walk toward the other side, I shake my head. "She's married, you dickhead," I remind myself as I step into the elevator. Seeing her again was something I thought would never happen. I mean, chances are we would have crossed paths again thanks to Jaxon, Ariella, and Jagger, but I never expected to see her here. Just like the first time, her beauty literally took my breath away.

My eyes roam over Lexi as the elevator doors begin to close. She moves like an actor starring in a play. Every movement seems planned, thought out. Like she's not really existing in the real world. Her eyes are still just as guarded as they were the first time I met her. She looked like she was going to crawl out of her skin when she saw me. The ding sounds and the doors open, and I look forward, stepping off the elevator.

I walk down the white hallway toward the office I visit often when I'm in town. The door is open, so I knock on the brown door and see her head look up. Kylie immediately smiles at me. "Well, there he is"— she pushes away from the desk, walking around it and coming over to me—"my older brother."

"The best one there is," I gloat, wrapping my arms around her.

"If you are the best one there is, why didn't you bring me coffee?" She glares at me as she walks back around her desk and sits down. "The best one would have brought me coffee and a muffin."

I sit down in the chair in front of her desk. "Noted for next time."

"You said that last week when you came to visit me." She picks up her pen and taps the desk.

"I just came from practice," I tell her, even though the season is over, I practice year-round to make sure that I'm in tip-top shape. I do take two weeks off, sometimes more, but I always make sure to add a workout wherever I am. "I haven't even eaten anything, so why don't I go and visit with some of the kids and their families first." I point over to the door. "Then I'll take you for lunch."

"Oh, that's better than coffee." She rocks on her elbows.

"Besides, I have to still convince you to come and work for my foundation."

"You don't even have a foundation," she points out. "You have an idea to help people get on their feet after leaving abusive relationships."

"Yes, and you have all the smarts to make it bigger than just my idea." She rolls her eyes. "Kylie, no one knows what these people are going through more than you."

"Stop bringing up my childhood trauma"—she holds up her hand—"and my high school trauma. You act like we didn't both grow up in the same house, with the same stepfather."

"May he be rotting in hell," I add, smiling. "Actually, I think hell is a bit too good for the likes of him. What's under hell?"

"I have no idea, but I'm sure he's there." She leans back. "Now, if you can get out of here so I can do my job."

"Oh, by the way," I say, getting up, "I have tickets for the fundraiser they are doing next month."

"The bachelor auction?" she asks, her eyebrows push together and I nod.

"Dude, those tickets are a thousand dollars apiece," she gasps. "They have invited only the richest of the rich."

"Why do you act like you aren't sitting on a multimillion-dollar inheritance that grew twice in the last five years since you got it?" I point at her. "I also just got talked into being one of the bachelors, so I get the perk of two tickets."

"Oh." She laughs. "I know a couple of friends who would love to get into your pants."

"Eww." I wince and she laughs. "The last time I met a friend of yours"—I use fingers to do quotation marks—"she tried to tell me she could tie a knot with the cherry stem and then spit in my face."

She throws her head back and laughs. "It was a fifty-fifty chance. She's gotten way better now." She sighs deeply. "Besides, she can't afford that price." She points at me and winks. "But if you come on down to the local bowling alley, I'm sure someone would bet up to a hundred dollars for you." I laugh at her and turn to walk out. "I might need a dress."

"So go buy a fucking dress," I bark. "You have a credit card I gave you to use."

"I'm saving it for a rainy day," she bites back at my retreating form.

"Well, it's raining." I look over my shoulder. "Go get a dress."

I walk back to the elevator and head up to the pediatric floor. I pose for a couple of pictures as I meet with different families and talk about their struggles. I sit with a funny four-year-old who is battling stage 4 brain cancer, and my heart aches for her and her family.

My head is down when I walk out of the wing toward the elevators and I look up, seeing Cheryl and Lexi standing there, talking to a man with a white coat. A doctor for sure. "There he is, the star of the day."

"Dr. Visabell"—she looks to the doctor—"this is Kirby Materson," she says and I reach out my hand. "Dr. Visabell is the chief of surgery."

"It's a pleasure to meet you, Mr. Materson," he responds with a smile.

"The pleasure is all mine," I reply, looking at him and then glancing at Lexi, who has the same fake smile plastered on her face that she had before.

"We were just going over a couple of things for the auction and we thought about the best idea," Cheryl says. "Well, Lexi did." She gives her the credit and Lexi looks down at the floor instead of taking the praise. "A choreographed dance. Something like the waltz."

"Oh my." I laugh. "You thought of that?" I ask Lexi, who looks up and laughs.

"I just thought it would be nice to have the winner dance with her date," she explains and shrugs and then looks over my shoulder, and I can see right away that fear seeps into her. She quickly masks it and her smile fills her face. "Honey," she says and I look over to see a man walking out of the swinging door. He's wearing blue scrubs; his hair looks like he just styled it. He looks up, seeing Lexi, and I notice something in his face, but then he quickly looks at Dr. Visabell and his whole demeanor changes.

"I was just looking for you," he says to Lexi, coming over and bending to kiss her lips, then looks up at Dr. Visabell. "George," he greets, nodding at him, "nice to see you on my floor."

"I had a meeting with these two lovely ladies to discuss the auction," he replies.

I stand here waiting for him to look at me, and he finally does. "Hi, I'm Kirby." I hold out my hand for his and he reluctantly takes it.

"Dr. Yoder," he mentions his professional name like I'm his patient or something. I immediately dislike him; I've grown up my whole life with people like him.

"Have you two not met before?" Cheryl asks.

"No, we haven't had the pleasure," I reply. "I met Lexi at Ariella's baby shower." I see him look at her. "I'm Jaxon's teammate."

"Of course," he says, looking me up and down, the disdain for me written all over his face.

"Kirby is going to be going up for auction," Cheryl announces.

"Is that so?" he says, side-eyeing his wife.

"Cheryl asked him," Lexi quickly relays, and I want

to punch him in his fucking throat. "They were talking when I got here."

I reach for my phone and slap my jeans. "I must have forgotten my phone. Dr. Visabell, it was a pleasure," I say to the man and then look at Lexi's husband. "Nice to meet you." I refuse to say his name before I walk away and head back toward the pediatric wing.

"Hi." I stop at the nurses' station and the head nurse smiles at me.

"Are you looking for this?" She holds up the phone.

"Guilty," I say and she hands it to me. "Thank you for that."

"See you in a couple days." She smiles and walks away from me as I retrace my steps back to the elevator. I'm almost there when I hear voices.

"You made me look like a fool," he hisses and I know that voice. "Standing there flirting with that…that no-good-for-nothing thug."

I almost laugh until I hear her voice. "I was not flirting with that guy," she hisses in a whisper. "Besides, I'm too good for someone like him, and you know it. Why would I want to be with him when I have you? Don't insult me like that." My head turns to the side, and I see them in the corner, her standing in front of him. "Now, let's stop talking before someone hears us. Then the gossip will take over and you don't need that stress."

I move out of the way and duck into an alcove as they walk away, his hand in hers like she's his prize and her head held high right alongside him. All I can think of at this moment is how wrong I was about her. "What a bitch."

Three

Lexi

MY PHONE VIBRATES by my hand as I look down at the flower arrangement in front of me.

Trent: On my way back from New York. I'll be home by six, have dinner ready. I guess I'll have what you are having since we are watching what we eat.

Who is we? I think to myself since he has never once changed the way he eats. The pit of my stomach lurches. He hasn't been home for dinner in three days. The last time I saw him was at the hospital after he met Kirby. The memory makes my stomach burn even more. I close my eyes for a second, trying to erase the words I said, *I'm too good for someone like him.* Just thinking about them again, I cringe.

Me: I took out some salmon and was going to do it grilled with veggies.

Trent: Shouldn't you be eating white fish instead? It's better for you.

Me: I'll take out the cod and steam it. Would you

like the salmon anyway?

Trent: Sure, you have the time to do both. Taking off, see you at six.

"Sorry about that," I say, putting my phone back in my purse now that he's on his flight and I don't have to worry about missing his call or message. "Okay, so this is going to be the flower arrangement on each table." I look down at the mock-up table Mindy has prepared for me. There are five gold cylinder vases in front of her, the tallest on the outside and then going shorter to the middle and then working their way back up. She has calla lilies in two of them and then roses in the other three. "What if we put only four vases?" I question, taking one off and then start filling the other four vases with more flowers. "It's less on the table since there will also be a bucket of champagne, and then using the same amount of flowers, the vases look fuller."

"That actually looks better," she agrees. "We can take off more vases and redistribute the flowers and your cost will go down without the extra vases."

I smile at her. "Music to my ears," I tell her. "Now, let's look at cutlery."

It takes about two hours to figure out all the little details, with Mindy telling me she's going to do a mock-up of everything we changed and email me the pictures.

I put on my sunglasses before stepping out into the scorching sun and walking to my car. The phone rings from my purse and I quickly reach for it and see Cheryl is calling me. "Hi, Cheryl," I answer, putting the phone to my ear as I pull open the car door and get in. "Did you get the pictures I sent?"

"I did," she confirms and I can hear her walking on her end of the phone call with lots of people. "It's stunning and looks so much better than last year."

"I think so too," I agree with her. "She's going to send me a full mock-up tomorrow."

"That's great. Listen, the reason I was calling you was because I have to call Kirby today to discuss what the auction entails, and I got my times mixed up with tomorrow," she explains breathlessly. "I have someone coming over to the house to go over the plans for the remodel, and I can't cancel on him. It took me a month to get this appointment and Harold will kill me if I push it more."

"Oh," I say, turning on the car and putting the air-conditioning on, "I'm sure you can call Kirby tomorrow."

"It won't take you that long," Cheryl states. "I'll send you his number."

"Okay," I reply, not sure I want to do it, but if I say no, she might think I'm hiding something. The last thing I need is for gossip to get back to Trent about him. "Sounds good."

I disconnect the phone and pull out of the parking lot, looking down at the center console and seeing I have about three hours until Trent is back. I stop at the flower shop, ready to pick up my white roses for the week. Stepping in, I see the pink lilies right away. "Oh my, those are so pretty," I compliment, walking to the counter. "Hi, Rhonda," I greet to the owner of the flower shop.

"Lexi," she returns with a smile, "I have your roses in

the back to be delivered in an hour."

"I was out and figured I would just pick them up. Can I also get two dozen of those lilies at the front?" I say to her and she smiles even bigger.

"Aren't they gorgeous? You know what? Why don't you let me put those in a vase for you and I'll send Henry out with them now."

"Are you sure?" I ask her and she nods her head. "Perfect, I can't wait."

I turn and walk out of the flower shop at the same time my phone beeps, and I see Cheryl has sent me Kirby's number.

I close my eyes and decide I'm going to call him once I get into the house. Parking my car in the garage, I then walk into the mudroom. I slip off my beige sandals before walking into the house. Stopping in my office, I put my purse down on the coffee table in the middle of the seating area before I sit down and call him.

I close my eyes at the same time the phone starts to ring. "Don't pick up. Don't pick up." I look at the clock and see it's just after four thirty, so he might be out or practicing or even playing golf. My leg starts to move up and down as the second ring starts. "Please don't pick up," I whisper, and when the second ring stops and then the third starts, I think I'm in the clear until in the middle of the third ring, he picks up.

"Hello." He sounds out of breath, as if he ran for the phone.

"Kirby," I say his name, "it's Lexi, with the hospital fundraiser."

"Lexi," he says my name and I turn my head to look out of the window, the nerves in my body making me get up to my feet.

"Is this a bad time?" I ask him, not sure what else to say. It's like I've never been on the phone before.

"Nope," he confirms, his voice is tight and he's not friendly like he was the last couple of times.

"Oh good. I know you were expecting Cheryl to call you to go over the details of the auction, but something came up and she asked me to call you."

"Is that so?" he retorts. "I would think that you would be too good to call someone like me." The minute he says the words, I feel like I've been kicked in the stomach. The hatred for myself fills in even more. I close my eyes and I want to crawl into the corner, knowing he heard what I said.

"Kirby," I say his name softly.

"Lexi, why don't we just talk about what you are calling for?" he suggests. "Cheryl said she was going to call to discuss what the whole auction would be like."

"Yes, of course," I agree with him. He obviously wants to get this phone call over with as much as I do. "So, as she mentioned, we have ten bachelors." I start at the beginning of the pitch I've heard her say. "There will be a bunch of auction items throughout the night outside of just the bachelors and there are also silent auction prizes."

"Where do I come in?" he asks me, and I hear the sound of slamming coming from his end of the phone.

"The ten bachelors will be auctioned off at the end of

the evening. You will dance with your partner."

"The partner I'm bringing or the highest bidder?" he asks his question, and I don't know why I assumed he wasn't with anyone.

"The highest bidder," I tell him. "After that, the two of you will have three dates to choose from, and then you go on your date and it's over…" I trail off. "Unless you want a second date. That is up to you, but not mandatory."

"Good to know," he replies and I don't know if he's making a joke or not.

"All bachelors are expected to be wearing a tux. I'm assuming you have one. If you don't, we can recommend a tailor who is working with a couple of the other bachelors."

"I'm covered." That's all he says. "Is that all?"

"Pretty much. There is the dance schedule that should have been emailed to you," I tell him, getting up. "Did Cheryl take down your email?"

"I don't think she did, but if you don't want to be bothered, I can text it to her."

"Kirby," I say his name. "I—" I stop talking when the doorbell rings.

"If that is all you need to tell me, *Lexi*," he says tightly, "I think we are done with this conversation."

"Yes, have a good night, Kirby," I state and he just hangs up on me.

"Well, you deserved that," I tell myself as I walk to the front door, seeing Henry there with my roses wrapped in brown paper and the vase of lilies in the other hand.

"This is pretty heavy," he mentions of the lilies. "How

about I come in and set it down for you?"

"Of course." I move out of the way. "If you can just set them on the counter in the kitchen, I'll take care of the rest." He does what I tell him and quickly exits with a smile.

I take the vase from the front and cut the stems of the old roses, putting them in another vase since they are still thriving, and place them on the coffee table in the living room.

I finish placing the flowers and decide to put the pink lilies in the middle of the island and smile at them with their pop of color before I start to make dinner.

I'm walking in from outside with the grilled salmon on the plate when the side door opens and Trent walks into the room. I smile at him. "Hey," I say as he looks over at me, giving me a glance up and down my body. Back in the day, this would make my stomach flutter, but now it just makes my stomach clench.

"What are you wearing?" he asks me, putting down his bag by the door. I look down at my cream-colored pants that are rolled at the bottom to over my ankles and the white high-neck sleeveless T-shirt I'm wearing. "I've been gone three days, and you couldn't dress up for me a bit?" He comes over and gives me a chaste kiss on my cheek before moving away from me.

"I'm sorry, I got home and got busy with the fundraiser." I put the salmon down. "I'll go change quickly."

"Don't bother." He sighs as he pulls open the fridge and grabs a bottle of his sparkling water. The sound of the bottle opening fills the quiet room. He takes a sip, his eyes going to the flowers. "What the fuck is that?" he asks, motioning to the vase of lilies with his chin.

"I got them today." I smile. "Thought they would brighten up the room."

"Take them to your office," he commands. "They don't go with anything in this room."

"I will. Dinner's ready to eat if you are."

"Good, I'm starved." He walks over to the table I set up while the salmon was grilling.

He pulls out his chair, sitting down in his spot, as I walk over with both our plates, placing his grilled salmon with roasted asparagus and peppers in front of him while my baked cod is placed in the middle of my dish with three stalks of asparagus. I fill up my glass with water and sit down before looking at him.

"It's good to have you home." I smile and he nods, picking up his fork and taking a bite of his salmon.

"It's good to be home," he replies.

"How was New York?" I ask him as my phone rings from beside me, his eyes flying to it.

"Why do you have your phone at the table?" he asks me, and I look down to see it's my mother calling. I press the side button to silence the ringing.

"I was setting the table," I explain softly, taking a bite of my own meal, "and I had the phone next to me in case you called me." I shrug. "I must have forgotten it was here."

"Dinners are our time," he reminds me and I look up at him. "It's time for us to connect again. Talk about our day."

"Yes, of course." I smile. "I want to hear all about New York."

"You know you're lucky you have me, right?" he says the words I hear about ten times a day.

"I do," I agree with him.

"Your focus should be on me tonight, especially since I've been gone for the last three days."

"Of course." I take another bite. "I'll turn off the phone," I say, switching the phone off, my heart feeling very heavy in my chest as I do it. The screen shows my mother not only called; she also left me a voicemail. The screen turns black and the back of my neck burns but I fight it, turning to him. "So, tell me all about New York."

Four

KIRBY

I PRESS THE button on the parking meter, waiting for the machine to spit out a slip. Snatching it, I pull into the first parking spot I see. I take my phone out of the center console and grab the iced coffee, along with the white bag that holds a blueberry muffin in it, before slamming the SUV door shut.

The sun is high in the sky and it's already burning my head and I'm wearing a baseball hat. I walked out of on-ice practice twenty minutes ago with my hair wet from the shower and it's already dry. I make my way into the hospital, the glass doors opening when I get under the sensor, and the cool air hits me right away.

I'm making my way over to the elevators when I spot her. She's standing in front of her husband, who has his white coat on. His hands are in his pockets while he says something to her. She's wearing white pants that go all the way to the floor, but fall just short of it because of the brown wedges she's wearing. Her blue-and-white striped, long-sleeved button-down shirt is folded and tucked in with a big brown belt wrapped around her tiny fucking waist. She has two gold bracelets on her wrist with a gold watch and that big-ass fucking diamond on her finger.

"I have a reputation to uphold." I hear his voice as she nods at him. Her hair is parted today like it was the other day, but it's tied in the back at the nape of her neck in a ponytail. "Don't embarrass me. You know your role here."

"Trent," she says his name, "I have a meeting with Cheryl and thought I would bring you coffee. I didn't think it would be that bad." Her voice wavers and she looks a bit uncomfortable as if she did something wrong by coming to visit her husband at work. She's saying what he wants to hear and I have to think if she maybe said what she said about me just so she could placate him.

"It's not bad," he says softly, holding the cup in his hand. "I just don't like you surprising me at work. We went over this. I like to know when you are coming."

"Well, it was a last-minute meeting and I didn't want to disturb you," she murmurs and she looks over and sees me. Her eyes flash with something before she looks back at her husband.

"Hey, you two," I say, stopping by them, not even trying to hide the smile on my face, knowing that he thinks he's better than anyone here. "Nice to see you guys here." She looks at me, not saying a word, and I have to wonder if she even knows who she is. Is this the real Lexi or was she forced to be this Lexi? "I'm here to visit with some of the kids," I announce, even though neither of them has asked, "and then I think we all have a meeting with Cheryl, right?" I look right at her, knowing she has to answer.

She puts one hand in the other. "Yes." She gives me a fake smile. "Cheryl and I will be meeting with all of you in an hour."

"Sounds good." I turn back to look at her husband, who is just watching. "I'll let you go save lives." I chuckle and smack the side of his arm, knowing he will probably fucking hate it. "The real hero of the place."

I nod to both of them before walking away, hearing her words again as I press the button to go up to my sister. *I'm too good for him.* I don't even know why I'm still harping on it a week later. I should care less; I've been called worse. Far worse by people who lived in my own house.

I step into the elevator, pressing the fourth-floor button before going to the back and waiting for the doors to close. My head turns to where I know they are, or at least were, finding them still standing there. He leans in and kisses her cheek and I have to roll my eyes. Who the fuck kisses their wife like that? She smiles at him and then turns to walk away. Instead of watching his wife, he turns to walk away from her and dumps the coffee cup in the trash.

I look down at my feet, trying to fight back the anger that is creeping up in my blood. Looking up when the elevator doors open, I walk toward my sister's office.

She's on the phone when I stick my head in, and she holds up a hand to say hello. Her eyes go big when I place the iced coffee on her desk with the white bag next to it. Her hands go into the shape of a heart. "I have you down for next Thursday at noon," she confirms. "I will see you then." She puts the phone back on its receiver.

"Who is my best big brother," she says, grabbing the coffee, "ever?"

"That would be me." I sit in the chair, taking off my hat and tossing it in the chair beside me, before running my hand through my hair. "Let me ask you something."

"Ugh, I know," she starts, grabbing the bag, "three thousand is a lot for a dress. But it's gorgeous and was literally made for me." My eyebrows pinch together. "If it makes you feel better, I bought the shoes myself."

"What the fuck are you talking about?" I ask her and she takes a piece of the muffin.

"I'm talking about the dress I bought on your credit card this weekend," she explains, leaning back in her chair. "What are you talking about?"

"I didn't even know you used my credit card. I also don't give a shit."

"Good to know, I should have also charged the shoes to you," she mumbles. "What has you all uptight and shit?"

"I'm not uptight." I glare at her. "Anyway, I have a question for you."

"Obviously, I'm a woman, so I have all the answers." She smiles at me and then winks.

"Do you think Mom knew Mac was a narcissist when

she met him?" I mention my stepfather, who came into our lives when I was eight and my sister was three. Our father passed away from a heart attack, and six months later my mother started dating Mac. The way Lexi acts around her husband reminds me of how we used to walk on eggshells around Mac and cater to his needs. How we would make sure to act the way we thought he wanted us to act. How we would say what he wanted to hear. How it didn't matter what we wanted; it mattered what he thought we wanted.

"No." She shakes her head. "She definitely didn't know. Did we know?"

"I figured it out in high school, I think," I admit to her. "We were so…" I snap my fingers to think of the word.

"Manipulated," she offers and I shake my head.

"Brainwashed," I correct and she shrugs. "Gaslighted is another word."

"Why are we talking about this?" she asks me. "We all got out from under him."

"Because he died," I snap.

"What difference does it make?" she questions me. "She met him six months after Dad died. She was lonely and Dad did everything for her, so she had no idea what the fuck she was doing. I love her, but she was a bit of a space cadet. Meeting Mac, she changed to make him happy, and along the way we changed also. The good news is, we all got out of it. Why are you bringing all this up again?"

I can't even begin to understand it. The last thing I want to do is tell her for the last week my head was all over the place, thinking about Lexi and wondering when she became who she is. Why she was so nervous when Trent was around and thinking about her reactions after he called her at the baby shower. "I don't know, maybe it's being home and shit." I get up. "It's fucking with my head."

"Well, don't come over here and yuck my yum." She takes a sip of her coffee. "It took me a year to come to terms with the fact that it's okay to cry when you aren't feeling well."

"I'm sorry, I should have—"

"You had no idea either. We grew up that way. I guess it was sort of cult-like. Worshipping him and making sure we never triggered him and always did what he said."

"Probably is," I agree. "I'm going to meet with the kids and then I have a meeting with the fundraising committee. Want to have dinner with me at my house?"

"Yes, I would like that very much."

"Love you," I tell her and she smiles.

"I love you more." I turn and make my way toward the pediatric wing. Spending an hour with them, I take a couple of pictures, less than last time, which is what I like. I get to color with one of the girls. My phone buzzes in my back pocket, telling me my meeting is going to start in five minutes.

When I walk out of the pediatric wing, I stop when I see Lexi's husband standing with a woman. He smiles at her, unlike the way he was smiling with his wife. The two of them share a laugh, and she turns her head to the side bashfully. "I only speak the truth," he says to her and then he looks up and spots me. His smile goes tight and he gives me a short nod, and I totally look the other way going to the elevator.

I press the button, waiting for the elevator to get there. "You seem to be all over this place," a grating voice says and I turn to the side, seeing him standing there, his hands in the pockets of his white jacket. I see his name stitched on the side of it, Dr. Trent Yoder.

"I don't know about that, Trent." I use his name, knowing he probably wants me to call him Dr. Yoder. "I'm just here for the summer. In a couple of months, it'll be time for me to head back to LA."

He doesn't say anything else as we both get into the elevator. He's a touch shorter than me, and where I'm buff and toned, he's lean. I press the second-floor button while he presses the first. Neither of us says anything to each other until the doors open, and I'm taking a step out. "Say hello to my wife for me."

I turn and smile at him with a little smirk. "Oh, I will," I assure him, fucking with him. His eyes go into slits before the doors close. "Asshole."

I make my way over to the conference rooms, seeing a couple of guys lingering outside. I introduce myself to them and they are all athletes also. There are four golfers, which is normal for this area. Two guys play for the NFL, and two are tennis players. I'm the only hockey guy here, again making me wonder why Lexi's family isn't more involved.

I look over and see Cheryl walking with Lexi at her side, the two of them talking about something. Cheryl looks over and sees us standing here. "Now if this isn't the hottest bachelor auction, I don't know what is."

My eyes go to Lexi, who walks over to a couple of the golfers. "Hi," she says, kissing one on his cheek. "How are you? How is your sister, Bernetta, and the kids?"

"Good," he replies. "How is Trent? I haven't seen him at the club in the last couple of weeks."

"He's so busy," she praises him, and I almost roll my eyes. "He was in New York at a medical conference last week."

"Busy man," he says.

"Shall we get started?" Cheryl urges us inside the conference room. "I know how limited your time is."

I wait for the other guys to head in and then I follow, stopping next to Lexi. "Your husband says hello, by the way." I look at her and her mouth opens and, fuck, if she's not the most beautiful woman I've ever laid eyes on. If there was someone who would ask me who the perfect woman is, I would say her. "I saw him in the elevator on the way down."

"Oh," she says, "thanks." I nod at her and walk into the conference room, sitting in one of the empty chairs closest to the door. Cheryl sits in the chair beside me while Lexi walks to the other end of the table. "Thank you all for coming, we won't take up much of your time." She smiles and sits down right when there is a knock at the door.

Trent sticks his head in. "Sorry to interrupt," he says with a smile, and seeing a couple of the golfers he gives them a chin up as hello. "I need to borrow my wife. I forgot an important file at home and I'm about to do rounds, so I was hoping she could go home and get it."

I swear I almost laugh at him, typical behavior from a narcissist. His work is always more important than anyone else's and he makes sure she knows it. "Of course," Lexi agrees, standing up. "I'm sorry about this." She avoids looking at anyone. "I'll try to get back as fast as I can."

"Take your time," Cheryl advises, as she walks out of the room.

I don't even know what the fuck they talk about, the only thing that keeps repeating in my head is the scene that just played out. No one else batted an eye at what happened, but not many people can see the signs. They can be so subtle you don't even know they are happening.

"We have the dance appointment next week," Cheryl announces. She looks over at one of the golfers. "Darryl will send you a reminder since he's the liaison."

"About that," Darryl starts, "I'm going to be deep in training." He looks around the table. "If anyone else has extra free time to be the liaison, I'd owe you big if you took it on."

"I'll do it." I don't even know why I offer, it's enough that I'm doing the auction. "Just tell me what to do."

"Thanks, man," Darryl says, "appreciate it."

"No worries," I reply, nodding at him and then turning around, trying to tell myself it's for a good cause, while the other side of my brain is thinking it'll be more time to spend with Lexi.

Five

Lexi

"AND GIVE ME eight," Chelsea instructs as I hold myself up on my elbows with my hands together, pushing the machine out and into a plank, and then piking back up. "Seven," she counts down the set, and by the time I get to one, my whole core is shaking. "And we're done," she says. "Let's start the cooldown."

"Finally," I pant out and get off the reformer, grabbing my bottle of water before lying on my back and stretching out my legs. I close my eyes, following her instructions.

"And we are done," she repeats. I open my eyes and take a deep inhale. "You killed it today." I look over at her as she packs up her stuff. "I pushed you harder than I normally do and I thought you would give in."

"No pain, no glory." I roll to my side and get up, walking over to my shelf and grabbing the disinfecting spray. "Thank you so much for coming."

"Of course." She smiles at me. "I'm sorry it was so early, but I have to teach at six."

"I'll take whatever time you've got," I tell her. "Let me know if you are available tonight also. I have a fundraiser coming up, and I need the help."

She laughs at me. "The help for what?" She grabs her bag. "You've never been in this type of shape before."

"We could maybe work on my arms," I suggest to her, thinking of how Trent wanted me to cover them up a few weeks ago, "and my shoulders. The dress I bought is a one-shoulder gown, and I could use the help making these spaghetti arms look toned."

She looks at me as we walk to the front door. "You are crazy." She laughs. "I'll look at my schedule and let you know. If not, I'll see you again tomorrow at four thirty."

"Amazing. I'm going to do another workout at eleven," I tell her. "One of the taped ones you did for me."

"You are going to have a better ass than I have," she jokes, opening the front door. "You could probably teach a class if you wanted."

I laugh politely as I hold the front door open, knowing Trent would never let me have a job, especially one as a fitness instructor. "Drive safe, Chelsea." I watch her walk out and only start to close the door when I see her car driving away.

I wait an extra second, seeing headlights turn into the driveway. Then I hear a truck door closing before I see him walking around to the front of the house. His white shirt is open at the collar and his sleeves are rolled up to his elbows, with his suit jacket in his hand. "What the fuck are you doing up at this time?" He moves into the door.

"Chelsea could only come and teach me at four thirty," I inform him. "Are you just getting home?"

"No." He scoffs at me, kissing my cheek. "I got called in for an emergency surgery." He walks into the house, not bothering to kick off his shoes at the front door. As he makes his way toward the kitchen, he tosses his jacket on one of the sitting chairs in the family room that no one ever uses, because it's the most uncomfortable furniture in the house. No, that's a lie. The sitting area behind the fireplace is the most uncomfortable.

"Are you going back to bed?" I ask him as he opens the fridge and grabs a bottle of his water.

"No, I have a tee time at six thirty. So I'm going to play a round and then head back to the hospital." I nod at him. "What do you have planned for the day?"

"I have a final fitting for my gown this afternoon," I tell him, smiling. "I love the dress."

"You didn't tell me you got a dress." He puts the bottle of water down on the island. "You didn't even show me a picture."

"I'm pretty sure I did." I try to remember if I did or not. "It's a blush-pink color."

"You really think that is a good color for you?" he asks me as I pull up the picture on my phone. "You are a little pale and it'll drag you down."

"I don't think so," I reply, handing him the phone to look at the photo of me wearing the dress. It's a blush pink that is off one shoulder, then it's ruched together at the chest. A gold-and-silver beaded belt ties at the waist and it flows straight to the floor.

"Do you think this style is good for you?" He looks up at me, handing me back the phone. "What other dresses did you try on?"

"This one." I pull up the picture of me with a darker pink, long-sleeved chiffon gown. The neckline scoops down a bit, but the whole top has light-purple crystals all along the front, and the sleeves go just past my stomach and then trail off. I don't mention to him that the whole back of this dress is open.

"Now this," he starts, "this is the dress that screams class and head of the committee." He smiles. "Don't you think?"

"I guess so." I grab the phone from him. "It's more expensive than the other one." I look down at the phone, swiping through the two pictures.

"That right there should have been your first clue, but you choose the one you want to choose. I'm just giving you my opinion."

"Okay, I'll call and make the changes today."

"That's my girl," he praises. "I'm going to go shower and get dressed."

"Okay." I watch his back walking to his side of the house. "Don't forget your files," I mention and he laughs, ignoring my comment.

Last week he came into my meeting and forced me to go home to collect his files that were here, except they weren't, they were with him the whole time. He said it was a slight oversight, but I knew better. He wanted to make sure everyone knew he was my husband and his job was more important than mine. And by everyone, he meant Kirby.

He comes out of his bathroom thirty minutes later, while I'm sitting down and having two poached eggs on a bed of spinach. "I have clothes that need to be dropped off at the dry cleaners," he states, "and I need you to make sure my tux is ready for your little fundraiser thing."

"Tux is ready, I checked last week," I tell him. "And I'll drop off the clothes when I go out to my meeting today." I don't bother telling him it's me going to a dance studio to make sure the bachelors are there and look proper. That would just upset him or make him find something for me to do so I couldn't go to that.

"I can't wait for this fundraiser to be finished," he remarks, annoyed. "It's taking a lot of your time."

"It's good for the hospital," I remind him, "and it'll make you look good too if it's as successful as I think it'll be."

"Always thinking about me." He smiles at me. "Why don't we go out for dinner tonight?"

"I'd love that. Anywhere special I can book?" I ask him.

"I'm golfing with a couple of people today, so let me ask them and I'll text you later."

"Sounds good," I tell him, taking a bite of my eggs. "Have a good round."

He nods as he walks out of the house. I finish eating and clean up the kitchen, even though I have a cleaning crew come into the house every two days. It's a bit extreme, but Trent refuses to see one speck of dust anywhere.

I walk back into my gym and decide to do a yoga workout and then another Pilates workout. I shower and get dressed in white capri pants that are tight on my hips, but then flow loosely all the way down, pleated in the front from the iron. I grab the dark-blue, sleeveless silk shirt with the ruffles around the shoulders and then opt to wearing my hair down and not tied back. I snatch a pair of nude platform wedges with an open toe and tie around the ankle.

I walk into Trent's room, expecting to see the bed unmade but it looks like it hasn't been slept in. I walk over to the side of the bed where he usually leaves papers that he accumulated in his pockets during the day, finding it empty. I turn my head to the side and see if he has his sleep pants tossed on the chair and find those aren't even there.

The knot in my stomach forms as I walk to his walk-in closet and see a pile of clothes on the floor, not on the chair like I asked him to put them, or in the bag that is hanging on the hanger. I grab the bag and start putting the clothes in it. I spot his white shirt with a brown mark on the collar. I rub it and it looks like it's foundation, I shake my head and put the shirt in the bag.

Anger fills my body and I pull the shirt out of the bag and place it on the chair where he dumps his clothes, with the mark on the collar showing. I know he's going to blame me again for it. It's always my makeup that dirties his clothes, except I stopped wearing foundation when the summer season started since it's just too hot for it.

I put the bag in the trunk of my car, heading straight to the dry cleaner before driving over to the dance hall. I park my car in the parking lot next to a charcoal Land Rover, a car I wanted but was told it was too big and bulky for me. I slip my phone in my purse as I make my way to the door, pulling it open and seeing the room empty with only one person there, Kirby. He's standing in the middle of the room, wearing another pair of blue jeans with a white T-shirt. With his tattoos on full display, his arms look tanned and golden. His hair looks like he walked out of the shower and just ran his hand through it. His head turns toward the door and his blue eyes find mine.

"Am I late or am I early?" he asks me and I look at the time on my watch, three steps into the room.

"You are right on time," I answer, looking around. "Did Darryl send out the invite to all the guys?" I pull up his name on my phone. "He is the liaison between us and you guys."

"I'm the new liaison," he states and I take a step back. "He says he's busy training or something, so I took it over."

"Oh." I try to hide my shock. "No one told me."

"It happened in the meeting that your husband interrupted," he fills me in, "when you had to run home." I swallow, trying not to let that dig get to me, but also knowing that I need to clear the air somewhat from what he heard me say.

"Kirby," I say his name, "I want to apologize for what you overheard." His eyes stare into mine as my heart hammers in my chest and I try to calm it down.

"It's fine, Lexi," he says. "It wouldn't be the first time someone thought that of me. Won't be the last."

"They would be wrong," I quickly add in. "We should never judge a book by its cover. We never know what the other person is going through."

"I guess we don't," he says and all I can do is nod at him, not sure what to say, when the back door opens and the dance instructor comes into the room. "The beauty has arrived," he tells me, coming to me, putting his glasses on top of his head, and kissing me on both cheeks. "How are you, darling?"

"I'm good, David." I smile at him. "How are you doing? How is Ivan doing?" I mention his husband.

"He's probably at home in his garden." He rolls his eyes. "Who do we have here?" he asks, looking over at Kirby. "A man with muscle." He folds one arm across his front and puts the other hand to his face, his finger on his chin. "So big and buff." I can't help but throw my head back and laugh when Kirby just smirks at him. "I'm going to have fun watching you wiggle those hips."

"I look forward to showing you that these hips don't wiggle," Kirby retorts as David turns his head to the side and shrugs one shoulder. "They have never wiggled in their life."

"Well, prepare to be fascinated," David tells him and then stops talking when the back door opens and five of his female dancers come into the room, while the front door opens and the guys all come trickling in.

"Don't you dare leave my side," I hear Kirby say in

my ear.

"Aww, what's the matter, Kirby?" I surprise myself by teasing him with the biggest smile on my face. "Afraid of what your hips can do? I'm sure you'll be fine."

His eyes are light and he just smiles at me. "Are you going to dance?" he asks me and I shake my head.

"Dancing and I don't go hand in hand, sadly," I admit to him, "and it's not for the lack of trying. I've watched almost every season of *Dancing with the Stars* and each time I think I can do it, I can't." I shrug.

"I find that very hard to believe," he counters, putting his phone in his back pocket. "You seem to excel in everything you do."

"Well, I'm here to say it's just an illusion." I fold my arms over my chest.

"I don't know about that." He looks around, his eyes dancing, knowing that his next words are going to make me do something I don't want to do. "I dare you to prove me wrong."

KIRBY

I WATCH HER eyes and see the guard she always has up slip away. In its place is a lightness I don't think she knows is even there anymore. A lightness that was probably there a while ago but has been dimmed because of the piece of shit she's married to. The type of man who needs to dim her light in order to shine.

"I don't know about that." I look around us to make sure no one else is listening and it could get back to her husband, hoping my next words aren't going to push her back into the timid person she is around other people, but instead let her have fun. "I dare you to prove me wrong."

She rolls her eyes. "Oh please, I dare you." She shakes her head. "You sound like my brother or better yet one of my cousins."

"Lexi," David says her name. "I want you to come here and be my muse," he adds, and she immediately shakes her head.

"Absolutely not," she retorts, "you have professional

dancers right there." She points to the group of women off to the side who are standing around waiting for his instruction.

"Come, come, come." He motions with his hand to her.

"Let's see what you got, Petrov." I use her maiden name and wait for her to correct me, but she just puts her shoulders back and takes a step toward David.

"David," she says his name, looking around, and the guard is back in her eyes, "this is…" She looks at the guys, then looks back at David. "I have two left feet."

"You do not," he scoffs at her words. "Who told you that?"

I can answer right away who told her that, but instead, I stand here watching her be scared of doing something that should be fun. "Now," David says, flicking his wrist and holding it up straight, "we waltz."

"Waltz?" Darryl questions. "That sounds complicated."

The guys laugh. "It's simple," David assures us as we watch him with Lexi. "Basic steps," he lists, looking at the guys, "box step, closed step, and a natural turn." He acts as if we understand. "We start with box step." He grabs Lexi. "Man starts with the right foot forward." He does the move and Lexi moves her right foot back. "Left foot slide to the side, right foot follows."

"Okay, that doesn't look too bad," one of the guys states.

"It's easy, now you do it backward," David instructs, "left foot back, right foot slide, left foot close." Lexi follows him elegantly. "We do it again. Ladies, grab a partner." I look around, seeing we are one woman short, so I stand to the side, not telling anyone I already know how to dance the waltz. "One, two, three," he counts, doing the first set. "One, two, three." He does the other set, then looks at me. "Come here," he urges me, calling me over and stepping out of Lexi's arms. "You can take my place. I will put my hands on your hips and guide you."

"Here we go," I mumble as I step in front of Lexi and she rolls her lips.

"You put one hand here." He takes my hand and places it right under her shoulder. "You put your hand here." He places her hand on my shoulder. "Then hold hands," he instructs us. "Perfect." He leaves us to go and make sure the other couples are all paired properly.

"Do you know how to do the waltz?" I ask her and she nods her head. She looks around and waits for David to come back to us. "So why did you say you don't know how?"

"Because I always end up messing up the steps," she replies softly, "and then I'll step on your foot because I have two left feet."

"I bet you don't," I assure her and she looks up at me, the heat of her hand searing through my T-shirt.

"Okay and start," David says.

"Ready?" I ask her and she shakes her head, making me laugh. "And go," I urge, moving my foot and she moves hers. "See? Told you, you're fine," I joke with her as we do the series of steps four times. I see a couple of the guys calling David's attention to them.

"Do you know this dance?" she asks me and I nod.

"I do," I admit to her. "My stepfather used to attend these fundraisers for the bank he worked with. He used to take us with him and I got forced into it." She smiles as we continue dancing. "How long have you lived in Phoenix?"

"It'll be about ten years, I think." She thinks about it. "I moved here with Trent when he was twenty-five and got his residency here. We thought it would be for four years, but he excelled here. He climbed the ladder quickly and became the best in his field."

"I bet he's the best," I mumble and she just tilts her head to the side.

"What about you? Why Phoenix for your off months?" she asks me as we waltz, and I even lead us in a turn.

"Born and raised here," I reply, surprising her.

"Really?" she says, shocked. "But there isn't even ice here."

I laugh at her. "My father moved here from New York," I tell her. "Started me skating when I was three. When he passed away, I made it a point to always skate."

"I'm sorry," she says softly.

"Thank you. He passed away and six months later my mother married my stepfather." I look into her eyes. "He tried to pull me out of hockey." My body tightens and she must feel it, her eyes search mine. "Said I could only play hockey if I took up golf. Golf, after all, is the all-American sport."

"I think that's baseball," she tries to joke with me, "or

maybe it's a toss-up between football and baseball."

"But deals are made on the golf courses," I repeat some of the words my stepfather drilled into my head, "not on the ice."

"He doesn't sound like a nice guy," she states softly. "I'm sorry, that was rude and I shouldn't have said anything." Her eyes search mine. "It was out of line."

"You're right, he wasn't a very nice guy," I admit to her. "We didn't see it though until many years later." I share a look with her, hoping she understands the meaning. "It was always about him and never about us. He was a hedge fund manager. Made deals with some of the important people. Lots of mergers made because of him and many of those were made on the golf course. Of course, he thought I would be following in his steps." I smile. "He passed away the day I signed my hockey contract." I chuckle, my hand slipping from her shoulder to the middle of her back, and I pull her even closer to me. "Even in his death, he had to take away one more thing from me."

"Well, you showed him," she says softly. "You are on the ice making the deals happen." She smirks at me. "Pretty sure there have to be some deals being made on the ice."

I smile at her. "I tried to make deals with half my team to make sure we beat your cousins, Michael and Dylan, a couple months ago. Asked them to make sure they did not kick our asses. I even made a deal with your best friend, Ariella, that if she had another baby and it was a boy, she would name it after me."

She shakes her head. "She really isn't one of my cousins," she shares and I stop dancing, making her step on my foot. "Oomph."

"What did you just say?" I ask her, confused.

"She isn't really my blood cousin," she repeats the words and I look at her because everyone knows the Stone family. "She's cousins with my cousins."

"I can bet if you say that in front of your uncle Matthew, he might have something to say to that." I glance at her and she just looks down, avoiding looking at me. "I've only met him a couple of times, but each time it was like—make no eye contact."

She laughs and looks up. "He's the best. He pretends to be this big bad wolf, but he's a softie."

"I dare you to tell him that to his face," I tease and she just throws her head back and full-on belly laughs. "I want to be there when you do."

"I don't think we'll ever be in the same room at the same time," she replies softly and I can hear something in her voice. It's a sort of longing. "But if we ever are…"

"I don't know when Jaxon and Ariella are getting married. I'm pretty sure we are all going to be there," I respond and she just smiles tightly. I have to wonder if she'd miss the wedding if Trent didn't want her to go. "You can do it then."

"We shall see." She turns to look over at David to see him talking to two of the guys.

"What do you think?" I ask her and she turns back to me. "Think we can incorporate a turn in this dance?"

"Oh, that's a little bit…" She looks unsure of herself.

"It all depends."

"On?" I ask her, getting bored just going back and forth.

"Are you going to go right or left?" she asks me, becoming stiff in my arms.

"I'll go whatever way you want me to go," I say softly. "Which way do you want to go?" I ask her to make her choose. Something I don't think she gets to do at all.

"Um." She hesitates. "I don't know, should we go right?"

I laugh. "It's not that big of a deal, and there is no wrong answer. You either go right or left."

"Okay, let's go right."

"Lead the way," I urge her and I can see her guard slip, and her eyes light up. "I'll follow your lead."

I follow her the whole way, and when she turns, she does it flawlessly. The smile on her face reaches her eyes for the very first time I've seen. It takes my breath away.

We turn around in a circle twice and David claps his hands. "Look at those two." He points. "Try that."

It's two hours later when we finally get dismissed. "I will be here if you guys need more lessons," David announces. "Otherwise, have fun."

"Okay." Lexi looks at all of the guys getting ready to head out. "If I can have your attention for just five more minutes," she says as we circle around her, "or less." She holds both of her hands in front of her. "Now, I don't know if Cheryl told you, but we've decided we are going to film a short video of each of you." She looks at us, doing a sweep from left to right. "It'll play before the auction, sort of a 'get to know you.'"

Some of the guys groan. "It'll be quick, I swear, fifteen minutes tops," she promises. "It's for a good cause."

"You're lucky that I like you," Darryl declares, "and I promised Bernetta I would be on my best behavior."

"You are the best, Darryl, and I'll be singing your praises the next time I see her." She smiles at him. "And who knows, you might actually get a real date with this auction, and then dare I say the B word."

"If you say bride," Darryl teases her.

"I was going to say a birdie," she jokes back to him, "but a bride might be good also. Next Tuesday, I'll be texting you all the time sheet." They say their goodbyes and turn to walk out of the room and I look over at her. "That didn't go as bad as I thought it would," she says with a chuckle, "and I didn't step on your feet."

"I call that a win for today," I reply. "Have a nice night, Lexi." I walk out of the dance studio, reminding myself that not only is she a married woman, but married to someone dimming her light little by little until she snuffs out.

Seven

LEXI

I WALK INTO the kitchen wearing my silk robe, my hair wrapped in a towel on the top of my head, wet from the shower. "Good morning," I greet when I spot Trent sitting at the island with a bowl of yogurt and fruit in front of him.

"Morning," he replies and I stop by his chair to kiss him. I wait a full minute before he realizes I'm here and then chastely kisses me. "You're up late."

I press the side of my phone and see it's a little after seven thirty, before placing it on the top of the island. "I know, it feels like I've wasted the morning away." I open the fridge to grab my homemade almond milk before heading over to the coffee maker. "Chelsea couldn't teach me this morning so I decided to sleep in." I pour the coffee in my cup and then add a splash of the milk to it, taking a sip. "It was glorious."

The phone rings from the counter and I see it's my father calling. A picture of me and him, side by side, both of us smiling at my mother who was taking the picture. "Good God, why is he calling so early?" Trent huffs and I reject the call, sending it straight to voicemail. Not really wanting to answer it in front of him anyway, since he likes to sit down and time how long I talk to my family members.

"He knows I wake up early and I usually get busy during the day, so it's the best time for us to talk."

He rolls his eyes. "He's always in your business, it's overbearing," he grumbles and I take another sip of coffee, but it tastes bitter in my mouth. "Thank God we only have to see them a couple of times a year." I put the cup down on the counter. "You're lucky I love you so much." He laughs, pushing away from the island and leaving his plate there before grabbing his suit jacket and shrugging it on. "Don't forget we have dinner tonight with Bernie and his wife." He mentions his best friend.

"I know, at seven, right?"

"Yes." He pulls his shirt cuff out of the sleeve and then goes to the next one. "The last time you dressed a little, how should I say this without hurting your feelings? It was a little slutty," he declares and my eyebrows pinch together. "So how about tonight you dress better?"

"What are you talking about?" I ask him, remembering I wore a one-piece beige dress with little cap sleeves. The front had a pleated skirt and, sure, it was above my knees but slutty is a stretch. It went up to my neck. I didn't even give off a hint of cleavage. "Joyce said she loved the outfit and went out the next day to buy one for herself."

He laughs at the statement. "She said that to your face, but in the end, she probably was talking about you to her friends." I shake my head, looking down at my coffee that looks light brown because I didn't put much almond milk in there so that I could limit the calories added in it. "How about we go into your closet now and choose an outfit?"

He turns and makes his way into my bedroom and into my closet. He opens one of the closet doors and then the other. He takes out one of my tight beige skirts with a slit on the side and then tosses it to the side. "When did you buy that?" he mentions of the skirt.

"My aunt bought that for me," I tell him, my aunt Zara owns Zara's Closet and to this day she sends me clothes once a month that she thinks I would look amazing in. She does it for everyone, but I always look forward to it.

"Figures," he mumbles, and for the first time ever, tears well up in my eyes. I blink them away as fast as they came before he pulls out a light-pink skirt that is very loose and then walks over to the hanging shirts and pulls out a white silk button-down top. "There, this is perfect, don't you think?"

"Yes," I agree softly, "it's very pretty." He hangs it on the stand in the corner. "What shoes do you want me to wear with it?"

"Nude pumps would work and use the new Hermes bag I bought you."

"Okay," I say softly.

He comes over and wraps his arm around my waist. "You're the best," he says softly and I look up at him, "and you know we have to put our best foot forward." I nod. "One of these days I'm going to be the head of the hospital, and I don't want anyone to have a bad thing to say about my wife."

"Of course." I brush away the little piece of lint from his jacket. "I'll try not to wear any foundation tonight"—I look up at him, eyes searching his—"to make sure I don't get it on your shirt. You probably didn't notice it on your shirt last week. You were probably busy and running out."

"Yeah," he says and I see his eyes change and then he smiles. "I should get going, I'm going to be late."

"Have a nice day." I look up at him and he kisses my lips.

"You know, maybe we should go away," he suggests. "After you finish with the fundraiser, we should go away to St. Barts or something."

"That would be nice," I admit to him and he lets me go and walks out of my closet. I hear his shoes on the tile floor before the garage door shuts.

I exhale deeply and turn to walk out of the bedroom and back to grab my phone to dial my father. He answers after one ring. "Hi, baby girl," he says softly, "how you doing today?"

"I'm good." I push down everything and act like I'm fine. "Sorry I missed your call. I was in the shower."

"No worries, I was just calling to check up on you. The family vacation is not the same without you here." I close my eyes, trying not to think that I'm missing another family vacation.

"It just didn't fit into Trent's schedule, and I'm knee-deep in this fundraiser that's happening next week. I just couldn't leave," I explain. "Is everyone there?"

"Yeah," he says. "Your sister is here with the twins and one of them is sick, so we're trying to help her out."

I smile and the lone tear escapes my eye. "I am going to check and see when I'll be able to go and visit her."

"Yeah, she said it's been a while since she spoke with you." I know he wants to say more but he's stopping himself.

"It's hard with the time zones and stuff, but I'll make more of an effort," I assure him. "I have to go get ready so that I can be at the hospital by ten."

"Okay, sweetheart, I love you."

"I love you too, Dad. Give a kiss to Mom for me."

"I will," he says and I quickly hang up the phone. I wish I still had social media so I could see some of the pictures from vacation, but after we got married, Trent thought it was good for us to be off social media.

I walk over to the fridge and take out an egg. I think about making myself a bagel with the poached egg, but then I think of the fundraiser next week and instead grab the bag of spinach.

I pick up the phone as I sit down to eat, bringing up the auction group chat I have going.

Me: Good morning, gentlemen, today is video day. Don't forget to be there at the time you signed up for to make this run smoothly. I have a camera crew setting up, starting at nine thirty. See you all later.

I put my phone down and take a bite of my egg when

my phone buzzes. I look down to see Kirby has answered me privately. I know it's him because he is the only one who I stored under Bachelor Auction.

Bachelor Auction: Not sure if it matters or not, but the guys moved around their times. Here is the revised copy. See you at three.

I look at the list, seeing he's the last one for the day. I respond to his text.

Me: Thank you. See you then.

I finish eating my breakfast before heading back to the bathroom. Pulling the towel from my hair, I apply leave-in conditioner in it. It takes me an hour to do my hair and makeup before I walk into my closet and pick up the skirt he tossed to the side. I hold it in my hand for a couple of minutes before I open the closet and put it back inside. Even though I know I can never wear it with him, I don't want to donate it. I push it to the back of the closet before closing it and heading over to my pants.

I move the hangers across the rod until I settle on a pair of dark-blue pants. Shedding my robe, I then slip the pants on. I walk over to the blouse closet, grabbing a blue silk one with long sleeves, and a sash around my neck to tie into a bow. I tuck it in and button the blue button with the silver ring around it. The blue of the shirt makes my blue eyes pop even more. I'm the only one of the three of us who got the blue eyes. My sister, Zara, has green eyes exactly like my mother, and Matty, my brother, is the stamp of my father with brown hair and brown eyes. I smile thinking of them and missing them a little bit more today.

I tuck my hair behind my ears before sliding on my royal-blue shoes with a chunky heel. Nothing too high since I'll probably be standing the whole time. When I pull up to the hospital, I reach over and grab the two shopping bags I have on the passenger seat.

I move my hip to the side to slam the door shut before walking into the hospital, heading straight for the office set up for the fundraising committee. I open the office door and put my purse down on the desk before turning back toward the conference room, where the camera crew is setting up.

"Good morning," I greet them as I see the cameraman adjusting the height of his camera. "I brought snacks." I put the bags that are in my hands on top of the table, taking the boxes out of the bags and setting them up. "I got some pastries and some muffins," I tell them. "There is juice and water as well." I take the bottles out of the second bag. "Please help yourself."

I nod at them before going back into the office to print out the time sheet Kirby sent me. I print it out, along with some of the questions that I'm going to ask them. I walk back into the room and see the camera guy and the sound guy in the corner having pastries and an orange juice. "Thank you all so much for doing this. I'm going to spend about twenty to thirty minutes with each guy, asking them questions. If you can just let the tape run the whole time, we'll edit it later."

"You're the boss," the camera guy says. I smile at him as the knock on the door has me turning to see Darryl there.

"I'm here," he announces and I smile as I take him in, wearing his golf attire.

"Coming or going?" I move my finger up at his outfit and he laughs.

"The guys decided that we'd play a round today," he says, shaking his head. "I should have said no when the tee time was fucking five thirty."

"What?" I ask, shocked. "I thought the earliest you can get is six thirty."

"Yeah, unless you are Kirby, who knows someone and he did him a favor." He shakes his head, and I can't help but laugh. "Half the guys are still there."

"Isn't that nice bonding," I joke with him and he glares at me.

"It's fine playing against the football guys, but you play against Kirby and it's…" he states and my stomach flutters for a split second. "His swing is insane and you know he can putt like a motherfucker."

"Good to know." I put my hands in my pockets. "There is water and juice if you want, and we'll get started when you are ready."

"Let's get this over with," he says, sitting on the stool set up in front of a green screen. "Let's get me a B."

I laugh at him. "I don't know if we should use that letter anymore," I joke with him. It takes me twenty-two minutes of asking him questions before he gets up and walks out of the room. The next bachelor is waiting to take his place. I stand as I listen to their answers, rolling my eyes a few times and then shaking my head more times than normal.

Cheryl comes in to check on things and then rushes out. I see some of the players stopped by the janitor as they leave. He tries to talk to them and they smile and hold up their hands before rushing out of the hospital.

Kirby walks in with ten minutes to spare and the stool is ready. He's wearing golf attire also. "Hi," he greets, running his hands through his hair, "hope it's okay I'm early."

"More than okay. We are ready for you," I tell him. "Do you want a coffee or a juice before we start?"

"No, thank you." He holds up his hand. "I just finished lunch with the guys." I smile at him. "It was supposed to be one game and then they doubled down. Good news is, I have money to bid on some items at the fundraiser next week."

"Did you trick them?" I ask him.

"Me?" He puts his hand to his chest. "I would never do that. It's not my fault they assumed I didn't know how to play golf." He walks over and he's the first one who introduces himself to the camera guy, even sharing a handshake. "Make me look pretty." He winks at him as he sits down.

"We are ready when you are," I tell him and he just smiles at me.

His blue eyes light up. "I'm always ready."

I look down at the sheet of paper, avoiding looking at him longer than I have to. It's inappropriate, to say the least. "Are you a morning person or a night owl?"

"Depends," he answers to the camera. "If it's a game day, then I'll probably be a night owl, but other than that, I think I'm more of a morning person. Sort of get everything out of the way and then you can relax."

I nod at his answer. "Speaking of relaxing, what do you do to wind down after a day at the office?"

He laughs at the question. "I'm a homebody," he admits. "I've always been a homebody. I travel so much during the year with my schedule that any time I'm home, I want to be in my home."

"What do you consider the perfect date?" I ask him the same question I've asked everyone else.

"That would depend, really," he starts and I just look at him. "Well, it's not just up to me. It's a date, so it would also depend on what she wants to do." My ears ring and the back of my neck starts to heat up. "If I want to take her to a restaurant and then a movie, that's great. But if she wants to go bowling instead, it's something I need to consider. If I would have to be spontaneous about the date, I would ask her questions about her likes and dislikes and then base it on that. I mean, what if I want steak and she's a vegetarian?" He laughs. "That wouldn't be a great date, would it?"

I nod, not sure I can say anything, the lump in my throat is bigger than it's ever been. The idea of someone asking me what I like or what I would want to do feels so foreign. I look down at the sheet. The words look like they are all over the place as I try to get my heartbeat down to normal. I have five other questions to ask him, but I suddenly just need to get this over with. So I just go to the last question. "Why should these ladies bid on you?"

"Well." He smirks. "Besides it being for a good cause"—he shrugs—"I have this amazing quality—I know useless information. Like the most random stuff. But it's probably because I used to watch *Jeopardy* with my grandmother when I was younger. Now I just watch it with my cat. I actually have it set to record when it's on." I can't help but chuckle at that information which makes him smirk at me. I see his leg move up and down nervously. "Secondly, I'm loyal to a fault, if you hate her, I hate her." He shakes his head. "I'm kidding." He looks at me and I can't help but smile again. "You can cut that out." I just shake my head as he looks into the camera. "I think I can converse well. I am a fun guy to be around, and I can pretty much guarantee you'll have the best time. We'll go on the date you've been dreaming about"—his eyes come to mine—"because I'll let you choose what we do and when we do it." My stomach feels like it's going to my throat as he looks back at the camera guy. "That's all I've got."

He gets up and the sound guy goes over to him and unclips his microphone. I look down at the paper, wishing I could just walk out of the room and have a minute to compose myself. "If you guys are ever in LA, hit me up, I'll get you tickets to a game." I close my eyes, wanting to stop my ears from hearing what he says. He's literally the nicest guy I think I've ever met. He's humble and kind, and he is everything I thought I would want in a guy. It's what I thought I had in my husband.

"Okay," he says, coming to my side, "if that is all. I have to go and shower this sweat off of me."

"Yup," I reply to him, still affected by the past thirty minutes. "Thank you for your time."

He nods his head at me and I turn mine, watching him walk out of the room and the janitor is there again. I see him stop Kirby, and instead of just holding up his hand and saying hello, like the other guys did, he actually stops to talk to the guy. He holds out his hand and shakes his hand and then poses for a picture for him. He spends a good five minutes talking to him before nodding his head and walking away.

"If that is all," the camera guy says to me, "we're done."

"Yes." I put my head back and smile at him, the fake smile I've become a professional at. "That will be all." I grab my papers before I head back into the office, closing the door behind me, and collapsing in the chair.

Eight

KIRBY

I WALK THROUGH the doors of the hospital and look down at the two cups of coffee in my hands. Each of them with a white bag that contains a muffin or a chocolate croissant. I'm making my way to the elevator when I look to the side and see Lexi sitting by herself at a table in front of the coffee area.

She's got her laptop in front of her and her head is down. I should just go toward the elevator and ignore that I saw her. I should do a lot of things when it comes to Lexi, but instead of doing what I should do, my feet make the decision for me. Getting closer to the table, I see she's wearing another pair of cream pants and a black shirt, but this one has big beige flowers on it. She has high heels on her feet, finishing the outfit. I don't think I've ever seen her wear jeans. I don't think I've ever seen her not looking perfect.

"Hey," I greet, once I get to the side of the table. Her head comes up and I see she has her earbuds in. She moves her hand to take an earbud out of her ear.

"I'm sorry, I didn't hear you," she says.

"I just said hey," I reply, moving to the seat in front of her and sitting down. "What are you doing here?" I look around seeing some of the tables taken.

"Cheryl had a meeting with Dr. Visabell about the next fundraiser. I should have just gone home, but we are meeting with the event planner in about an hour to go over the final plans."

"How excited are you for the day after?" I ask her and she laughs.

"I might not get out of bed," she states. "It's been so nerve-wracking, I can barely eat."

I don't love hearing that, she's already so small, so I place the coffee down in front of her with the white bag. "Why don't you take a break?" I urge her. "Keep your strength up."

"I couldn't." She shakes her head, looking at the bag.

"Come on," I push, putting the other bag next to it, "I dare you to pick one and eat at least half."

She glares at me, a little bit of fire coming back into her eyes. "Fine." She opens one bag and then the other. "Chocolate chip or croissant."

"I know decisions, decisions," I tease, leaning back in the chair. "It's win-win if you ask me."

"Well, the muffin probably has less calories than the croissant," she reasons and I shake my head.

"Lexi, you could eat both of them and still be okay," I tell her as she smiles up at me and then chooses the croissant.

"There is one latte and the other one is just plain black." I point to the two cups. "The one with the sleeve is the one that is just black."

"Why do you have two coffees and two sweet treats?" she asks me, taking a bite of the croissant. I swear her eyes almost roll in the back of her head.

"Good?" I ask her and she nods her head. She looks like a kid who is given a treat after doing something good.

"I don't even remember the last time I ate one"—she looks down and takes another bite—"but it should be more often." She laughs and I have to wonder if she was this carefree before the prick fucked her up. "So why two sweet treats?"

"I usually bring it for—" I stop talking when she raises her hand and her eyes go big.

"You are dating someone who works here?" she asks and looks at the bite she took out of the croissant. "Oh my God, does she like this or the other?"

"I'm not dating anyone here," I confirm to her. "They were both for me," I lie to her. "I was undecided, so I thought, you know what, why not get both?" I look down at her laptop and motion with my head. "What are you working on?"

"I'm editing the video," she answers, picking up the croissant. "I have to get it to the DJ."

"How's it turning out?" I ask her.

"Good. Some of the guys are funny, so I'm hoping that it gets a lot of interest." She takes another bite. "What are you doing here?"

"I come and visit the kids twice a week," I explain to her and her eyes go big.

"Twice a week," she repeats before she reaches for the water in her purse and takes a sip. "That's a big commitment."

"Some of the kids have no other adults who visit but their parents or guardians. It's good for everyone to get a break for a bit." I shrug. "Plus, I'm doing a Lego set with one of them and I'm excited to finish it."

"You are just full of surprises, aren't you?" She takes a bite and looks like she's about to laugh when she hears someone say her name.

She looks over and her face goes white. "I thought it was you," the woman says, walking toward us. Lexi gets up from her seat as she greets the woman with a kiss on each cheek.

"Joyce," she says her name softly, "this is a surprise."

"I had an appointment," she states, looking at her and then at me. "Were you two having coffee?"

"No," Lexi quickly refutes, "he's one of the bachelors for the auction."

"Hi," I say, reaching over to extend my hand, "I'm Kirby."

She smiles at me and nods her head, extending her hand. "It's nice to meet you. I'm Joyce Baron."

"Ms. Baron," I use her last name because she either wants me to or she thinks her last name means something to me. "It's a pleasure."

"Well, I'll let you get back to your"—she looks at the table—"meeting." She nods at me before turning and walking away.

Lexi slinks back into the chair, all the light that had entered her eyes gone. "Everything okay?" I ask her, knowing it probably isn't.

"No," she declares, putting the rest of the croissant in the bag and crunching the top shut.

"What happened?" I ask her and she grabs the white case that holds her earbuds, putting them both in there before shutting her laptop.

"I have to go." She grabs her laptop and places it in her bag. "This is…" She shakes her head. "That was Joyce," she fills me in, "Trent's best friend's wife." She gets up and grabs her bag. "She'll probably tell Bernie I was having coffee with you." She looks up and exhales. "Thanks for the croissant."

"You did nothing wrong." I can't help but say the words. "We were discussing the fundraiser, and I offered you something to eat." I get up and grab the two bags and the cups of coffee. "Don't let anyone spin it into something it isn't." Meaning don't let your husband fuck with your head.

"I'll see you at the fundraiser," she says, putting the bag on her shoulder, turning, and walking away quickly with her head down. I fight back the anger that escapes me as I walk toward the elevators, giving her a head start. The last thing she is going to need is us getting in the elevator and having someone else see us together. I turn and opt to take the stairs instead of the elevators, going to see my sister.

I walk into her office and she turns from her computer

screen to look at me. "I love these visits," she says, reaching out her hands to me. I hand her the latte and the two white bags. "You ate this and then gave it to me?" She tosses it to the side. "I'll save it for the car ride home."

I laugh as I sit down in the chair in front of her. "What do you know about a Dr. Yoder?" I ask her and she looks out her door and then back to me.

"How do you know him?" she asks me, and I see the worry on her face.

"I'm fine," I assure her. "Just did my physical this morning and all is good."

She does a deep sigh. "Don't fucking do that."

"Do what?" I ask her.

"Start with how you know the top neurosurgeon in the world," she hisses out, "instead of, I had my physical and I'm fine. But how do you know him?"

"Duly noted for next time to not start at the beginning." I laugh.

"Thank you." She takes the bottom of the muffin off and starts eating it. "Now, why do you want to know about Dr. Yoder?"

"Just wondering," I reply and she gets up, walking over to her door and shutting it.

"Cut the bullshit with me. You have been here a little bit too often, even for you."

"Kylie, there is no bullshit," I try to tell her. "I just I know his wife."

"Obviously, doesn't her brother play hockey?"

"Yeah and practically everyone else in her family

too," I confirm. "What do you know about her husband?"

"I know he's an asshole and you don't want to piss him off." She leans back in her chair. "I also know he's not exactly a model husband."

"What does that mean?" Even though I know exactly what it means.

"It means that he fucks pretty much anything that walks." She shrugs. "At least that's the gossip around the water cooler. No one has actually confirmed they fucked him, but you can see his wandering eye." Even knowing it was coming, I wasn't ready for her to actually say it.

"He's such a fucking piece of shit," I growl, shaking my head. "Has he ever tried to come on to you?"

"We don't run in the same circles." She laughs.

"Stay away from him," I warn, getting up from my chair, "and keep out of his sight." She looks up at me. "He's not a fan of me." She gawks. "We've shared a few words."

"Kirby," she says my name, "I have to work here."

"Not if you take me up on my job offer," I remind her. "Then you won't have to worry and you can just be free." I go to open the door. "Think about it."

"Well, by the sound of it, I probably won't have a job once you're gone. It's a good thing we don't share the same last name."

"Told you not to change it," I tease.

"He adopted me when I was eight," she snaps at me. "It's not like I had a choice in the matter."

"Then you'll be safe and no one will know we're related." I smile at her.

"Well, I am prettier than you." She laughs, making me laugh. "And you"—her face grimaces—"from what Angela told me, you are ugly both inside and outside." She mentions my ex-girlfriend, who I dumped when I figured out she was a bully to Ariella.

"Yes, because you really need to listen to what she says." I look over at her. "She also said you were a spoiled brat and I shouldn't be paying for your car."

"That bitch," she retorts. "I never liked her anyway." Now I laugh out loud. "What time are you picking me up on Saturday?"

"It starts at seven, so probably seven thirty," I reply and she nods.

"Make an entrance, I like it. Also, I'm getting glam done. Thank you for that."

"Anything for you…always," I say, walking out. She blows me a kiss. I head to the children's wing, and instead of listening to the kids, the only thing I can think of is Lexi and how pale her face got. Hoping maybe, just maybe, she breaks free one day.

Nine

Lexi

I LOOK AT the clock and see it's just past five o'clock. Picking up my phone I call Trent, who went golfing this morning and has yet to be back. I sit on the bed, listening to the phone ring once and then he picks it up. "Hello."

"Hey, it's five o'clock and the car is going to be here at five thirty," I remind him. "Are you on your way back?"

"The car can wait," he says, his voice low. "I'm at the club, I'm going to leave in a bit."

"I have to be there by six. I told you that this morning."

He sighs. "Relax, Lexi, it's not like you're saving lives." He takes a deep inhale. "I'll be ready when I'm ready."

"Trent," I reply, my voice tight, "I've worked hard for the last six months for this one day and I've done it for you and your status at the hospital. What do you think they will say if I show up late? It'll be a bad reflection on you."

"I'm on my way," he retorts, disconnecting the phone.

I walk back into my bathroom and sit down on the chair to get the rest of my makeup applied.

"Sorry about that, husbands and golf games." I make an excuse as she asks me to look up.

It's five minutes later when I hear the slam of the front door. Then the sound of his sneakers squeaking on the floor before he's in my bathroom. "Oh," he remarks, surprised, "the glam squad." He smiles and I look at him in the mirror with a smile on my face. "Not that she needs it," he praises, coming to me. "Oh, that's a bit too dark on the eyes, don't you think?" He looks at the makeup girl. "Can we lighten the eyes a bit? Her eyes are so beautiful without makeup, I feel like you can't even see them." He looks at me. "Don't you think?"

I look at light-pink eyeshadow on my lids and the darker plum on the outer corner of my eyes in the mirror. "I think they look fine," I reply, "but maybe we can lighten it."

I look at the makeup artist, who nods her head. "Of course." She walks over to get the makeup brush.

"I'm going to go shower," he announces, bending and kissing my lips and I can taste the booze on them. "I'll be ready at five thirty," he assures me and I smile at him.

"Thank you."

He walks out of the room and the makeup girl applies a light coat to the dark edges. It takes her ten more minutes to make the edges lighter and then she applies my lipstick. My hair is slicked back and tied into a tight bun at the base of my neck. "I'm going to go and get dressed. Can you zip me?" I ask her and she nods at me.

"I'll be closing up," she says and I rush to the closet and slip off the robe and grab the dress, sliding it on over my hips, before working my arms into each sleeve. I hold the front to my chest and turn to walk back to the bathroom. "Oh my gosh," she gushes breathlessly, "you look like a goddess." I smile, turning so she can zip the zipper closed to the base of my back.

My phone buzzes, letting me know the driver is at the door. I rush out to slip on the open-toed satin shoes that match the dress, tying each one around my ankle. Then I slip on the pink diamond earrings my parents gave to me on my twenty-first birthday. "I'm ready," I hear Trent as he comes into the room wearing a black tux, "and you aren't."

"I am," I confirm, grabbing the little clutch purse, walking out of my closet, and waiting for him to say something.

"We should go," he urges, motioning with his head. "Don't want you to be late."

"Yes," I agree, feeling a little bit disappointed that he didn't tell me how pretty I look. I walk out of the house following him, wondering when he stopped holding the door for me or waiting to follow me instead of me following him. The driver has the door open, and again, instead of waiting for me to go in first, he gets in and tells the driver to shut the door. "Go around to the other side."

I look at the driver. "Good evening," I greet the driver. "How are you doing?" He rushes to the other side to open my door before I put one foot in and then the other one. "Thanks for waiting for me."

"You're welcome," Trent replies, his phone in his hand as he types away.

I look out the window with my hands in my lap and I try and focus, going over the list I must check once we get there. But instead, I hear Kirby's voice from when we recorded the video, "It's not just up to me. It's a date, so it would also depend on what she wants to do." That one sentence stuck with me and I can't get it out of my head.

My head is spinning with everything that went on in the past month. Everything I've worked so hard for is finally here, and I should be celebrating it. But instead, I'm dreading it and I don't know why. The car comes to a stop and I look over at Trent. "Let's get this fucking over with," he mumbles, opening his own car door, while my car door is opened.

A man reaches in to help me. I slip my hand in his, getting out and smiling at him. "Thank you," I tell him and see Trent standing by the door, waiting for me. He waits for me to be beside him before he walks into the banquet hall.

The sign in the entranceway sits on a gold easel, telling guests to walk up the steps. He folds his arm for me to slip my hand in his before walking up the steps. "I hate your makeup," he starts. "She made you look like a fucking showgirl instead of a doctor's wife. Don't hire her again. She does nothing for you. You could have done your makeup better," he chides. Then his scowl turns into a smile when he gets to the top of the steps and sees Cheryl there with her husband and Dr. Visabell standing with them.

"There she is," Cheryl states, looking over at me, her face a bright smile wearing a light-blue, off-the-shoulder gown. "I don't know how you did it"—she throws her hands up—"but it's so pretty." I can't help the smile that fills my face. The nerves from today are going away a bit, as I look around, seeing the little seating areas I fought for. They are scattered all around the little lounge area. A cast-iron railing is in the middle of the room and you can see five doors that lead to the outside where the big terrace is. We even have seating out there if people want to get away from the noise.

"It's the best we've ever seen," Dr. Visabell declares proudly.

"I mean, they aren't saving lives like us," Trent jokes, laughing and the other men share a look and then chuckle, "but they help with the budget."

"That they do," Dr. Visabell confirms.

"Why don't we go and get something to drink?" Trent suggests. "I'm going to need all the help I can get to stay awake tonight."

"It'll be a fun night," Cheryl assures him, "and we get to dance with the bachelors tonight to help show them off."

"Is that really necessary?" Trent questions. "A couple of them might not bring in any money but—"

"Yes," Cheryl says, laughing, "it's necessary. We have to make sure those bids are up there. We already got a million-dollar donation from one of them."

I gasp in shock. "What?" I put my hand to my stomach.

"Yes, and that was on top of the two million he

donated to the children's wing," she shares. "That Kirby Materson is a gem."

My eyes go big and they immediately go to Trent, whose jaw gets tight and he snorts. "Can he really afford it?" He chuckles. "Isn't he just a hockey player?"

"They get paid pretty well." Dr. Visabell laughs. "I think I saw someone who signed eight years for one hundred and twelve million dollars," he says and then looks at me. "Doesn't your family play hockey?"

"They do," I confirm proudly. "My grandfather is the all-time leading scorer to this day. But my cousin Dylan is biting at his heels."

"He's adopted," Trent retorts and my head whipping to him.

"He's my cousin," I declare and then look back at the group. "If you will excuse me, I need to make sure everything is done before people arrive." I look at the group before I look back at Cheryl. "Shall we go and bask in our success?" I ask her and she smiles at me.

"We shall." She nods and we walk away from the men. I try not to let Trent and his attitude get to me tonight. I don't know why I thought it would be different. When it's not about him, he doesn't really think anything is important.

I walk in and see all four walls are covers in a white drapery, the drapes pulled away from the door as you step in. Fifty tables are all scattered around the room, around the big dance floor that has been covered and is white, with the hospital's foundation name in gold across it. I walk past the tables with the white-and-gold chairs to the back of the room, seeing the long tables filled with silent auction prizes. I look over toward the doors, seeing the men come in and head over to one of the eight bars we have set up all around the room.

The DJ is on a stage at the back of the room, right next to the door. "We did it, Cheryl," I tell her and she smiles at me. "We need champagne." I spot one of the waiters walking around with a tray and hold up my hand. He comes over and I grab a glass for me and then one for Cheryl. "To an unforgettable night," I toast to her, not knowing just how true it would be.

I take a sip and then spot the event planner. We walk outside, seeing the seating chart being placed in front of the open doors. "Here we go," Cheryl says, once people start arriving.

I'm standing by her at the front door, making sure to greet everyone. I look up to see the television screens we had put up, playing the video of the bachelors on a loop. I even added a clip of the sport they play so you would be able to see them in action.

Darryl is the first of them to arrive, smiling at us. "After tonight," he says, leaning down to kiss my cheek, "we are even."

I laugh. "And you walk away with a—" I point at him, not saying the B letter.

I am joking with him when I look over and see Kirby walk in, a tall brunette on his arm. She's wearing a gold satin dress that fits her every curve. My stomach gets tight when I look over and see him looking at me. He's wearing a custom tux, no doubt, because it fits his broad shoulders like a glove. He walks up to us. "Hello," he greets us, leaning to kiss Cheryl's cheek and then coming over to me and I think I hold my breath, feeling his bearded cheek on mine. "You look beautiful," he whispers in my ear and I close my eyes, and just like that he's taking a step back. "This is Kylie," he introduces his date. "This is Cheryl and Lexi."

"You look familiar," Cheryl says to her and she smiles.

"I work at the hospital, fourth floor. Day surgery coordinator," she explains softly, then looks at me. "I love your dress, it's stunning."

"Thank you," I reply softly. "You look just as amazing."

"Please check and see what table you are sitting at," Cheryl urges him, "and keep a dance open for each of us."

He looks at both of us. "It'll be my pleasure." He nods before walking into the room.

I stand up with Cheryl, smiling and greeting everyone, and when I finally go in, the music is in full swing. I'm making my way to the table when I look to the side and see Trent with a group of his friends, walking out of the room toward the outside, probably to go and smoke the cigars he usually has. He hasn't even come to look for me or check in on me once.

"If I can have everyone's attention," I hear Cheryl in the microphone, "and if I can get my co-chair up here." She looks around. "And, of course, our ten bachelors up for auction." She laughs as I make my way to the middle of the dance floor where she is. I look to the side and see Darryl coming from one side with Kirby beside him. "Our two co-chair bachelors," Cheryl introduces them and Darryl goes to stand at her side and Kirby stands by mine. The rest of the guys line up beside them. "Thank you all for coming." She starts her speech. "When Lexi and I came up with this idea, we didn't know if we could pull it off. But Darryl was our saving grace." She points to him. "He helped get us in touch with these fine men so that we can have what I think will be the best bachelor auction ever put on." She laughs and I nod my head. "So get your checkbook ready." She holds up her hand. "We will be opening the dance floor with the bachelors." She nods to the DJ, who waits for her cue, starting a soft ballad. "Darryl," she says his name, "you are my number one dance."

I see Darryl put his hand out for her, while he puts his other hand on his stomach and bows just a little. "It would be my honor." I watch them and then I hear him from beside me.

"So what do you say, Lexi?" Kirby says my name. "Care to open the dance floor with the second co-chair?" He holds out his hand. I look around to see if I spot Trent, then look back to him, the twinkle in his eye making my heart speed up. "I dare you."

Ten

KIRBY

I STAND NEXT to her as Cheryl starts talking and I've never in my life felt a pull to someone like I do to her. Even though I know it can never go anywhere. Even though I know she's not that person who would ever step out on her husband. Even though I know in a few weeks I'll leave here and I won't see her. The thought alone makes my stomach lurch.

I hear clapping and then look over to see Cheryl reaching for Darryl's hand, leading her to the dance floor when I turn to Lexi. "So what do you say, Lexi"—she stops mid-clap to look at me—"care to open the dance floor with the second co-chair?" I smile at her, holding out my hand as she nervously looks around her. No doubt looking for that piece-of-shit husband of hers, who's been mingling the whole fucking time, not once going to check up on his wife. Her hands are in front of her, one hand in the other, as she contemplates my question when I tease her, "I dare you."

She smiles and looks down at her hands before she looks back up at me, side-eyeing me while she tries not to smile too big. "I mean, if it's a dare," she replies, reaching out her hand to put in mine. "I sort of have no choice but to dance with the bachelors." She steps into me as my hand goes to the middle of her back. "I guess so."

"Well," I laugh, "I'll take it." She puts her hand on my shoulder as I sway her to the side. "On a scale of one to ten, how nervous are you?"

She chuckles. "A million." She looks around at the dance floor that seems to be filling up faster and faster. "I think I'll only be able to do a sigh of relief once the bidding is over, and we see how much we've raised."

"I don't know how the last one went, but from the looks of this place"—I look around at the decorations—"it's kicking the last one's ass." I laugh.

"You just said you didn't know how the last one even went." She shakes her head. "So you can't compare it."

"Well, I think this one is going to be better than the last one because you put your heart and soul into it." I pull her even closer to me. "All of the touches with the dances, the videos, the silent auction. Look around, everyone is having a great time and you did that. It's just—" She looks up at me and I can see the compliments are all new to her. "You look beautiful," my mouth says before I have a chance to stop the words from coming out of it. Her smile goes sideways as if she's embarrassed.

"Thank you," she says softly and my thumb moves on her back up and down. "You look very handsome," she adds and immediately looks down at our feet.

"I mean, it's not what I would usually wear." I try to make a joke out of it.

"Oh no," she joins in on the joke, "you don't like dressing up in a tux every Saturday?"

I laugh. "I mean, I'm usually suited up on Saturday nights." We sway side to side. "But that is only because I have no choice."

"I forgot, you guys have to dress up before the games." She softly laughs. "We used to call it the thirst traps."

"What?" I can't help but laugh at her.

"Yeah, the guys dressing up before the game and being filmed walking in. The swagger you guys have because you are being filmed." She's laughing now, and not a fake laugh, it's a real fucking laugh. A laugh that makes her eyes crinkle at the sides. "Matty was the biggest one. Then Michael was second, for sure, no doubt about it. He would even give a little smirk. Dylan did it, not even aware he was doing it. Franny's husband, Wilson, used that as his personal fucking Tinder." She mentions the men in her family with so much love and pride.

"I never even thought of it like that," I admit to her, "but you might be right. I have to check next season when I do it if my follower count goes higher when I swagger in there."

"I bet it does, for sure," she assures me and she's about to say something else when we both look to the side, hearing Cheryl speaking.

"Okay, time to switch out," she says, letting go of Darryl and smiling at me. "Come here, handsome." She motions with her head, and I let go of Lexi's hand almost unwillingly.

"Be careful with that one," Darryl warns, "she's handsy." He winks at me as he laughs at the joke, making Cheryl gasp.

"You should be so lucky." She turns her head to the side.

"Burn, Darryl," Lexi jokes with him, holding out her hand for him. "Come on, let's get this over with."

"I am feeling so much love right now," he mumbles. "I don't know what to do with it all."

The three of us laugh as I walk to Cheryl and take her hand in mine. "How amazing is tonight?" she asks me. I look back over at Lexi and see her in her gown, and again, she takes my breath away. When I walked in and saw her, it was as if she was the only one in the room. Her blue eyes shone even brighter as she talked to people coming in, and when our eyes finally met, it was as if the earth shifted under my feet. For the rest of my life, I will be looking for that moment, and it scares the ever-loving fuck out of me, because I am petrified I'll never find it.

"I've attended my fair share of fundraisers throughout the years, and this has to be the best one." I smile at her.

"I totally agree and I wish I could take half the credit, but Lexi," she says, her face filling with the biggest smile, "she is the one who did it all."

"It's always a team effort," I remind her, "and knowing Lexi, there is no way she would let anyone think otherwise."

"You know her well," she observes and I want to

answer that I wish I could get to know her even better.

The song ends and she lets go of my hand and I bow my head. "That was the best dance of my life." I put my hand to my chest. "Thank you."

"Oh, you are smooth." She shakes her head. "Very smooth. Now get to your seat because the auction is about to start."

I look around to see if I can spot Kylie when I see Lexi standing at the side next to Trent, who has a glass of whiskey or scotch in one hand, while the other is in his suit pocket instead of holding his wife's hand. The two of them are chatting with Darryl and one of the other bachelors.

"If I can get everyone to their tables, please, we are going to be serving the first course and starting the auction."

I walk over to my table and find Kylie walking back from the bar with a glass of champagne in her hand. The smile on her face is from ear to ear. "I feel so fancy." She sits down next to me, putting her purse in front of her name. "Table two." She wiggles her eyebrows. "You're a big deal."

"It's only because they are auctioning me off." I lean back in my chair and look over at the table beside me, seeing Lexi is sitting down next to Trent on one side, who is busy talking to the lady beside him, while Lexi just looks around the table.

Darryl pulls out the chair next to Kylie and introduces himself to her. "I'm this guy's sister," she quickly points out and I have to laugh.

"This guy has a name," I mumble, trying not to look at Lexi's table but failing miserably. He never fucking once tries to talk to her and she's stuck talking to Cheryl's husband, who is sitting with an empty chair between them, no doubt left for Cheryl.

"Did you bid on any of the silent auction items?" Kylie asks from beside me as the first plate is placed in front of me.

"I didn't see them all," I admit, grabbing my glass of water in front of my plate. "Why? Did you?"

"Not yet." She smiles, taking a sip of her champagne. "But I will. What's my budget?"

I can't help but snort when she leans in. "How much can I bid on Darryl?" she asks right before she leans back to her other side as she chats with Darryl, the two of them laughing at whatever she said.

I barely eat the food, nervously waiting for the auction part of the evening. Cheryl stands up when they are clearing the plates of the first course, with Lexi next to her. "Okay, let's get the bidding out of the way," she begins. "There are ten bachelors." She names us all.

She starts with the first bachelor and he goes up to the front and she makes him do a catwalk of sorts. "I'm not doing that," Darryl quickly states. "I'm drawing the line."

"I think you should," Kylie urges him, and I just look over at her with my eyebrows pinched together.

It takes no time to go through the eight bachelors, most of them going anywhere from thirty thousand dollars to fifty-five. "You can bid up to eighty-five thousand for me," I tell Kylie, who grimaces.

"Why would I bid on you?" she retorts, grossed out. "You're my brother."

"Okay, fine, you can bid on Darryl up to eighty-five and then seventy-five for me," I tell her and she shakes her head.

"Kylie," I hiss at her as Darryl pushes away from the table and tosses his napkin down on the table in front of him.

"Here goes nothing." He looks at me and I hold out my fist and he fist-bumps me as the clapping starts, and he goes to the center of the dance floor. He grabs the microphone from Cheryl. "Before you ask me to strut my stuff"—he looks at Cheryl—"I'm just going to say that whoever picks me won't be sorry." He makes everyone laugh as he hands her back the mic.

"Shall we start the bidding at ten thousand?" she questions and it quickly goes up to fifty-five.

"Sixty," Kylie says from beside me, and I can't help but close my eyes and shake my head, laughing. "It's for a good cause."

"Seventy," someone else bids on him.

"Seventy-five," Kylie bids. "Now it's personal."

"For who?" I ask her, and I hear Cheryl egging on the other woman.

"Sold." She points over to our table at Kylie, who claps her hands together. "Come and get your prize."

"Hold my beer," she mumbles, getting up and strutting over to Darryl, who runs to Lexi's table. He leans in to grab a flower from one of the vases and goes back to

Cheryl, who is standing with Kylie laughing, as he hands Kylie the flower before taking her free hand and bringing it to his mouth, kissing it.

"That's what you all missed out on." He looks at the crowd and it makes everyone laugh. The two of them come back to the table and she puts the flower down next to her purse.

"I'm going to need to borrow seventy-five thousand dollars," she whispers in my ear, making me laugh even more.

"And the final bachelor of the night is none other than our hometown hockey star, Kirby Materson."

"Go get 'em," Kylie urges, clapping her hands and cheering for me. I shake my head as I walk to the middle of the dance floor.

Lexi looks at me with a huge smile on her face, and I can't help but smile at her. Cheryl starts to talk and I grab the microphone from her. "Before you ask, I'm with Darryl on this one. You see what you paid for after." I look around the room. "And no refunds allowed." I hand the microphone back to Cheryl, who is laughing.

"Okay, shall we start at ten thousand dollars?" she suggests and it quickly goes to fifty thousand from Kylie and she winks at me.

"Kirby is a very generous donor already tonight," Cheryl pleads my case. "He's already donated a million dollars."

The crowd gasps and then I hear shouted out, "One hundred thousand dollars!" I look over to see Dr. Visabell's wife holding up her hand. "It's the least we can do."

"One twenty," someone else calls out. I look at Lexi, who has her mouth open and both hands in front of her, the happiness is written all over her face.

"Two hundred," his wife says and then Cheryl closes the bidding.

"Going once, going twice. Sold," she screams, "for two hundred thousand dollars!"

"Oh my," Lexi yells, "this is incredible!" Her hands are over her head clapping. "That was incredible."

I look over at Trent, who looks like he's sneering, and I don't know if he's sneering at her or at me. Either way, he should be up here celebrating with her. My eyes go to the lady walking over to me and I smile at her. "I don't have a flower to give you," I tell her and then look over at the DJ, who gives the head waiter a nod of his head. "I just have this." The waiter comes out with a bouquet of roses, making everyone aww.

"Thank you for bidding on me." I hand her the flowers and then look over at Cheryl and Lexi. "How about we give a round of applause for the co-chairs of the event?" I say loudly as another waiter comes and hands Cheryl a bouquet of roses and then one to Lexi. "You guys can do better than that," I tell the crowd and they get onto their feet and cheer for them.

Cheryl comes over first and she leans up to kiss my cheek and then I look at Lexi, who is just shaking her head in disbelief. "Thank you," she says softly, "for everything." I lean down and kiss her cheek, wishing it was her lips.

I escort my future date back to her husband. "I promise to be a gentleman," I assure him and he laughs as I look to the empty seat where Trent was sitting.

"I'm sure you will," Dr. Visabell replies. I look over at my table and tell Kylie I'm stepping out to get some air. I need to get away from Lexi before I do something stupid that will make a fool out of me.

Walking out of the room, I head to a door that leads outside. I push one open and see Trent there in the corner, his head bent, talking to a blonde. The woman is way too close to him, closer than she should be. Her front is practically plastered against him. Their eyes are locked on each other as she says something to him and all he does is smirk at her.

"Wow," I blurt, not even sure why I said it, "this is rich." They jump apart from each other and the blonde moves her hand up to put her hair behind her ear.

"I'll just," she blusters, "excuse me."

"I didn't mean to interrupt a private moment," I state when she walks by me. "This is his wife's event, after all." The color drains from her face as she slinks back inside.

"What the fuck are you doing out here?" Trent sneers, coming close to me. "You're just like one of those fucking annoying fruit flies we can't get rid of."

"I'm out here getting air," I reply to him, "while you are out here disrespecting your wife."

"*My wife*," he hisses, stepping in even closer to me, "is none of your fucking business." He puts his head back. "She's a fucking nobody without me." His words make me ball my hands into fists. "She was a nobody when I met her. For fuck's sake, her father is a fucking drug addict. She should be thankful I took pity on her." The gasp should have me turn my head around to look, but all I see is black in front of me. The last few weeks of treading on thin ice when it came to him. The whole time wanting to kick his ass.

It happens so fast, my hands come up to grip the lapels of his jacket. "Shut your fucking mouth," I tell him at the same time I hear her voice scream my name.

"Kirby," she says and I see her standing beside us now, her hand on mine holding her husband's jacket, "stop this right now." She looks over her shoulder. "You are making a scene."

I let go of his jacket and give him a shove back, and he stumbles. "I'm sorry, Lexi," I say softly.

"I think you should go." She avoids looking at me and instead looks at her husband. I feel a tightness in my chest as I look over and see a couple of people watching and then what looks like security rushing out of the door, ready to break up the fight.

"I'm so, so sorry." I look back at Trent. "You deserve better than him."

"Like who?" He straightens his jacket. "Like you?"

"Like anyone who will treat her with respect," I retort. "Who will raise her up and not knock her down to make themselves feel better." I hit the bull's-eye right in the center. "Anyone but someone like you." I see she is wiping a tear off her cheek, and I know in that moment I've lost her. Not that I ever had her, but whatever it was is over. "You deserve better, Lexi." That's the last thing I say before I turn and walk away from her.

Eleven

LEXI

"I'M SO, SO sorry," Kirby says, his voice filled with regret. "You deserve better than him."

"Like who?" Trent sneers at him as he smooths down his jacket that not two seconds ago Kirby fisted in his hands. "Like you?" He motions with his chin.

"Like anyone who will treat her with respect." He looks at me, but I can't turn and look into his eyes. "Who will raise her up and not knock her down to make themselves feel better." My eyes watch Trent's face as he says the words. Wondering if he's going to say anything back to Kirby. "Anyone but someone like you." The tears were stinging at my eyes when I stepped outside of the door and heard Trent's words about my father. I wipe one away from my cheek, forcing the others back at bay. I will not let him see that he's hurt me. "You deserve better, Lexi," Kirby declares, and I wish I had the balls to look up at him but I don't. I don't have the balls to do anything. Instead, I listen to him walk away. "Excuse me," he says and I look back and see this little altercation has drawn a crowd.

My eyes are on the security people turning and telling everyone there is nothing to see here. "Now look at what you have done." I hear his voice and look back to see him standing closer to me. "Look at the fucking scene that you've caused." He shakes his head.

"The scene I've caused?" I point to my chest and look down to see if I'm bleeding through my dress because that is the pain I'm feeling. Like someone has just taken a knife and stabbed me in the heart. "I wasn't even out here."

"You," he growls between clenched teeth, "were the root of this scene. Did you fuck him?" I gasp and take a step back away from him. "You better tell me now before I find out."

"How could you even ask that?" I hiss at him. "How could you think I would do that?"

"I don't know anything anymore," he grumbles. "All I know is you've made a laughingstock out of me tonight."

"Me?" I point to myself. "I made a laughingstock out of you?" I can't help but repeat his words because, surely, I've heard him wrong. Surely, my ears are playing tricks on me.

"We need to get back inside"—he puts his shoulders back—"and make sure no one is talking about this shit. Should have fucking laid his ass out," he mumbles about Kirby and I want to laugh in his face. There would only be one person laying the other one out, and it would not be him laying Kirby out. He grabs my hand and pulls me with him back into the room.

People mingle everywhere and not one person looks over at us. I walk back into the room with a smile on my face. My eyes go to table two, hoping to see Kirby sitting there with his date. But the two seats are empty. I let go of his hand as I make my way back to my own seat, sitting down and smiling at Cheryl, who is eating the second course. "How is the food?" I ask her, putting the linen napkin back on my lap.

"Better than the taste testing." She smiles. "Everyone is having such a good time."

She doesn't even mention the altercation that took place not ten minutes ago. "That is amazing." I fake smile at her as Trent sits next to me, putting his glass of bourbon in front of his dish.

"Isn't this amazing?" Cheryl asks Trent.

"Perfect," he replies, leaning and kissing my cheek, "just like my wife."

"Isn't he sweet?" she says and all I can do is smile at her. The smile feels like it's plastered on my face. The smile I have no choice but to give right now. The whole night all I do is put on this front when I am crying inside.

People come up to me all night long, telling me how incredible the night is. Even the silent auction blows up. People start trickling out, and when it's just a handful of people left, Trent stands up. "We should get going," he announces and I get up, grabbing my purse.

"Don't forget your flowers," Cheryl reminds me of the bouquet of white roses Kirby had given to both of us to thank us for tonight, something that made me stand there speechless.

"She doesn't need more flowers at home," Trent declares. "You should donate them to the hospital with all the other flowers."

"Of course," Cheryl says as she watches Trent walk over to Dr. Visabell to say goodbye. "You should at least get the card he wrote," Cheryl urges, her voice low and I nod at her, not willing to make another scene.

"I'll be right back," I tell Trent, who in front of Dr. Visabell doesn't say anything. I walk over to the back of the room where the silent auction table is, seeing the two white bouquets of flowers on the table. I look in the first one and see Cheryl's name on the card and then see the next one, my name written across the middle of the white card. I open my purse, shoving it in before turning and walking back to Trent.

We wish everyone goodnight as we walk out of the room. "Thank fuck that is finally over," he grouses, walking in front of me. We get to the bottom of the stairs as the doors open.

"I need the car for Dr. Yoder," the valet guy says into the walkie-talkie. "We'll be right out."

"I need another car also," Trent says to him and he nods his head and I look at him.

"What do you need another car for?" I ask him, holding my purse in my hands in front of me.

"I'm going to stay at the apartment near the hospital." He looks around to make sure no one can hear him. "After the shitshow of tonight, I need to think."

"You need to think," I repeat, my voice not as low as

his was.

"Lower your voice," he warns. "It'll also give you a chance to think about the scene you caused tonight," he adds. When our car gets there, he walks to the back door of the car and opens it for me. "I'll see you tomorrow and we can talk then." He leans down to kiss me, but instead of waiting for it, I duck my head and get into the car. He sticks his head into the car. "I can see I made the right decision." He doesn't wait for me to say anything, instead shutting the door in my face.

I sit in the back of the car, looking out at him shaking the valet guy's hand as he walks toward the car he got for him. The driver gets into the car. "Are we going straight home, Mrs. Yoder?" I look at him as he watches me in the rearview mirror.

"Yes," I confirm with a smile, "take me home." I swallow down the lump in my chest as I look out of the window. It was supposed to be my night. I worked my ass off to make tonight the most successful fundraiser the hospital ever had and, in the end, he ruined it for me.

My eyes go dry as the tip of my nose stings. I put my hand on my stomach as I watch the city fade away as he drives me closer to my house. The last thing I want tonight is to fall apart in the car in front of a stranger.

I close my eyes as I blink away the tears. My head goes back to that moment outside with him and Kirby, I will never in my life forget. A moment I will never in my life forgive him for. The minute I got the flowers and I took a step back, I looked toward where Trent was supposed to be sitting but saw it was empty. I smiled at everyone as I handed the flowers back to the waiter, and he told me where he would put them until I was ready to leave. "He's so thoughtful," Cheryl praised Kirby, and all I could do was nod because it was more than that.

I looked over and saw his date was chatting head to head with Darryl, and instead of sitting down, I walked out of the ballroom, coming to a stop when I saw Tatum, one of the surgery coordinators, walking in from outside. Her red dress hanging too low in the front, low enough that you could see her fake, round tits. Her face was pale, as if she was caught doing something, as she hurried back into the ballroom. She stopped when she saw me. "Is my husband out there?" I asked her and whatever color was in her face was totally gone. She couldn't even answer me, all she could do was nod her head and quickly run away.

I rolled my eyes and wondered if I should even go out there. I knew I should have turned and walked back into the ballroom, but instead I was pulling the door open at the exact moment I heard the words that would change everything, *"For fuck's sake, her father is a fucking drug addict. She should be thankful I took pity on her."*

Everything happened so fast after that, I had to make sure Kirby didn't do anything he would regret in the morning.

I open my eyes when I feel the car coming to a stop and the sound of the door being shut. Looking out of my window, I see I'm in front of my house. The door is pulled open as the driver holds out his hand. "Thank you." I nod at him once I'm out of the car, and he lets go of the door. "Have a nice evening."

I walk into the house, not bothering to take off my shoes or even turn on the light as I make my way to my bedroom. The purse slips from my hand and smashes onto the floor, making it spring open, my lip gloss skidding across the floor and the white card falling out.

I squat down in front of the purse and take the envelope in my hand. My finger moves over my name before I turn it over and open it.

Pulling it open, I see Kirby must have written this.

Lexi,

Our deepest fear is not that we are inadequate, but that we are powerful beyond measure. It is our light, not our darkness, that most frightens us.

That's my favorite quote and thought I would share it with you.

I dare you not to let anyone darken your light.

K.

The minute I read the last sentence, I'm sobbing out loud. Bringing the card to my chest, I can't help but cry. The pressure is so much that I'm knocked on my ass. My head feels like it's a washing machine spinning around and around.

"You're beautiful." I hear his voice but then at the same time I hear Trent. "She should be lucky she has me." I close my eyes to not hear the words. "You deserve better." That is the last thing I hear before I open my eyes and I grab my phone.

Pulling it up and not even thinking about what time it is, I call him. It takes him four rings to answer the phone, and when he does, his voice is filled with sleep. "Lexi," he says and I can't help it; instead of saying anything, all I do is silently cry. "Lexi, honey." The worry is filling in voice.

"Daddy," I say, the tears rolling down my cheeks, one after another. "Daddy."

"Lexi, baby, where are you?" His voice that was worried is now filled with a more frantic tone.

"I'm home." I look around the room. "Dad, I need your help." My hands shake as I say the words. "Dad, I need help."

"Baby," he says tightly, "where is Trent?" He's probably fucking some girl in his apartment I almost say, but I stop myself.

"Daddy," I repeat and I can feel the panic starting to come as my breathing is starting to get a bit harder. "Daddy, I need to—"

"Lexi," he says, snapping my name, "where the fuck are you?"

"I want to leave him, Dad," I tell him and close my eyes. "He—"

"Did he touch you?" he asks and I can hear the fear and anger in his voice.

"He says I'm not good enough. That I need him."

"He's lying to you."

"That without him, I'm nothing." The words come out. "I don't dress good enough. I don't smile enough. I am not skinny enough." My body shakes uncontrollably, my teeth clattering as if I'm in ice-cold water.

"Baby," he soothes. "I'm calling Uncle Matthew and

the two of us are coming to get you."

"I won't be anything without him." I feel like I'm in a trance. "But I don't want to be with him. I'll be nothing, but I'll be without him."

"I'm going to be there in five hours, in five hours."

"Okay."

"Can you wait in the house or do you want to go to a hotel?" I lie down on the floor in my room.

The card in one hand, the phone in the other as I just stare out. "Okay."

"Lexi," he says my name, "I'm going to hang up on you now, and I'll call you back."

"Okay, Daddy," I reply and then he waits for me to say something. "I love you, Daddy."

"I love you too, angel"—I can hear the softness of his voice—"more than my life."

"I'm sorry." I close my eyes. "I'm so sorry I wasn't strong like you taught me to be."

"I'm coming. I want you to do something for me. Can you do something for me?"

"Yeah," I say, not sure I can even move.

"I need you to lock the door of your bedroom and not open it until I get there."

"He's not coming home," I tell him.

"I'm coming. I promise you I'm coming." I nod my head. "I'll call you back."

"Okay." He hangs up as I close my eyes. He calls me back every single thirty minutes to check on me, and I vow each time I'll get up and change. But I just close my eyes and drift off to sleep.

The pounding makes me open my eyes, and I look around the room before getting up on my side. "Lexi." I hear his voice and then I get up, walking toward the front door. I unlock it, and when I pull it open, I'm in his arms. "Lexi." He breathes me in. "I'm here."

"Daddy," I cry just like I did when I fell off the bike the first time I rode on two wheels. Just like when I busted open my chin skating and he took me in his arms, protecting me the whole time.

"Lexi," I hear softly and then look over to see my mother standing there. She's wearing jeans and a white top, a baseball hat on her head. "Lexi." She brings her hand to her mouth and I can see she's shaking.

"Why don't we get her in the living room where there is more space and talk?" My uncle Matthew puts his arm around her shoulders. My mother nods as my father carries me into the living room. I almost turn around and tell them to take off their shoes, but I just shake my head as he guides me to the living room and sets me on the couch. My mother and Matthew sit in front of us. "Okay, talk," Matthew demands and I can see his jaw is tight as he looks around and then back at me.

"Matthew," my father warns tightly.

"Lexi," my mother urges, "we need to get you out of that dress and get your clothes packed." She stands up. "Then we are taking you away from here and the hold he has on you."

She holds out her hand. "Come and choose what you want to take with you." I put my hand in hers and we slowly walk to the bedroom.

"Mom," I say softly as she unzips the dress, "I should have been stronger, like you."

"My beautiful girl." She puts one hand to her stomach and I see that she's about to completely lost it. "You are not strong like me. You are stronger than me. Picking up that phone and making that phone call you are in a category of your own. Don't you dare," she snaps and grabs ahold of my face. "Don't you dare let him have one more fucking minute of you." Her tears roll down her face. "Now, my beautiful girl"—she smiles—"let's get you packed."

I nod my head and look at her. "Do you think I'll be okay without him?"

"I think you'll thrive without him," she assures me, going over and grabbing one of my suitcases. "I think he's the one who isn't going to be okay without you."

"But he's a doctor," I retort and I giggle at the stupidity of it as she laughs with me. "He told me so many things, Mom," I say as I slip on a pair of yoga pants. "He made me believe so many things."

"Viktor!" my mother shouts his name as I slip a T-shirt over myself and he comes jogging into the room.

"I need those boxes we just hang the clothes in," she says, then looks at my uncle Matthew. "I need you to pack her office."

"It's four thirty in the morning," my father replies. "Where do you want me to get those types of things?"

"Don't you know people?" she snaps, looking over her shoulder as she pulls open one of my closet doors.

"In Arizona?" He shakes his head.

"I can call someone," Matthew offers, and just like that I giggle again.

"You're the best, Uncle Matthew," I declare, feeling like I haven't in a while. Most likely in shock, but I'll take this feeling.

"We'll get you out of here," he assures me and I can see him swallow.

By ten thirty, I'm walking out of my house with my hand in my father's. The emergency movers my uncle got are pulling out of the driveway with all of my clothes in it, along with all my office stuff. I left everything else, not wanting to take anything.

"Where is he?" Dad finally asks me once I'm sitting on the private plane and the doors close.

"At his apartment in the city," I tell him, looking out of the window.

"I need a drink," my mother announces from beside me and the phone rings from my purse.

"Put it on speaker," Uncle Matthew urges once I pull it out and see it's him.

I close my eyes before I press the connect button and place it on speaker. "Hello."

"Morning," he greets, "how did you sleep?"

"I didn't," I answer him honestly.

"Well, that's because you had a lot to think about. I hate fighting with you, Lexi, but you left me no choice." I hang my head and feel my mother put her hand in mine. "Don't you think you could have acted better?"

I hear hissing and look over to see Uncle Matthew holding on to the armrests with his head back as he looks up at the ceiling of the plane. "I don't," I finally reply.

"I can see that you are upset. You have to admit, Lexi, you have no one to blame for this besides yourself."

I close my eyes. "I'm leaving you, Trent."

He laughs as if I just told him the funniest joke he's ever heard. "Yeah, right." I wait for him to get over his stint of laughter. "What's gotten into you?"

"Nothing has gotten into me," I refute. "I finally saw what was right in front of my face."

"Lexi, I'm going to take a shower and then I'm going to come home and we are going to talk about things. And you are going to see how much different things would have gone if only you—"

"I'm done." My voice cuts him off. "I'm done letting you darken my light, and I'm not coming back, not now, not ever, Trent."

"You can't leave me!" he roars.

"Yes, I can." I finally inhale deeply. "And I did. Goodbye, Trent."

Twelve

KIRBY

Three months later

I WALK INTO the lobby and head straight over to the elevator. There is a man sitting behind the desk in the middle of the path leading to the elevators. He looks up from whatever is in front of him and he points at me. "Are you Materson?" He uses my last name, and I nod my head.

"I am." I stop at the side of his desk and hold out my hand. "Nice to meet you," I tell him.

"You guys going to bring the Cup home this year?" he asks, and I am almost tempted to roll my eyes in the back of my head.

"That's the plan," I politely answer, instead of answering him with the real answer. The season hasn't even started, so how the fuck does anyone know who is going to win the Cup? "It's never over until it's over."

"Isn't that the truth?" He shakes his head. "Who

would have thought Edmonton would have kicked you guys out of the playoffs."

"Not us," I tell him. "Especially since at Christmastime they were dead last." I start to walk toward the elevators. "But you never know. Playoffs are a different beast."

"They sure are." He nods. "I look forward to watching."

"Have a great day." I finally break the conversation, walking over to the elevator and pressing the button to go up. I look up at the two elevators in front of me and then the two behind me to see which one is going to get here first. When the doors swing open behind me, I turn and head into the elevator and press the button for the fourteenth floor.

I take a step back in case someone else comes into the elevator and wait for the doors to close before it starts to move up. It stops on a couple of floors before it finally opens on mine, and I have to move around two people before stepping out into the hallway. I step out to face the other elevators and there is an office on one side and another on the other side. That's it, two offices per floor. I make my way over to the office that has fourteen zero two on it before turning the handle and pushing it open.

"Hello." I take a step into the empty office space and look around at the small space—gray carpet all around, four walls all painted a sterile white. A couple of windows in between to give the place more natural light, but not much, and the only overhead lights are the eight square bulbs in the tiled ceiling.

"Hey," Kylie says, walking out of one of the two

offices in each corner of the room, a smile on her face. "Finally." She makes her way to me and I give her the biggest hug.

"I feel like I haven't seen you in forever."

"Relax." I kiss the top of her head. "It's only been three months"—she steps away from me—"and we FaceTimed at least once a week."

"I want to say you look horrible." She folds her arms over her chest. "But you look good. You even have a tan. I guess Canada agrees with you." I shake my head. After the fundraiser, I knew I had to get the fuck out of town. That night I sent a couple of trainers messages to see who had a place on their roster and was lucky I had someone in Toronto who could take me. I booked a house on the lake.

We would do on-ice practice every single morning and then in the afternoon. I would do my training outside in the sun, since it wasn't a hundred and fifty degrees. I flew back to Arizona two days ago when I took out Mrs. Visabell's granddaughter to fulfill my part of the auction, and I was officially free of all obligations. I didn't even spend the night in Phoenix. I couldn't stomach it, so I landed in the morning and took a private plane out of there the same afternoon.

"I wish you would have come out," I tell her. "The house even came with a boat and a Jet Ski."

"I was busy"—she rolls her eyes—"quitting my job and then packing my shit and moving."

"I told you we could hire you movers to do all of that." Now that she finally caved and took up my offer to start up the foundation.

"Why are you so extra? Hire movers? Who are you, the Rockefellers?" she asks and then holds up her hand. "I don't want to know. What do you think of the office?"

"It's an office." I shrug my shoulders. "I'm sure you are going to make it less like a psych ward and more like a welcoming space for people."

She throws her head back and laughs a full belly laugh. "Yes, I have Ariella coming in tomorrow to go over some plans."

"That sounds great, and then we need to hire a couple of people," I tell her and she looks to the side.

"Listen, I think we should start small." She walks to the other side of the room. "I think we should hire one more person."

"You think it'll be enough with just two of you?" I run my hands through my hair. "I don't want you to bury yourself in your work."

"One of us can call around and speak to different organizations to see where we can offer help, and the other can call around and see which corporations can donate to our little foundation." She cocks her hip to the side. "First order of business is a bachelor auction."

"Fuck that. We know how the last one ended." I shake my head as the phone in my back pocket rings. "That's my alarm; I have to get to the rink. It's the first day back."

"Okay," she replies and then claps her hands and shrieks, "How exciting is this!"

I open my eyes and try not to laugh at her. "I couldn't sleep last night thinking of the excitement." I pull the phone out of my pocket and turn off the alarm. "Let's have dinner tomorrow after your meeting with Ariella."

"Sounds good," she says, "skate bag."

"Nope." I shake my head. "Still not using it right." I laugh. "It's bag skate and it's a term when the coach is punishing us."

"Whatever." She uses her hand to shoo me away. "Go and leave me with my four white walls."

"You settling in okay at your place?" I ask her of the two-bedroom apartment I rented for her without her knowing. She would never have taken the place if she knew the real price of the apartment.

"It's gorgeous and it has its own gym and a rooftop pool." Her voice goes higher. "And I know it's not twelve hundred dollars a month, jackass."

I laugh. "I have to go. I don't want to be late on the first day."

"Leave me if you must." She turns and walks into one of the offices. "By the way, I'm taking this as my office."

I don't even bother answering her, instead I just walk out and head down to my SUV. I get in and put my phone in the middle of the cupholder as I head straight to the rink. I stop at the black garage door, before pressing the sunglasses holder on top of the rearview mirror. It falls down and I grab the white parking pass, sliding it in front of the scanner. The garage door slowly starts to open and I replace the card before driving in.

Cars are parked everywhere and there is the valet, Clive, waiting for us. He gets off his stool and smiles when he sees it's me. "Look at who decided to join us," he jokes with me as he comes over and extends his hand. "You look uglier than you did last season," he adds when I shake his hand. I can't help but laugh. "I thought they would have fired you by now."

"It's day one and you are already busting my balls." I shake my head and look around. "Got to say, it's good to be back."

"Yeah, I'll remind you of that when your old ass is limping to your car in December." I slap his shoulder as I start to walk away.

"I know you will." I walk toward the black stainless-steel door, pulling it open. Taking a step in, I look into the first office that has the door open, but no one is inside. I turn the corner and see a couple of the offensive coaches in one office. "Hey." I smile and give a chin up. I walk into the office and extend my hand to each of them. "How's it going?"

"How it always goes during training camp," Zane states. He just joined the Warriors, so he's still green around the collar since he's so young. "It fucking sucks." I laugh at them, knowing how hard it has to be to be the one who tells a hockey player that even though they probably gave their all, they are not going to make the final cut for the team.

"See you guys out there." I turn and walk back out of the office. I stop when I see the equipment manager, Barry, putting out some of the hockey sticks. "You have mine?" I ask him and he nods his head. "I have the new one coming next week."

"I got the email," he replies of the brand I work with

who develops my stick every single year. "I have a couple from last season and two from the two seasons before."

"Why don't you take those two sticks and I'll sign them and we can donate them to whoever," I suggest, knowing I hated the stick from two years ago anyway.

"Sounds good. I have your gear in your locker, ready for you."

"We couldn't live without you, Barry." I slap him on his shoulder before walking over to the locker room.

"Holy fuck," Knox, one of the forwards and also a veteran, says when I walk into the room. He's sitting on the bench right under his name, in between Stevie and Lane. "Did you only work out on break?" I shake my head and walk over to them, slapping each hand and then fist-bumping them. Knox gets up and gives me a hug also. We've been on the LA Warriors for the past eight years, and I consider him one of my closest friends.

"Did you only eat on break?" I slap his stomach and he yelps.

"I went to Italy with the family," he mentions his wife and three kids. "What else do you do in Italy besides eat and drink?"

"You stayed in Italy for four months?" I ask him, making him laugh.

"No, but Josephine," he mentions his wife, "took a pasta-making class and she has made pasta every single day since. I can't seem to tell her if she makes pasta one more time, I am going to literally throw up."

"Oh, boo-hoo." Lane makes fun of him. "Your wife cooks for you and makes you homemade fucking pasta.

Cry me a fucking river." He shakes his head, getting up and walking over to his spot.

The three of us all laugh at him. "Thankfully, I get to eat more meals here than at home now."

I walk over to my own side of the room and put my phone on the shelf where my workout clothes are folded.

"Look at who decided to join us." Martin, our head coach, walks into the room wearing a tracksuit. "You guys are about six weeks behind everyone else, so I don't want to see anyone else dragging their asses out there." I kick off my shoes. "Welcome back, boys." He claps his hands. "On the ice in ten."

He turns to walk out of the room and stops when he comes face-to-face with Jaxon. "Why are you fucking late on the first fucking day?" He puts his hands on his hips as he scolds him in the middle of the doorway.

"I was walking out of the house"—he pulls off his baseball hat and scratches his forehead before replacing it on his head—"and I went to pick up Jagger and kiss him. When I held him over my head, he literally threw up in my mouth." He closes his eyes and shakes his head. "I wish I was fucking lying about that."

Everyone in the room grimaces. "That's fucking disgusting," Martin says. "You have eight minutes before you need to be on the ice."

"Got it." He nods at him, coming into the room now.

"One minute of suicide laps for anyone who's late," Martin throws over his shoulder, making everyone rush to get dressed and get on the ice.

"Hey, boys," Jaxon greets, holding up his hand and

then coming over to stand beside me where his locker is.

He holds out his hand to me and I slap it, give him a fist bump, and then we go in for a hug. Both of us slapping the other on the back. "Shit, it's good to see you."

"Good to see you too," I reply, letting him go. "You look fucking exhausted," I joke with him as he puts his phone exactly on the shelf where I put mine.

"I am, fucking teething is not for the faint of heart." He shakes his head. "Honestly, I don't know how we would do it if we didn't have Lexi with us."

My head about whips off of my shoulders as I turn to look at him. The name I didn't let myself say in the last three months. The name I would say in my dreams every fucking night. The woman who I would go to bed thinking about and then wake up thinking about, but then force her out of my mind. "Lexi?" I say her name and my stomach gets tight at the same time my chest feels like an elephant is sitting on me.

"Yeah, man," he confirms, pulling off his shirt, "she's been living with us for the past three months I think."

I blink my eyes, not sure I am actually awake or maybe I'm still sleeping. Maybe this is another dream I've having. "She's living with you?" I repeat the words as I stand here transfixed on him as he gets undressed.

"Yeah, she left her husband," he explains. "I don't know the details because I don't really want to ask her. But she left him and Ariella offered her a place to stay."

"She left her husband." My head feels like it's spinning and I have to sit down on the bench.

"What the hell is the matter with you?" he asks me and I just shake my head. "Why the fuck are you repeating everything I'm saying?"

"I," I start to say, "I'm just."

"Listen, you two lovebirds," Knox interrupts, "as much fun as it is watching you fuck with Kirby with whatever it is you are saying, I do not—and I repeat—I do not want to do suicides." He looks at both of us, dressed in his full gear. "I don't think I could handle it, to be honest with you two. So can we finish whatever this is"—he uses his finger to move from Jaxon to me—"after practice, when I'll probably be throwing up in the garbage can?"

Jaxon laughs at him. "Don't worry about the defense," he assures him, looking over at me and I get up to start undressing. "We'll be on the ice when we need to be on the ice."

"Yeah," I agree, still trying to catch my bearings and not freak over the fact she left her husband. I can't help the smile that now fills my face for two reasons. One, it's good to be back to work, and the second, she finally fucking did it. "What he said."

Thirteen

Lexi

THE SOUND OF crying wakes me up and I blink twice before I turn my head to the side, seeing the sun isn't even up yet. I get up on my elbow and reach over the side table. I press the top of my phone and see that it's just after four thirty in the morning. Tossing the covers off me, I get out of bed and walk toward the door, turning the handle and slowly pulling it open. The crying gets louder and louder. "I know." I hear Ariella's voice in a whisper as she says, "Shhhh shhh shhh." But the crying just gets louder and louder.

I walk down the hallway toward the nursery, the little night-light illuminating the room in a soft yellow. Ariella is in the middle of the room with Jagger in her arms, one hand under his bum, the other on the back of his head, as she bounces from side to side. Jagger's crying is getting a touch louder. "Hey," I say, stepping into the room.

"I'm so sorry we woke you," Ariella apologizes to me as I step into the room and Jagger rubs his face in the middle of her chest. "He just won't get comfy."

"Do you want me to try?" I ask her and hold out my hands to him. "Do you want to come to see Auntie Lexi?" I ask him softly as Jaxon comes into the room.

He's wearing black boxers and nothing else, a baby bottle in his hand as he rubs sleep out of his eye. "I got a bottle." He holds it up and then sees me there. He looks at me with one eye closed. "What are you doing here?"

"I heard the crying and thought I would help," I reply, grabbing Jagger from them and kissing the side of his head. "What's all this fuss, little man?" I hold out my hand for the bottle and Jaxon gives it to me. "You two go back to sleep and I'll come and get you if I need you guys."

Ariella looks at me and then at Jaxon, who reaches forward, grabs her hand, and pulls her out of the room. "You are a godsend," Jaxon mumbles to me.

"You come and get me if he—" She stops talking because he's got her out of the room and the door slams shut behind them.

"Listen, little man," I soothe, putting him on his side as he looks up at me, "don't make us go through sleep training again." He whimpers in my arms. "Remember that?" I ask him, walking toward the rocking chair in the corner of the room. "You cried for a full hour," I remind him as I tease his mouth with the bottle. "Your mother cried the whole time and I thought your father would go bald." He takes the bottle and starts drinking. "I know you're in pain, little man." I move the rocking chair with my foot back and forth. "Teething pain can be the worst." I put my head back and close my eyes, listening to him gulp down his bottle as if he didn't have a bottle at midnight when he woke up for the second time. I open my eyes and look down at him, seeing his eyelids close halfway, his chubby fist closed and lying on my chest. I wait for him to finish the bottle, but he falls asleep before the nipple slips out of his mouth.

I put the bottle on the side table before placing his chest on mine, his head resting on my shoulder, as I gently tap his back. "All I need is a burp from you and we can both go to sleep." I rub his back in a circle before going back to tapping it. It takes him a couple of minutes, between tapping and rubbing, for him to give me a burp before I'm able to stand up and walk him back over to the crib. "Now I'm going to place you down, and you are going to either wake and then drift off or you will just still be sleeping," I say, placing him gently on his back, trying not to wake him. I slowly disengage from him, stopping mid-movement when he jerks his arms. When my arms are fully out from under him, I look in the crib, seeing him on his back with his hands by the side of his head. "Sleep tight, angel," I tell him and turn to walk over and turn off the night-light, before turning on the sound machine and tiptoeing out of the room and closing the door halfway behind me.

Making my way back to my bedroom and sliding into the bed, I look out of the window at the darkness. It's been three months since I left Trent. Three months of being free from him, but at the same time still feeling the pull to him. Guilty for leaving him and then unsure that I did the right thing. He didn't think I had really left him, but then he came home and saw I was gone.

He blew up my phone, but at that point I was in New York at my parents' house. I ignored his calls until I finally caved and answered him. "Lexi," he said with so much anger in his voice, it felt like his whole body was shaking, "what the fuck is going on?"

"I think it's pretty much self-explanatory, don't you think?" I sat in the middle of my bed. My legs pulled to my chest, my arms wrapped around them. "I left you, Trent."

"I want you to get your ass back here right now!" he screamed. "I'm not kidding with you, Lexi. You let those people come into my house!" he roared.

"Those people?" I asked him, knowing he probably checked the Ring cam as soon as I called him. A Ring cam that I wasn't given the code to because it didn't matter to me. I shouldn't bother myself with it. His words, of course, and probably because I would be able to see when he would actually get home, or maybe he was sneaking out more times than I knew about. "You mean my parents."

"Lexi," he hissed, "get your ass back home now."

"Why?" I asked him the question instead of giving in to his demands like I usually did.

"Excuse me?" His tone had gone down.

"Why do you want me to come back?" I repeated the question.

"Be careful," he threatened. I don't know if it was because I was past the point of being exhausted or I was

just happy to be rid of him, but I let out a laugh. "This isn't funny, Lexi."

"It is, actually," I replied. "It's funny that it took me this long, don't you think?" I didn't wait for him to answer. "I should have left you the first time I found out you cheated on me."

"Is this what this is all about," he huffed out, "because you found out I spent the night with Tatum?" I wish it would have hurt hearing that, but deep down I knew he never stopped being unfaithful. "I ended things with her this morning. I want to focus on us."

"You want to focus on us?" I said, hoping he could hear the venom in my voice. "You're a little too late for that, don't you think?"

"It's not too late. We can do the couples counseling you wanted to do. Then we can finally try for a baby. It's about time, don't you think? It's been ten years."

"I'm not going to couples counseling with you." The bitter taste hung in my mouth. "And I am definitely never having a child with you." I sighed deeply. "I'll have my lawyer contact you in the next couple of days."

"Don't do this, Lexi," he said, his voice back to being tight. "I would hate for you to do something and then regret it. Don't you think this has gone on long enough?"

"I do," I agreed with him, "way too long. Goodbye, Trent." I hung up the phone and blocked his number.

A lone tear escapes from the side of my eye and rolls onto the pillow. The confusion about leaving him always hits me at night when the quietness comes. He's made me feel so reliant on him and his thoughts that I second-guess myself. It's at these times I have to think about what my therapist has said from the beginning. You are rebuilding your life starting at step one. Step one is me not second-guessing myself because there are no wrong ways to live my life. Her words repeat in my head as I close my eyes and drift off to sleep.

The sun hits me smack in the face when I turn over on my other side, and I groan before holding my hand up to stop it from blinding me. I turn over again and snuggle back into the covers for a full second before I throw them off me and get out of bed. The bedside table clock shows it's almost ten in the morning. I stretch my arms over my head before making my way over to the bathroom, starting the shower before brushing my teeth. I take a shower and then brush out my hair before walking to my closet and grabbing a pair of sage-green linen pants with an elastic waist and a white sleeveless button-down shirt that has a scoop neckline, something Trent would never approve of. I tuck the front of the shirt in before I walk over and make the bed and open my door.

I look over at the nursery and see the door is open, and so are the shades, before walking down the steps to the kitchen. I walk in, finding Ariella sitting on one of the stools at the island with the highchair beside her.

"Good morning," I say cheerfully, walking in and starting my coffee before going over to the highchair.

Jagger has his hands up and is moving them excitedly in a circle. "Good morning, sweet boy." I bend to kiss his blondish-brown hair. "How did we sleep?" I look over at Ariella, who picks up her cup of coffee and brings it to her mouth.

"After you put him down, he just woke up," she tells me and I smile. "I call that a good stretch, don't you?"

"He wore himself out." I walk back to the coffee machine and grab my cup while I walk over to the fridge to grab the milk. Not almond milk for me, straight-up cow's milk. "Do you want me to make you something for breakfast?" I ask her as I pour the milk into the cup.

"You have to stop acting like you are my personal chef," she hisses. "You don't have to always cook for me."

I snort as I grab my cup of coffee and take a sip. "How about I make some sausage and eggs on English muffins?"

"I want to say no, but I have literally no energy to get up and cook."

"Can you at least let me do this?" I ask, walking over to the fridge and opening it, grabbing the white plastic egg container from the shelf before opening the freezer and taking out the frozen sausage patties. "I already feel like I'm overstaying my welcome."

"What?" Jaxon says, coming into the kitchen dressed in a T-shirt with the LA Warriors team logo in the middle of it and basketball shorts. His hair is wet from the shower and pushed back with his hands. "Why would you even think that?" He walks over to Ariella, leaning down and kissing her lips. "Morning, baby," he murmurs softly before he turns to Jagger, "and you, little pain in the—" He unsnaps him from the highchair and picks him up, Jagger slapping his chest. "Neck." He kisses his neck.

"I'm going to need you to go back to sleeping through the night, please." He puts his cheek on the top of his son's head before turning his face back to me. "Why do you feel like you are overstaying your welcome?" he asks as I turn to the stove, placing a pan on top of it, and then adding water and two of the sausage patties.

"It's just that you already have a little baby to get used to, and then all of a sudden a roommate." I shrug. "It's just, it's a lot."

"We love having you here," Ariella declares, "and Jagger especially loves having an extra set of arms to hold him." I laugh at her as Jaxon hoists him in the air.

"I wouldn't do that if I was you," Ariella warns. "Remember yesterday when he threw up in your mouth?"

"Don't remind me. I have to get going," he says. "I have off-ice practice with Kirby in twenty."

The minute he says his name, I turn toward the stove where he can't see my face. My eyes close as my heart speeds up to the point where it's hard to breathe. The sound of my heart beating echoes in my ears, along with Jaxon saying goodbye in the distance. I swallow past the lump in my throat before looking over my shoulder. "Bye," I say softly, listening to him walk out of the house.

It's been three months since I've seen him or spoken to him. The only thing I have of him, besides the memories of those two months, is the white card I keep folded in my wallet—a reminder of how Trent constantly dulled my light and why I should never go back.

I keep my mind busy by making us breakfast. Toasting the English muffins before placing the scrambled eggs on the top of half of it, followed with a slice of cheddar, and then a golden fried sausage patty, before topping it with the other half of the muffin.

"Here you go." I hand her the plate as she grabs a fussing Jagger and places him on her breast. "You both get to eat," I make a joke as I pull out the stool and sit down.

"What do you have planned for today?" she asks me, taking a bite of the hot sandwich and then huffing out the heat.

"I have therapy at noon," I tell her, "and then nothing at all."

"How is that going?" she asks me softly, and I just smile at her. The minute she heard I left Trent, she opened up her home to me. I stayed with my parents for three days before I caved and took Ariella up on her offer to stay with her. I thought I would come and hang out with her for a couple of weeks, but now it's going on three months and I am feeling like I need to get out of their hair. Which is what I'm going to be discussing with my therapist during this session.

"It's going good," I assure her. "I like her, so that's a good thing." I take my own bite of my sandwich. "I'm still working out not having what he says bother me."

"Fuck that bitch," she snaps, making me laugh.

"Yeah, well, I got a text from Cheryl the other day." I mention one of the only people I still talk to from the hospital.

"What story is he making up this time?" she asks me and I laugh. The minute I left, he started the smear-

Lexi campaign. It started with me being away at a spa, and then when I didn't go back to him, he said I had a nervous breakdown from planning the fundraiser. When that story got old, he said I was traveling the world, finding myself. That he gave me everything on a silver platter, but all I did was throw it back in his face.

"He said I was going crazy because I couldn't get pregnant, and I was taking extra hormones and that drove me crazy."

I can't help but laugh at the stupidity of him. "He's something all right," I mumble. "What about you? What do you have planned today?"

"I have a meeting with a new client who's starting a new foundation," she tells me, "at one thirty."

"Do you want me to watch Jagger so you can go without having to worry?" I ask her and she looks over at me.

"Are you sure?" she asks and I can see the relief on her face. "I don't want you to think I'm taking advantage of you." I laugh at that.

"I literally have nothing to do. I mean, I was going to go online and search for houses."

"Good, then that will stop you and you'll never leave us," she states as Jagger slips off of her breast. Her top falls to cover her as she places him over her shoulder and he turns his head to the side to sleep on her shoulder. "I'm going to go and take a shower. Leave the stuff, I'll clean it after." I nod at her, knowing there is no way I'm going to leave it. "I'm not kidding," she warns softly, rubbing her son's back. "I don't know how I would have done these last couple of months without you."

I blink away the tears. "You would have been just fine."

"I don't know about that," she says. "I don't want you to leave"—her voice trembles—"but I know you have to eventually."

"Yeah," I agree with her, "but just think about how much fun it'll be. You get to help me pick and decorate a house."

Fourteen

KIRBY

THE LAST FIFTEEN minutes of practice is always a scrimmage game. First team to score gets off the ice first. After a two-hour on-ice practice, plus the three hours off ice we did before, I'm ready to take a shower, collapse on my couch, and not move for the rest of the fucking day. The sweat pools at the top of my helmet as I skate around in a small circle at the blue line, looking over at Jaxon, who has his stick on the ice, both arms folded and leaning on the stick as he waits for the forwards to get into position.

"Knox," Jaxon calls his name, "if we lose this because you're skating like your grandmother, I'm going to kick your ass."

"I'm getting better." He moves his skates forward and back as he waits for Coach to drop the puck so we can start.

"I want to trade Knox for Lane!" I shout and Knox just side-eyes me. "You better fucking skate; we lost the last game because you thought you were having a heart attack."

"My chest was hurting!" he yells back, defending himself.

"It's all that fucking pasta and meat," Jaxon declares. "Chicken, steak, fish. Broiled, no carbs."

"You're one to talk. You got here yesterday morning and you looked like you were six months pregnant," Knox fights back.

"That's Lexi's fault; she made chicken parm. Don't worry about the back of the house, worry about the front of the house." The minute he says her name, my body feels like it's being jolted. I hide my mouth with my gloves as I try and breathe normally. Did I sit in bed last night for a full two hours and pull up her name to text her? Why, yes, yes, I did. Did I write something and then delete it over a thousand times? Also, yes. Did I ever send anything? The answer is, fuck no.

I ended up reading and rereading our text thread, even though there was nothing personal there. The whole conversation was dry and just about the fundraiser, but I couldn't help but recall all the conversations we had face-to-face, when I saw her slowly coming out of her shell. But then the only thing I could see in my head, replaying on repeat, was her face the night of the auction. The tears in her eyes as she held on to my arm, begging me to stop. I tossed my phone to the side, telling myself if she wanted to get in touch with me, she would have.

The whistle blowing has me grabbing my stick in both hands and then placing it on my upper thigh as the coach drops the puck and the battle at center ice begins. I watch Knox turn his body, blocking Lane from getting the puck, as he wins the face-off, passing the puck back to Jaxon, who receives it the middle of his blade. I start to skate up the ice with him, Knox, Patrick, and Mike, the rookie, and wait for him to skate into the zone to cross over the blue line. Jaxon looks straight ahead like he's about to dump it in and lets them chase it, but with the flick of his wrist, he sends it across the ice to me. It shocks the other team, who doesn't stop me at the blue line from skating in. Knox hustles to the front of the net and I raise my stick, about to slap shot it in, but instead I pass it over to Jaxon, who lifts his stick midair, and then with the perfect hand-eye coordination slaps it over the goalie's shoulder and to the back of the net.

The whistle blows and Jaxon comes over to me, holding up his glove. "And that's how it's done." He winks at Knox, who just stalks over to the bench huffing.

Taking off my gloves, I unsnap the chin strap and push the helmet back to sit on the top of my head as I walk down the tunnel and toward the locker room. I place my stick against the wall with all the other sticks before walking into the locker room. I toss one of my gloves into one of the big gray bins in the middle of the room.

I then sit down on the bench, grabbing a bottle of Gatorade before I untie my skates, taking one off and then tucking it under my bench, followed by the other one. I slip my feet in my plastic slides and, when I'm undressed, head to the shower. If it wasn't a two-hour practice and I hadn't been off ice before, I would probably attempt to go home and shower, but not wanting to kill anyone I come in contact with with my stench, I decide to shower at the rink.

I'm dressed in basketball shorts, a white T-shirt, and my baseball hat turned backward when I grab my phone and my keys. "See you tomorrow, boys," I say before I walk out of the locker room and toward my SUV. Clive is there at the valet stand as he spots me and tosses me my keys. "I moved it." He motions with his chin toward the front of the row. "You're welcome."

"I got your son's opening-day tickets," I tell him, seeing him smirk. "You're welcome."

I pull the Land Rover's door open and get in before starting the engine. I hold up my hand toward Clive, who gives me a chin up before I pull up and the garage door opens. I pull out of the parking lot, looking at the radio. I see it's just after two in the afternoon. Knowing Kylie is going to be at the office until about four, I decide to head over to the small coffee shop I like. I have to circle the shop twice before I can park five doors down.

I lock the doors and head toward the coffee shop, walking past a flower shop, Pilates studio, and a doggy daycare, most of the dogs sniffing the front window, right next to the coffee shop. *Talk about torturing animals,* I think to myself as I pull open the pink door. The bell on the top of the door rings. I look around, seeing the five tables they have are mostly open, only one is taken.

I head toward the pink counter that matches the door and look in the display case, seeing homemade apple, carrot, blueberry, and chocolate chip muffins on one shelf and then the good stuff under it. There are fresh giant cinnamon rolls right next to a pile of danishes and then under those are the croissants: chocolate, almond, and regular.

The woman walks out of the back, wiping her hand on her apron at the same time someone comes out from the side. I see the dark hair first as she looks forward and then turns to look at me and our eyes meet. "Lexi." I'm the first one to speak. She stands there, mid-step, her mouth open as she stares at me. I step away from the counter and go to her.

"Kirby," she says, shocked. Shocked and nervous from the looks of how her chest is rising and falling. "This is…" She shakes her head, no doubt trying to find the same words I'm trying to find.

"Holy shit." I chuckle. "It's you. You're here."

"I'm here." She finally snaps out of her daze and laughs. "I was next door doing Pilates," she says and I finally take in her outfit. She's wearing tight yoga pants in like a dark blue, almost black, and a cream-colored long-sleeve zip jacket. The sleeves are pulled up to her elbows while the zip is halfway, showing me she's wearing the same-colored tight top under it. My eyes immediately go to her left hand to see if she's wearing her wedding ring, but it's hanging by her side and I can't see it. I'm almost tempted to grab her hand and look at it, but then I think about how crazy that would make me seem.

"This is…" I shake my head. "It's very unexpected to see you here." My heart speeds up. "Do you want to sit down and have a coffee with me?" I blurt before I can think too much about it, turning to face the empty tables. I have never been this nervous in my whole fucking life.

She inhales and shakes her head. "No." My heart plummets to my stomach and I'm sure, after I ruined her night, she's never going to talk to me again.

"Okay." I try not to sound as devastated as I feel. "Fair enough." I smile at her, trying not to turn and storm out just to get away from doing more damage to whatever this is by kissing the ever-loving shit out of her. "It was good to see you." I stare into her eyes. I nod and turn to walk out of the shop without even getting anything.

I'm two steps away from her when I hear her voice. "That's it?" I turn back to look at her.

"Well, you said no." I put my hands on my hips. "So yeah, that's it."

"Wow," she says, moving to the front of the counter and to the girl who has been waiting for my order and watching this awkward exchange. "I was waiting for you to dare me."

My pulse picks up again and I move back to stand beside her at the counter. "Fine," I concede, trying not to smile too big. "I dare you to have coffee with me."

She puts her hands on the counter right in front of her. "Ugh, if you put it like that, then I guess I'll have coffee with you." She shakes her head and finally lets out a little laugh. "Hi." She looks at the barista, who now is trying to hide her smile. "I'm going to have an iced coffee with whole milk." She looks over to the display case, eyeing the cinnamon rolls.

"And she'll have one of the cinnamon rolls." I order for her and she looks up at me smiling.

"I really shouldn't," she says and I laugh.

"You should eat whatever you want," I tell her and the girl behind the register smiles at us.

"Do you want that warmed up?" the girl asks her and her eyes light up. I swear I'm going to buy her cinnamon rolls every single day, just to see that smile on her face.

"Yes, please," she replies, and the girl reaches for a pair of silver tongs before she places one of the rolls on the plate and then turns to put it in the oven.

She presses a couple of buttons before coming over to me. "What can I get you?"

"Can I have an iced shaken espresso?" I order. "No milk, no sweetener." She nods her head and I hear noise coming from beside me and turn to look at Lexi.

"That sounds so gross." I can't help but laugh at the cute face she's making. "Why didn't you order something to eat?"

"Did you see how big that roll is? It's the size of your head. I don't think you are going to finish it."

"I'm not sharing with you." She gawks at me. "You asked me to have coffee with you. You didn't say let's have coffee and share a cinnamon roll. Besides"—she turns and leans her hip into the counter—"I'm going to take home the rest and have it in bed later tonight while I watch my reality television."

"You won't share even a bite with me?" I ask her and she just shakes her head. "I'll take my chances." We stare at each other, the lightness of her eyes making them pop even more.

The girl comes over and places the tray down in front of us as she tells us the total. "If you reach for your wallet," I threaten, grabbing my own wallet from my pocket, "I'm definitely going to take a bite of your cinnamon roll. I asked you to have coffee with me, I pay. Next time you ask me to have coffee with you, you can pay." I hand the girl my card and she takes it, swiping it on her machine, and then handing me the white receipt. "Why don't you grab a table and I'll bring the tray over."

"You think there's going to be a next time AND I'm going to leave you alone with my cinnamon roll? You are crazy." She shakes her head, trying not to laugh at the whole silly exchange. I can't help but smile back at the light in her eyes that already looks so different from three months ago.

I grab the tray and then walk over to the table in the corner, facing the window outside. I take off my baseball hat and toss it on the ledge of the window, in between the potted plants, before sitting down. She sits in front of me and grabs the fork on the tray. "Thank you for the sweet treat," she says, right before she sinks the fork in the side of it.

"Lexi," I say her name and she looks up at me. The way I said her name was a bit harder than I wanted it to be, confusion fills her face. "Before we talk about anything else"—I swallow—"I want to apologize for ruining your fundraiser," I tell her as I rub my hands on the front of my shorts, the nerves making them sweat. "I shouldn't have let him get to me, and I know you worked so hard to make everything perfect, and I should have—”

She smiles at me and shakes her head to stop me from talking. “You didn’t ruin the night.” I take a deep inhale, grabbing my plastic cup with the black straw. “Other things that night ruined it, but you definitely didn’t.”

She takes a bite of the cinnamon roll and avoids looking at me. “How have you been?” I ask her softly as she chews and then takes a sip of her own coffee.

“Okay.” She moves her head side to side, still avoiding looking at me. “Rough.” The only thing I can see is she looks even better than she did before. Her eyes don’t have that haunted look. Her guard isn’t up at all, she’s still a little standoffish, but considering it all, that’s to be expected. “You knew something was off.” She finally breaks the silence and then looks up at me. “You knew I was going through something.”

“I did,” I admit to her. “I didn’t tell anyone.”

“I know you didn’t.” She puts the fork down. “Because if you did, my family would have swooped in like a SWAT team sent in to extract me.” She tries to laugh, but I can see her lower lip tremble. “How?” she asks me softly. “How did you know?”

“It’s a long story,” I tell her. “But yeah, I had a feeling.” She doesn’t push it. “What was the breaking point?” I ask her.

“That night.” She exhales. “That night when I stepped out onto the balcony and heard him say those things.” I look up at the ceiling and she reaches over and puts her hand on mine; her hand is cold as ice, and I wonder how nervous she is about this conversation. “It’s not your fault. You didn't say them." I turn my hand over to have her palm in mine. "He blamed me about the scene and then sent me home by myself."

"What a piece of shit," I hiss and turn to look out the window. "He's such—"

"Your note," she says and I turn my head back to look at her, "it was exactly what I needed at that moment."

Fifteen

LEXI

"THAT NIGHT." I exhale, my whole body feels like it's being jolted by a taser as I recount a bit of that night to him. "That night, when I stepped out onto the balcony and heard him say those things." He looks up at the ceiling and I can see his jaw getting tight, and I reach over and put my hand on his. Feeling the heat from his hand under mine, I worry if it is too forward, and before I can even snatch it back, he looks back at me. I'm drawn into his eyes, drawn into him. "It's not your fault. You didn't say them." He turns over his hand and now my small one is in his. "He blamed me about the scene and then sent me home by myself."

"What a piece of shit," he hisses before he looks out the window. "He's such—" The pain in his voice is too much for me to hear.

"Your note," I say softly and his head whips back my way, "it was exactly what I needed at that moment." I tell him the truth. "It was a light in the darkness."

"Lexi." His voice sounds broken.

"Anyway." I pull my hand from his. "I called my father and that morning I was out of my house."

"You could have called me too." He grabs his plastic cup of coffee and takes a sip. "But I'm happy you made that call and you're here now."

"Yeah," I reply, grabbing my fork and taking another bite of the cinnamon roll and then cutting a piece off and holding out the fork for him to grab it. Instead, he smirks at me and leans down to grab the piece from the fork while I'm holding it. "Don't say I didn't share."

"You look good, Lexi," he compliments and I look down right away when my cheeks heat up. "You looked amazing before this, but now you just…" I look up at him as his words penetrate. "I'm so fucking happy you left him."

"How did you know?" I ask him, even though I asked him before and he didn't answer. I vowed not to, but I can't help it.

"Well, you know my dad died," he reminds me, and I nod and see his Adam's apple rise and fall.

"You know what?" I hold up my hand. "I'm sorry I pushed it."

"No, not at all." He shakes his head. "My stepfather was exactly the way Trent was. He was a grade A narcissist and then the head of the gaslighting association." He tries to joke, but I can see the pain in his eyes. My hand moves again, automatically going to his to hopefully give him the same strength he gave me. "Of course, when you're ten, you don't know it's not normal. I was, I think, fifteen or sixteen when I figured it out. My friend's house was nothing like mine. I saw them have a relationship with their parents that was loving and caring, and I knew just by the way they spoke to each other that something wasn't right in my own home. We were almost like robots. Whenever we got out of line, he would turn it around and tell us how to act but, at the same time, make it like we wanted to act that way." He turns his hand around again and this time my fingers slip entwined with his. "When I left for college is when I sort of broke free of him and I became 'the enemy.' He passed away three years later."

"I'm sorry that that happened to you. Thank you for sharing that with me. It means a lot…" I say softly as I look into his eyes with a small smile. "Enough heavy talk," I tell him. "How was practice?"

He smiles, but his hand never leaves mine. "It's good. I was just coming from there," he tells me and the phone in my bag rings.

I slip my hand out of his as I reach in and pull it out. "It's Ariella.

"Hey," I answer, putting my phone to my ear, looking over at him grabbing his cup of coffee and wondering if it would be totally insane to lean over and just kiss him. Obviously, I would never do it, but there is nothing wrong with imagination, is there?

"Are you okay?" she asks me, and I can hear worry in her voice and I close my eyes.

"Yeah, sorry, I got out of class and stopped to have a coffee. I should have called."

"Oh my God, I'm annoying." She laughs. "I was just worried."

I smile. "All good, I'm on my way home now," I tell her and look over at Kirby, even though I don't want to leave him yet.

"Okay, see you soon," she replies, hanging up the phone and I put it back in my bag.

"I should go." I push away from the table. "I'm going to go and get some things for home," I tell him. "You don't have to wait for me."

"I'll be here," he assures me and I nod at him, getting up and walking back to the counter. The girl comes out from the back.

"I'd like to have two cinnamon rolls to go," I tell her, "with a couple of other things you think would be good." I smile at her. "And if you can wrap up an extra cinnamon roll in a separate bag," I ask her and she smirks at me. "Can I also have a container to wrap up the one I have? Sorry." I hold up my hand. "I know it's a lot."

"You're fine," she assures me and prepares my order and hands me the two bags before swiping my card. "Have a good one," she says and I nod, walking back to my table, sitting down and grabbing my cinnamon roll, placing it in the takeout container before licking the stickiness off of my fingers.

"Ready?" I ask him, wiping my hands with napkins and putting the container in the bigger bag.

"I guess," he says, grabbing his empty plastic container while I grab my half-full one. He puts his hand on my lower back as we walk to the door. Stepping out before him, my heart races quickly as we stand in the middle of the sidewalk. "Where are you parked?" he asks me and I point to the white Land Rover parked right to the side of him. "Oh, okay." He takes a deep inhale. "It was good seeing you," he says nervously as he leans in and kisses my cheek. "It was better than good seeing you."

"It was better than good seeing you too." I laugh at his choice of words.

"We should do this again sometime," he suggests and I can't help the smile that fills my face. "Whenever. As soon as possible."

"That sounds good," I agree, my hand gripping the bags tighter. "Oh," I say quickly, "I almost forgot." I hand him the bag with the single cinnamon roll. "For you." I hold it up for him and his hand comes out to grab it. Our fingers graze each other and I swear my body shivers. "For later."

He looks into the bag and he laughs. "I'll think of you the whole time I eat it," he teases, and I bite my lower lip, trying not to giggle like an idiot. He takes a step closer to me and hugs me with his free hand. I close my eyes as I inhale his musky scent. The hug lasts a little longer than it should, but I'm not complaining. He lets me go and I reluctantly walk over to the new car I bought for myself the month after I was in California and decided I would be making this my home. I get into the SUV and put my things on the passenger seat before I put my hand on my forehead. Letting out a huge exhale, I then look to see him walking away. "That was not on my bingo card for today," I mumble, starting the car and pulling away from the curb.

I'm halfway down the street when the phone rings. I look in the center console to see my lawyer calling me, her name in the middle of the screen, Marley Schrimmer. I press the button on my steering wheel. "Hey, Marley," I say her name as I turn and head toward Ariella and Jaxon's.

"Lexi," she says my name. almost sighing, "I have news."

"Oh," I say, surprised. It's been two months since I hired her. I know I should have called Ryleigh, my cousin's wife, but I was still a little embarrassed about everything that happened. She used to be in the DA department in Chicago and then fell in love with my cousin who played for Nashville. She quit the DA department and is now doing family law. From what my sister has said about her, she's cutthroat. My parents don't even know I hired a lawyer yet. It was something I did without telling anyone. It was step one after I got a therapist.

"His lawyer called today and he wants you to sign an NDA and he'll give you twelve million dollars." I look at the screen. "But you can never, ever talk about him or the relationship."

"What do you mean?" I ask her.

"No interviews, no gossip, nothing," she fills me in. "Basically, your relationship is like it never happened."

I shake my head. "Okay, I'll think about it."

She gasps, "It's twelve million dollars! What is there to think about?"

"Right, but if I take it, then he again has control over what I do." I shake my head, knowing I'm going to have to fire her. We are obviously not on the same page, and she didn't listen to a word I said when we had our meeting.

"Gotcha," she replies as I pull into the driveway. "Well, how about you think about it and let me know?"

"Will do," I say, disconnecting the phone and turning off the SUV. I grab the bags from the seat next to me, getting out and shutting the door with my hip.

Walking up the steps, I open the door and listen for a second before announcing I'm home. I hear Ariella's voice coming from the family room. "I'm back here."

I kick off my shoes on the mat and put my bag down at the step before walking back into the family room. I spot her sitting on the couch with Jagger nursing. "Hi," I say to her and the sound of him unlatching from her breast fills the room as he looks over at me, giving me a smile and then going back to his meal. "Now that's the smile of my dreams." I squeeze his foot, making him kick me away.

"He's a charmer." Ariella grabs her water jug and takes a deep sip of water as I walk over and place the white paper bag in the middle of the island. Then I walk back over to the family room and sit on the floor next to Jagger's toys, stretching out my legs. "What's in the bag?" she asks over her shoulder.

"The most amazing cinnamon rolls I've ever tasted in my life," I declare and she laughs.

"I'll be the judge of that," she retorts. "You spent the

last ten years without sugar, so you don't really have the perfect palate for that." I can't help but laugh and it interrupts Jagger again, who unlatches and looks over at me. He squirms in her arms and she pulls down her tank top before getting up and handing me Jagger, who now has his fist in his mouth as he gives me a gummy smile.

"Hi, my chonker," I coo softly, kissing his neck before looking at the table, seeing there are pictures scattered all over. "Did you have a good afternoon?" I ask him and he gurgles at me. I turn and place him on his back in the middle of his activity mat. He knows right away to kick his feet to hear the piano by his feet sing the music. "What are all these?" I cross my legs and pick up a picture of an office.

"That—" Ariella starts, taking one of the containers out. "You brought me a half-eaten cinnamon bun?"

I laugh at her face. "No, that's for me after. I brought you a whole new one. One for Jaxon also, so you don't have to share."

"You love me!" she shrieks, turning to grab a fork and then coming back to sit on the floor next to Jagger. I watch her take her first bite and see her eyebrows go up at the same time her eyes go big. "Okay, this is good," she praises mid-chew and I laugh at her looking at the pictures. "That"—she points to the pictures with her fork—"is for the office I'm designing. Actually, I was going to talk to you this morning about it." She used to do marketing with social media but always dabbled in design. She decided to get her interior designing degree while pregnant. Now she just does that and she makes her own hours.

"You need help designing?" I snort. "My whole house was cream and beige."

"No." She shakes her head. "It's for the new foundation that I had a meeting with the other day. Helping women and children leave toxic and abusive families. Really small for now," she says. "One person works there, and they're looking for someone else."

"Okay," I say, unsure of why she is telling me this.

"I think you should apply for the job." She puts the roll to the side as "Mary Had a Little Lamb" plays in the background.

"What?" I ask, shocked, not sure I really heard her.

"You can help people like you, who don't know what steps to take. Why don't you go on the website and see what their mission statement is?"

"I don't know." She gets up and walks over to the front door as I look down and see how bright and colorful she is making this office. She comes back a couple of seconds later and hands me a card. I look down and see K. Hayes and her phone number under it. The name of the foundation is in the middle of the card, Make the Choice. "I haven't had a job in over ten years."

"You have nothing to lose," she tells me, taking another bite of her roll. "You apply for the job and then see if you're a good fit. No harm, no foul." I turn the card around, my hands shaking. "The first step is to apply. Then you see what happens next."

"I'll think about it," I reply and then Jagger lets out a huge shriek and we both turn to look at him.

Later that night while I'm in bed, wearing my plush robe, I open my laptop and type in the foundation name. The website pulls up right away and I see the mission statement right in the middle of the screen.

Our Mission:

Abuse happens in all different types of environments and in different forms.

Our mission is to help people impacted by this. To help them survive and thrive through awareness and community engagement and education.

I look over at the top where the contact button is and press it, and it brings me to an email page.

I swallow down the lump as my hands fly over the keyboard composing the email.

Hello, Ms. Hayes,

I came across your website and was wondering if you were looking for anyone to help at the foundation. I would like to set up a phone call if you do have anything available.

Please feel free to contact me at any time.

Lexi Petrov

(602) 521-1002

I press send before I can take it back, then shut the top of the laptop at the same time the sound of swooshing ends, telling me the email has officially been sent. "Well, here goes nothing."

Sixteen

KIRBY

I SIT SLOUCHED on my couch, my feet on the coffee table in the middle of the room. The television is playing in the background. One of the shows Jaxon told me is a must watch is on, but all I have been doing for the past hour is sitting down and staring at my phone.

The text app is open to Lexi's name, and I must have composed about a thousand different text messages in that hour. My eyes read it over and over again before I press send.

Me: The best part of my day was seeing you. Thank you for the cinnamon roll. I dare you to come over to my house right now.

"You can't send that," I tell myself after I write the last part. I go back and erase it all. "Just be natural."

Me: Thanks for the cinnamon roll. It was good seeing you today. We should do it again soon.

"Yeah, that's good, right?" I ask my cat, Jefferson, who is sitting right next to me, but not so close that we are touching, because that's not the type of relationship she wants. "Should I press send?" I take a deep breath in, looking over at her and seeing her with her eyes closed. I move my hand to rub down her black back and she opens her eyes and gets up to move away, turning around and giving me her back. "Does that mean I should?" I'm about to press send when the phone rings in my hand.

Kylie's face appears on the screen, her eyes closed as she makes a pufferfish face. I took the picture when she turned twenty-one and she thought she could drink with the big boys. I got her a shot of moonshine and that was the face she made right after. I swipe my finger across the screen and then press the speaker button. "If you are calling me to discuss paint samples again, I'm blocking your number."

The sounds of her laughing fill the room. "No," she pants out, "I am calling because we just got an email."

"Okay," I say, not sure I'm following what she is saying. "Were we expecting to get an email?"

"No," she sings out loudly, making Jefferson look over. Then she decides this isn't her vibe, so she jumps off the couch and starts to walk over to the back door, then turns and gingerly walks up the steps toward the bedrooms. "Total surprise."

"Are we going to play twenty questions or are you going to tell me who the fuck the email is from?" I chuckle.

"I mean, playing twenty questions will make my night," she teases. "Especially since you said you were going to be my right-hand man, but the minute that a decision needs to be made, you take off."

"I don't give a shit what type of carpet you want in the office or even what color you want to put up on the walls. I couldn't care less, that is totally up to you. I'll only be in there a couple times a month."

"Whatever." I can hear the eye roll from my side of the phone. "Okay, start with question one, but there is no way you will ever guess."

"Is this a woman?" I ask her and she laughs.

"It is," she confirms. "Now you have to choose between one and three point nine billion women. And go."

"Is this a woman I know?" I ask her and she hmms. "Is this a woman we know together?"

"I met her, yes," she says, and I think of the next question.

"Is it someone we know from back home?"

"I guess," she says and I groan because I'm already over this fucking game.

"It's a yes-or-no question, Kylie."

"Fine, then yes, we know her from back home," she snaps out.

"Have I slept with this woman?" I close my eyes and silently laugh when she makes vomit noises.

"I'm going to go out on a limb and say no, but I'm really hoping you didn't, or else it will be really fucking awkward for all of us."

"Okay, I'm about done with this," I bark. "Just tell me who it is, and what it's going to cost us?"

"You really are no fun." She snorts. "It's not going to

cost us anything. Well, it will cost us something if you hire her."

"Hire her?" I repeat.

My phone pings with a notification and I look down to see Kylie just sent me an email. "Go read what I just sent you. I'll wait here."

"This must be really fucking good," I say, pressing the email logo and then clicking on the one that has Kylie's name on the top. My eyes go big and I sit up when I see Lexi's name. I scan the email quickly before gasping out.

"That's what I said," Kylie says, her voice going loud.

"Did you call her?" I quickly ask.

"Yeah, sure, she sent it about four minutes ago and I already called her."

"You need to call her."

"I am going to call her; it's just I don't know what to say," she backpedals, and I hear how nervous she is. "I've never had to hire someone."

"Okay, how about you call her and set up a meeting, and I'll go?"

"I don't need you scaring her off," she counters and now I'm the one rolling my eyes.

"I'm not going to scare her off," I assure her and I'm not even sure of myself. "We have a connection."

"You have a connection," she repeats the words like she didn't just hear them. "Can you not fuck this up by doing something stupid?" she hisses out. "Lexi single-handedly raised over ten million dollars for the hospital with two fundraisers. Can you imagine what we could do with that type of money?"

"I would never fuck this up," I say softly. "This foundation means as much to me as it does to you."

She waits a couple of minutes before she answers, "Fine. What do you want me to ask her?" She doesn't even wait for me to answer. "Forget it, I'll just wing it. I'll call you back."

"No," I about scream out. "Don't wing it!" But she's already hung up on me, but I still talk to the screen. "Don't wing it." I grab the phone in my hand and shake it. "You better not fuck this up, Kylie." I toss my phone on the table and get up, going over to the fridge. I pull it open and then close it before walking over to the pantry. I step in and take a look around, and my stomach churns, feeling like I'm going to throw up. I never in a million years thought she would reach out. I had a plan to get her to work for the foundation. The plan would be to bring it up to her in a couple of months. That is after I finally convinced her to date me. But this works out way better, but now I have less time to convince her to take the job.

The phone rings and I run back out, seeing it's Kylie again. "Did you fuck it up?" I put the phone to my ear as I run my hand through my hair.

"If fuck it up means she's going to meet you tomorrow at one to discuss what the job entails, then yes, I fucked it up."

"Okay," I reply, fisting my hand in the air and shooting it up to the ceiling. "Send me the details. Did you call and make a reservation?"

"Yeah, in three seconds since I hung up with her and called you back, I also called and made a reservation," she retorts. "Also, I'm not your secretary. My job was to get her to come to the restaurant. Your job is to seal the deal." She groans. "And I don't mean seal the deal by taking her back to your place and doing naked Twister."

I laugh at her. "I'm not going to do naked Twister with her," I assure her, leaving out the yet or that I wish I could actually play naked Twister with her.

"Seriously," she says softly, "I don't know what happened between the two of you. But the rumors around the hospital about her were not good when I left."

"Rumors around the hospital?" I sit down, my legs not sure they can actually continue to stand. "What rumors?"

"That she went crazy."

"She didn't go fucking crazy!" I practically shout into the phone. "That's a bunch of bullshit."

"I know," she agrees. "There were so many different ones." I fist my hands, ready to punch a hole in the wall. "One of them was that she was traveling through Asia on sort of an *Eat, Pray, Love* trip. Another couple were that she found him cheating." She laughs. "That we all thought was for real since someone heard they caught him and some girl in the stairwell making out." I close my eyes. "Anyway, she's obviously here now." I don't say anything else, my stomach tightening when I think of the lies that he no doubt started to save face. "Don't fuck it up."

"I won't fuck it up," I confirm. "Okay, I'll call you tomorrow after I meet with her and give you the details."

"Great. Also, I'm going with an ecru for the walls."

"Great." I smile. "That was the color I wanted you to

go for, but was testing you." She laughs. "You passed."

"Good day, sir." She hangs up the phone and I pull back up the text thread. I delete the text and start again.

Me: It was great seeing you again. Thanks for the cinnamon roll.

I press send before I overthink it and make it more complicated than it has to be. I don't think she's going to answer me at all, and I'm definitely not ready for her to answer me right away.

Lexi: It was great seeing you again also. Hope you warmed up the cinnamon roll, it's better that way.

I look down, wondering if I should answer her when Jefferson comes back down and jumps up on the couch beside me. She takes one look at me before turning and lying at the opposite end of the couch, away from me. "She asked me if I warmed it. Should I answer her?" I ask Jefferson who just blinks her eyes closed. "Solid answer," I tell her. "I'll answer her tomorrow in person."

I toss my phone to the other side of the couch before I do something even more stupid, like call her.

I PULL IN the parking lot with ten minutes to spare. Getting out of my black Land Rover with my phone and my keys in one hand, I walk into the restaurant, pulling open the door and seeing the hostess behind the stand smile at me. "Good afternoon," she greets when I walk in.

"Good afternoon," I reply, taking off my sunglasses. "I have a reservation under the name Make the Choice."

I smile at her as she looks down at the paper.

"For a party of two?" she asks me and I nod my head. "The other party is already here," she says, shocking me. "Right this way." She turns and leads me past the walk and into the restaurant. Half the tables are filled and I do a quick scan of the room when I see her. She's sitting down, her head turned to the side, looking out the window. She must feel me staring at her because she turns her head and spots me. Her blue eyes go big as I get closer and closer to the table. "Right over there," the hostess says, stopping two tables before and holding out her hand to the table Lexi is sitting at.

I nod at her. "Thank you." I make the rest of the way to the table with Lexi. She is wearing a white button-down shirt with blue stripes. The top three buttons are undone with a gold necklace hanging around her neck. The long sleeves are pushed up to her elbows and I can see she's wearing a gold watch with two Cartier bracelets. "Lexi," I say once I get to the table. She looks at me and the need to bend and kiss her lips is like the need I have for air to breathe. "Thank you for meeting with me."

"Meeting with you?" she asks, confused, and then sits back in her chair. "Wait a second, are you Make a Choice foundation?"

I pull the chair out and sit down in it, placing my phone and keys beside me. "I am," I confirm. I'm about to say something else when the waiter comes over and introduces himself.

"I'll have a sparkling water," I tell him and then look at Lexi. Holding my breath, I wonder if she's going to get up and storm out. Maybe I should have told her it was me.

"I'll have the same," she tells him with a smile and waits for him to walk away before turning back to look at me. "I'm going to need you to explain this to me."

"I will explain whatever you need me to explain, but then you have to tell me how you found out about us."

"You go first."

"Okay, we talked a little yesterday about my stepfather, and after playing hockey for years, I've wanted to start a foundation. Something meaningful that I'll have a hand in when it's time to step off the ice for the last time. I finally took the leap and hired Ms. Hayes." I use Kylie's name, not sure I want to tell her she's actually my sister. She might think it's a family business and not want to get involved. "Now, you can tell me how you found out about us?"

"Ariella," she says and I chuckle.

"Of course. She's the one designing the office."

"She is; she said they were looking for someone else," she explains and stops talking when the waiter comes over and puts our glasses down with the bottle in the middle of the table.

"Have we looked at the menu?" he asks us and we both shake our heads. "I'll give you another minute." He walks away.

I wait for a second, reaching for the bottle and pouring some in her glass and then some in mine. "Ariella is right," I start. "We are looking for someone else. And I think you would be perfect for the job." She doesn't say anything, so I continue my pitch. "I don't know the full extent of your relationship with Trent. And frankly, I don't really want to know. I saw what I needed to see. We need someone who has been there before. We need someone who has compassion for what they're going through. We need someone who isn't going to judge the people we're helping because of their situation. We need someone who can guide them through the most difficult time of their lives."

"Those are big shoes to fill," she states, reaching for her water, and taking a sip before going on. "I don't even know if I'm qualified for all of that."

"I'm going to disagree with you on that," I counter and her eyebrows shoot up. "You took the biggest step of your life. You made the call. Many people don't even take the first step. You know what they feel, why they are feeling what they are feeling. We are looking for someone to reach out to different organizations and become a liaison with them. Then we get to find those who need the most help."

"I don't know," she says softly.

"I mean, there is no harm if you try it out. Maybe you won't like it. Maybe we won't like you," I reply and she gasps, making me laugh. "Or maybe"—I lean in—"maybe we're a perfect fit."

Seventeen

Lexi

"I MEAN THERE is no harm if you try it out. Maybe you won't like it. Maybe we won't like you," he replies and I just gasp, and then it's followed with a quick chuckle by both of us. "Or maybe"—he leans in and my stomach literally flutters at his words—"maybe we're a perfect fit."

I put my elbows on the armrests of the chair. "I don't know," I say honestly. "I barely know what I'm doing with my life. How can I help people change theirs?"

"Well, you aren't going to be the only one." He puts his hand on the armrest and I can see the ink on his wrist. The white button-down shirt goes tight around his biceps when he sits like that. "We'll be working as a team. We will have weekly meetings, or monthly, that hasn't been decided yet, and you'll work closely with Ms. Hayes. Basically you'll help us find where we're needed the most."

"That sounds better than just me." I laugh nervously.

"I would just give help to everyone. Like Oprah," I joke with him. "You get a car." I point over to the waiter. "You get a car." I point to the hostess and he laughs.

"So are you going to do it?" he asks me and I shrug. "How about you think about it and let me know?"

"That I can do," I answer him. The way my heart is beating in my chest, it's a miracle I can even hear his words.

"And if you have any questions while you are deciding if you are going to do this or not, you can call me or Ms. Hayes," he offers.

"Fine," I agree and then he looks over at the waiter.

"We still going to have lunch?" he asks and I just laugh. "We still need to eat."

"You already lured me here under false pretenses," I tell him and look at my watch to see I have two hours before I have to meet my mother. "I should have left already."

"Technically I didn't." His blue eyes go lighter.

"You texted me last night after I had already taken the meeting," I point out and he looks up, probably trying to think of what else to say. "So you knew I had emailed her."

"I did." He doesn't lie to me or try to spin the truth. "But I texted you on a personal level."

I can't help the chuckle that comes out of me. "I can't even argue with you."

The waiter comes over and we both order a salad. "So on a scale from one to a hundred, how shocked were you when you saw me?" He puts his elbows on the table and

I follow his move, entwining my fingers together and resting my chin on them.

"A million," I answer him and he grins. "Your mission statement on the website was the thing that pulled me in."

"That was all Ms. Hayes." He doesn't take the credit. "You two will work well together."

My eyebrows shoot up. "I didn't say yes yet."

"But you didn't say no either." He points at me and the rest of the lunch is spent with us talking about how his back-to-the-ice training is going.

When I push away from the table and stand up, his eyes go down, a full sweep of my outfit, and I'm suddenly happy I chose this outfit. The white wraparound skirt hits me mid-thigh, shorter than I would ever wear three months ago, but also one I was dying to wear. I hold my nude-colored purse in both hands as I wait for him to stand up. He grabs his things, putting his aviator glasses on the top of his head as he extends his hand out for me to walk in front of him. I walk toward the front door, smiling at the hostess when she tells us to have a nice day.

The wind blows my hair over my face as I step out and wait for him to follow. I look at the black Land Rover on the other side of my white one. "Well," I say, stopping in the middle of the parking lot, "thank you for meeting with me."

He extends his hand for me to shake and I reach out, my hand sliding into his. "Thank you for your interest in our foundation," he replies, so official.

"I guess I'll be in touch," I state, our hands still in each other's, moving up and down.

"I am very much looking forward to that." His eyes stare into mine. "And for working with you." I don't know why but those words make my insides shiver.

"I'm going to need my hand back, if you expect me to be in touch with you," I joke and he just smirks, squeezing mine once before letting it go.

"Have a good day, Lexi," he says and waits for me to walk over to my SUV before he walks over to his. I get in at the same time my phone rings, and I see it's my mother. "Hey, Mom," I answer, looking in my rearview at his ass as he walks to his own vehicle. The tight black dress pants fitting him perfectly. "Did you land?"

"We just landed," she says breathlessly. "Do you want to meet us at the first house?"

"Yeah," I reply with a smile, "I'll be there in fifteen." I watch him back out of his parking spot and look over at me. The aviator glasses on his face make him even more hot. I shake my head. "I'm excited."

"Us too," she says. My phone rings and I see he's calling me.

"I'll see you soon," I say, hanging up and answering him, "Hello."

"Everything okay?" he asks me and I turn to look out the back window at him.

"Yeah, why?"

"You haven't left yet," he notes and I wonder if he can see me, "just making sure you are okay."

"All good," I assure him. "My mother called."

"Sounds good." He holds up his hand and waves. "Talk later," he adds, right before he disconnects. I watch him drive out of the parking lot when I add the address of the house in the GPS. I replay the whole conversation we had at lunch as I follow the directions to the house, stopping when it tells me I've reached the destination. I get out of the SUV and walk toward the house. Stepping onto the driveway, I see the black double garage door. I look up at the house and it looks like it's all concrete. I look over my shoulder when I hear a car approaching and then smile when I see my mother in the passenger side, waving. The car comes to a stop and I walk toward them.

My mother gets out and comes to me while my father trails behind her. "Hey," she says with a huge smile on her face as she comes to me and gives me a big hug, and we sway side to side. Letting me go, she then grabs my face in her hands. "You look so good," she praises, "even better than the last time we saw you."

"You see me every day during our FaceTime calls," I remind her as my father walks around and grabs me in a hug. "Hi, Dad," I say, putting my head on his chest and listening to the sound of his heart beating.

He rubs his hands up and down my back. "You ready to see this house?" he asks me and I nod my head.

"This is my favorite one," my mother shares, walking over to the gate and putting in the code. The door unlocks and she steps in. "I like that it's got a cement wall so you can't see the front door." She looks over at me as we step in and I look at the house.

"That's because if not, you would be able to see right in the house," I say of the big window in the front. "Like I see everything." I smile as she walks up the steps to the door and puts in a code on the lockbox for the key as it pops out. She opens the door and I step in behind her, seeing a three-piece sofa set facing the door. The high vaulted ceiling slants down and you see it's filled with windows, showing you the sky. My eyes go up past the couch set to what is the upstairs loft area. The bottom part of the railing is white and the top is a dark-chocolate brown, almost black. It has a brown sofa pushed up against it.

"This is spacious," my father observes, walking in behind me and closing the door. I slowly take steps into the house and stop at the staircase that is the same color as the railing upstairs.

Walking more into the house, the ceiling ducks down to a normal height but I stop when I see the back of the house has full floor-to-ceiling windows overlooking the ocean. "Oh, wow." I move past a little seating area that faces the family room.

My father walks into the family room and goes up the two steps to the dining room that is just off the kitchen. "This kitchen is the perfect size." I follow him in there to see the L-shaped counter with two stools at the head.

My eyes go to one side of the wall that is all windows but facing a cement wall with vines all over it. "That's a bit scary," I say of the sink that faces the wall. "Imagine you are washing the dishes and a head pops up."

My father laughs, walking around the island that has

another sink. The cabinets are a dark brown. "This house has three bedrooms," my mother says, "and although it doesn't have a pool, it has a newly remodeled jacuzzi."

"Her backyard is literally a pool." My father points toward the ocean.

"Two out of the three bedrooms have private balconies facing the ocean."

"How much is this house?" I ask them as I take the steps back to look out the windows to the ocean, seeing some outside furniture.

"What difference does that make?" my father asks, putting his hands in his pockets. "The question is do you like it?"

"What do you mean 'what difference does it make?' It makes a huge difference. I have a budget," I inform him and he looks at my mother. "Mom, you know my budget, right?" I question. I didn't want anything too big, nor did I want to go over two million dollars. I don't know how much I'm going to get from Trent, but that was what I had in my bank account that I'd accumulated over the years.

"I do," she confirms, "and this is in the budget." She looks at my father. "Should we go upstairs and see the bedrooms?"

I follow them up the stairs and step into the loft area. Built-in custom cabinets are against the wall, with a brown love seat that faces a television. "This is cozy," I say, looking to the left where two big double doors are open and I see a long brown chaise. I walk across the wood floor to the bedroom. Stepping into the room, on the left-hand side is a long dark-brown built-in lining the hallway with a cream-colored counter that faces the entry of the open bathroom. The floor looks like it's little seashells glued together. My heels click on it as I look to the left side and see the massive shower that could fit about fifteen people, with the bathtub against the glass shower wall.

"This is a little—" my father says, taking in the glass windows that face the same cement wall that is in the kitchen. "Can you see in here?" he asks my mother, who laughs.

"It's frosted from the outside," she assures him. "You can look out, but they can't look in."

The shower faces the double vanity, and if you walk deeper into the room, you are taken to the walk-in closet. "It's so dark," I mention of the dark cabinets. "Do you think we can swap this out for white?"

She nods her head. "That's an easy fix. Go and see the balcony." She motions with her head toward the bedroom. Walking past the king-size bed, I open the door and step out, seeing the beach right under my feet, and the sound of the waves crashing onto the shore. "The view is everything."

My mother steps out, followed by my father. "This house is two million dollars?" I ask her and she looks over at my father.

"It's five," my father admits and I gasp.

"Why would you show me a house that is over my budget?"

"Because it's not over your budget," he refutes.

"Consider this your wedding present"—I laugh—"and your divorce present."

"What are you talking about?"

"Well, you and Trent eloped," he explains. "I mean, not eloped, you had a small wedding without us there." I am not getting into that right now. I don't want to upset him by telling him Trent wanted just five people there because he didn't want the uproar of my family to take the focus away from me. That is what he went with, and that is what he had me believe. Looking back on it now, I can't believe I ever agreed with him. "We gave your sister a house in New York before she even got hitched, and now, she doesn't even live in the city."

"I'm not going to take your money."

"Okay, then if we buy it, will you stay in it for us?" I roll my eyes when he asks me that. "What? It's an investment and we want to make sure it's taken care of, and what better person to do it than you?"

"I'm supposed to be buying this house myself," I remind him. "It's a big step for me."

"Okay, so what if we go halfsies?" he counters. "And when you take Trent to the cleaners, then you can pay us back."

"Do I want a five-million-dollar home?" I ask them. "It's so big." They both look at me like I have two heads. "Okay, fine, it's a third of the house I had in Phoenix but—"

"You wanted a three-bedroom house on the ocean." My mother cocks her hip to the side and puts her hands on her hips. "This is it."

"I mean, it doesn't have a pool," I try to joke with them, "but this is high on the list."

"Now, let's go see the other two," my mother urges and my father wraps his arms around my shoulders and kisses my head.

"Love you, Lexi," he says softly, "more than life."

"Who is the most handsome boy in the world?" I ask Jagger as he bounces down on my legs, going to blow kisses in his neck. "You." I rub my nose against his. "You are the most handsome boy in the world."

"You tell no lies," Ariella says, walking into the living room, her hair fresh from the shower. "Was he good?"

"When isn't he an angel?" I ask her as he squeals.

"Last night," she retorts. "That was not an angel thing to do by being up every hour on the hour." She sits with us and looks over at him. "I bet you are going to miss that when you finally move out."

"Can I take him with me?" I ask her. "I don't think I can live without him."

"Did you choose which house you wanted?" she asks me. It's been three days since we went to visit the houses and up to today the best one was the first one. "Are you still going over it in your head?"

"You know I am," I reply as the front door opens and then a couple of seconds later slams shut.

"Oh, they're here," she states, getting up and walking over to the entrance, and I have a spilt second before it dawns on me she says they're here.

"Hey." I look up, seeing Jaxon come into the room. I smile at him and my eyes go behind him to two more blue eyes, my smile slowly fading at the same time my palms start to sweat. "Kirby," he says his name, "you remember Lexi."

Eighteen

KIRBY

I FOLLOW JAXON into his house, my heart speeding up just a touch when I know I'm going to see her again. This afternoon, when I picked up Jaxon to go out to office training, I looked for her SUV and saw she wasn't there. My mind wondered where the fuck she was and what she was doing. But I didn't dare ask. Then when I got here and Jaxon asked me if I wanted to come in to say hello to baby Jagger, I jumped at the chance.

"Hey," Jaxon says, walking into the family room. He goes straight to Ariella and bends to kiss her lips, as I make it into the room and spot her in the middle of the couch. She smiles at Jaxon and then her head turns just a touch, as I watch Jagger standing on her thighs, bouncing up and down. Her smile fades as she sees me. "Kirby," Jaxon calls my name and I look over to him, "you remember Lexi."

I grin, then turn back to look at Lexi, who looks like she's in the middle of the street with a car coming straight for her. "I do," I confirm. "We met at the baby shower." Not sure what she told them, so I play it safe, for her.

"We did." She nods and then looks at Jagger before getting up and holding him on her hip. She's wearing a pair of cream-colored linen baggy pants with three brown buttons down the front and a white cropped tank top that falls in the middle of her stomach, but shows off her defined abs. This is the first time I've seen her dressed in something that shows off her figure and I, for one, love it. "Do you want your daddy?" She smiles down at Jagger, who just gives her a gummy smile.

"Hey there, big guy," Jaxon coos, taking him from her and kissing his cheek. "Did you have fun with Auntie Lexi?" He looks at Jagger as if he's going to answer him. "Want to go see your uncle Kirby?" he asks him as I stand here, wanting to get closer to Lexi. "I wouldn't want to either," he tells him, making all of us laugh, "but he said he missed you."

I chuckle and reach out my hands for him. He looks at me and then my hands before turning back to look at Jaxon and then back at me. "He's not as scary as he seems." Jaxon tries to encourage him. But he turns back and smacks Jaxon's chest. "He seems to only like three people." Jaxon tries to make me feel better. "Lexi is his favorite."

She isn't only his favorite, my mouth almost says, but I bite my tongue. "That's only because she takes him in her bed and cuddles with him instead of letting him cry in his crib," Ariella says.

"I'm moving out soon," she states, shocking me but I

try to not show it on my face, "and I'm not going to have any Jagger cuddles." She rubs his back gently and he plunges toward her and she catches him laughing.

"Am I your favorite?" she asks him, blowing bubbles in his neck. This is a side of Lexi I've never seen before. I've never seen her this carefree. I've seen her let loose before, a little bit, but not like this. Not the way she is with Jagger, and as I stand here, I find myself jealous of a twenty-pound baby who has no teeth.

"You want something to drink?" Jaxon takes off his baseball hat and tosses it on the couch before heading into the kitchen.

"I'll have a water," I tell him and Ariella follows him into the kitchen.

"Fancy seeing you here," I remark softly as I walk to Lexi, who looks up at me and tries to hide her smile.

"Well, considering I live here, it's not that surprising," she says, looking down at Jagger. "Be careful of this one." She looks up at me as she whispers in his ear, "He's very sneaky, and whatever you do, don't fall for his dares." I can't help but throw my head back and laugh.

I hold up my index finger and Jagger reaches out to grip it in his fist as he moves it up and down. "I'm not as bad as she says I am." I look at her. "She's just mad she can't say no to me."

"Oh, I can say no to you." She rolls her eyes.

"We were just about to eat dinner," Ariella interjects. "Kirby, you want to join us?"

I stare into her eyes. "Sure," I reply, then turn to her. "Never a third without a second, I guess."

"Who says I'm staying for dinner?" she retorts, and now I'm the one who looks like a deer in the headlights. "I could have a date."

The minute she says those words, I feel my whole body turn almost to stone. "Do you?"

"Obviously"—she looks at Jagger—"I burn up the town." She then turns to me and chuckles. "Especially when someone, who shall remain nameless"—she looks at Jagger—"keeps me up most of the night."

I don't ask her anything else because Ariella comes into the room and Jagger whines for her. She comes over and grabs Jagger from Lexi. "I'll go and set the table," Lexi says, walking away from me and up the steps toward the kitchen.

"What can I do to help?" I offer, following her into the kitchen.

"You can sit down." She looks over her shoulder and I cock my hip against the island.

"It's four plates, I can handle it." She turns to reach for said plates and my eyes can't help but roam down to her ass.

"I have no doubt you can handle anything." I fold my arms over my chest. "Just trying to help."

"You can help by taking your ugly face to the table," Jaxon teases, "and leaving her alone."

Lexi and I both let out a little laugh as I wait for her to turn around and then grab the plates in her hands. "You can get the cutlery while I do this."

"Do not play tug-of-war with my plates," Ariella warns, walking into the kitchen.

Lexi looks like she wants to murder me, but she lets go of the plates before turning and going to get the cutlery. I turn and head to the table that has four chairs on each side and one at each end. "Do you guys ever have ten people over for dinner?" I put one plate next to the other and then two more across from them.

"Yes," Ariella confirms, "my family is huge. Well, our family is huge," she says of Lexi, "and they are always dropping in."

Jaxon comes to the table, putting down a platter of salmon and then placing the platter of veggies beside it. "This looks so good," I say of the roasted veggies that are placed neatly next to each other. Red and yellow peppers, next to asparagus, and then Brussels sprouts at the end.

"It's all Lexi," Ariella praises and I look up at Lexi, who is placing the forks and knives by each place setting. "Another thing we are going to miss when she moves out."

"You guys are more than welcome to come over to my house every single day." She looks at Ariella, who is putting Jagger in his highchair.

"All of us?" my mouth says before I can take it back.

She looks up, biting her lower lip. "Most of you." She puts her head to the side and we all laugh.

I sit down in the chair in front of Ariella and wait for Lexi to sit beside me, as Jaxon puts bottles of water on the table in the middle. He pulls out the chair next to Ariella, as Lexi pulls out the chair beside me. "Dig in," Jaxon urges. Lexi grabs the platter of veggies, putting some on her plate before handing it to me.

"So where are you moving to?" I ask her and she shrugs.

"It's still up for debate," she says, grabbing the platter of salmon and taking a piece with two pieces of lemon on it, before handing it to me. "We went to see three houses." I try not to fixate on the we. Who the fuck is we? "I liked the first one but it's, again, over my budget." She pours herself some water. "Like almost double."

"Your parents want to help," Ariella says. "Let them."

"My mother is going to lowball an offer and see what they say," she mentions and I look at Jaxon.

"Her mother is a real estate agent," he fills me in and I just nod my head.

"It's nice and the nicest, but is it worth the money?" She takes a bite of her salmon. "I had the big-ass house. I'm not sure I want that again."

"You can have a big-ass house and make it comfy." I take my own bite of my salmon and she just looks at me.

The rest of the night's conversation is light as we discuss the upcoming away schedule. We leave tomorrow for three days and I'm already dreading it.

"That was perfect," I praise once I get up and grab her plate to take it into the kitchen.

"It really was," Jaxon says. "Are you sure you have to move out?"

"I've never lived alone," she admits. "It is time."

"Ohhh," Ariella says as she takes Jagger in her arms, "we should do a round of never have I ever." Jaxon groans while I try not to laugh, as I place the plates in the dishwasher before going back and taking my spot. Ariella now has a cover hiding the fact that she's nursing. "Lexi, you go first."

She leans back in her chair. "I don't know, never have I ever"—she looks up at the ceiling, then looks back at us—"gotten a speeding ticket."

I roll my eyes. "Stop taking the easy way out," I tell her. "You always do that." I catch my words right as they leave my mouth, but no one calls me on it. But I do see Jaxon and Ariella share a look with each other.

"Fine," she huffs, raising her eyebrows. "Never have I ever had a one-night stand." She smirks at me.

"I have," I answer her and she rolls her eyes to the side. "I was young."

"Whatever," she dismisses me, looking over at Ariella and see her mouth hangs open.

"You?" She points to her.

"Have you met Jagger?" She points to her son in her arms. "The definition of a one-night stand gone wrong."

"Not wrong," Jaxon retorts, "gone off the rails."

"Whatever it's called," Ariella says, "I have."

"Okay, Jaxon," Lexi calls him.

"Never have I ever," he starts, "wanted to play this game." The bark of laughter fills the room. "Never have I ever gone on a blind date."

"I have," I say, "and then I never went on another again."

"Oh, I want to hear more," Ariella states and Lexi sits up and puts her elbow on the table, and then holds her neck with her hand as she listens to the story.

"I think I was twenty-two, I don't remember how old I was," I explain, trying to remember the little details, "went out. We were having a great time until her husband showed up at the table. She was not twenty-three like she said she was but instead thirty-five, and trying to convince her husband to have an open relationship." I hold up my hands. "I vowed to never do that again."

"So no to open relationships?" Lexi asks me and I think even she's shocked that she asked me the question.

"It's a fuck no to open relationships." I stare into her eyes for longer than I should, my hands aching to cup her cheeks before kissing her.

"Okay, Ariella." Jaxon breaks the moment between us.

"Never have I ever…" She thinks for a second. "…had sex in a movie theater."

Lexi snorts out while Jaxon gasps and whips his head to look at her. "What is wrong with you?"

"I'm just saying I have never, have you?"

"No," he answers her like it's the most ridiculous thing he's ever answered.

"I have not," Lexi adds and all eyes are on me.

"No, I have never."

"Okay, your turn," Lexi says to me.

"Never have I ever ridden a roller coaster," I admit to them and her hand drops from her neck.

"What?" she asks me, shocked, and the smile fills her face. "What do you mean, you've never ridden a roller coaster?"

"I don't think it's anything I need to do," I declare and

I hear Jaxon snort-laugh from his side of the table. "Do you know if you are stuck up there, it's like hard to get out?"

"Why would you be stuck up there?" He shakes his head.

"Mechanical issues." Both my hands go up. "It's more common than you think."

"I have never been to an amusement park and seen one get stuck," Ariella says.

"Well, count yourself lucky," I mumble.

"That is so random," Lexi notes, "and so unlike you." She smirks and then turns back, her face to the table. "Roller coasters," she repeats.

"You are all welcome. Now it's going to show up on your algorithm and then you can message me and thank me for opening your eyes." I lean back in my chair and fold my arms to the side, placing my hands at the back of my neck. "Back to you, Jaxon."

We laugh through the never have I ever until I see Lexi yawn more than twice. "I should get going." I stand up. "As much as I want to hear about all the places Jaxon has had sex in, I'm going to head home and try to wash my brain."

"We should do this again," Ariella suggests. "It was so much fun."

"Was it?" Lexi asks her and then she laughs. "I can't believe none of you have gone skinny-dipping." She shakes her head. "Especially you." She points to Jaxon.

"Why me?" He points to himself, insulted. "What about the Mr. I Played Strip Poker before?" He points over to me as we make our way to the front door. I reach for the handle before turning to look at the three of them. Jaxon is standing next to Ariella with his hand on her shoulder and pulling her to him.

"This stays here." I motion with my hand and wish she could walk me out to my truck so I can kiss her. "Lexi," I say her name and she looks up at me, and I wonder if she was maybe perhaps thinking the same thing. "Good luck with the house hunting."

"Thank you," she says. "Fingers crossed I can pick something."

I hold up my hand and walk out into the warm night. The soft breeze runs through me as I get into my SUV. I pull out of the driveway before I do something stupid like go back and ask her to take a walk on the beach, or literally anything that would prolong us spending time together.

I get home and toss my keys on the island in the kitchen as Jefferson comes in and jumps up on one of the stools. "Hey," I say, walking over to her and rubbing her neck, "how was your night?"

I pull out my phone and text her before I chicken out.

Me: Have you thought about the job offer?

I press send and then look at Jefferson. "I might have a friend who might come over and see me," I tell her, smiling.

My phone beeps and I see that it's her.

Lexi: I have…

Me: What does that … mean?

Lexi: I think you want to give me the job because

you feel sorry for me.

I snort and my fingers fly over the keyboard, and before I can even contemplate what I said, I press send.

Me: Trust me, I feel a lot of things for you but sorry isn't one of them.

"That was too forward." I look at Jefferson, who jumps onto the island and stretches her two front paws before turning and walking away. I walk upstairs to my bedroom, and she still hasn't answered me. I pick up the phone and text her one more time before shutting my phone off.

Me: I dare you to do it.

Nineteen

LEXI

I SIT HERE in the middle of the bed, my legs folded, the television playing in the background. My hands shake and my stomach flutters as I read the text thread over and over again.

Me: I have…

Kirby: What does that … mean?

Me: I think you want to give me the job because you feel sorry for me.

Kirby: Trust me, I feel a lot of things for you but sorry isn't one of them.

I close my eyes and lean back on my pillows before stretching out my legs in front of me. The phone in my hand feels like it's a fifty-pound dead weight.

"You have to answer him," I mumble to myself when the phone vibrates again in my hand and I look down at it.

Kirby: I dare you to do it.

My fingers move before I can think, and the next thing

I know, I'm putting the phone to my ear and listening to the sound of it ringing. It feels like it's been ringing for five hours when not even one whole ring goes by when he picks it up midway. "Yes?" he says, not even bothering with hello.

"You can't dare me to take a job," I huff out at him.

"Why can't I?" he asks and I hear him moving on his end, and I wonder what his house looks like. "Is there some rule somewhere that I don't know about that says I can't dare you when it comes to a job offer?"

"Kirby," I say his name softly and then close my eyes.

"Lexi," he says my name back in the same tone, and I don't answer him. Both of us just sit here listening to the other person breathe. "Why don't you want to take help from your parents?"

"Because it's embarrassing," I finally admit. "I'm almost thirty and my parents have to buy my house."

"Did you ask them to buy your house?" he asks me and I don't answer him, because he knows full well I would never. "Are you sitting at home doing nothing but wasting the day away, not bothering to work or taking the steps to get a job?"

"Okay, I get it."

"I don't think you do. Accepting help doesn't mean you failed."

"I know that also, but I just should have had things organized before."

"What would you have done differently?" I listen to his question and I seriously have to think about it. "Would you have stayed longer, just so you could save up money?"

"I don't think so." My voice trails off. "I didn't even know I was going to leave him that night." I close my eyes.

"What was it that made you want to break free?"

I swallow the lump. "I think it was a bunch of little things that just accumulated and pushed me over the edge." I sink down in the bed, to where my head is now on the pillows. "I worked so hard on the fundraiser that would make him and the hospital look good, and he ruined it."

"I had a hand in that also." His voice is soft.

"Why did you go out there?" I ask him. "What happened?"

"He didn't tell you?" he asks the question and then I hear him sort of hiss. "Of course he wouldn't. I walked out there to get some air. I just needed to…" He trails off and I close my eyes. "And he was there with this blonde."

"Tatum." I fill in her name.

"Whatever her name was, and they were…" He doesn't want to say it, no doubt not wanting to hurt me. Even though he owes me nothing, he's still not going to say it. I wait for him to tell me what happened before I tell him my side of it. Each word feels like it hurts him more than it hurts me.

"He tried to turn it around and say I was the one who let this happened."

"Shocker."

"He didn't come home with me that night," I tell him.

"Ordered another car and told me he needed space to think about what happened. Needed me to think about what I did. It was supposed to punish me. The whole time in the car I thought about how this was my big night and he should have supported me, but instead he made things about him." The tear escapes. "He spent the night fucking Tatum, and when I called him in the morning to tell him I left, he said he would stop."

"I'm going to need you to stop talking right now," he grumbles between clenched teeth, "and I take back the dare. I'm not daring you."

"What?" I chuckle. "Why?"

"Because it'll be me trying to force you to do it and it's not right," he admits and I hear the sound of a meow.

"Do you have a cat?" I sit up in bed.

"I do," he confirms. "Jefferson. She's an acquired taste." His laughter fills the phone. "She chooses when she wants to be rubbed. She likes to be escorted to her food plate, even though there is always food in it." I slowly put my head back down on the pillow, the smile filling my face as he talks about his cat. "She also hates to be held."

"She sounds delightful."

"She is," he agrees, "in her own way." He exhales deeply. "Seriously though, I want you to come and work for the foundation because I think you would make it that much better. But I'm not going to dare you to do it."

"Okay," I say softly, "I won't take into account the dare."

"Thank you," he replies and then silence lingers

between us. "I'll let you go."

"Okay." I don't want to let him go but I'm not sure how to prolong the conversation. "Have a good night."

"It's one of the best nights I've ever had. Goodnight, Lexi," he adds quickly and then hangs up.

I look down at the phone and then do something I haven't done in ten years. I start a social media account. The first thing I do is search his name and then see the first picture of him is of him on the ice. I scroll down and stop at a couple of videos to hear what he is saying. Each time it's an interview about the game. There is a picture of him at a blackjack table with a caption of Casino Night, with Jaxon in the back of it. I scroll until I see a picture of his cat. She's sitting down with the cutest face I think I've ever seen on a cat; she's all black with a little patch of white on her chest. The caption says it all, Meet Ms. Jefferson.

I smile before shutting it down and placing my phone to the side. Sleep comes easy to me, so easy that I'm shocked when I open my eyes nine hours later and I'm literally in the same position I was when I fell asleep. I stretch my hands over my head before tossing the covers off me. I wash my face and brush my teeth before grabbing my robe and making my way downstairs. "The wheels on the bus go round and round," Ariella sings softly as I walk into the kitchen.

She's sitting on the stool with Jagger beside her in his highchair, as she is feeding him his cereal. "Morning," I say with a smile on my face. Jagger turns his head to my voice and smiles. "Morning, handsome boy. How did we sleep?"

"He woke up once at three and then went back down again," Ariella shares. "It was magical."

I make a coffee before going over and standing on the other side of the counter, leaning over it with my elbows on it while I take a sip. "Is Jaxon gone?"

"He is," she confirms and then turns her eyes to me. "Last night was fun, wasn't it?"

"It was," I admit to her.

"You and Kirby." I look at her, not saying anything, and then I shock the shit out of her.

"Me and Kirby have a history."

The gasp fills the room. "Not that type of history." I rethink my words. "But he—" I smile. "We became friends when I was in Phoenix."

"When?"

"After your baby shower." I clear up the timeline. "We came face-to-face with each other at the hospital. He was there to volunteer, and he got roped into being one of the bachelors at the fundraiser I was throwing."

"And," she eggs me on.

"And nothing, really, we became friends. He—" I take a sip of my coffee. "He figured out I was going through something with Trent."

"How?"

"Not sure," I say, not willing to give away his past. If he wants anyone to know, he'll tell them. "But he knew I was going through things and he was…" I shrug. "…there."

"I had no idea," she says softly.

"No one did." I smile at her. "I didn't tell anyone."

"Well, I'm glad he was there to help you through it then." She reaches across the island and puts her hand on mine and squeezes it.

"I applied for the job," I tell her and her eyes go big.

"What job? The one I told you about?"

"The foundation Kirby owns," I point out and she shrugs.

"I didn't know you two had a history or I wouldn't have mentioned it." She scoops some cereal in the blue plastic spoon before giving it to Jagger. "How did it go?"

"Well, after getting over the shock that it was him, I think it went well." I smile at Jagger.

"Are you going to do it?"

"I think so," I admit to her, standing up now and placing one foot on top of the other. "I love what they stand for, and it's someplace that I would feel like I'm actually making a difference in people's lives."

"I think you'd be perfect for the job," she encourages me, "and you'd have a kick-ass office. We are just getting the stuff delivered now and it's so pretty."

I smile. "Now all I have to do is decide if I'm going to take the house."

"This is so exciting." She looks at Jagger. "Isn't this exciting, little man?" Then she turns to me. "A new job and a new house." She whistles. "Watch out, world, Lexi Petrov is back."

A SHORT WHILE later I'm sitting in front of the house I

fell in love with when I came across it online. I didn't tell anyone about it when I went to do a secret visit. The minute I walked in I fell more in love with it. It's a two-bedroom house and comes right in my budget. I see the brown-stained door with the matching one-car garage. I smile as I walk up and put the code in the lock pad as the bottom springs out with the key. I turn the key in the lock and step in a little closed-in patio and I smile at how cute and charming it is. I walk over to the real front door, open it, and I suddenly feel like I'm home. A small entranceway is there, and when you walk in a bit more, you have the kitchen to the right. It's nothing grand. No island in the middle, just a stainless-steel fridge, next to two ovens against the wall, with a stove top next to it. A small counter space before the sink. It's small and quaint and perfect.

I walk into the open space that's the living and dining room and head straight to the back of the house; the thing that made me want to seriously consider this house. I push open one of the two doors and stand out on the wooden balcony. The sounds of roaring waves hit right away as I smile, walking over to the glass railing. Looking to the left, I see the bedroom that leads onto the same balcony. This is where I'm planning to have my coffee in the morning. I can see myself doing yoga in the middle of here once I push the table and couch to the side.

I take my cell out of my purse and FaceTime my mother, who answers after one ring. "Hey, sweetie."

"Hey, Mom," I say as the wave hits again.

"Are you at the beach?" she asks me and I nod.

"I think I found a house," I tell her and her eyes go big. "And," I say with an even bigger smile, "it's in my budget."

She laughs. "Well, let me see it," she urges me eagerly, waiting for me to take her on a tour.

"Okay, but remember this is for me and I think I love it," I say and she nods her head.

"The kitchen is small," she notes, "but you're one person." After the tour, she states, "You can use the second bedroom for extra closet space. Unless you knock down the wall and just make it one giant space."

"I don't know, it might be better for resale purposes if I keep it two bedrooms," I mention and she agrees with me.

"I want to make an offer," I tell her and she smiles and then I see the tears in her eyes. "Do you not like it?"

"I love it," she says. "What's more, I love that you love it." She wipes away her tears, making me cry.

"Also, I went for an interview for a job with a foundation that helps relocate victims in abusive relationships."

Her eyes go big. "I think that you are going to help a lot of people, Lexi." She sniffles. "I feel like if there was ever a job made for someone, that job was made for you."

"I think so too," I agree with her. "Look at all these changes." I giggle. "I thought I would be overwhelmed and it would weigh down on me. Making all the choices on my own and not being steered in the direction that I should go." I wait for my chest to feel the tightness, but it's not there. "Now, please get me this house."

"I'm on it," she says and then smiles. "I'll call you back."

"I look forward to it," I tell her and she disconnects the phone and I pull up his number.

I press the phone button and listen to it ring once, twice, three times when his voice now fills my ear. "You've reached Kirby." I smile when I hear his name. "Leave me your name and number and I'll get back to you as soon as I can." I wait for the beep before I talk.

"Hey, Kirby, it's Lexi," I start to say and then hear I have another call coming in, and when I look down, I see it's him calling me back. "You're on the other line." I laugh. "Bye," I say, pressing the switch-call button. "Hello."

"Lexi," he says and it sounds like he just woke up.

"Are you sleeping?" I look at my watch and see it's three in the afternoon.

"Yeah, we have a game tonight before we leave, so there is always the afternoon nap," he explains and I sit back on the outside chair. "Where are you? It sounds like you are in a tunnel."

"I'm sitting on my hopefully soon-to-be balcony," I tell him, "but I was calling for something else."

"What's up?" he asks as I hear the covers rustle from his side of the phone and I wonder if he sleeps with boxers or naked. The thought of Kirby naked makes the back of my neck heat up and my mouth water.

"I've decided to take the job," I start, "with one

condition." I bite my lip, wondering how he'll take this condition. "We ride a roller coaster together."

He huffs out, "Fuck no." I can see him shaking his head side to side.

"Come on, Kirby," I say teasingly, "I dare you."

Twenty

KIRBY

WHEN THE PHONE rang from my bedside table, I knew it was one of four people, and four people only: Kylie, Coach, Jaxon, or Lexi. They are the only ones on my favorites list, so even when I put it on do not disturb, they can get through to me.

I jumped up when I heard the vibration, and then I thought my eyes were playing tricks on me when I saw her name. I turn over in my bed, surprised. "What's up?" I ask her when I hear her backpedaling and then her voice changes, and I can almost hear the smile in her voice and the shyness.

"I've decided to take the job," she says and I sit up straight in bed, "with one condition." Whatever it is, it's going to be yes, but I don't tell her that. My heart picks up speed, thinking about what the condition will be and secretly hoping it ends up with us naked and in bed together. "We ride a roller coaster together."

I huff out and collapse back onto my bed. "Fuck no."

I shake my head side to side.

"Come on, Kirby," she says teasingly, "I dare you." I will give this woman whatever she wants, whenever she wants it. Even going out of my own fucking comfort zone to make her happy.

I close my eyes and all I can see is her face smiling from ear to ear, and my mouth is quicker than my brain. "Fine," I concede, "but I want it in writing."

She laughs and it shoots straight to my dick. "Fine, we will get it in writing."

"When do you want to do this?" I ask her, trying to tell myself it's going to be two minutes of torture, but in the end it'll be worth it.

"How about Saturday?" she asks. "I know you guys come back on Friday and there is no game on Saturday."

"Fine," I agree, reaching out my empty hand to the side, wishing she was here. "I will make plans for Saturday."

"It's a date," she states and I sit up in bed, wondering if she thinks it's a date-date, like I get to hold her hand and at the end of the night I get to kiss her, or it's an I'll meet you there and I'm not inviting you in after.

"It's a date," I repeat with the biggest smile on my face. "Now that we got that out of the way, should we discuss work?"

"Sure," she says and I hear the waves crash in the background and wonder how far away she is from me.

"Do you want to come over to my house and we can get the contract signed, and then we can discuss all the things?"

"Um," she hesitates and I close my eyes and pinch the bridge of my nose. "I would but I promised I would watch baby Jagger so Jaxon and Ariella could have a date night before he leaves."

I turn to the side. "Okay, so how about we discuss it on Saturday? Right before I sign away my life."

She laughs. "It's not that big of a deal."

"It is that big of a deal," I say tightly, "and I hope you know there is no one else in this whole fucking universe I would do this for besides you."

"I know," she says softly, "and there is no one else in this whole fucking universe I would go to work for besides you."

"I'm glad you are going to be part of the team," I say, wishing I could be in front of her when I say this, "a very important part of the team."

"Okay, just so I'm prepared," she says, and I can hear her walking on her end of the phone, "when do I start?"

"How about Monday?" I inhale. "No time like the present."

"Oh wow, but you are right, no time like the present."

"We can prolong it." I toss the cover off myself and get up.

"No," she snaps, "Monday it is."

"Eager." I chuckle, walking down the steps to the kitchen. "I like it." She laughs. "Okay, so how about this? We do that stupid roller-coaster thing and then come back to my house and we can go over your contract."

"Fine," she agrees and I don't know why I feel like jumping up and tapping my heels together. "Why don't you call me when you guys get back on Friday, and we can set up a time and a place to meet?"

"If it's easier, I can pick you up or you can come here and leave your car here." I give her different options instead of saying what I really want to say, and that is, I'll pick you up.

"Might be easier to just leave my car at your house. Now that I start work in less than a week, I have to get my ass into gear." My cock springs to life when I picture her ass. "Okay, I'm excited," she says gleefully. "Have a good trip."

"I'm sure I'll talk to you while I'm there," I mention hopefully. "If not, I'll speak to you on Friday." I reluctantly hang up the phone and call Kylie right away.

"Hello," she answers after two rings, "you've reached Kylie, who is busy—" I laugh when she pretends to be her answering machine.

"Hey," I cut her off mid-sentence, "she's taking the job."

"Lexi?" she asks me.

"No, the mayor of Munchkinland." I roll my eyes. "Yes, Lexi."

"Wow, someone chose violence today," she hisses. "No one likes a smart-ass, Kirby."

"Noted." I grin. "Now, she starts on Monday, so be ready."

"Are you going to bring her in beforehand to introduce her?"

"Nah, I'm leaving tomorrow and I'm only back on Friday. She's taking the job under one condition."

"Do I even want to know? Will my ears bleed?"

"I ride a roller coaster with her." She gasps so loud my ear hurts.

"You hate those," she reminds me.

"I know." I shrug. "But how bad can it be? I can close my eyes and think of my happy place."

"I honestly do not want to know what your happy place is. That's a no for me." I hear the sound of her pretending to vomit.

"That is not my happy place."

"Oh please, then what is?" The way that question is followed with probably an eye roll makes me almost burst out laughing.

"My house. Sitting on the beach." I start to name a couple of things and she groans.

"Okay, this therapy session took a nosedive. I will have everything set up for her to start on Monday. It'll be good." She snickers. "Try not to die on that death trap." I groan out and just hang up the phone before I rub my hands over my face.

"The things I do for you, Lexi," I mumble. "The things I do for you." I look out the window and start the countdown until I get to see her.

I SIT ON the steps outside in the front, waiting for her to arrive. She texted me twenty minutes ago, telling me she was on her way. I spot her SUV from the distance and get up to my feet with the gate open for her to drive in. I can't help the smile that fills my face when I see her. She has her hair down and is wearing a pair of gold-rimmed aviator glasses. I walk over to the driver's side door and pull the handle. "Hi," I say, trying to contain how happy I am to see her.

"Hey," she greets, taking off her glasses and giving me her eyes. "How excited are we?" she asks me, reaching over to the passenger side and grabbing her blue crossbody purse.

"On a scale of one to a hundred"—I move out of the way so she can come down—"it's at a minus ten." She shakes her head. "Which is a lot better than this morning when I almost cancelled."

"You didn't," she says and closes the door and I take in her outfit. She's wearing a pair of loose, light-blue jeans, with a long-sleeved white top, her midriff showing off her tanned skin. But it's the sneakers on her feet that have me gawking. My eyes go back to her midriff and the hint of skin she's showing.

"I'm sorry if I'm staring," I apologize in advance. "I didn't think you owned jeans or sneakers." She smirks.

"Let's just say that I got a refresher in my clothing department." She puts the crossbody around her top. "I still have stuff for work, but I have a lot more casual me clothes."

"Well, you look good in anything," my mouth says before I can stop it, "but I really like you in the jeans."

"Thank you, and you look comfortable." She takes in my outfit of black joggers and a long-sleeve white shirt that is pushed up to my elbows.

"Figured if I throw up, this will absorb more than jeans," I answer her honestly. "You ready to go so we can get this over with?"

"It's okay to not be okay," she tells me. "I'm so excited."

"Well, at least one of us is," I mumble as I walk over to my own SUV and open the door for her. "After you."

She stops and puts her hand on the door. "I'll be right there with you the whole time." She gets in and I close the door.

"You better be." I walk around to the driver's side. "I keep thinking about the rides," I tell her as I pull out and head toward the amusement park. "I even went and watched videos of them."

"Of course you did," she states and the whole car already smells like her, a bright citrus scent. "Why does this not surprise me?" I look at the road and pull into the parking lot, pulling into the first spot I can find. "Here we go," she chirps and I just close my eyes before getting out of the SUV.

She waits for me in the back. "Do you want to start slow?" she asks me as we walk with people toward the front gate. "I also already bought us tickets"—she takes out her phone—"and the fast pass so we can go right to the front of the line and you can't back out."

"I'm not going to back out," I assure her nervously, "and we should probably just get it over with." I look around as she walks to one of the booths as she scans her phone.

"Here," she says, handing me a bracelet, "today is on

me."

"That's a very intriguing offer," I tell her and I can see her eyes get a touch darker, and her cheeks turn a hint of pink as she looks down and avoids my eyes. "Thank you."

She shakes her head, putting on her own bracelet. "I meant, it's cashless, so whatever you want, it charges my card."

"I'm too nervous to argue with you," I admit to her, looking around and she tries to hide the smile by biting her bottom lip. "How was your week?" I turn to her and I can't help but smile when she smiles.

"I got the keys to my new house," she declares proudly, "and I moved in, mostly." I follow her to the entrance as she scans her bracelet and it beeps, letting her in.

"Please don't work," I joke as I scan my own bracelet and it beeps, letting me in. "This is happening," I say and I feel her hand slip into mine.

"I promise you, I'll be here the whole time," she assures me, and with her hand in mine, I think I'd do whatever she asked me to do. Roller coaster, jump out of a plane, swim with sharks, in a cage, obviously, but I would do anything.

"Okay, so which one do you want to do?" I ask her as we walk hand in hand through the throngs of people. I see a couple of people do a double take when I walk by them.

"Shit," she swears, stopping and looking at me. "I didn't even think people might recognize you." Her hand slips out of mine and I want to grab her hand back.

"Does it bother you?" I ask her, seeing her eyes looking around. "It really doesn't bother me. Worst case, I have to take a couple of pictures."

"No," she says, stepping in close to me, and I swear I stop breathing, "worst case is you throw up on the ride and it goes viral."

"That pretty much is a worst-case scenario," I admit, looking around and smiling at a couple of people who have stopped to look. "Now before I run out of here with my tail between my legs, let's get this over with."

I slip my hand in hers, this time our fingers intertwined and it feels more intimate. "Okay, so I think we just do the Goliath and call it a day."

I don't answer her as she pulls up the park map on her phone. "I think it's over there." She points and I try to collect myself.

She zigzags through people, the whole time holding on to my hand until we get to the ride. "Are you tall enough?" she jokes over her shoulder, going through the line of fast pass and I can hear people yelling.

"I think I'm going to be a little sick," I tell her and she turns back to me, stopping me in my tracks but making her bump into my chest. My hand comes up to grip her hip, while she puts her hand on my chest.

"We don't have to do this," she backpedals softly. I move my hand from her hip to the small of her back, and I pull her closer to me. "I'll still take the job."

"A deal is a deal," I tell her, looking into her eyes and then down at her lips before looking back up at her eyes. "We do scary things all the time."

"You are one of the bravest people I know," she says softly, and I wonder if she can feel how fast my heart is beating under her hand. I can blame it on the ride, but the reality is that it's her.

"It's funny," I reply, as if there aren't a thousand people around us, "I was thinking the exact same thing about you." I let go of her hand and move it to the side of her neck. Both of us staring in each other's eyes.

"Sorry," someone says from behind me, interrupting the moment, "are you guys going or can we go ahead of you?"

I chuckle, hanging my head before looking back at him. "We're going," I tell him and then drop my hand from her neck to slip back into her hand. "Let's go." I walk ahead of her and go to the front of the line.

"This is the line for the first car," she tells me, looking at me with big eyes.

"Go big or go home, right?" I tell her and she just opens her mouth and then quickly closes it. "Besides"—I pull her closer to me—"I never back down from a dare."

Twenty-One

LEXI

I WATCH HIM walk until the end of the row and then he turns to get in line at the first railing. "This is the line for the first car," I tell him, trying not to freak out and make him even more nervous.

"Go big or go home, right?" he declares and I open my mouth to say something, but then close it again when I feel his thumb rub mine. He pulls me close to him, our chests practically touching, making my stomach flutter as if it's in a washing machine cycle, spinning it back and forth and then around and around. "Besides, I never back down from a dare."

All the words I have ever learned in my whole life are erased from my memory. The only things I can focus on are his eyes. His smile. The heat from his hand that is in mine and on the base of my back. "It's your turn," the guy behind us says and I close my eyes, trying not to die from embarrassment. I also want to turn around and tell him to fuck off already, we are all going to get a chance to ride the fucking roller coaster.

"We're going," I throw over my shoulder, "relax."

"Here we go," Kirby mumbles as he steps into the front seat and moves over to sit. He sits down and the man comes over and pushes down the harness over his chest. "Shit, this is getting real." He looks over at me and I can see his foot moving up and down with nerves. I reach my hand over to put it on his leg, his hand covering mine. "I think I'm going to vomit."

I don't want to laugh at him; this big strong man who gave me courage to take the biggest leap of my life is scared of such a small thing. "It's okay, I'm here." I turn my hand over in his and he shocks me by raising our hands to his lips as he kisses my fingertips.

"If I die, at least I'll have kissed a part of you," he says. I don't know if he knows he's said it out loud, as I try to calm my own nerves that are coming on for a whole different reason.

The sound of the lock clicking into place makes it even more real. The attendant comes over to make sure we're securely in our seat. "Shit, I should have maybe kissed you for real if I'm going to perish." He then closes his eyes as the roller coaster starts to move. "Shit, I can't believe I'm doing this," he repeats and I see him swallow as he squeezes my hand. "Oh my God!" he yelps as we move up toward the top. The clicking the whole time is louder than it should be. "In case we die"—he looks over at me—"I should tell you that you are the most beautiful woman I've ever seen in my whole life, and I thought that the very first time I saw you."

"We're not going to die," I tell him. "It's going to be—" I don't have a chance to say another word because it drops down and the only thing I can do is watch the fear on his face. He closes his eyes at the same time he screams out, and I feel suddenly horrible for making him do this. The ride lasts maybe two minutes, at most, and when it slows down, I look over at him and see him blinking open his eyes. It comes to a stop and the sound of the lock clicking has my chest decompressed from the harness. I let go of his hand as I push up the red harness, and I'm too ashamed to look at him.

"Wow," he says, standing up and holding out his hand to me. "That was—" he starts and I blink away the tears.

"It was." I swallow the lump and step out with him, trying not to freak out the whole time. We walk down the exit route and stop when we see the pictures come on the screen and he bursts out laughing.

"Oh wow," he says and I look up, seeing the picture of him with his eyes sealed shut so tight his nose is scrunched up and his mouth is wide open. "We are going to buy it," he states, walking up to the counter. "We are going to need two of those." He points to the picture on the screen. "Oh, can we get it on a mug also?"

"I don't think we need it on a mug." I try to persuade him to not buy it since it will be a reminder of what a horrible person I am. How I manipulated him into doing something he didn't want to do.

He gets the plastic bag as we walk out, and then he pulls it out of the bag and I can't help but laugh when turns it to face me. "Look at my face."

"Kirby," I say his name and hold on to his wrist, "I'm so sorry." He just looks at me, his eyebrows pinched together. "I don't know, I thought it would be funny but—" I shake my head and look down. "I shouldn't have forced you to do this."

"Hey," he says, stepping closer to me and putting his finger under my chin to lift it. I try and blink away the tears that have pooled. "What are you going on about?"

"That." I point to the ride. "It was wrong and I shouldn't have done it. You were so scared."

"Well, yeah," he says. "But hey…" He smiles as he makes sure that he steps even closer to me. "A couple of good things happened out of it."

"What?" I shake my head, not sure I understand what he is saying.

"Okay, one, I got to hold your hand." He grins. "And two, I got to kiss you."

"My fingers," I start to say and then stop when his free hand comes up, his fingers touching my cheeks as I start to pant. My eyes stare into his as he moves his hand up my cheek, gripping the back of my head. His thumb rubs my cheek, as he tilts his head to the side.

"Well, my life just flashed before my eyes and all I got to kiss was your fingers." He smirks. "Might as well go all out and ask for the big one. Can I kiss you?" he asks me, and all I can do is nod my head before his lips are on mine.

There, in the middle of a crazy theme park, with thousands of people around us, it feels like it's just the two of us. My heartbeat drowns out the sound of my breathing as my eyes want to stay open to make sure I see him, but the minute his tongue slides into my mouth, my eyes automatically shut as I lean farther into him. My hand comes up and I slide it to the back of his neck and into his hair. While my other hand grips his arm, he deepens the kiss. He drops the bag with the picture by our feet to wrap his arms around me and pulls me so my chest is flush to his. *It's the single best kiss I've had in my life* is the only thing I can think of when he slowly releases me.

"Jesus fucking Christ," he pants, his hand still buried halfway in my hair and half on my face. "How can you be so fucking perfect?"

I can't help but smile at his words. "It's a gift," I joke softly, not sure I can say anything more clever, and also not wanting to sound like an idiot.

He laughs before he kisses me softly once more and letting me go to bend to grab the bag and the picture. "Do you want to ride any other rides?" he asks me and I look around. "I'll even go on the Goliath if it means I get to kiss you again. I would really rather fucking not." I snicker, bending my head and tucking the hair behind my ear nervously. "Actually, I think I've reached the breaking point of trying to be all macho. So if it's alright with you, I think we should grab a couple of burgers and then head back to my place where we can—"

"Make out more?" I ask him and his eyebrows go up.

"We can totally do that." He slips his hand in mine. "I was going to say discuss work, but I like the way you think." He walks toward the car, opening my door and holding my hand to help me in, and I am a little bit disappointed when he doesn't try to kiss me. He gets into the SUV and tosses the picture bag into the back seat before handing me his phone. "Here," he urges, "order food."

"You are giving me your phone?" I ask, shocked, looking down to see the screen saver is of his cat.

"Well, how else are you going to order food?" He laughs as he pulls out. "Unless you want to use your phone, but then you have to enter my address and it's a pain in the ass." I look down at the phone and try not to compare him to Trent, who refused to even let me see the weather from his phone.

"Is that okay?" he asks me when all I can do is stare down at it.

"I wasn't allowed to touch Trent's phone," I admit to him. "He kept telling me it had confidential things on it."

"I bet it did," Kirby retorts, "and some things he probably didn't want you to see."

"Oh, most definitely things he didn't want me to see." I snort. "It's just…"

"There is nothing on my phone that needs to be under lock and key," he assures me. "The password is twenty and then sixteen." I put in the password and then turn to him.

"What do you want to eat?"

"Don't care," he says as he makes his way to his house. "Even though I'm pretty sure we almost died, this was one of the best days I've had in the longest time." My hands clench the phone even more as I try not to show him how much that means to me.

We pull up into his driveway at the same time I place the order for two burgers, fries, onion rings, fried pickles, and a bunch of other things. I hand him the phone. "Thank you," he says and I just smile at him and I'm so nervous. "Do you want to come in?" he asks me and I nod my head. "No, I don't think you understand what I'm saying right now." He steps in closer to me and I raise my hand to his shirt.

"I actually do think I understand what you are asking me right now," I counter, looking up at him, never thinking I would be here in this moment.

"What am I asking you?"

"You are asking me to come in," I tell him and stare at him. "I would like to come in and for you to give me a tour."

"I can do that." For the first time in my whole life, I take a leap without basing my decision on what anyone else wants.

I giggle. "I've had one boyfriend," I share with him, "and I was married to him for ten years." My fingers tap his chest. "So I might be really bad at this whole thing."

"Shut up, Lexi," he mutters through clenched teeth. "The first time I saw you, I wanted you." He shocks me. "That was even before I knew what an incredible person you are, how strong you are, how beautiful inside you are." He shakes his head. "Then I got to know you, and this might make me sound like the biggest piece of shit, but I wanted you, knowing you were married."

"Kirby," I say his name.

"I will never force you to do something you don't want to do," he assures me, "or pressure you in any fucking way."

"I want to come in." I get on my tippy-toes and hope he bends his head to kiss me. "Show me your house." He bends his head and kisses me. The kiss is very different from the one before. This one is full of need, his hand gripping my hip tightly as I slide my tongue in with his. He wraps his arm around me and pulls me up, my legs wrapping around his waist. He turns, and with his mouth still attached to mine, he makes his way down the walkway to the front door. "Is this safe?" I put a hand on his cheek as he walks up the steps to the front door.

"I've never tried to walk into my house with my eyes closed," he admits before pushing open the front door, "but I have once arrived drunk and stumbled my way to the bedroom." I laugh as I look behind me at the foyer. There is a big mahogany table on the side with a huge mirror before he takes three steps up. "After, I'll give you a full tour," he says, then stops, "unless you want one now."

"Is that where your bedroom is?" I point down the hall, hoping I chose the right way and he nods his head. "Then I want to tour that."

He chuckles as he walks down the hallway to the stairs that lead to the second level. Both his hands are holding my ass as he walks up six steps and then turns on the landing to walk up another six steps. He steps into his bedroom and I unclasp my legs from his waist. "This is exactly like I thought you would live." I look toward the cream-colored see-through drapes that are floor to ceiling and open halfway for you to see the ocean in the distance.

His bed, which must be custom-made because it's bigger than a king, sits in the middle of the room. The headboard against a fabric wall goes from floor to ceiling too. A plush seating area is to the side and another bench is in front of the bed, with what looks like the clothes he must have worn yesterday. "It's very modern, very masculine," I say, not wanting to go on the beige-colored rug that covers the dark-brown wood floor, "yet very classy."

"I've thought about you here," he says, "in this room."

I can't help the smile. "Have you?"

"In that bed." He points to his bed that has a beige cover folded over and then another cover draped in the middle that falls to the floor.

"Show me what you thought about," I tell him and he just walks to me. It's all hands at that point. He's gripping the bottom of my shirt at the same time I'm gripping his. He pulls my shirt over my head before I get his off. My hands roam up his chest, as my nails score his skin. His abs contract as he bends his head and kisses my neck, right where my pulse pounds, before his hand unclips my bra. He hisses when I move my shoulders and the straps fall, the bra now at the base of our feet. His hand comes up to cup my breast, his fingers rolling the nipple before he sucks it into his mouth. My whole body feels like it's on pins and needles.

"Fucking perfection," he mumbles before moving to

the next nipple. "It should be illegal"—he looks up at me—"to be this perfect."

My hands go to the elastic at his waist. "I'm really glad you didn't wear jeans." I move his pants down past his hips, leaving him in his black briefs. I then push him backward until he falls on his ass on the bench. "Shit, get up," I tell him and he does and then I slip his briefs down over his hips. His cock springs out and I look down at it. "Now you can sit down."

"Lexi," he says, his voice tight.

"I'm asking you to please sit down," I rephrase and then take a step back, "unless you don't want that." He sits back down, his hand coming out to grab mine and pulling me back to him.

"I want this more than I want to breathe," he confirms and I get down on one knee first and then the other one. "Jesus." He leans back as I grip his cock in my hand, and I don't waste time as I suck it into my mouth. We both moan out as I try to get him deeper into my mouth. My hand comes up to jerk him before I let the head of his cock go and kiss his hip.

His eyes fixate on my every single move, and I know it's just the two of us in this room. "I take it back," he starts as I lick from his balls up his shaft to the tip of his cock, "this might be the best thing that has ever happened in my life." The whole time his teeth are clenched. "Watching you take my cock in your mouth." I smile as I take him back into my mouth, working him with both my mouth and my hand. He puts his hand in my hair as he watches me, and I've never been more turned on in my life. He grabs my face and pulls me up to kiss my mouth, his tongue sliding into my mouth. "If I hadn't stopped you," he says between kisses, "I would have come down your throat."

"You act like that's a bad thing," I state, my hand still working his hard cock, trying to reach around the thick base. He cups the back of my head, bringing me even closer for a kiss. "Your kisses make me forget what I'm doing." He lifts his hips to help push his cock in my hand. "Almost."

I move my way back down, kissing his stomach before taking his cock back into my mouth. I close my eyes as I swallow as much of his cock into my mouth as I can, lost in the way his body moves with mine. "You fucking drive me crazy." He moves the hair away from my face so he can watch me. "Seeing my cock so far down your throat." I look up at him. "You need to tell me now," he encourages, his breathing coming in pants. "You want me to come in your mouth," he says as my hand grips his cock tighter, "on your face." My eyes must lust over because his eyes do the same. "Or your tits?" His hands reach out to pinch both my nipples when he says that, and I swear I close my eyes and feel myself get wetter. "Where do you want it?"

"Where do *you* want it?" I let go of his cock enough to ask him the question.

"Mouth this time, pussy the next time, then your tits in the shower, and your face in the kitchen," he lists and I watch his Adam's apple rise and fall as he shoots down my throat, my name on his lips. "Lexi."

Twenty-Two

KIRBY

I WATCH HER swallowing my cock and I swear I feel like it is made out of stone. I've never been this hard before, and I mean never. In a split second, I'm about to blow and she needs to decide where she wants me to do it. "Where do you want it?" I grit my teeth, watching her is torture and makes me want to come faster.

"Where do *you* want it?" Her mouth rises off my cock for her to ask the question before she sucks the tip back into her mouth.

"Mouth this time, pussy the next time, then your tits in the shower, and your face in the kitchen." I try to keep it at bay, but her hot mouth, that smooth tongue. "Fuck." I swallow and then hiss out her name, right before I shoot into her mouth and she swallows all that I have to give her. "Lexi."

Her head bobs up and down as she makes sure she takes it all. She lets my cock go and I sit up as she moves back, placing her ass on her heels. I take her mouth in a kiss before I stand up, taking her with me. My kiss leaves her lips, going to the side of her mouth and then trailing down to her jaw. "That was," I tell her as my hands grip her tits in both hands, rolling her nipples, "the best fucking blow job." I kiss her collarbone before trailing my tongue along it. My hands move down and to her sides. "Of my fucking life." My head also moves down, my tongue coming out to twirl around one nipple as my hands go to the button of her jeans.

"I thought I was going to come the minute I felt your mouth on my cock." The button pops open and then the sound of the zipper fills the almost silent room. "Took everything inside me not to hold on to your head and fuck your face." I kiss the middle of her chest, over her beating heart. I can feel how fast it's hammering and I look up at her. "I want my mouth on you," I tell her. "If that's okay with you?"

She grins and then it turns into a smirk. "It's rude not to return the favor." Her eyes twinkle in the sunlight that is coming through the blinds.

"Is it now?" I ask her, pushing her jeans over her hips as I get down on my knees in front of her.

"I want to memorize every single part of your body," I inform her as I rub down the back of her legs and move one foot out of her pants. I kiss her stomach and then trail my kisses left to right. My hand works to free the other leg. "I want to cherish every single part of your body." I look up at her and her hand comes to play in my hair. "Every fucking part I want to kiss, lick, and suck." I move my hands to her hips, gripping her lace panties in my hand before moving them down her legs slowly. I stop myself from just ripping them in my hands and then eating her pussy while she stands up with her leg over my shoulder. "The things I want to do to you." I watch her eyes watching me. "The things I've thought about doing to you"—I wink at her—"all started with you in my bed." I get up and put one hand around her shoulders and the other under her knees before carrying her to my bed.

I place her head down on the pillows before bending my head to kiss her. Her hands come up to hold my face as my tongue fights with hers. I move my legs over her to get between them, letting her mouth go and then moving my lips down, stopping at her right nipple first. Her hand moves to the back of my neck as I move down to her stomach and then finally where I've wanted to taste the minute after I kissed her. I move her right leg back as I feel her move her left leg back before her pussy is in front of my face, and the only thing I can do is kiss her right on the little strip of hair she has there.

My eyes find hers, right before my tongue comes out, and I lick from her clit down and then back up again. Her taste on my tongue is one I know I'll crave every single day. Her head goes back onto the pillow and her eyes close when I slide my tongue inside of her.

Her hands move from the side of her to beside her head. "Oh my God," she pants when I move my tongue. With the tip, I flick her clit side to side before sucking it into my mouth. "Oh, God. I—" Her hips move up as I feast on her. I slide my tongue back into her and she moves one of her hands to the back of my head as she puts her left heel on my shoulder. She stops talking when I suck her pussy into my mouth.

"Not God, Lexi," I say, "it's Kirby. Say my name when you come." She looks at me. "Going to make you come with my tongue." I slide it back into her. "Then with my fingers." She writhes under me while my tongue plays with her clit. "Then with my cock." I lick around her hole twice before sliding my tongue back in. My tongue fucks her and I wish it was my cock. She's hot, wet, and tight, and my half-mast cock is now hard and ready to fuck her. "You like this?" I ask her, even though I know from her moaning and her pants that she likes this. She doesn't answer me with her words, but instead she puts her hand on the back of my head and shoves my face deeper into her pussy. I chuckle. "Take what you want, baby." She moves her hips up and down my tongue until the tip is at her clit.

She rolls her hips side to side, her hand moving behind her head as she grips on to the pillows. "I'm coming," she calls out as my tongue plays with her clit. "It's—" She arches her back and moans out her release. My hand grips her hip to stop her from moving out of my reach. "Kirby," she whispers my name.

"Yeah, baby," I answer her and watch her face at the same time I slide a finger inside her. Her eyes flutter open, the lust written all over her face. "Time to make you come with my fingers," I tell her. "Open your legs wider, baby." She moves her hips back and her legs widen to the sides. "So fucking wet." I watch my own finger slide into her, becoming coated with her juices before I slide another one in. "Is my girl ready to come again?"

"Yes," she pants.

"Ride my fingers." I curl my two fingers up and rub against her G-spot and she about shoots off the bed. "Use my fingers to make yourself come." She moves her hips up and down.

"Faster," she hisses out, "need more."

"Okay." I move my fingers with her hips now, my fingers slipping into her up to my knuckles. "You about to come again?" She doesn't have a chance to answer me; she moves her hips to the side and then moans out her orgasm. Her pussy convulses on my fingers, over and over again. She clamps her legs shut around my hand, her hips riding out her orgasm. "Fuck me," I mumble, my cock aching to slide inside of her.

"Need to get inside you, baby," I tell her and she moves her hips back and then opens her legs. "Get a condom." I motion to her with my chin to the bedside table. She takes the new box out, rips it open, the condoms flying on the bed as she takes one and then looks at me.

"I've never," she starts to say, "put one on." I move over her, pushing her back to the bed and I devour her mouth.

"Let me teach you." I sit back and tear the top off in between my lips, taking it out and handing it to her. "Hold the base of my cock," I instruct her and she grips it with my hand. "Put the condom on the top of my cock, baby." I watch her hand place it softly on the top. "Roll it once." She does as she's told. "Squeeze the tip."

She looks down at my cock, full concentration. "That's perfect"—she looks up at me—"now roll it down." She rolls it until the base of my cock. "There." The smirk on her face as if she just figured out the biggest secret in the world.

"Is that okay?" she asks me and I don't answer her, instead I kiss her like I've never kissed anyone before. I hold her jaw as I move my face over to the other side, trying to get the kiss deeper.

I let her go when she arches her back. "Want to fuck you slow," I state before I kiss her again, "but not sure I can."

"Then fuck me fast." She holds my face in her hands as we kiss, the heels of her feet already at the back of my thighs, digging into them. "I don't care how you fuck me." She moves her head to the side, her hand now reaching in between us as she jerks my cock in her hand. "As long as you fuck me."

She places my cock at her entrance and I just sink into her. The head of my cock feels her heat and wetness and then every thought leaves my head and I slam into her. She's so fucking tight, it takes me a second to breathe before I move my hips. I place my hands on the bed as I fuck her. Her hands are on my face, our mouths open but not touching as we both pant out. Her eyes are closed for half the time and all I can do is watch her. She licks her lips and then calls my name, "Kirby."

"Right here, baby," I say, my tongue coming out to slide into her mouth once as my cock pounds into her. She holds on to my arm with one hand and wraps the other around my shoulder. Her left leg moves over my shoulder, making my cock sink into her deeper. Both of us groan out when I get deeper in her. "I don't know how much longer I can last," I admit to her between clenched teeth, the hand on my arm now on my shoulder.

"Don't hold back," she urges. "Show me how much you want me." Her eyes move from mine to between us, making me look down.

"Look at how your pussy takes my cock." The minute I say that, she gets tighter. "So tight for me." I pull out and then slam back in a couple of times. "So fucking wet." She closes her eyes for a second before opening them back up. "You going to come on my cock?"

"Yes." She nods her head and my forehead falls to hers as I fuck her with everything I have. I move my right hand from beside her to over her head, gripping it in my hand as I fuck her harder than I want to. The harder I fuck her, the tighter she becomes. She arches her neck and moans out before coming back and sliding her tongue into my mouth at the same time she comes on my cock. Her pussy's so tight it's hard to pull out, even an inch. She holds on to my face, her fingertips gripping me as she gushes over my cock. "I can't," she mewls, shocked. "It's happening again."

"Let it," I urge her. "Ride it out, baby." Before she even finishes riding the first orgasm, she comes again. This time I can't fight it back; my balls tighten as I come. Our eyes lock on each other as if she knows I need to see her eyes. Her eyes lock on to mine as if she needs to see mine. My mouth devours hers as my thrusts slow down, until I'm just planted to the root inside of her. "Jesus," I say, turning to the side and taking her with me, "you've fucking ruined me." I look at her face as she looks at me, her eyes going down as she tries not to smile but fails. My arms wrap around her, not wanting to ever let her go. I kiss her nose before she buries her face in my neck.

"I want to stay like this forever, but I have to get rid of the condom," I inform her as I slide away from her, "and then we need some food." I stand on the side of the bed, watching her turn to her side to watch me. Her perfect fucking body is on display and my cock, which should be going down right about now, wants a round two, then probably three and might settle after four. "You want to come with me?" I motion with my head toward the bathroom. "Or do you want me to bring you a rag?"

"I'll come with you," she says, getting off of the bed and standing next to me. "Um, is that normal?" She points to my cock that is still hard.

"No." I shake my head and slip my hand in hers as I make my way over to the bathroom. "But then again, nothing with you, Lexi, is normal." I walk into the bathroom and she looks around. "Give me a second and I'll get out of your way and you can do your thing." I walk over to the toilet and pull the condom off of me, before grabbing tissues and tossing it in the trash. "I'll meet you downstairs." I stop beside her and bend to kiss her neck.

"Okay," she says and I walk over and slip on my briefs before walking down the steps and to the front door where our food is waiting. Turning, I walk back into the open-concept room. The dining room off the massive kitchen is right in front of the four big couches that face the television. The whole back of the house is floor-to-ceiling windows, showing you the ocean. It's the same view from the bedroom, but I don't have any shades in this room. The windows also all slide open if you want. I walk to the cabinets, taking out two plates and look over when I hear footsteps. She walks into the room wearing one of my Warriors T-shirts. "I borrowed this," she says. "I hope it's okay."

"It's more than okay," I reply as she moves to the island and her eyes go to the water.

"You might have one of the best views I've seen in my life," she compliments.

"I'm looking at the best view right now," I tell her and her eyes come back to find me looking at her.

"We should talk," she says and I already hate the way she is starting this conversation.

"We should." I am not sure if I agree with her, but I say the words anyway.

She pulls out one of the stools as I grab two bottles of water from the fridge, and I wait for the other shoe to drop. I sit down beside her. "So where should we start?"

She snags the bag and opens it up, grabbing a burger and then handing me the other one. "I think we should start with me saying I really, really, like you."

"Oh, for the love of everything." I look up at the ceiling. "If this is the 'it's not you, it's me' talk." I hold up my hand. "I think we can skip over it."

She laughs. "It's not that." She looks at her food. "But

it is that." I open my burger; not sure I can look at her without saying something she isn't ready for. "And it's a little bit more than that." I take a bite of my burger as she continues, "You are going to be my boss."

"Okay." I look over at her.

"And, well, I'm not going to sleep with my boss." She taps the counter next to her burger as she grabs a cold fry. "It's just, I can't do it." I turn to her now. "This job is a big deal to me," she says softly. "It's the first job I've had, really. Trent never wanted me to work because I had to be ready in case he needed me." I raise my eyebrows. "I know it was his way to control where I was and what I was doing. But I always wanted to get a job and being able to be on the fundraising committee, even though I didn't get paid, to me was like working. But this"—she shrugs—"it's my first big-girl job, and I just can't be sleeping with my boss."

"I see." I take another bite, but the whole time it's a struggle to swallow it.

"I shouldn't have started this." She trails off and I can hear the quiver in her voice. "I would never lead you on."

I put my hand on hers. "You are one of the best women I've ever met. There is not a mean bone in your body." I smile at her. "I wanted this as much as I have ever wanted anything in my life." I lift my hand from hers to move her hair behind her shoulder for me to be able to kiss her neck. "And I respect your decision a thousand percent. I'm not happy about it, but that's only because I'm selfish and want you." She smiles sadly. "But if that is what you feel like you need to do, then I'm going to respect your decision." She looks back at me when I say, "However, it's Saturday and you only start work on Monday, so until then, I'm not your boss."

"I guess that would be correct." She sits up straight.

"Which means we have a day and a half." I turn her in her chair.

"We do." She smiles big before she rolls her lips and her eyes go big.

"So will you stay here until tomorrow night?" I ask her. "I would like Monday morning, but I know with you in the bed, I'm going to want to fuck you the first thing in the morning, so Sunday night it is." I trail off. "If that is okay with you?"

"Sunday night." She nods at me and I don't bother finishing my meal or letting her finish hers before I drag her back to my bedroom for rounds two and three.

I LIE IN the bed, the sheet covering my bottom half as I watch her slip her jeans back on. The pit in my stomach is getting bigger and bigger as she reaches for the shirt and covers the rest of her body. The body I spent the last thirty hours committing to memory. I want to tell her I hate this, but instead I toss the sheet off me and get out of bed. Neither of us says a word to each other as she puts her sneakers on and I grab a pair of boxers and basketball shorts.

She stands up and looks at me, and I wonder if she's feeling as shitty about this as I am. "I guess I should go." She motions over her shoulder with her thumb.

"I'll walk you out," I tell her and she nods, turning to walk out of the room. I follow behind her, the whole time it feels like my feet are getting heavier and heavier. She grabs her purse from the entryway table as I unlock the front door and pull it open, the sun already down for the night with the stars in the sky.

I walk her to her SUV as she opens the door and tosses her bag onto the passenger seat. "I guess this is it," she says softly and I take a step toward her, wrapping my arms around her and pulling her to me. I bury my face in her neck and she does the same, except she gives me a soft kiss, and out of all the kisses we've shared the past two days, it's the best kiss I've gotten.

"Thank you for this weekend," she says, letting me go and stepping away from me. I fucking hate every single second of this. I hated it from when she told me yesterday to every single second after.

"Thank you," I reply, putting my forehead onto hers, "for giving me an incredible weekend." The lump in my throat feels like it's getting bigger and bigger. My lips kiss hers lightly before I let her go and step away from her. "You, Lexi Petrov," I say, using her full name, even though I know her last name is Yoder, "are one in a million."

Twenty-Three

Lexi

"THANK YOU"—HE puts his forehead on mine—"for giving me an incredible weekend." My hands move to his bare chest and I take in his heat. "You, Lexi Petrov…" I try not to smirk that he doesn't use Yoder, but nothing, and I mean nothing, could prepare me for the next five words. "…are one in a million." He gives me the softest kiss we've shared this weekend as he lets me go and I step into the SUV.

I close the door and pull out of his driveway, thinking I'm going to be strong, but then the lone tear escapes and rolls down my cheek as I make my way over to my new house. These past two days have been what fucking dreams are made of. It's what you wish would happen when you meet someone. It's what I have been wanting my whole life. A man who respects me, who listens to me, who is all fucking that. I sniffle, not wanting to wipe the other tears that come because it's okay for me to cry over him. If there is anyone in my life I should have cried over, it's Kirby. Even now, after everything that I've been through, I still can't have the one thing that I want.

I make it to my house, parking in the garage before opening the door and stepping out. The phone pings from my purse, so I take it out and see his name.

Kirby: Can you at least text me that you got home so I don't worry?

I close my eyes. "Why can't you date him on the off hours?" I ask myself and then shake my head. "Because if you suck at your job, he's not going to tell you and then he'll just keep you because you guys are banging each other," I answer myself before getting out and texting him back.

Me: Just got home. Thanks for checking on me.

I press send before I add in, *Want to come and see my new place? And maybe bang me one more time?*

I walk into the house and dump my bag on the table by the door before I kick off my shoes. I'm pulling open the fridge when my phone pings and I rush over, thinking it's him but then feeling a little disappointed when I see it's Ariella and she sent a picture.

I open the text thread and see a picture of Jagger with his big gummy smile.

Ariella: Someone misses Aunt Lexi and her nighttime snuggles.

I answer her right away.

Me: How about I come by after work tomorrow so he can see I'm alive and I can get some wet kisses from him?

She answers back right away.

Ariella: He'll be waiting with drool and all.

I close the fridge and walk back to my bedroom and then straight to my bathroom. "Might as well wash away the evidence," I state, opening the glass shower door and turning it on. Slipping my jeans off me, I toss them into the laundry basket in the corner before the shirt, bra, and panties join them. I put my head back when I step into the warm water and close my eyes. Memories of last night and all day today play over in my head. Me in his lap, his cock buried in me, our arms wrapping around each other, our mouths attached. It was the single most erotic thing I've ever done. Every single time with him just got better and better. He really made sure he kissed every single inch of my body. From the top of my head to the tips of my toes, he's had his mouth or tongue on me.

I shake my head to stop thinking about it, getting out and doing my nighttime routine. Sliding into bed, I take my phone and I'm itching to text him that I'm thinking about him, but knowing it's not right for either of us. So, I put it down and turn off the lights until the alarm rings softly the next morning at 6:00 a.m.

I stretch my arms over my head, my muscles still sore from all the work it did the day before. Even getting out of bed I feel him, and I knew I would. He didn't just take me to bed and get it over with. Nope, not Kirby, he took me to bed and properly fucked me until I couldn't move. The ten minutes I was used to, which by the end of our marriage had dwindled down to two minutes, was not even a comparison.

"Okay, you are going to have to stop thinking about

him," I scold myself as I take a sip of coffee. "He's your boss and you made the decision." I walk to the outside couch area, sitting down and watching the sun rise. "Doesn't mean you have to like it."

I finish my coffee before getting up and heading back inside, my phone ringing at exactly seven, and I look down to see it's my father calling. "Good morning." A smile fills my face.

"Morning, sweetheart," he greets. "I just got in the car to go to the gym and thought I would call and say good luck today."

I take a deep breath and my stomach flutters nervously. "Thank you, I'm so nervous."

"I don't know why; I think this will be good for you. They should be lucky to have you."

"You have to say that, you're my dad." I roll my eyes, rinsing the cup and then opening the fridge to grab the eggs and then the freezer for a sausage round. "But I'm honored either way."

"How was the weekend? Did you unpack?" he asks me and I look at the boxes in the living room.

"I'm almost done," I lie to him. I couldn't really unpack this weekend; I was having the best sex of my life, and now I'm probably ruined for all men. "Just a couple more to go."

"Okay, honey, call us tonight and let us know how it went," he tells me. "Love you."

"Love you more." I disconnect while I make my breakfast sandwich and eat it with a smile on my face.

I head to the bedroom next and grab the exact skirt

that would probably piss off Trent but makes me happy. The skirt he tossed to the side and told me to give away is now the outfit I'm going to wear for my first day at work. The tan skirt with a slit on the side, making it classy but with a hint of sexy. I slip the black, long-sleeve button-down cotton shirt off the hanger, tucking it inside and leaving three buttons open before folding the oversized cuffs.

I get into my SUV and try not to let the nerves fill me, but the closer I get to the destination, the more nervous I become. I park in the underground parking where the email the secretary sent me instructed me to.

I look around and I don't spot his SUV, and I have to wonder if he's even going to show up today. I grab my purse and follow the signs for the elevator, pressing the up button and then waiting. "He's probably avoiding coming into the office because he hates you," I mumble to myself, the thought making me feel like I'm going to throw up.

I don't have a chance to turn and head back to my SUV before the elevator opens up and I step in. My hand shakes as I press the number to the floor. I step in the back as it stops on the first floor and people get in the elevator. I have to squeeze my way out when it's my floor. I step out, looking right and then left before I see the name on the door. I walk over and take a huge inhale before I turn the handle. "You've got this."

As soon as I push the door open and step in, I feel a sense of calmness. The waiting area on the side has a long green couch with two different shades of pink pillows and two single green chairs facing the sofa. In the middle of the wall on top of the couch are three words.

Make The Choice. The Make and The is in gold and the Choice is in a green. Above the words are what look like green leaves with pink flowers covering the top half of the wall, like you stepped into a garden.

I hear movement from the side and look over and blink once, twice, three times and the back of my neck starts to heat up. It can't be. Would he really? "Hi," the woman says, "I'm Kylie. I don't know if you remember me." Her green eyes stare at me. "We met."

I swallow down and put on my fake smile. "Yes," I confirm, moving to the side, "you were Kirby's date." I stop talking when the door opens and the man of my dreams and who's now on my shit list steps in.

He's wearing dark-black jeans with a white T-shirt and a caramel button-down shirt open and with the sleeves pushed up. The hat on his head hides the silky hair I spent most of two days with my hand buried in. "Hey," he says, looking at me and all I can think of is he's the most handsome man I've ever met. "I wanted to get here before you," he mentions to me and then holds up the tray of three coffee cups and a see-through bag with a pink box in it. "I guess I'm late." His eyes find mine and all I can do is stand here transfixed on him.

"She just got here." I hear Kylie and turn back to look at her as she steps to him and grabs the coffee. "She gets coffee and sweet treats on her first day. I got a phone call."

My eyes go from her to him and then back to her.

"Ignore her," Kirby states, walking in and putting the box on the brown desk on the side. "She's been giving me shit her whole life." He takes off his hat, tossing it onto the desk. "Lexi, meet my younger sister," he says, smiling at her, "Kylie."

"Sister?" I repeat the word. "I thought you two dated."

"Ew," Kylie says, making me laugh. "I bid on another guy at the event."

"I know, I just thought you were trying to make him jealous."

"The only thing it did was make me poorer," Kirby deadpans. "Shall we get started?"

"I haven't even given her a tour," Kylie says, taking one of the cups of coffee out and then looking at the label. "How do you take your coffee?"

"I'll take whatever is left," I tell her and she smiles.

"I love working with her already," she remarks, making me laugh.

"Yeah, Lexi is amazing." He exhales and looks at me for a second, the second enough for my stomach to flutter, before turning his head. "Do the tour and I'll wait here." He walks over to the single couch, sitting while he takes out his phone.

"Okay, so we have two offices," Kylie says, "and if it's okay with you…" She looks over at me. "I kinda love that one." She points to the office on the right.

"I don't think I need an office," I tell her and turn to look back at Kirby, who gets up to grab one of the coffee cups, not even listening to our conversation. "I just need a desk."

"And you will have one in this office." She ushers me to the office in the corner. "Anything you don't like, Ariella says she will change, but she sort of said you would love this." I step in and see there is an L-shaped desk pushed into the corner and facing the outside. A white fabric chair is pushed in, facing a desktop computer. "We also got a laptop for you to use if you don't want to come into the office." She steps to the side where the cozy part of the office is. Two big plush ivory-colored couches face a dark green wall. In the middle of the wall are six frames.

The first one reads: "Everything you've ever wanted is sitting on the other side of fear."

The second reads: "The question isn't who is going to let me; it's who is going to stop me."

The third reads: "I have not failed…"

"I love it," I say, turning to her, "and those quotes." I point to the wall. "I might steal that for my house."

"I took a couple for mine also," she admits. "Just a little affirmation makes you remember what the big picture is, I guess." She looks over at Kirby. "We should have the weekly meeting so he can get to work." She takes a sip of her coffee. "There are only two offices, and he refused to take one, so we have to have the meeting in the waiting area." She calls him over her shoulder, "Okay, brother?" Kylie walks out to the waiting room. I follow her, seeing him sitting in the chair, his ankle on his knee, and now I can't look at him without knowing he's even more perfect naked.

"Welcome to the first weekly meeting." He sits up and puts down his coffee. My eyes go to his hand and his fingers, wanting to sit next to him and hold his hand, but opting to sit in front of him with a coffee table in between us. His eyes go to my legs when I cross them, and I see his jaw get tight. "I have no idea what to say except welcome, Lexi." He smirks at me. "Thank you for taking the job." I smile at him. "If you have any questions, feel free to ask me or Kylie." He chuckles. "I don't even know what else to say or discuss." He looks at me, then at Kylie. "Maybe we can go over what you plan to do this week." Kylie snickers at him as she goes over what she plans on doing this week. It lasts maybe thirty minutes before it's an awkward silence for a couple of seconds before he looks back over at Kylie. "I guess that ends our first meeting. Kylie, be nice." He gets up and Kylie also gets up, shaking her head.

"I'm nice to everyone but you." She walks away from him to her office, leaving us by ourselves.

"She is nice to everyone but me," Kirby admits, bending and grabbing his cup of coffee. "If you need anything, please don't hesitate to reach out to me," he says. All I can do is nod because in this moment with him right here, I'd give anything to kiss him one more time. To feel his hand on my face, to put my hand on his. He takes a step toward me. "I guess I'll see you next week," he states and my heart sinks. "I'm really glad you took the job," he says when he is right beside me. Then I look up at him and wait for him to say something else. I can almost bet he wants to say something else, but he just gives me a smile before he walks to the door. "Bye, Kylie!" he shouts toward her office, then looks at me.

"I got you one of those cinnamon rolls." He motions toward the box and then he's gone, the sound of the door clicking behind him. I close my eyes and I'm about to go after him when Kylie comes out of her office.

"Now that the big mean boss is gone," she starts, holding a notebook in one hand and the coffee in the other, "how about we have our own meeting and get to know each other a little?"

I smile at her, pushing all thoughts of her brother out of my mind, at least for a little bit anyway. "I would really like that."

"Okay," she says, "first rule of business, I have to know"—she slinks onto the couch and kicks off her heels—"how much did my brother scream when you took him on that ride?" I laugh and any self-doubt I had about working with her is now washed away. "And did you get it on video?"

Twenty-Four

KIRBY

"OKAY, EVERYBODY," MARTIN, the coach, says, coming into the room. He's wearing his usual tracksuit with a whistle around his neck, swinging back and forth. "I want you guys all to rest up." He looks over at all of us. "We leave tomorrow on a five-day road trip." Half of us groan, while the other half snickers. The rookies look at each other as if they found their favorite toy under the tree at Christmas. Little do they know that their look will slowly fade as we get later in the season. It's all fun and games traveling at first, having a girl in every city and parties to go to, but it quickly becomes old. When you get to be my age and you've played as long as I have, those days away from home are the most dreaded of all the season. "We are spending Saturday night in Vegas."

"Coach, are we going to have a curfew?" One of the rookies, Owen, puts up his hand stupidly, and half of the old guys just look over at him, giving him a glare.

"We leave the next day at eleven," the coach replies.

"Anyone who throws up on that plane signs the *whole* team up for skating practice that night and the next morning."

"If any of you fuckers," Knox warns, "even think about getting shit-faced and throwing up, I will personally kick your ass." He looks at all the young kids.

"Got it," Owen confirms. "Go out, but don't drink."

The coach just shakes his head. "No one wants to skate after a six-hour flight." Knox stares at Owen. "Especially not me." He shares a nod with him. "You get me?"

"Got you, Coach," Owen says, "loud and clear."

"Jaxon," Coach snaps his name. "Kirby," he says my name right after.

"It's your turn to babysit."

I look over at Jaxon, who puts his head back and closes his eyes. "I might sleep the whole time we aren't on the ice," he mumbles, making everyone laugh, and then his look goes to Owen. "If you guys make me skate, you also get to babysit Jagger through the night." He points at them. "And news flash, he's teething, so he likes to be up all night and he does all of this wailing." He makes sure he makes eye contact with all of us. "So keep that in mind if you want to pick up that drink."

"See you all tomorrow," Coach says, turning and walking out, followed by the rest of the coaching staff.

"Listen up," I say, leaning forward and looking at Owen and his crew, "if you think I'm going to babysit you guys in Vegas on a Saturday night, you are mistaken. There is nothing more torturous than weaving through the mounds of drunk people. So, you guys are going to get dinner after the game that ends at five, and then you are going to sit in your fucking hotel room until we leave the next day." Owen stares at me. "Are we clear?" They nod and share a look before they get up and head to the shower.

"You think they are going to listen?" Jaxon asks and I shake my head.

"Nope," he replies, "and I think it's a fifty-fifty chance we have practice on Sunday night." I get up and take off my practice jersey, tossing it in the big gray bin in the middle of the room. The away bag is already open at my feet for me to put my things in it.

"I hope Ariella will be okay," he says softly. "First time I'm gone and she's by herself since Lexi moved out." I try not to look over at him when he says her name. Instead, I pull the Velcro off my chest protector from the right and then the left, tossing it into the bag. "So you hired Lexi?" Jaxon asks me. I look over at him, seeing him still sitting down in his gear, a protein shake in his hand.

"Yeah," I answer, sitting down and finally taking off the skates I untied as soon as I sat down. "She applied for the job."

"She has no job experience." I look over at him as I place one skate in the bag.

"What are you saying?" I will not play this guessing game with him. "If you want to ask me something, then ask me."

"You two…" He puts his drink beside him and all I can do is look at him. The whole locker room is filled with noise from different conversations going on all around us, but it feels like it's just the two of us. "You guys acted like you knew each other more than just meeting for the second time when you had dinner at our house."

"Yeah," I say and take off the other skate, and I know he's waiting for more. "We"—I place the skate in the bag—"ran into each other in Phoenix." His eyebrows shoot up like he was not expecting that answer. "She was doing a fundraiser at the hospital I volunteer at."

"No way." He takes off his own skate now and places it in the bag in front of him. "So you met her husband?"

"Oh yeah." I nod, the lump in my throat getting bigger as I think about him.

"Is he as big of a piece of shit as I think he is?"

"Even bigger," I confirm, taking off my hockey pants. "Listen," I say, stopping the conversation when it comes to Lexi, "I don't want to sit around and talk about her and her life back there. I won't do it. You're my best friend and I love you like a brother and would fight right next to you, but I can't." I shake my head before tossing my pants in the bag. "I am not going to talk about her or her dickhead of an ex."

"Wow," he says, chuckling, "so Ariella was right." He gets up and folds his arm backward to grab the back of his jersey. "There is definitely something going on between you two."

"I can confirm that," I start, pushing down the lump that is growing in my throat, "that is not true. She works for me and I'm her friend. It's nothing more." I leave out the word sadly, because I'm fucking sad it's not more.

But I also have to respect her wishes.

"I'm happy she has you at least," he states, shocking the shit out of me. "I didn't know her that well when all of that was going on, but knowing her now and seeing how amazing she is, I'd love to meet her ex…with my fist in his face."

"Trust me"—I shake my head—"he's not worth it." I toss my shin pads in the bag. "People like him feed off attention of other people. The more you ignore him, that's what really gets him." I stop talking because just the thought of him makes my blood boil.

I finish my shower, getting dressed in my black joggers with matching black T-shirt before putting on one of the team sweaters with the logo in the middle of it, my number seventy-seven on the upper left side.

I get into the SUV and pull out of the parking lot, the garage door opening as soon as I drive up the ramp. I pull out and look over at the center console, seeing it's just after one in the afternoon. I stop by and pick up lunch before heading to the office. I take the brown bag off the passenger seat before reaching into the back seat and taking out the blue bag with white handles and a white ribbon on it and shutting the door with my hip. I look and see that Lexi's SUV is here and then see the space beside her empty. Kylie told me she would be working from home today, but I wasn't sure if things had changed.

I press the elevator button and bounce on my feet, waiting for the doors to open. It's been four days since I last saw Lexi, and four days that I've done nothing but tell myself this is the way it's going to be until she makes a move. The doors open and I step in, pressing the button and then stepping back. A couple of people get on when I get to the lobby floor, and by the time I get to my floor, I'm the only one left.

I take a deep inhale when I open the door and step in, hearing soft music coming from her office. "Hello," I call out and then hear the music stop before she sticks her head out of the doorway. My heart speeds up for a whole different reason when I see her face. The tightness of my chest comes on full force now; it's a tightness I'm getting lately whenever I think of her and not having her.

"Hey," I say and a smile now fills her face. Her blue eyes light up and then she comes into the room and my eyes stupidly give her the once up and down. My cock springs to action the minute I see her legs in that charcoal miniskirt she's wearing. It hugs her hips perfectly and looks like it's been folded over. It's total class, just like her, and the black silk button-down shirt she is wearing is tucked in and the sleeves have these big cuffs that are tied to make the sleeves puff out.

"This is a surprise." She steps closer to me and then her scent hits me and my cock becomes even harder. I'm thankful I wore track pants and not jeans.

"I brought lunch," I mention, holding up the bag, "and I got you something." I hold up the other bag.

"Kirby," she says my name softly, just like she said it that night when I slipped into her from behind. When she was on her stomach, I lifted her hips a bit and then slid in. "That was not necessary."

"The lunch or the gift?" I try to joke with her and she

chuckles.

"Both, I think." She shakes her head. "Kylie isn't here."

"Oh, really?" I look over at her office and see that it's dark. "I thought she was."

"You're lying." She calls me on it right away.

"Okay, fine, I knew she was working from home," I admit, walking over to the couch and tossing the food bag on the table, "but I'm leaving for five days and I won't be here for the Monday morning meeting." I put the other bag down on the table. "So, I thought we could talk about your first week."

She comes over and sits on the couch, leaning forward. "Okay, all valid points." She reaches for the blue bag. "But the gift?"

"It's a welcome-to-the-team gift," I tell her, sitting next to her but not too close. She pulls the white ribbon off and then puts it gently to the side. I look at her beauty and I want so badly to put my hand on her leg, but I want more to put my arm around her shoulders, pulling her to me. Just to kiss her softly and have her next to me. I would be happy with just that.

She takes out the white tissue paper and then unwraps the gift, laughing when she turns it over. "It's a gift that even Kylie will like," I say when she shakes her head and turns it to face me. It's a mug that has the picture we took from the ride. "She saw the picture when she came over two nights ago," I fill her in, "and she took a photo of it with her phone." I shake my head. "I think she even called and asked if they did live shots."

"She did," Lexi says, putting down the cup. "On Monday, after you left, she asked me if you yelled for your life."

"Anyway, it's a gift that you can both use, I guess." I put my hand on the back of the couch instead of around her shoulders.

"No way," she declares, picking the cup up again, "this is mine. If she wants one, she needs to find out what you want and barter for it."

"Don't give her any ideas," I tell her, leaning forward and opening the bag of food. "I didn't know if you had eaten," I mention, handing her one of the wrapped burgers, "so I brought lunch since I just left practice."

"I actually haven't stopped." She reaches for the burger and our fingers graze each other and both of us stop moving. Her eyes fly up to mine to see if I'm as affected as she is. The moment lasts maybe two seconds before she is the first to move away. "Thank you."

She folds one of her legs under the other before opening the wrapper and taking a bite. "Wow," she says mid-chew, "this might be the best burger I've ever had."

"Yeah," I agree, grabbing my own. "It's a small spot that only the local people know about. They use all fresh ingredients, which is why their burgers are more expensive than others, but you can taste the freshness." I bite my own piece. "So tell me about this week," I urge, wanting to know everything she's done, and not just at work.

"Hold that thought." She puts the burger down and gets up and walks to her office, and I make the mistake of watching her ass swing side to side and my cock literally groans.

"Yeah, I know, buddy." I look down. "Trust me, I'm in pain more than you are."

"Did you say something?" She comes back out of her office with two bottles of water, handing me one.

"I said I think they forgot to put bacon on mine." I look down at the burger, seeing the bacon clear as day. "Nope, it's there."

She comes back to sit next to me. "Like I was saying, I spent the last two days looking at local churches."

"Churches?" I ask her, confused.

"Yes, they are the first place people go to for help," she explains something I didn't even think about. "Strangely enough, my therapist gave me the idea." I want to know everything about her. I want to know all of the things. The need to ask her everything is at the tip of my tongue, but I'm respecting her and her boundaries. So, if she is going to give me anything, it'll be her play. "Anyway, I reached out to about twenty-five of them"— she grabs her burger—"and told them about us and what we are planning to do. Some were skeptical, which is only normal since we haven't been open long, but a good chunk of them have already responded to my email."

"What are your next steps?" I ask her.

"The next step is to reach out to some of the local shelters before hitting up the hospitals." She takes a bite of her burger. "Then we check and see how my lists are."

"Well, it looks like you have everything under control"—I smirk at her—"just like I knew you would."

We finish eating, then I stand up and she stands up with me. Standing at the same time, very close to me, so close I can't help myself. "I miss you," I say softly and she looks up at me, her eyes looking at me the exact way she did on Saturday night, full of wanting and need, "so fucking much." I step in an inch, just to be closer to her. "But I understand why we're doing this." She turns to face me, our chests almost touching, and if I squatted down and leaned in even a little, my lips would be on hers. My heart speeds up, my fingers move to touch her, and my body aches with the need to hold her. "I'll see you next week." I turn and walk out of the door before I do something I'll regret and lose her forever.

Twenty-Five

LEXI

ARIELLA: I CAN'T wait for tomorrow.

Gabriella: I wish I was in town.

Zoey: I wish I could cancel on the date that Nash has planned for us.

Ariella: Well, it sucks you won't be there, but I will. Well, me and Jagger but he doesn't count since he's attached to my boob for most of the day.

Me: Guys, I live here now, so we can do it any other time.

Zara: You think I can fly in for the night and then fly out?

I smile at Zara's last comment. It's been a while since I've been active in the group chats between the girls. My cousin Gabriella always makes me laugh as much as my sister, Zara.

Me: If you want, I am sure someone can lend you a plane. Doesn't Gabriel's family have one just waiting in the wings?

Zara: Don't tempt me. Okay, I'm going to have to pass on this girls' night, but I'm coming down in about a month and I expect girls' night two-point-O. So clear your calendars.

Me: It's a date.

I push away from my desk and walk out of my office toward Kylie's. Seeing her behind her white desk with a pink chair, she looks up from her screen and smiles at me. "Are you taking off?" Kylie asks as she leans back in the chair and puts her hands over her head.

"I'm about to," I reply, "but I was also coming in to invite you over to my house tomorrow."

"Oh," she says, the smile on her face going bigger and bigger.

"Nothing big, just the girls are coming over for a housewarming party and we are going to watch the hockey game." I hold up my hands after she shoots me an amused look. "Ariella has to since Jaxon is on the team, so we are supporting her. But there will be pizza and sushi, along with wine and whatever it is you want."

"Girls' night?" Kylie shrieks. "I haven't had girls' night in well…a long time, since I moved here and don't know anyone. And girls' night was dwindling even more by the time I moved from Phoenix, so it's been forever and a day."

"I didn't know you moved here just for this job," I tell her.

"Yeah." She leans her hands on her desk. "He's been wanting to start this foundation for a while." I smile when I think of Kirby's smile and then my heart literally skips a beat, but then it gets tighter knowing I put the brakes on the whole thing.

"Well, it's going to help a lot of people," I affirm to her.

"Then it's good I jumped on the train. Besides, I think I'm finally in the headspace to help. You know, since I'm over the trauma." I smile at her sadly.

"Don't we all have trauma?" I lean against the doorjamb. "Or at least that's what everyone says."

"We do." Kylie folds her arms on the desk. "Some of us just don't see the trauma before we know it's trauma."

I smile at her. "Isn't that the truth?" I push away from the doorjamb. "It's a good thing I wasn't going to take no for an answer."

"I wasn't going to turn down the offer, so there is that." Kylie laughs. "I'll bring dessert."

"Perfect, I'll see you tomorrow, then." She nods. "I'll text you my address; you can come whenever you want."

"Don't say that." She points at me. "I literally have no life, so I'll be showing up at noon."

"We can have no life together." I point back at her. "Plus, you can help me decorate."

"Ariella is coming over to your house." She gawks at me. "You think I'm going to put anything anywhere where she can ask why I put it there, and then she tells me how wrong of a decision it was?"

"I never thought about that," I say, thinking about all the decorations I put out. "Thanks for that, now I'm going to spend all night overthinking everything."

"You're welcome." She pushes away from the desk

and shuts her laptop. "That's what friends are for."

I shake my head and walk back into my office, shutting down my desktop and packing my laptop. I walk out of the office at the same time as Kylie walks out of hers and we head down to the garage at the same time. She gets into her own SUV while I wave at her and pull out at the same time my phone rings and I see it's my lawyer.

"Hello."

"Hey." Her voice fills the car. "I'm just following up on my previous call. Trent's lawyers are breathing down my neck with calls daily."

"I can imagine," I mumble as I pull onto the highway, heading to my house. "I'm still thinking about it," I tell her, except it dawns on me that I haven't thought about it once since she called me.

"I don't know if that answer is going to be good enough for them," she huffs.

"It's the only answer I am going to give them right now." I stand my ground.

"I'll let you know what they say," she says and disconnects. I look at the display screen and I know exactly what I should do, but I also am afraid of doing it.

I pull into my garage at the same time the phone pings with a text.

Marley: They will give you until the following Monday for an answer and then the offer is off the table. It's twelve million dollars, it should be a no-brainer.

"You know what also should be a no-brainer?" I say, getting out of the SUV. "Firing you and actually getting someone who is on my side." I shut the door and head into my house.

"Look at this view," Ariella gasps, walking out from the living room to the patio while I hold Jagger in my arms. "No wonder you wanted to move out so fast."

"Oh, would you stop?" I kiss his head and he looks up at me. He's been in my arms since they got here over twenty-five minutes ago. "I was in your hair."

The doorbell rings and I look over at her. "Make yourself at home."

I turn and walk back to the front door, Jagger on my hip as he looks around. I open the door and smile when I see Kylie there with two clear bags, holding four boxes of what is probably dessert. "Hello," she greets, smiling big. "Am I too early?" she asks me and I shake my head. "Good. Here, take this, I have more in the car." She hands me the bags and runs back to her SUV that is parked in the driveway.

"Is she silly?" I ask Jagger as he hits my chest a couple of times and he blabbers at me.

I watch her walk back to me with two big boxes and another bag. "What are you doing?" I ask her, moving out of the way so she can come into the room. "What is all that?"

"This"—she holds up the bag—"is a present from the office." I laugh at her. "And then these"—she holds up the two white boxes—"are from our boss."

I swallow when she says our boss instead of saying Kirby's name. "Presents," Ariella says, coming into the house. "Hi." She smiles at Kylie. "We meet again," she says, holding out her hand to Kylie, who goes to shake her hand. Jagger decides he's done with me and launches himself toward Ariella, who catches him as if it's no big deal. "This is my boy, Jagger."

"He looks exactly like Jaxon," Kylie says, rubbing her finger over his cheek.

"That he does." She raises her eyebrows. "I spent nine months carrying him for him to come out looking like his dad. Actually, the only one who said he looks nothing like his dad was Angela." When Ariella says that name, Kylie fake vomits making her laugh.

"Who is Angela?" I ask them.

"Kirby's ex," they both say at the same time and my stomach literally clenches. "She was vile."

"She was," Ariella agrees and they both look at me. "You okay?"

"Yeah, I'm fine," I lie and put on my fake smile. "So, what is all this?" I look at the boxes, hoping it will change the topic of Kirby and his ex.

"The champagne and glasses are from the office, which means they're from me," she replies of the box wrapped in blue paper and the bottle of champagne with a blue ribbon around it. "These"—she puts her hands on the boxes—"are from Kirby."

"Isn't that nice?" Ariella says. I look over and she is trying to hide her smile with Jagger's head. "You should open it."

"I'll open it," I say, "and you"—I point to Kylie—"pour yourself a glass of wine."

"Say less," she says, making us both laugh, walking into the kitchen and grabbing a glass and filling it with white wine.

I untie the white ribbon and open the box, folding the white tissues over to see that he's got the quotes in my office printed and framed. I gasp and look at Ariella. "You knew about this?"

She rolls her eyes. "He might have called and asked where I got them."

I take all of them out of the box and stop when I see the last one. "Wait," Ariella says, looking into the box, "there were six." Her eyes go to the last one.

It is our light, not our darkness, that most frightens us.

"Wait." She turns and walks to the living room and picks up the frame I put there yesterday, his card from that night in the middle of it. "It's the same quote." She reads it and then gasps. "K is Kirby?"

"K is for Kirby." I nod at her. "The two of us—"

"Are a couple," she quickly fills in, and I shake my head but look down at the picture in my hands.

"We got close when he was in Phoenix," I admit to her. "He was there when I needed him." That's all I will say. "And I will be forever grateful for that."

"I think it's more than that," Kylie breaks into the conversation, "but it's none of my business." She takes a sip of her wine. "Well, at least that's what he told me when I asked him about it."

"There is nothing to say," I agree with him, even though my head screams there is a lot to say. "He's my boss and I'm his employee."

"Yes, but you were friends before you started working for him," Kylie states, "so does that count?"

"It doesn't," Ariella refutes at the exact time I say, "One thousand percent. He's my boss; it's wrong."

"I mean, if we are being technical…" Kylie looks at Ariella, then back at me. "I'm your boss." I shake my head. "I mean, technically, there is no boss."

"He signs my paycheck."

"No, he doesn't"—Kylie shakes her head, laughing—"the foundation does."

"Where do you think the foundation is getting money from?" I argue with her.

"From our trust fund," she says and I take a step back. "Actually, it's the interest from our trust fund."

"I'm sorry, what?"

"Our stepfather," she explains softly, "the one who adopted me, which is why we don't have the same last name anymore—something that I'm going to change back—left us both a trust fund of a loooottt of money," she sings out as Ariella gasps. "And then my mother passed away"—she blinks away tears—"and she left us the rest of what our stepfather left her. I'm not talking about the M word; I'm talking about the B word and it makes me uncomfortable to even say it!"

"Wait, so you guys are Richie Rich rich?" Ariella asks, making me laugh and all I can do is laugh at her.

"Yeah, it took a while for Kirby to even want to touch the money," she says, looking at me. "I live off the interest and just let the money sit there. He makes fun of me all the time at how cheap I am." She takes a sip of her wine. "But, yeah, he's not your boss."

"Well, you are both my bosses," I declare, turning and walking away from the kitchen and the girls as they talk, carrying the frames with me to my bedroom. My head is spinning at finding out things about Kirby, but I was feeling like I was invading his privacy, so I walked away.

The rest of the night the three of us sit in my small living room, watching the game. My heart speeds up every single time they say his name or they show his face. We half watch the game, half talk as I keep filling up the trays with snacks. I walk them both out when they leave and give them both a hug, and we make plans to go to the next home game the guys have, which is next Friday.

Ariella pulls out first, waving at me like crazy, before driving away. She is followed by Kylie, who holds up her hand and then stops and rolls down her window. "I want to try the Pilates thing you were talking about."

I clap my hands. "Want to do a class tomorrow at ten?"

"Yes," she says. "Send me the details and I'll meet you there."

"Will do." I hold up my hand and take my phone out to reserve our spots for the class.

I clean up the little bit of a mess when I get back into the house and then head to my bedroom. I look up and see the pictures Ariella had put up during the first and second period. I smile when I see the one in the middle, with the six of them hanging all around that one.

Pulling out my phone, I pull up his text and close my

eyes before I start writing the text.

Me: Thank you for the pictures. They are the best.

I press send and then take a picture of them and send it to him.

I look at the clock, seeing it's just after eleven thirty and wondering if he's sleeping or not. I slip into my shorts and tank top, and I'm sliding into bed when my phone pings with his reply.

Kirby: You are more than welcome.

I laugh and then decide to call him but after half a ring I hang up.

Kirby: Are you drunk calling me?

I laugh and call him again and this time he answers within the first half of the ring. "I'm not drunk," I state before he even says anything and his laughter makes parts of me ache and then tingle.

"It's girls' night, you're supposed to let loose."

"Is that what you are doing in Vegas?" I ask him and then I hear a ring and look to see he's trying to FaceTime me. I smile and press the green button, and his face fills the screen with his naked shoulders.

"We didn't even go out for the team dinner." He laughs. "We were going to and then we saw two girls in the corner puking and decided room service was the best plan."

I can't help but laugh at him. "Are you dating anyone?" I ask him and the back of my neck burns and I feel like I'm going to throw up.

"Are you crazy?" he asks me, his eyebrows pinching together.

"I'm asking you a serious question." I turn on my side and lie down, pretending he's here with me.

"How the fuck do you want me to be dating anyone when the only one—" He stops talking and then tilts his head to the side. "I'm not. Are you?"

"No, of course not!" I shriek, not adding that if I would be dating anyone, he's the only one I would want to date. "See? I miss this," I tell him. "I miss talking to you." Admitting it to him pushes me out of my comfort zone.

"No one is stopping you from talking to me." His voice goes soft.

"I just—" I start and then stop.

"We're friends, right?" he adds in.

I want to be more than friends, I almost say out loud instead of in my head. "We are."

"So, friends talk," he says, leaning against the pillows in his bed. "What's on your mind?"

I think about it and tell him the first thing that is on my mind. "I hate that I missed so much stuff when it comes to my family."

"Like what?" he asks me. I turn and sit up myself, propping up the pillows behind me.

"Like fucking everything." He laughs at my answer. "Like the fact I wasn't there when Matty and Sofia got married because Trent had just graduated and said he booked us tickets to Europe." Kirby just rolls his eyes. "And I missed the gender reveal and the birth of my sister's kids." My voice gets angrier. "One, because he was going into his first clinical trial and the other because he took me on 'our much-needed vacation,' away from everyone."

"Okay," he says, "but that was then." He tries to make me feel better. "You can't change that, but you can change what you do going forward."

"I want to do it all," I declare. "Birthday parties, I'm there. Gender reveal, sign me up. Wedding, yes, please." He laughs at me. "I'm not kidding, I feel like I just missed out on so much."

"Lexi," he says softly.

"Did you ever feel like this?" I ask him and he nods his head.

"When I left home for college, and I started living my life, and wasn't under his thumb, I stayed away from my mother and my sister," he admits softly. "I missed birthdays and Christmases. I even missed Kylie's graduation, and I'll never forgive myself for that."

"Well, you definitely turned it around," I tell him. "Now the two of you are closer than ever."

"We are," he confirms, "and I would die for her."

"She's an amazing human."

"She is," he agrees with a smile, "and she got the brunt of what that asshole did. She tries to pretend she's okay and that nothing bothers her, but it's a front. She's never let anyone in for them to see how amazing she truly is. She's afraid, and I hate that for her." I suddenly feel so sorry for Kylie, and I make a mental note to open up to her more, hoping that maybe in some small way I can help her move forward.

"So I heard about your ex-girlfriend today." I snicker

at him and he groans. "Angela was her name."

"My nightmare." He shakes his head. "She was the complete opposite of you. She was a horrible human, a mean girl through and through."

"Why did you date her, then?" I ask him, not sure I really want to be sitting here talking about his past girlfriend.

"Fuck if I know." He runs his hand through his hair and he laughs. "I was young and stupid."

"It was last year." I laugh at him.

"Was I not younger then?" he points out. "I like this," he says softly, "talking to you after the game while I wind down."

"I like it too," I admit to him, "but I'm going to let you go so you can get some sleep."

"Okay, I'll talk to you soon, Lexi." He looks into the camera and into my eyes, as if he's looking into my soul, sucking the air out of my lungs. "Sweet dreams."

Twenty-Six

KIRBY

"I'M HOME," I say into the phone as soon as I get into my car. "The eagle has landed."

"Wow," Kylie says, "you really think highly of yourself."

"What?" I ask as I make my way to my house. The last five days have been excruciating and long, so fucking long, it felt like two weeks and I'm happy to be fucking home.

"The eagle is a very well-respected bird—" she starts to say, half laughing. "I can't even say it with a straight face. Welcome home, Mr. President."

"I'm going to be home in fifteen minutes. Want to have a late lunch with me?"

"I guess since I'm working from home I can come over. Just don't tell my boss," she whispers. "I'll get food." She disconnects and I have the urge to call Lexi and tell her to join us, but I'm not going to pressure her. I also haven't spoken to her since she called me Saturday night. I thought she would text me the next day, but the only thing I saw was Kylie's social media post with a picture of the two of them at some exercise class and then having coffee at an outdoor café. Her smile was so big on her face, her eyes so light and free, the picture was everything.

I pull into the gated driveway and press the button for the garage, driving in and then shutting the door. Grabbing my luggage from the trunk, I make my way into the house. "Honey, I'm home!" I shout to the almost empty house.

Walking to the staircase, I take the steps two at a time until I'm in my bedroom. The shades are half open, so I dump my bag before pressing the button and having the shades open wide. The minute there is more light in the room, I hear Jefferson's little bell coming closer and closer. "Well, hello there." I look over my shoulder and see her sitting at the entry to the bedroom. She sits as her eyes get used to the bright sunlight that is now coming into my bedroom. She blinks a couple of times, her look staring at me like I deserted her. "I'm sorry, I had to go work." I sit on the bed, kicking off my dress shoes and then the jacket. "Trust me, I didn't want to go either."

She comes in gingerly, taking two steps before stopping and stretching out her two front paws and joining me on the bed. Her soft meow I'm sure calling me an asshole. I pet her head and expect her to come and sit beside me, or at least that is what I would like, but instead she turns around, gives me her back, and then goes to lie at the edge of the bed in the sun. Like she's a Grecian goddess. "I'm happy I'm home too." I get up and walk into my closet with my suitcase, emptying it before I slip into a pair of jogging pants and a T-shirt.

I'm walking down the steps when the front door opens and closes. "Hello, eagle!" Kylie shouts and I join her in the kitchen. "I've also just landed." She looks at me and snorts, pulling out one of the stools and sitting down.

"I got us some salad with grilled chicken," she says, while I pull out my own stool and sit down. "This is yours since it is the full size." She hands me the container before taking out hers, which is half the size.

"Let's trade," I suggest to her. "I ate on the plane."

She shakes her head. "I have dinner plans." I side-look at her. "I don't want to be too full."

"Dinner?" I ask her as I open my container. "With who?"

"Don't get all excited, it's the HOA meeting." She takes a bite of a piece of chicken. "Listen, I have to talk to you about something." She avoids looking at me. "And, well, you might be pissed."

"Might be or am going to be?"

"That's in the eye of the beholder," she tries to joke but doesn't look up at me, and I can tell it's serious if she's avoiding looking at me. "What happened?" I ask her right away. "Are you okay?"

"Oh yeah," she replies, "it's really not that big of a deal, but it might be for you."

"Would you just tell me?"

"Well, I was at Lexi's place for girls' night, right?" I nod, listening to her. "And, well, it came out that you are "sort of rich."

"Explain, please."

"Well, she was going on and on about how you were her boss and then my boss." She looks at me. "You are not my boss."

"I'm not anyone's boss."

"That's what I told her also, but anyway, I don't know why but it came out that you are Richie Rich rich."

"We are Richie Rich rich," I correct her. "You really have to stop putting it all on me. And you are richer than I am."

"Anyway, I just thought you should know. Now it's off my back and I don't have to avoid talking to you."

"You were avoiding me?" I ask her.

"You called me twice and I didn't answer," she gasps. "What did you think was going on?"

"I don't know," I answer, flabbergasted, "that you were busy?"

"Wow." She pushes away from the island. "It's like you don't even care."

I can't help but laugh at her. "I have to go. My lunch break is finished and my boss is back in town, and he's an asshole."

I shake my head, snorting. "I heard otherwise."

"From who?" she retorts. "Say their name." I don't answer her. "Exactly, I'm gone. Tell Jefferson she's a little bitch for eating the string to my bikini."

"That was two months ago," I shout to her back, "and I got you a replacement!"

She doesn't answer, she just shuts the door with a

bang. I look at the phone next to me, seeing it's after four. I pick it up and decide to just call Lexi. She answers after two rings. "Hey," she answers and I can almost see her smile on her face.

"Hey," I say back to her, looking at the salad in my bowl and pushing it in front of me.

"How are you?" she asks and then quickly follows up with another question, "Are you back?"

"I'm good. I'm back," I reply. "Got back a little bit ago.

"Are you at the office?" I ask, not really caring but figuring I can perhaps keep her on the phone longer.

"Nope," she replies, "it was a work-from-home day."

"How come you haven't invited me to see your house?" The minute I ask her the question, I close my eyes and I want to kick myself in the balls.

She laughs. "I don't know, I guess I haven't had the opportunity to. Would you like to come over and see my house?"

"Now?" I ask her, wanting to go and see her desperately.

"If you are free." She chuckles. "You can come over now."

"Drop me a pin," I tell her. I wait, looking at the phone for what feels like five years but is actually a couple of seconds. "I'm about twenty minutes away."

"Okay, I'll be here."

I hang up the phone, rushing to my bedroom and grabbing my keys before running out and into my SUV. I stop at the place where I saw her for the first time after she left Trent and she got the cinnamon rolls I know she loved.

When I pull up to the house, I take a second to look at it, smiling when I get out and see her in the doorway. "Wow," I say to her, pulling the sunglasses off my face. "She owns more jeans," I say of the jean skirt she's wearing. It's all the way to her ankles but has a huge V split in the front, showing her legs. Her midriff is out again because of her white, sleeveless tank top.

"I have a whole row of jeans now," she announces, a smile on her face as she moves away from the door. "Kirby," she says my name with a sly smile, "welcome to my home." She moves away from the door for me to step in and all I can do is smile at her. Lucky for me the box of cinnamon rolls is in my hand, so I don't wrap my arms around her and give her the biggest hug—followed by kissing the ever-loving shit out of her—and then fucking her against the wall. "Let me give you a tour, and then we can sit down."

"I brought you these," I say, holding up the box. "They're the cinnamon rolls you love."

She gasps, "I was literally craving one this afternoon and then told myself that if I was good all week long, it could be my treat on Saturday. But if they're here, it's rude for me not to eat one." She looks at me. "Right?"

"It shouldn't be a treat on a Saturday," I tell her. "You should eat it when you want to eat it. Like on a Tuesday night or a Wednesday lunch. You don't have to justify it," I reply as she walks sideways.

"This is the kitchen," she says of the little kitchen off

the entrance. "It's nothing big but—"

"It's perfect," I tell her as I follow her into the living and dining area. I see a round glass table with her laptop on it and her notebook beside it with writing scribbled all down the page.

"I was working before I was so rudely interrupted by someone." She points to the table and I roll my eyes. "It's only two bedrooms." She walks to the small hallway off the dining area, and I stick my head in the spare bedroom, seeing there are just racks of clothes and then stop when I look at the other side, seeing her bedroom. The big king-size bed is in the middle with two bedside tables, but my eyes go to the frames I had made for her above her bed. "The best part is here." She grabs my hand and drags me back to the living room and then out the glass door to the balcony area. "I do yoga right there every single morning." She points to the side where there is a rolled-up yoga mat lying. "Right when the sun is rising." She lets my hand go and I want to snatch it back. "It's small compared to your place."

"It's perfect for you," I tell her softly, "and exactly how I thought it would look."

The smile on her face is worth all the money in the world. "It's windy today," she mentions. "Let's go inside." She turns and walks inside. "Sit down." She points to the couch. "I'll go get the cinnamon rolls."

I walk over to the couch and stop when I see what's in the frame next to the television. I walk over to it, picking it up. "You saved it?" I ask her and she looks over at me from the kitchen, grabbing a plate out from the cupboard.

"I did," she confirms, coming back into the room with a tray in her hand, containing two plates with two bottles of water, as she places it on the coffee table. "It's special. It was the one thing that made me see the light. It's gotten me through some tough times. You probably had no idea when you wrote it how much it would change my life." She sits on the couch, grabbing a plate, and then leaning back tucking her feet under her. "I have news," she says and I walk over and sit beside her, but not close enough for me.

"Tell me."

She takes a bite of the cinnamon roll before she leans over and places the plate on the table. "I was thinking about what you said on Saturday, so on Sunday I reached out to Matty and Zara,"

she shares, and I can see the tears well up in her eyes. My hand automatically goes out to rest over her curled-up legs. "I apologized to them for not being there," she says through a shaky voice. "I'm not sure I can say this without crying."

"It's okay," I encourage her softly, and she puts her arm on the back of the couch.

"It was therapeutic, I think, for all of us. I told them how sorry I was for missing all of the most important events in their lives and then, in return, they told me they were sorry for not being there for me. For not seeing the signs, for not pushing it more. Zara and I basically sobbed to each other for a full five minutes before I was even able to finish and then she said that she felt guilty for not seeing it." She chuckles. "Matty had some other choice words about going to Phoenix to kick his ass and Sofia said she could make sure no one knows it's him. His exact words were 'If I see this fucking clown anywhere, he's going to have a broken nose and a busted lip, and then I'm going to knee him in the balls just for fun.'" She smiles through the tears.

I can't help but smile at that. "I'll help," I tell her and she laughs. "I'll drive the getaway car." She smiles as she puts her elbow on the back of the couch. "How did that make you feel?"

"Stupid," she admits, "like I knew what Trent was saying half the time was wrong, but then I doubted myself and all my choices without his input."

"It's what they do, it's like they tell you how you should do things and then turn it around and make it seem like it was your idea."

"Yes." She shrugs. "I'm just sorry I didn't see it sooner."

"Everything happens when it's supposed to happen," I tell her.

"It was that night," she says softly, "hearing what he had to say about my father." She shakes her head and the tear that she has kept at bay this whole time escapes, and my other hand comes up to catch it. "It was like you threw cold water on me."

"Lexi," I say her name softly, the ache to kiss her is almost too painful to bear, "you beat him at his own game." I cup her cheek in my hand. "For the rest of his life he's going to know he lost the best thing to ever happen to him." I stare into her eyes and take a second before I let go of her face.

"Thank you, for everything."

I nod at her; not sure I can be in her space much longer. I get up and she follows me. "I should get home and get my things sorted."

"Of course," she says. "Do you want me to pack up the roll?"

"No." I shake my head. "You have it." I wish we could be eating it in her bed after I fuck her senseless. "Thank you for the tour," I say when I get to the door and take a step to her to hug her. I wrap both arms around her, closing my eyes and feeling her in my arms; it's my own brand of torture. "Have a good night," I say when I finally let her go and walk out the door.

She stands at the door, watching me drive away, her hand held up with a smile on her face, my heart feeling like it's being crushed in my chest. "This is not good for you," I tell myself, "and it's not good for her." I swallow the lump down, knowing I'm going to have to just walk away from her. "You have to let her go." The thought alone crushes me. "You just have to hope she comes back to you." I blink away my own tears. "But even if she doesn't, you know she's finally fucking safe, and that means everything."

Twenty-Seven

Lexi

MY PHONE BEEPS and I look down.

Marley: I have to give them an answer on Monday. Let me know if you can talk tomorrow.

I'm about to answer her when the phone rings and I see it's Kylie.

"I'll be there in ten minutes," Kylie says. "Is that enough time?"

"I'm putting on my shoes now, and I have to grab my jacket," I huff out, tying my shoelaces. "I'll be outside, you don't even have to stop. Just open the door, I'll jump in."

"Open the door." She snorts. "I thought you would challenge yourself by jumping through my sunroof."

"Ohhh, that's even better," I joke, standing up when both white sneakers are tied. "See you soon." I hang up the phone, walking back into the bathroom. I pick up my perfume and spray some on my shirt, two on each side of my neck, and then one on each wrist. I step into the spare bedroom, taking one more look at my outfit of black jeans that fit me tighter than they did last week, and I can't help but smile big. The black T-shirt is tucked into the front as I grab the short, blue jean jacket, putting it on and rolling the cuffs before grabbing my small black Chanel bag and putting it across my body.

"This screams, yay sports." I turn and see how good my ass looks in these jeans. "I hope it also screams, please grab my ass, Kirby," I mumble, then stop thinking that when I hear the sound of the horn honking. "Shit." I run out the front door. "Sorry," I say and she looks at me, "I was trying to find my shoes with springs so I could jump into your SUV."

She can't help but laugh at me as I get into her SUV and then lean over to kiss her cheek. "You look so good." I look at her cargo jean pants with a white, long-sleeve shirt that shows off her stomach, a baseball hat on her head with the Warriors logo across it. At the side it has his number 77 and his name stitched in it. "Like the hat."

"I stole it from Kirby," she states, pulling out and making her way over to the arena. "I wore it to see if he notices," she says and I shake my head. "I bet you five hundred dollars he doesn't."

"I'll take your word on it." We laugh as we talk about what we did after leaving each other not too long ago. We've been spending more and more time together and, I have to say, she's quickly becoming one of my favorite people.

"Where are you going?" I ask her as she drives up to a garage door.

"It's for the players and family members." She looks over, taking out her parking pass and scanning it. We drive down the ramp, and when we stop, it's near a valet booth, one guy in a red jacket is instructing the four guys who are running around. One of them comes to my car door while another goes to Kylie's side. He hands her the white ticket and I wait for her to see where to go.

"That door"—she points to the door in the corner—"is for the players." I look over and see there is a camera crew set up. "The family goes over there." She points to the other door as we walk toward it. I step in and then we go up an escalator toward a floor that looks like there are office doors across it. A man sits on a stool and looks at us. Kylie takes out her badge and he scans it. "It's for the both of us," she tells him and he just nods as she walks over to one of the doors. "This is Kirby's suite," she announces, pushing open the door and stepping in. "Jaxon's is next door." She points to the wall where I see some action shots of Kirby. A round table sits in the middle of the room with four leather chairs around it. There is a long table by the wall with trays of food on it. "Usually, it's full of people from the hospital," she tells me, and I look over to see Ariella walking up the steps where the seats are.

"There you guys are," she huffs. "He was looking for you," she says of Jagger, who is on her hip wearing a team jersey and black headphones over his ears. "He's not a fan of the headphones," she shares and I smile at him.

"Hello, my boy," I say, holding out my arms and he

flings himself into them. "Hi," I say to him and he gives me the biggest smile as I kiss his neck.

"We should head down there," Ariella directs. "Jaxon will be looking for him."

"I'll carry him," I offer her and she nods as I follow them out the door. "This feels like déjà vu," I tell them. "My most memorable nights were the ones where we would all get together for the game." I look over at Ariella, who just nods in agreement. "And then going down to the glass, watching them skate around and waiting to catch one of the pucks." I smile big at the memories. "My favorite part would be catching them and then giving them to one of the fans and they would go nuts." I laugh as we go down the escalator and then through one of the doors and head down the steps toward the glass. People are already lined up, waiting for the team, some with boards in their hands with messages.

I stand in the corner, in the middle of Ariella and Kylie, waiting. "Look at that one."

I turn to the side to see two women dressed in jeans and leather jackets, one of them holding up a sign that says: Materson, Rock, Paper, Scissors for Your Number.

I can't help but snort out a laugh. "She's not getting a puck if I get one." The girls just laugh and then I spot something out of the corner of my eyes. It looks like the players are coming onto the ice. Jagger jumps when someone bangs on the window and he reaches back out for Ariella.

The lights go on and then the players take the ice, my eyes watch to see if I spot him, and the minute I do, my smile must get even bigger. He is walking out with Jaxon, his helmet not on, the two of them talking about something, and then they both burst out laughing. Jaxon gets on the ice first and then waits for Kirby. The girls with the sign bang on the window for Kirby's attention, but he just looks over when Jaxon points our way. His eyes find mine and the smile fills his face even more.

Jaxon comes over and Ariella holds Jagger in front of her at the glass as Jagger smacks it, trying to get to Jaxon. "Hey," I hear before the glass is knocked with a hockey stick and I look over at Kirby, "you aren't even wearing anything to support the team."

"I'm wearing black," I tell him and he shakes his head.

"I dare you to go wear my jersey," he states, standing in front of me, his eyes on me and me alone.

"Don't you have pucks to shoot?" I tell him and he just laughs, and fuck, does it make my knees weak and my pussy wet. Everything about him turns me on, but especially his laugh. He turns and skates away, not even making eye contact with the girls.

My eyes follow him until he skates to the bench and I see him talking to a guy as he is taking off his jersey and disappearing into the tunnel.

I look over at Kylie. "I have to go to the merch store," I say and she just laughs. "A dare is a dare and I'm not going to let him win."

We walk back up the steps and the three of us head over to the store. I spot his jersey right away and buy it. "Are you sure about this?" Ariella asks me. "You know what it means when you wear the guy's jersey."

"I saw fifty girls wearing his jersey walking here," I tell her as I grab the bag and we head back to the suite. "It doesn't mean anything."

"I don't know about that," Kylie refutes. "He didn't want them to be wearing his."

I take off my jacket when I get into the suite that is now filled with people, some of them Kylie recognizes and introduces me to. I slip on his jersey and then go to sit in one of the chairs, when the door to the suite opens and I see the man that Kirby was talking to as he looks around. A bag is in his hand as he sees Kylie and then she points over to me. I get off my stool and head over to him.

"I have something for you." He holds up the bag and tries to hide his smile. "But I don't think you need it."

I grab the bag from him and look inside seeing the note on top.

I dare you. -K

I pull out the jersey with his name and number and I laugh shaking my head. Bringing it to my nose and smelling him, knowing that this is the one he took off after he skated around.

"Of course he did." Kylie laughs as she heads off with a group of guys she knows that she met when she and Kirby went to volunteer at the hospital last month, and Ariella and I watch the game. Jagger drifts off to sleep at the end of the third period after the horn blares.

"Hey," Kylie says, "I'm going to head out to the bar with the guys. Do you want to take my SUV?"

"No." I shake my head. "I'll get a ride with Ariella," I

say—*or your brother*—I don't say that part. "Have fun."

"I will." She turns and walks out. We sit and watch the arena empty before she gets up.

"Let's go wait downstairs," she suggests. "I can put him in his car seat." I follow her out of the suite, my jacket in my hand, nervously waiting for Jaxon to come out and hoping Kirby is with him.

We get to the garage at the same time the door opens and Jaxon walks out, followed by Kirby, who is wearing a black suit with a white button-down but his shirt is open at the collar. He looks down and then looks up when he must feel me staring at him, his hair still wet from the shower. "Hey," Jaxon says, softly looking down at Jagger in her arms and bending to give her a kiss.

"Hey," she says, looking up at him, "we have to drive Lexi home."

"I'll take her," Kirby offers and I look over at him, trying to hide my smile, "if that's okay with you?"

"Works for me," I say, my stomach fluttering like it's home to a million butterflies. I give Ariella a hug and then look up at Kirby. "That was a good game."

"It was"—he nods—"but seeing you in my jersey might be the best part."

"A dare is a dare," I remind him and he puts his hands in his pockets as we wait for his SUV. I hold up the bag. "Although now I have two."

"What do you mean now you have two?" He looks at the bag, then the jersey on me.

"I went to the merch store before I got the official one," I tell him and his eyes go big and then his face fills with a huge smile.

"Are you hungry?" he asks me and I nod my head, hoping I can just spend more time with him, even though there is no way I can eat another thing. "Come on," he urges with his head toward his SUV, "I know a good spot."

He opens the door for me and I get in, rubbing my palms on my jeans as I watch him walk around the SUV and say something to the guy in the red coat. He opens his door and gets in, looking over at me. "Kylie ditched you," he says, taking off, his voice tight.

"She didn't ditch me," I counter. "She got a better offer." He shakes his head. "I could have taken her SUV if I wanted," I inform him as he makes it out of the parking lot and some of the fans yell his name. He stops the car, rolling down the window and signing a couple of things before continuing.

"How did you like the game?" he asks me.

"I forgot how much fun it is," I say honestly.

"It's only fun because we won." He chuckles. "It would be a lot different if we lost."

"Oh, for sure. It brought back lots of memories."

"Your dad played for LA," he says and I nod.

"This is where he started," I state, my chest proud. "Do you know he was traded while he was in rehab?" I add and he gasps. "Yeah, and my uncle Matthew was the one who picked him up and took him to New York."

"I didn't know that," he says and then stops in front of a diner. "That's wild." I open the door and step out.

"Yeah, it is," I agree. "What's even wilder is, my

parents fell in love with each other, and he refused to tell her or even act on it until his one year of sobriety hit." I wait for him to join me on the sidewalk before walking to the door. He opens it and holds his hand high on the door for me to step in before him. "Only then did he tell her."

"You can't fight love," he declares, looking around at the almost full diner, the only seats are the stools at the counter. "Let's sit over there," he mentions at the end.

He sits on the last stool and I sit next to him. A woman comes out to take our order and I order a side of fries and he just looks at me. "I'm stuffed."

"So then why did you say you wanted to eat?" He turns his stool toward me, his legs opening with mine in between his.

"I figured you were hungry," I admit to him.

"I would have much preferred to go to my house," he says and I look around.

"We still can. How about we take it to go?"

"You sure?" he asks me and I just nod my head. He holds up his hand, telling the waitress we are going to take our food to go, and then we make our way to his house.

"We can sit out on the deck. I have heaters."

He walks into the house and I follow him and halt when I see the cat coming down the hallway and stopping when she sees me. "Well, hello there, Ms. Jefferson." I bend to pick her up and hold her in my arms.

"She doesn't like to be held," he throws over his shoulder.

"She's purring," I remark as she looks up at me and I bend to kiss her, but her back paws push my face away. "Well, she lets me hold her," I say, putting her down as I follow him into the house and out to the back patio. I hear the sound of the waves hitting the beach, but all I can see is blackness. He turns on the heaters before tossing his bag of food onto the table by the L-shaped oversized couch in the corner.

I sit down and watch him take off his jacket and toss it to the side before rolling up his sleeves. "So what's new?" he asks me, taking a bite of the burger.

I sit back and turn my body to him, putting one leg up and even turning my hips to face him. "I have to talk to my lawyer tomorrow." He stops chewing after I say what I have to say.

"Why?"

"Trent offered me twelve million dollars to sign an NDA forbidding me from speaking about us and our relationship."

"Of course he did," he mumbles, taking another bite. "Do you want to do it?"

"I don't know," I answer him. "In a way I don't, because fuck him and trying to silence me again, but then again twelve million is twelve million." I trail off. "I don't want to though."

"Then fuck it, don't," he encourages. "Actually, I'll give you thirteen million bucks to be the one to tell him that you aren't taking it and to fuck off."

I bite my lower lip thinking of how much Trent would fucking die if that happened. "My lawyer thinks I should." He smirks, making my mouth water.

"You know what that means? Time for you to get another lawyer." I throw my head back and laugh.

"I was thinking the exact thing," I admit to him, "but for that I'm going to have to call in my cousin Stone's wife, and well, again, I'll have to turn to my family."

He tosses his half-eaten burger down. "You know that is what family is there for, right?" he states. "It's a give and take. What would you do if the roles were reversed?"

"I would help in whichever way I could," I reply and he points at me. "Fine, I'll call her and talk to her."

He leans back and puts his arm across my leg. "That sounds like a solid plan. Now, tell me something that no one else knows about you."

I put my elbow on the back of the couch and fist my hand to lay my head on it. "I don't know if I can," I answer him honestly. "I don't want you to think any less of me."

He puts his head back on the couch. "There is nothing, and I mean nothing, you could say that will make me think any less of you." His words warm my soul, and for the first time in my life, I tell him two secrets no one has ever known. Secrets I've kept to myself out of fear. Secrets I vowed to never tell anyone else. But with him, he makes me want to bare my soul to him. "So tell me, Lexi, what's your biggest secret?"

Twenty-Eight

KIRBY

"THERE IS NOTHING, and I mean nothing, you could say that will make me think any less of you." I know things are different with her. I know I told myself I would stay away from her, but walking out and seeing her in my jersey, it just shifted it all over again. I can't give up on her. I won't give up on her. I'm going to be here and be patient as she weaves her way through whatever she needs to do. She's the one for me, so I'm okay doing things in her timeframe. "So tell me, Lexi, what's your biggest secret?"

I turn my head on the back of the couch, watching her. "Well, it's kind of a two-part secret." She holds up her hand with two fingers up. My arm that is draped over her leg moves to the side when she tucks her second leg on the couch. But I just bring it back on her. "Okay." She takes a deep inhale. "First big secret. I found out Trent cheated on me when he came home one day and gave me a prescription to take." I close my eyes, trying to keep myself calm. "He said they were vitamin C tablets to help fight off cold symptoms." She laughs and then wipes the tear from the corner of her eye. "I didn't believe him, obviously, and when I pushed it, he finally caved and told me that when he was in Vegas, he got drunk and slept with someone by accident. It was a one-time thing and he had no idea who she was or any of that." I look up to the sky and hold my breath. "He fucking caught chlamydia and gave it to me."

I sit up, not sure I can even breathe. "I went behind his back and went to my own gynecologist, and he confirmed I had chlamydia." She puts her hand on my arm. "Then I did something I vowed to never tell another soul."

"Your secrets are safe with me, Lexi," I tell her in a whisper and she smiles through the tears.

"I know." She tries to hold it together. "That day at the doctor's office, I asked him to give me a prescription for birth control," she shares in almost a whisper. "For the last nine years I've been taking birth control so I wouldn't get pregnant." She snorts. "The irony is, for the last year he hasn't even been around to try. He sort of gave up after the second year. I was afraid he would want to go and talk to a fertility specialist, but I figured out that it would mean admitting maybe he was sterile, and he just couldn't admit that to anyone."

"Lexi," I say her name and it pains me to say it, knowing she has been shielding herself from him for the past nine years.

"One time when he was away on who knows what, I asked him what he was doing." She laughs. "And he said he was making himself a tea. Well, the idiot sent me a picture of the teakettle, but it was a stainless-steel one, and I saw him standing in front of it and there were girls there beside him naked, playing with his dick."

"Okay." I shake my head. "I don't know how much more of this I can take," I inform her and lean with my elbows on my knees, as my hands hang between my legs.

"Okay," she says, sitting next to me, "now you have to tell me something that no one else knows."

"Um, the biggest one is," I say, looking over at her, "I found out my stepfather was dying. He had stage 4 mesothelioma and was in palliative care. My sister called me crying that he was dying. I flew up there that night, no one knew, and I went to his bedside and told him I was happy he was dying and I hoped he suffered to the bitter end. He died four hours later while I was on the plane back to my house. I showed up at the funeral and I was the last one to see him before they closed the casket, and I told him to rot in hell."

I'm expecting her to jump up to her feet and run away, but instead she scoots closer, our hips touching as she slides her hand in between my elbow and my arm, letting it dangle in between my legs, until she can slide her fingers through mine. "Thank you for sharing that with me," she says softly, "and for listening to my secrets without judgment."

"I said I would let you make the next move. I would wait for you to be ready." I pull her face close to my shoulder. "But fuck it, I dare you to kiss me."

She leans in her face, her other hand coming up to cup

my jaw as she whispers, "Okay," right before her lips are on mine. I close my eyes when her tongue slides into my mouth and my own hand reaches across and cups her cheek. The kiss is soft and perfect; she lets my mouth go with a soft kiss.

"Stay with me tonight?" I ask her with a plea.

"You're still my boss," she reminds me, this time trying to hide her smile.

"Fine, you're fired," I tell her and she laughs, "until Monday. Actually, how about you are fired every night until the morning at eight? Then Friday from five until Monday at eight a.m."

"Wow." She drops her hand from my face and gets up. "And to think I was just going to say I don't care anymore. I'm tired of holding back."

"That works even better," I say, getting up. "Now will you stay with me tonight?" I'm one second away from dragging her into the house over my shoulder. "I would never do anything to hurt you or mess up my chance with you. I've been waiting a long fucking time for you to come into my life." I look at her. "I would also never jeopardize your position with the foundation if things didn't go like I wanted it to. I would become a silent partner and only work through Kylie. You never have to worry because I will never take anything out on you or use you as a pawn in a game."

"I don't know." She turns in my arms. "What are we going to do?" She bites her lower lip, as she places her hands on my chest.

"Well, the first thing that's going to happen is we are

going inside." I push her hair over her shoulder. "Then I'm going to take you to my bedroom."

"Yes, I like where this is going."

"Should I just show you?" I lean down and kiss her lips, her chest melting into mine. My hand grips her hip before going to grab her ass. "I have another secret," I say when I let go of her lips. "This might be a really big one and you might be upset."

"Okay." She looks at me waiting.

"I dared you to wear my jersey tonight so you covered that amazing body of yours and I'd be the only one able to see it when I took it off you later." She throws her head back and lets out a big laugh.

"I have a secret also," she announces and I see her eyes are dancing in the moonlight. "The two girls who wanted your number…" She mentions the two girls who were trying with everything to get my attention, and I made sure I didn't even stop anywhere near them. "Well, they saw you hit the glass with the stick, and when we left and I went to buy your jersey, I gave them a smirk and a shrug and might have mouthed, 'Better luck next time.'"

"You didn't?" I shake my head.

"Okay, I didn't mouth 'Better luck next time' but I thought it," she retracts. I pick her up and carry her into the house, her legs crossing behind me. "It served them right."

"Baby," I say softly as I lock the door behind me, "you have to know I only have eyes for you." I turn off the light in the kitchen and head toward my bedroom.

"The minute I ran into you at the baby shower I was done or so I thought. I knew I was for sure done when I skated onto the ice and saw you," I admit to her. "Even after I vowed to stay away from you yesterday." She gasps. "I know, but it was so hard to be with you and not be able to touch you or to kiss you."

"I have a secret," she murmurs, dislodging herself from me when we get into my room. The strips of lights are all on softly along the wall with my bed, and the other wall with my curtains. Her hands cross over in front of her as she pulls my jersey over her head, leaving her in a black T-shirt and her jeans. "I wanted you to kiss me yesterday." She then pulls the T-shirt from her pants, repeating the same action with the jersey. "I was sad when you left and you didn't try."

"I could have been driving into my garage and if you would have called and told me you wanted me to kiss you, I would have broken every single traffic law to get back to you." I see her swallow as she kicks off her shoes, then her hand goes to the button of her jeans and I watch her strip for me. She kicks her jeans off to the side and stands there in front of me wearing a black lace bra and matching panties.

"Fuck, you look"—I step to her—"mouthwatering." I walk to her, bending to take her mouth with mine as my hands come up to cup her tits. I move her back until her knees hit the side of the bed and she falls back on it at the same time I get on my knees in front of her. "Put your leg on my shoulder," I tell her and she does it while I move her black thong to the side. "Fuck, I need to taste you,"

I say right before I lean and lick her all the way from entrance to her clit. "Tastes like fucking heaven." I push both her legs back and suck her clit into my mouth. Her moans fill the room with a heavy pant.

"Oh, God," she sighs when I slide my tongue and finger into her. "Yes," she pants as I move my tongue up to flick her clit. Another finger slides into her and this time I watch her back arch as it rubs over her G-spot.

"I want to know your body inside and out." I suck her clit into my mouth. "I want to know what you like, what you don't like, and what you can't live without." My fingers move faster and faster in her as her pussy gets wetter and tighter. "Every single night I want to worship you." I bite down on her clit gently and then harder until she moans out her release. "The question though"—her wetness runs down my knuckles as she clenches over and over—"is what do you want?" I suck her clit into my mouth and my fingers don't stop fucking her until I feel her body sink deep into the bed and her legs fall beside me.

"I want. I want everything." She gets up on her elbows, looking at me, her eyes a darker shade of blue. She sits up, my fingers sliding out of her as she brings them to her lips and licks herself off of me. "I want to suck your cock." She stands and pulls me up off the floor before kneeling back on the bed. I reach around her to take off her bra, leaving her in just her panties. Her hands go to my shirt, pulling it out of my pants. "I want to get to know your cock." Her hands go to my belt as she unbuckles it before going to the button of my pants. "I've never wanted to pleasure someone more in my life." She pulls the zipper down and all I can do is watch. "I want you to fuck my mouth." She opens the front of my pants. "I want you to let loose with me. I don't want you to hold back."

"Lexi," I hiss between clenched teeth.

"I want you to grab my hair in both hands and fuck my mouth." She grips my cock in her hand and then slowly, ever so fucking slowly, she licks my cock up the shaft with the tip of her tongue. "I've never had someone just lose it to fuck me." She takes the head into her mouth. "I've never been ravished before"—she takes a little bit more into her mouth—"and I want it with you. I want you to lose control with me." Her tongue twirls around my cock.

"I," I try to say as she jerks my cock and then slides her mouth halfway down, her hand going to the base of my dick. "If that's what you want, baby." I grip her hair in mine and pull it a bit, and I can see her eyes go light before lusting over.

"I dare you to fuck my mouth like it's the last thing you're ever going to do." The twinkle in her eyes is back, and this time I just shove her head down onto my cock.

"Open that throat up," I tell her. "Let my cock slide into it." I move my hips faster and faster, her hands gripping the edge of the bed. Her back is arched, her ass in the air, and I have to close my eyes as she gags on my cock. I let her mouth go and she fights me to get my cock back into her mouth. "That's it," I praise as I touch the back of her throat and she tries to take me to the root. I let go of her hair and reach over her, slapping both ass cheeks with my hands. The moan from her throat vibrates through me as I knead her ass and then smack it again, making her throat open up more. "You like when I slap your ass and fuck your face?" I ask her but slap it again. This time her throat opens and my cock is buried all the way, her throat gagging after a second.

"Fuck, no one has ever taken me as deep as you. Going to coat your mouth with my cum." I move my hand down her ass and into her dripping, wet pussy. "Going to watch you swallow every single drop I have to give you." She moves her ass side to side, my balls wet from her spit. "Tell me you want it."

I let her go for a split second, and she pants out, "I want it."

"Then take it," I say, another finger sliding into her. "Suck my cum from my balls." I close my eyes when my balls tighten and I shoot into her mouth. Her hips move back against my fingers as she comes again. Only when I finish coming in her mouth does she let my cock slip out of her lips. "I might need a minute." I look down at her and see she is licking my shaft, the smirk on her face making my cock jerk. "I think I just died."

Twenty-Nine

LEXI

"I MIGHT NEED a minute." His chest rises and falls as he pants before he looks down. My hand is still holding his shaft and I want more of him. I lick the back of his cock, smirking at him. Never in my whole life has someone literally lost control with me and done that. "I think I just died."

I get up on my knees in front of him, kissing the middle of his chest and feeling the pounding of his heart beating. "Was that okay?" I move my nose back and forth, trailing my tongue to his nipple, flicking it. "Because I have to say"—his hand comes up to push the hair away from my face—"that was the most erotic thing that has ever happened to me." I move to the other nipple.

"Night is still young," he teases and his hand grips mine on his cock. "Get a condom."

"I'm on birth control," I blurt suddenly, "and I'm clean. I got tested monthly after...well, you know. Besides, it's been a while before that. Seems since I wasn't getting pregnant, there was no use in us being intimate."

"Have I mentioned he's a fucking idiot?" he deadpans, and I can't help but laugh as his hand comes up to hold my jaw while he kisses me. His tongue is on mine and I can taste myself on his lips and hungrily suck his tongue into my mouth. His hand falls from my chin and, in a blink of an eye, I am on my knees, my chest on the bed, and his mouth is now buried between my legs. I close my eyes, feeling his warm, soft tongue slide into me and I push back at him, hoping to get it deeper inside me. "Tell me what you want."

"I want you to fuck me," I throw over my shoulder, "like you have never fucked anyone before." He moves my hips back a bit, getting up. He holds his cock in his hand and I feel it rub up and down my slit. He puts one of his feet on the bed beside my knee. He teases me as he rubs it up and then stops to slip it in, for just a split second, before continuing back to my clit, where he rubs it with the tip of his cock. "My whole body feels like it's on fire."

"Good," he says right before he slides his cock into me and the feeling of fullness overwhelms me. He puts his hand at the base of my back and pulls me away from him and then back to him, making me move to fuck him. He doesn't move, never burying himself fully inside me. Just stopping midway and then pulling back out. I get up on my hands and twist to look behind me and his eyes are fixated on his cock sliding into me.

"What are you doing?" I ask him, semi-frustrated, semi-ready to push him down and ride his cock, taking what I want.

"I'm watching your pussy swallow my cock." He doesn't even look up at me while he tells me this.

"Well, my pussy would like a good—" I don't say another word because he slams into me and I swear I think I see either stars or the lights of heaven. The jolt rushes right through me and I can't help but orgasm all around his cock. He doesn't even give me a second before he's pulling out and slamming in again, over and over. My moans and the sound of skin slapping skin fill the room as my hands grip the sheets to try to hold on before he fucks me off the bed. "Is that all you've got?" I bite down on my bottom lip and he leans forward, taking each of my tits in his hands and pulling me back on his cock. Kirby has lost control. I've made him lose control.

"If I fuck you any harder—" he grits between clenched teeth.

"If you fuck me any harder," I can barely say, his cock hitting the sweet spot over and over, "I'll feel you all day tomorrow." He fucks me with abandon, making me slam into him over and over again. My eyes roll behind my head when I come again. "It's right—"

"I feel it," he growls between clenched teeth. "Feel you strangling my cock." I try to keep my eyes open but I can't, I just go with the feeling. "Need to get deeper," he says and I'm about to say if you go any deeper, you'll be in my throat. He pulls out of me and I moan out in frustration, wanting him to get back inside me. He flips me like I'm a rag doll to my back.

Holding one foot in his hand and the other leg pushed

back, he slides his cock into me. "That's deeper." He pulls out slowly before he slams back into me again, letting go of my legs and leaning down on the bed. One hand is beside my hip, the other around my waist, pulling me up to him. His cock goes so deep in my pussy, I have to put my hands on the headboard behind me and my head falls back.

He moves his hand from beside me to hold my ass as he puts one knee on the bed for support before I sit on his lap. The hand around my waist moves up to the middle of my back, while my nose plays with his as he moves me up and down on his cock. His tongue slides into my mouth as I ride him, or rather, how he makes me ride him.

"I want to ride you," I tell him when he lets go of my mouth. He places his other knee on the bed, my pussy still impaled on his cock as he moves over to the headboard, turning, and sitting down with his back against it.

"Then ride me, baby," he urges, his hands coming up to roll my nipples as I put my knees by his hips. "Ride me good." I put my hands on the top of the fabric headboard beside his head and move myself up and down on his cock. His hands go to my ass, slapping one cheek, my movement speeding up a touch when he does that.

"Your pussy gets tighter every time I smack you," he states, sucking in one of my nipples that bounce by his mouth, biting down on it just enough for me to move faster and faster. I pant out and lean forward, our mouths connecting as his body rubs my back to my ass and back up again. I feel his hands everywhere, and I know I'm about to come again. I've never had more than one orgasm during sex, but with Kirby it's like he knows how to get more out of me.

"Going to come, baby, after you finish coming on my cock," he informs me and I can't even focus on what he is saying, I'm just chasing the feeling of exploding. "Going to flip you on your back, lick your pussy, and then come right on your landing strip."

All I can do is nod as my head falls back and I come on his cock over and over again, feeling like I'm floating out of this universe. He flips me to my back, his mouth going on my clit, sucking it into his mouth, but his fingers fuck me so hard it feels like his knuckles are trying to get into my skin. All I can do is try to open my legs wider to give him more space.

"Come on my tongue," he commands, his other hand coming up and pressing down on my clit, moving it side to side. Just like that, I'm jumping off this cliff I've never been on, so high I don't even care where I fall. "Fuck, you gushed all over me."

He moves his hand from my clit and then I slowly open my eyes, his fingers still in me slowly moving, but he's got his cock in his hand. I try to move my hand up to help him, but I'm spent. "Baby." He aims his cock for my landing strip and white cum shoots right on it. Once, twice, three times before he's pressing his cock down and moving his cum all around me, his cock still shooting some more. "Mine," he claims, "all fucking mine."

I smile when he collapses beside me on his back, his

chest rising and falling as if he just spent the last hour running a marathon. "I think you killed me."

One of my legs falls to the side and I move my hand to his hip. "I can't move," I tell him. "Tried to help you come on me, and I couldn't move my hand." I turn my head to watch him with his eyes closed, trying to catch his breath. "I think I've died and gone to heaven." I turn to look at his ceiling. "Or I'm having a stroke."

"You aren't having a stroke," he assures me and moves his hand to cup my breast, squeezing it, "but you might have killed my dick."

I gasp and sit up in his bed. "Not the dick! I'm fond of the dick." He can't help but laugh and I move next to him, kissing his neck and cuddling my face in his neck. "Kirby," I call his name softly, my hand on his abs moving it around in circles, "there is something we need to talk about."

"What is it, baby?" he asks, rubbing my arm up and down.

"It's serious, so I need your undivided attention."

"You're naked in my bed and I just had the most insane sex of my life." He chuckles. "You have all my attention." I chuckle as I put my hand on his abs and then place my chin on it, looking at him. He folds his arm under his head to look at me. "What is it?"

"Well," I start and I can see the worry on his face, "who is going to sleep in the wet spot?"

He barks out his laughter. "Well, you did it, so you have to sleep in it."

"Yeah, but you made me do it," I point out to him,

"so, technically, it's half your fault."

"I'll sleep in the wet spot," he offers, turns, taking me in his arms, "or we can sleep in it together."

"Or, we can sleep on one side until the spot dries."

"See?" he says, kissing my nose. "You are just a solver of problems." He squeezes me tighter. "I'm going to go and get cleaned up," he announces, slipping away from me. "Don't move."

"I want to get cleaned up also," I tell him, getting up and following him into the bathroom. "You smeared your cum all over me."

"Well, I had to make sure I marked you." He winks over his shoulder. "It's a man thing."

I stop at the sink beside him as he turns on the water. "I've never been marked before." He stares at me through the reflection of the glass. "I've also never had sex like that before." I avoid looking at him and instead look at the stream of water that is pouring out of the faucet. "It was—"

"Did you not like it?" he asks me and I can feel him staring at me.

"Did you not see the mess I made in your bed?" I joke with him and point over my shoulder with my thumb. "It was the most…"

"Lexi," he calls my name and I know he wants me to look at him, "I've never had sex like that either. And not to be an asshole, but I've had a lot of sex." I roll my eyes. "But that—" He points to the room. "That was like next level. I thought I died. Like my legs nearly buckled." I can't help but laugh. He shakes his head, reaching for a face cloth. "Then I almost forgot about making you come and just came by myself." That makes me laugh. "And for the record, I am not a fan of you talking about you with whatever his name is." I have to roll my lips because he knows exactly what his name is. "Or me with other women."

"Same," I say, "like, out of sight, out of mind."

"Yes. So can that be the last time I have to listen to you talk about what's his name and sex?"

"Just so you know, he never got me that turned on." I wrap my arms around his waist. "Sometimes I didn't even finish." The smile on his face goes big. "I definitely never had a wet spot." I kiss his chest and he picks me up, putting me on the counter. "What are you doing?"

"Seeing if you're still wet." That's the last thing he says before he slides his cock into me, fucking me on the counter in the bathroom.

MY EYES FLY open when I feel a heaviness on my legs and then the feeling moving up to my hip and then over my stomach. Raising my head off the pillow, I see Jefferson walking up my body. I look over and see Kirby with his back to me, somewhere along the way he let me go and rolled away. She makes her way up to my face, and then with the top of her head, she nudges my chin.

"What does that mean?" I whisper at her and she does it again, the sound of her purring filling the room. I slide my hand out from under the cover and rub her. She settles on my chest for a full two minutes before she gets up and jumps off the bed.

"Good morning to you too," I say, getting on my elbow and seeing the sunlight trying to come in from around the bottom of the shades. I toss the covers off me and head to the bathroom, snatching one of Kirby's T-shirts from the bench in his room. I tiptoe out of the bedroom and then head out to the kitchen.

Jefferson follows me down the steps and toward the kitchen. I open up the cabinets as I search for things to make myself a coffee and make sure Jefferson has breakfast too. I feel like I've had the workout of my life, and I can't help but smile when I think of the workout I had. The phone rings from the table and I run over to grab it. I open my purse and look down, seeing it's Zara calling me. "Hello," I answer, looking over my shoulder, hoping I didn't wake him.

"Good morning," she says, her face filling the screen. "Did I wake you?"

"Um, no," I say, shaking my head and walking into the kitchen.

"You aren't home?" She sticks her face deeper into the screen. "Where are you?"

"I'm at a friend's house." I avoid looking at her, but the smile and giggle that comes out of me makes it evident that I'm not really at a friend's house.

"At a friend's house, and what is this friend's name?"

"It starts with a K," I whisper, putting a coffee cup under the spout for the coffee.

"Oh my God, you had sex."

"I did," I confirm to her and she just gasps. "Good

sex. Great sex." I try to keep my laugh down. "The best sex."

"I want to hear all the details," she prods and I look over to the entranceway.

"He's a guy I've known for a while," I say softly, "and he helped me through a lot."

"Gabriel did that for me too," she replies and I laugh.

"You had a one-night stand with him and then snuck out on him." I walk to the fridge.

"Yeah, he helped me get over my cheating ex," she huffs, "and then his super sperm got me pregnant." I laugh louder, as I sit on the stool. "Anyway, tell me about this guy." I pour the milk in my coffee and tell her everything. I don't think I've ever been this open before. Even about meeting him in Phoenix and the dance class.

"So he plays hockey," she finally asks me, "and when does he play Matty?" I look over and then see him walking into the kitchen, wearing boxers and rubbing the sleep away from his eyes. "I have to go and make sure I am in LA when they play each other."

"Okay," I say, watching him, "call me later." I quickly hang up when I feel him wrap his arms around me, kissing my neck. "Good morning. Did I wake you?"

"Yes." He buries his face in my neck. "I reached over and you weren't there."

"Sorry, Jefferson woke me up and then," I start to say as he walks toward the fridge, "my sister called." I take a sip. "Ever since I left Trent, we have Sunday coffee dates." I'm waiting for him to say something as he grabs a small bottle of orange juice and shakes it. "Is that okay?"

"Why are you asking me this?" He leans against the counter. "She's your sister, you talk to her when you want to talk to her."

I shake my head, forgetting for a moment who I was talking to. He's not Trent and his support of me reconnecting with my family shouldn't surprise me. "I also spend most of Sunday catching up with everyone in the family."

"Okay," he says, as if he's missing something. "Are you asking me to go out so you can have private time with them?"

"No," I gasp. "I just—"

"Lexi, you talk to your family when you want to talk to your family, for however long you want to talk to them. I can be in the room, or you can go in another room if that makes you more comfortable. You can talk to them whenever they call you. I just will have to draw the line if you're blowing me. I don't want you using your mouth for anything else." Here, in the middle of his kitchen, I laugh like I don't think I've laughed before, and with the laughter is a lightness in my chest I don't think I'm used to just yet.

Thirty

Kirby

I LOOK AT her wearing my shirt, sitting on one of the stools in my kitchen, and the only thing going through my mind is keeping her here. "I promise to never answer the phone if your cock is in my mouth."

"Then we are on the same page." I open my orange juice, taking another sip. "So how is your sister?"

"I told her about you," she replies, leaning onto her elbows on the counter in front of her. "Like everything." She raises her eyebrows. "She asked when you play Matty next."

"Two weeks," I answer her and her eyes go big. "He's coming to LA."

"Shit, I think she is too."

"Are you okay with that?" I put the bottle of juice on the counter beside me.

"Well, I get to visit with my nieces and nephews, so yeah."

"There is casino night; it's a team fundraiser that we

do for the children's hospital next weekend," I tell her. "Do you want to come as my date?"

"Would that be weird?" she asks me and I shrug.

"It doesn't have to be weird. It's just the two of us, dressing up." I smirk. "We've done that before."

"What would we tell people?" she asks me and I just shrug.

"Whatever you want us to tell people," I answer, knowing I want to tell everyone she's mine. I want to yell it from the rooftops, but I know I can't push it. I know she is the one who is going to have to take that giant leap. "We can be there as friends," I say the word, feeling like it's bile in my mouth, "or we can say we're a couple."

She's about to answer me when her phone rings and she looks down at it. "It's my dad."

"Okay, well, as much as I want to be here for that conversation, I don't think I can stand here half naked while you talk to him."

She laughs and answers the phone, putting it on speakerphone instead of to her ear. "Hey, Dad." She looks at me. "What's up?"

"Nothing much," he replies and I swear I can feel the love through the phone. "Your sister just called me."

"Oh, she did?" Lexi pretends like it's no big deal, but she mouths, *What the fuck?* "I just got off the phone with her. We had our weekly sister coffee date."

"She told me," he says.

"Oh yeah, what else did she tell you?" Lexi questions and then looks at me whispering, "I'm going to murder her."

"She said she wants to come down and watch the game when Matty is in town so we can all be together." Lexi rolls her eyes. "I'm making the plans today."

"Oh, that sounds like fun," she replies and I walk to her, kissing her neck quietly before walking out of the room and toward the bedroom. I start the shower and take off my boxers before stepping in. I shower quickly and grab a white plush towel, wrapping it around my waist before I grab another one for my head. I walk out to the bedroom and see her sitting on the side of the bed, wearing one of my T-shirts and her legs are crossed under her. "When I was with Trent, he hated that I would talk to my family."

"Well, that is because he was afraid they would see what he was doing to you." I toss the towel to the side.

"He would hate when I was on the phone and I would always feel pressure to end the call." I hate that for her, hate she went through it. "It got to the point I would only call my father early in the morning before he was up, or when he left to go to work."

"Lexi," I say and she holds up her hand.

"I have a big family," she says.

"I know, I met most of them on the ice and some off the ice."

"And we are extremely close and sometimes overbearing."

"Okay. The only family member I have is Kylie. She's the only one I have and I would never stop having a relationship with her for anyone. She's a bit overbearing and she's in my business all the time. Does that bother you?"

"Of course not."

"Because it's normal," I say. "It's normal to speak to your family. It's normal for them to be in your business if they love you. It's also normal, and more importantly, extremely healthy for the other person to also be involved with your family."

"They are coming down for Matty's game, and we usually have Sunday lunch."

"Okay," I reply, not sure I want to know where this is headed. "You better not be asking me if you can go," I huff out, "because—"

"I'm not asking you if I can go. I'm going." I smile at her forcefulness. "I'm just not sure it's a good time for you to come."

"So I don't come," I say, trying to let her know I'm okay with it. "It's not going to be the only time I can meet them. When you feel ready, then we take that step. I plan on being here with you for a long, long time"— my whole life, I almost say—"I don't mind taking things slowly."

"Just like that?" she asks, shocked.

"Just like that," I assure her. I take off my towel. "Now, I'm off all day today and my goal is to continue getting to know every inch of your body." She nods at me, trying not to smile but then smirking and her blue eyes light up. "But I think we should go and get something to eat and then come back here, so I can get started on that."

"Fine." She rolls her eyes, getting on her knees. "If

you have to." She walks on her knees toward the end of the bed. "But I need to stop by my house and change my clothes."

"We can do that, but only if you grab something to wear to work tomorrow."

"Are you asking me to sleep over again?" She gets off the bed and bends to collect her panties.

"I'm hoping I can persuade you," I tell her as she puts on her panties.

"Is that so?" she asks me, taking off my shirt and tossing it to the side. "And how is that?"

"I mean, I could tell you, but it's so much better if I show you." I lunge for her, and after what feels like an eternity but is really thirty-five minutes, we are heading out and toward her house.

I walk out of the elevator with two cups of ice coffee in my hands, headed toward the office door. Opening it and stepping in, I look around and see that both lights are on in the office. "Hello!" I shout out and then hear a groan coming from one office while in the other office is a laugh.

"Ugh, you again?" Kylie moans. "You were here two days ago."

I shake my head and head toward her office first. "Does that mean you don't want the iced coffee I bought you?" I ask her and she looks up from her desktop. "If so, I can enjoy it."

"Give me the coffee." She extends her hands and then

winces. "Fucking Pilates workout," she mumbles. "Lexi, your boyfriend is here again." I shake my head. "He's being really annoying too."

A laugh comes from Lexi's office and I just smile and walk toward her. "Hi," I say, sticking my head into her office. She looks over her shoulder before she turns her chair around and my eyes travel up her legs that are crossed. "I was in the area."

"You were in the area?" She gets up and I take her all in. She's wearing a tight tan skirt around her hips that flares out and falls to the middle of her thigh, with a white short-sleeved, button-down shirt. "Is that so?"

"You weren't wearing that this morning when you left." I wrap an arm around her waist and pull her to me.

"I was wearing workout clothes," she states, putting one hand on my chest and the other hand on my shoulder. "You think I come to work in workout clothes?"

"She should!" Kylie yells from her office. "She comes into the office and looks all official each day. It's not good for the morale in this office." Lexi closes her eyes and laughs. "We're going shopping after work to buy me a whole new wardrobe."

"Is that so?" My eyes are on Lexi and her eyes are on me.

"That is so. I need a dress for tomorrow's casino night," Lexi says, taking a sip of her coffee before kissing my lips and moving away from me.

"So you are coming with me?"

"Obviously she's going with you," Kylie says. "She's got to make sure no one gets next to her man."

"That is not the reason, but yes, I'm going to go with you. Although, I am hoping to get lucky." She winks at me.

"The walls in this office are very thin and I just threw up in my mouth!" Kylie hollers.

I walk over to the couch area and sit down. "How is everyone's day going?"

"Good," Lexi says, sitting down in her chair.

"Did she tell you what she did today?" Kylie asks, and I look over when I hear footsteps coming into Lexi's office.

"I didn't tell him yet," Lexi huffs, "but I will tell him since I need him to post on his social media."

"I'll just give you the login," I tell her and she gawks at me.

"We can answer all those dm's that say I love you?" Kylie mocks. "Like yeah, you love him why? Tell me the reason?"

"I would never do that," Lexi informs her, "but you can be next to me, and if you answer them, then that is between the two of you."

"Okay, what did you do?" I ask Lexi.

"Well, I figured that a bunch of my family members will be down in a couple of weeks, so I'm going to ask them to bring me, like, a jersey or a stick. I'll get it and we can put it up for auction on the foundation website to bring in extra funds. So, like, not a big fundraiser but still something."

"That sounds good," I say. "If you want, I can ask a couple of the players to donate also."

"Look at us," Kylie says, "the dream team."

I get up then, walking over to Lexi and putting my hands on her armrests. "You coming over tonight or am I coming to your house?"

"I don't know when I'm going to be done shopping, and what about Jefferson?"

"She'll be fine." I smirk. "When you left the bed this morning, she came to sleep on your pillow." It's been a full week since we've started this thing between us and every single night we go to bed together. Usually it's been at my house, but once I showed up at her house after the game and she let me in.

"What time do I have to be ready tomorrow?" Kylie asks me as I kiss Lexi softly.

"We'll pick you up at six thirty," I tell her and then move away from Lexi. "See you tonight."

"Maybe"—she shrugs—"or maybe not."

I shake my head laughing as I leave, and four hours later, she's pulling up in my driveway with her outfit for the next night and a bag for the rest of the weekend.

"I'm going to need you to zip me." I look over and see Lexi walking into my walk-in closet at the same time as I fasten my cuff links in my white shirt. "I got it halfway up but I can't get it the rest of the way."

My pulse speeds up when I see her wearing a black lace dress. The sleeves are long and show her skin through the lace. The front goes high up to her neck, where there's black solid fabric backing the lace until her midriff and a few inches of her skin peeks out, making my mouth water. It's solid from there until her mid-thigh where two rows of ruffles accentuate her toned legs. Classy, with a hint of spice. Just like her.

She turns around and my cock springs up as if we didn't just fuck forty-five minutes ago. Her back is completely bare, the lace is the only thing covering it until the base of her back and then it's solid black again. She moves her hair to the side, giving me access to zip her up. I finish zipping her before I grab her hips and pull her against me. "My cock really likes this dress."

She laughs and looks over her shoulder at me. "Wait until I put on the shoes." She winks and walks back out as I readjust my cock and then slide on the black suit jacket. She comes back in with sky-high heels, a strap around her toes and then another strap around her ankles. "Aren't these sexy?"

"So sexy I'm going to fuck you bent over wearing just those shoes." I slap her ass as I walk past her and out of the closet. "Now if we don't leave, I'll forget that we have to get my sister, and I'll fuck you against the closet wall."

I look over, seeing her assess the room. "I've never been fucked against a closet wall." She comes to me, grabbing her black handbag. "Maybe we could try it tonight."

"Lexi," I moan, "you can't just say things like that."

She laughs as she walks to me and slides her hand in mine. "I'm sorry, but I think you banging my brains out against the wall would be a lot of fun." She shrugs.

"Now let's go before we're late."

She pulls me out of the room and somehow we make it in time to get Kylie. We pull up in the parking lot and see Clive dressed up in a suit instead of his red jacket. He smirks, pulling open my door when someone opens Lexi's and Kylie's. "Look at who decided he was going to join us."

I laugh. "I'm right on time," I tell him and see Lexi walk around the car and Clive's eyes come to mine. "Be nice," I mumble to him. "Lexi, this is Clive."

"Lexi"—Clive extends his hand—"it's a pleasure." He nods at her, then smiles big at Kylie. "Aren't they beautiful?" he says. "I have a son."

"They're not interested," I retort, slipping my hand in Lexi's and walking into the arena.

The locker room is closed, as well as all the office doors, as we walk toward the ice, which has been covered by a wooden floor. "Look at how fun this is," Lexi states, taking in all the casino décor. I look over to see Jaxon standing there looking at me, and then his eyes go to our hands that are linked. "Okay, there is Ariella. I'm going to go and say hello."

"Okay." She lets me go and she and Jaxon cross each other on their way. She stops and smiles at him, giving his cheek a kiss. I watch her until Jaxon is in my eyesight, his head shaking from side to side.

"Wow." That's all he says, standing beside me and my eyes find Lexi, who now has her head thrown back and she's laughing. Her eyes are light and her whole demeanor is free, so unlike the woman I first met. She's come so fucking far and I'm so proud of her. "You sure about this?"

I look back at him before looking back at Lexi, my answer coming so clear. "About as sure as my next breath," I vow, looking at him, "and I love to breathe." I nod. "So yeah."

Thirty-One

LEXI

"WELL, WELL, WELL," Ariella says to me once I get closer, "isn't this a surprise?" She smirks at me before coming in and giving me a hug and a side air kiss. She then turns to Kylie. "What the fuck?" She rolls her eyes. "It's enough that this one over here"—she points to me—"is all sexy and class, but then you come in as if you are queen of the fashion show."

"What are you talking about?" Kylie asks her. "It's just a skirt and a top," she says of her outfit, but it's more than that. It's a mini black-and-gold sparkly skirt, the gold shimmers in the light and shows off her ridiculously long, toned legs. The silk top has long sleeves tucked in, but is slightly open all the way down, showing off the black satin bra she has underneath it. It's barely open, but if she moves right or left, you get a glimpse of it. The strappy black heels on her feet that make the outfit complete. "You are the one wearing red." Kylie stops talking when one of the servers comes over to us and offers us champagne, and we each take a glass except Ariella.

"I can't, I'm still breastfeeding," she groans, "but the minute Jagger and I cut ties with breastfeeding, I'm going to have a whole bottle of wine. Not one glass, but the whole bottle." She smiles. "Even if I have to drink it by myself in a bathtub." I look over at Kylie, trying not to laugh at Ariella as she holds up her glass to her.

"I will then have to drink for both of us," Kylie announces. "It would be my honor." She takes a sip of her champagne, downing half the glass.

"Okay, so what's going on here?" Ariella turns back to me. "What does this mean?" she asks me, motioning with her chin toward the guys, and I can't help but put my head back and laugh at her.

"It means I'm here with him," I tell her, taking my own sip of champagne and avoiding putting a label on whatever this is. "We're friends," I say and Kylie, who is taking another sip of her champagne, starts to cough, making me roll my eyes. *Friends who sleep with each other occasionally,* I think instead of saying it out loud.

"So you don't mind if I set him up with someone?" The question earns her a little glare, at the same time the champagne I just took a sip of starts to feel like the bubbles are coming back up. "There is a super nice girl I know. I met her in yoga class; she's new in town."

I cough and almost choke on my spit, turning to glare at her and the notion that she would set him up with someone else makes me see red. Looking at her I see she's fucking with me as she tries not to laugh at my reaction. I put the glass to my lips again and can't help but smirk at her. "You don't do yoga."

"No." She shakes her head as she grabs a bottle of water from one of the trays that is being passed around. "I don't, but now you know that you don't want anyone else dating him." She untwists the cap and puts it to her lips. "You're welcome."

"Oh," Kylie adds, "that was a good one."

"That was not a good one," I disagree with Kylie. "That was not good at all."

"I don't know," Kylie pushes, finishing her champagne. "She was like, can he date my friend, and then you went all breathing fire out of your nose like a bull."

"I was not." I try to defend myself.

"Oh, you were." Ariella laughs. "Your face drained of color and then your jaw got tight and your hand gripped the glass."

I just stare at them, not bothering to say anything because they might be right. I was not happy thinking of him dating someone else; in fact, I sort of got this feeling I've never had before.

"Hey." I hear Jaxon from beside us, followed by Kirby, who stands beside me with his hands in his pockets, his shirt pulled across his chest, and I have this sudden desire to walk up to him and kiss him. My lips tingle thinking about it. I've never felt this need before. I've been to countless events with Trent and I smiled when I was supposed to smile and talked to a few people, but I never had this need to be beside him. I drink the champagne when I think about the reason why, telling myself it's crazy.

"How are you doing?" Jaxon puts a hand around Ariella and pulls her to him. "Are you okay?"

"Why wouldn't I be okay?" She looks up at him with a semi-smile on her face, then it goes into a full-blown smile.

"Okay, this was fun," Kylie states, staring at the four of us, "but I'm going to go mingle." She puts her empty glass of champagne on a tray and then takes another one. "I'm drinking for two tonight," she says to her brother, "and I'm going to go gamble." She looks around. "So I just tell them your name and they'll front me chips and you pay for it?"

I can't help but laugh. "Story of my life," he says with a sigh. "You know, you probably have more money than I do."

"Yes." She winks at him. "How do you think the rich stay rich? They spend other people's money." She smiles big at him and he wants to be annoyed with her, but the love on his face makes it hard to believe he's that annoyed. "Also, thanks for the outfit." She turns and walks away.

"Are you going to warn any of the rookies that Kylie's off-limits," Jaxon mumbles as we watch her move through the crowd.

"You think she's going to give them the time of day?" Kirby shakes his head. "She's a viper."

"If you think that, you would be wrong," I say and both of their eyes come back to me and Kirby gets what I'm saying.

"She looks soft on the exterior," he explains, "but she's locked up so tight, I just hope someone can get in there."

"I have faith in her," I reply as a man comes over to them. Kirby takes his hand out of his pocket to shake his hand.

"Martin," he says to the guy, "this is Lexi Petrov." He puts the hand that was just shaking the man's hand on the base of my back. "This is my coach."

"Petrov," the man says right away, "Matty." His eyes go into slits. "Viktor."

"They would be my brother and my father," I say proudly, extending my hand to him.

"It's nice to meet you," he says to me and then Kirby's hand slides down from my back, and I slip my hand in his.

"Matthew Grant is—" he starts to say and then stops. "Holy shit, Cooper Stone."

"That would be my grandfather," I reply with a fondness in my voice.

"Legacy," he declares. "It's an honor."

I look up at Kirby shyly, who is looking at me with the biggest smile on his face, and I can't help but lean into him a little bit. "Well, I have to go and talk to everyone," Martin says. "See you guys later."

"Let's go and see where I have to be," Kirby suggests, pulling me away from Ariella and Jaxon, who laugh.

We stop when he spots a couple of guys he knows. "Hey," he says to them, his hand never leaving mine as he introduces me to them. They all nod their heads, a couple of them do a double take when they hear the last name.

"Don't we play Matty next week?" one of them says and he snickers. "I've got your back."

"There will be no need for that," I quickly put in. "It's a game." They all laugh at me. "And may the best team win."

"The big question is," one of them asks me, "what jersey will you be wearing?"

I bite my lower lip, looking up at Kirby. "That would be a game-time decision," I joke, making them all laugh.

We turn and bump into one of his teammates and his wife. "Lexi," Kirby says, "this is Knox and his wife, Josephine. This is Lexi."

"It's a pleasure to meet you," I say to Knox and then turn to his wife, who is giving me the fakest smile I've ever seen in my life, and trust me, I know fake smiles when I see them.

"Yeah," she says, holding out her hand and I think she's only doing it because Knox is here.

"I love that dress." I decide I'm going to kill her with kindness. I actually do like her dress. It's a gold jacket dress, the top button is right between her fake breasts and looks like it's about to pop off and hit me in the eye. I just don't like her in the dress.

"Thank you," she says tightly. "I'm going to go and see the girls." She turns and walks away and I almost burst out laughing.

"Knox spent the summer in Italy," Kirby says, trying not to let me feel uncomfortable by the whole Josephine thing.

"Oh, that sounds like heaven."

"It was," he confirms. "The kids had a blast and they picked up so much Italian, it was cute."

"How old are your kids?" I ask him.

"We have three:ten, eight, and five. Two boys and a girl."

"Fun, my sister has three-year-old twins," I say, smiling at him when his eyes about come out of his sockets. "Boy and girl, both daredevils."

"I think having two boys first was a mistake. They are all fun and loving and then you have my girl, who I just knew was going to be chaos personified." He shakes his head. "The other day, her brothers told him it would be fun to use the top of the plastic bin to slide down the stairs." I can't help but laugh. "In case anyone is wondering, it's not fun. She about broke five bones in her body and her head smashed into the wall." I put both hands in front of my mouth. "You would think she would learn her lesson, but the only thing she learned is to put on a hockey helmet the next time."

"Sounds like a smart kid to me," Kirby pipes up, "unlike her father."

Knox is about to say something else when Josephine calls his name from across the room. "Excuse me, duty calls."

He walks away and I slip my hand in Kirby's, stepping a touch closer to him. "He's nice, I like him." He just nods as I stand in front of him. "Is this okay?" I ask, lifting my hand with his.

"Do you not want to hold my hand?" he asks me, and I roll my eyes when he kisses my fingers and then drops our hands to our sides. "You look beautiful," he tells me softly, "so fucking beautiful."

"Oh yeah?" I smile up at him and want him to bend his head just a bit to give me the sign he wants to kiss me before I take the big step and kiss him.

"Oh good, you're here." Our heads turn to the side where we see two blonde women coming toward us. "Kirby," one of them says as she turns to the girl beside her. Both are wearing little black dresses, one has red shoes on, the other one has electric blue shoes on. "I want to introduce you to my oldest friend, Belinda."

"Well, not old." The blonde looks at her as she tucks her hair behind her ear. "But we've been friends a long time." The minute she says that, I get the feeling she's trying to set them up.

I let go of his hand and he immediately turns to look at me, and I just smile up at him. "I thought you and Belinda would hit it off."

"Oh," Kirby says and I am about to turn around and head away from this conversation because, well, I am not sure I want to be here while he's being set up with another woman. I take a step to turn away and then stop, turning back and not willing to slink off into the background but instead letting them know that he's mine.

Turning back to him, I move into his space. "I'm going to go and get a drink at the bar, honey." I kiss his neck. "Do you want something?" I don't wait for him to answer before I turn to the blondes. Belinda looks like she wants to die on the spot, and the other one looks at me with a glare like I just ruined her evil plan. "Hi," I say, moving my hand from his hand to extend it to the women. "I don't think we've met, I'm Lexi."

"Oh," the girlfriend says.

"Do you want anything from the bar?" I ask them and they both shake their heads.

"I'm sorry," the blonde says, "excuse us."

I don't say anything to them as they turn to walk away, turning once more to look at us. I stand here staring at them until they disappear into the sea of people.

"What?" I ask when I look up at Kirby and he looks like he's about to burst out laughing.

"Nothing." He puts the hand that is holding my hand on my lower back, making my arm twist back. "I was just thinking, I like this Lexi."

He pulls me closer to him, and the smell of his aftershave makes my knees weak. "Is that so?"

"Well," he says softly, and even though we are in a room with about five hundred people, it feels like it's just me and him. His eyes are on mine. "I like every Lexi." I put my hand on his chest, my finger playing with his lapel. "The kind one, the soft one." I can see his eyes twinkling, and I know the next thing isn't going to be as sweet. "The one who lets me—" I put my hand on his mouth to stop him from saying the rest of whatever it is he was going to say, and he laughs under my fingers before kissing them. "All of them."

I shake my head and I'm about to say something to him when a man comes out rushing toward him. "Kirby, it's your turn at the blackjack table number seven," he states, "and there is a lineup waiting."

"Great, I need chips," he tells the guy, who nods his head and then looks at me.

"I'll have them at the table."

"Want to come with me?" he asks me.

"I guess so," I reply and he turns, pulling me with him as he looks for the table he needs to be at. I see the line of women there and I about gag out loud. "This is it." I point to the table. "Your harem awaits," I joke with him. "If only they knew you snore sometimes."

All he does is laugh at me as he lets go of my hand once we get to the table. "Hey there," he says to the chairs that are now filled with six women and one man. "Are we all having a good time?"

"It's better now," the lady at the end with red hair and green eyes says. "I've been waiting all night to meet you."

I hold my purse in both hands and I'm about to step away when he says, "Hey, baby." My head whips to see who he is talking to and I see him staring straight at me, getting a bit closer. "Can you hold my phone?" He takes the phone out of his suit jacket pocket and hands it to me. I reach for the phone and hold it in my hand, knowing that all eyes are on me. He smiles at me. "Thanks." I take one more step and put my head back and he bends and kisses my lips softly. I raise my hand and wipe the lipstick from his lips.

"Have fun, you guys," I tell the table of semi-glaring women. "I'll be over here"—I point to the side—"if not,

I'll be with Kylie."

"Okay," he replies, giving me another chaste kiss before slapping his hands together. "Who is ready to lose money?" he asks the table. I watch him for about fifteen minutes before Kylie comes up to me and asks me if I'm going to get something to eat.

We walk away together, going to a table and sitting down. She gets up to grab a plate of food from the buffet and then comes back. "Are you not eating?"

"I'm going to wait for your brother," I answer, looking over my shoulder at him.

"Friends wait for other friends," she mocks my words. "I'm not a good friend," she says, taking a bite of the slider she just got.

Ariella joins us a couple minutes later with her own plate, telling us Jaxon can eat when he wants to, she's not waiting. It's about twenty minutes later when Kirby comes to join us, the both of us going to get a plate and then Jaxon comes about fifteen minutes after that.

We spend most of the night at the table, biding our time until we can leave. Eventually, we walk to the garage where we say goodbye to Ariella and Jaxon and they offer to drop off Kylie since she is on the way to their house.

My hand is where it's been most of the night, wrapped tight in Kirby's, as we walk in the garage. "Do you want to come to my house or do we go to yours?" I ask him.

"Doesn't really matter to me, as long as you're with me. The more important question is are you going to blow me?" he asks me, and I can't help but laugh because his tone is so serious.

"No." I shake my head, but the minute he asked me the question, my pussy contracted.

He walks over to the SUV parked in his spot. He opens the passenger door, but instead of helping me in, he pushes me against the back door. "Yes, you are."

The air leaves my body. "No, I'm not."

He rubs his nose with mine. "I dare you."

I laugh and push him off of me. "That doesn't always work." I get into the SUV and I'm about to reach for the door when he just smirks at me.

"It will this time." He winks at me, closing the door for me. "It will this time," he repeats.

Thirty-Two

KIRBY

I GET UP the next morning, and when I reach for her, I come up empty-handed. The bed's still warm from her body as I listen to hear if maybe she is in the bathroom. No noise is coming from there, and when I look at the bedroom door, it's shut, so I know she's already up and out of the room. I toss the covers off me, grabbing a pair of shorts from the chair, and seeing the pieces of my suit from last night trailing all across the room, along with her dress that's in a heap on the floor too. Her one shoe is on one side of the room, while the other is on the other side. I pull open the door and hear her voice.

"It was fun," she says and then I hear another voice.

"Well, the picture you sent us of you and Ariella looked like you two were having fun." I walk down the steps and into the kitchen, seeing her on the stool with her phone propped up in front of her. She's wearing one of my workout shirts that falls to the middle of her legs. "I can't wait to be there on Friday."

"I can't wait for you guys to be here," she says excitedly. "Mom and Dad are arriving on Friday morning. Matty is getting here Friday afternoon, and now the Sunday lunch is going to be a Friday dinner, since Matty has to leave as soon as they finish the game to head to Vegas."

"I heard," her sister says, and I walk in quietly and she looks over at me. I point to the fridge and she just nods. "Hi, Kirby," she says and Lexi laughs.

"Hi, Zara," I reply, pulling open the fridge.

"When am I going to meet you?" she asks and Lexi motions with her head to go over to her. I walk around the island with the bottle of orange juice in my hand. "Hi," she says with a huge smile on her face when I stop beside Lexi, bending to kiss her head. "Aww, so when are we going to meet?"

"Whenever you want," I tell her and I can see some similarities with the two, but in my opinion Lexi is prettier.

"It would have to be Sunday morning since we have to head back on Sunday afternoon. Colson has to be back in school on Monday."

"Name the time and place and I'll be there," I reply and she smiles at me.

"Okay, it's time for me to get up and get my ass in gear," she states. "I'll see you Friday," she tells Lexi and then blows her a kiss. "Bye, Kirby."

"Bye," I reply, holding up my hand and she disconnects the phone call. "Morning," I say as Lexi looks up at me, "you snuck out of bed again."

"I did," she confirms. "I was going to surprise you

with a whole breakfast feast, but my sister called."

"Want to prepare it together?" I ask her and she shrugs. "How about you tell me what you want, and I'll make it for you?"

"You would cook for me?" She leans back in the chair.

"Baby," I say, bending to kiss her lips again, "I'd do anything for you."

"I need a shower." She gets up and grabs her cup of coffee. "How about I jump in the shower and then come and help you?"

"Okay." I know by the time she comes back out of the shower, breakfast will be all done. "Waffles or pancakes?" I ask her as she walks out of the room.

"Surprise me," she says with a wink and my cock stirs. I think about joining her in the shower and then turn back and start to make my waffles. I take out the waffle iron as I mix the batter, tossing in some brown sugar instead of white sugar and then adding a touch of cinnamon to it.

While the waffles are being made, I scramble up some eggs and then toss some sausage in the pan. She walks into the room twenty minutes later, with her hair wrapped in one of my towels on the top of her head and wearing a pair of her shorts and matching tank top. "It smells delicious."

"I made waffles," I toss over my shoulder as she comes over to me and holds my hips in her hands and leans in to kiss my back. "Surprise."

"Did you know," she starts, walking over to the fridge and grabbing the bowl of strawberries, blueberries, and blackberries she always has, "that Trent used to watch how many calories I took in?" I look over at her, my hand gripping the fork tighter. "He would do this thing when we first got together." She puts the bowl down and now leans her hip against the counter and then puts her foot on her other foot. "If my waist was bigger than this"—she hangs her hands down together with her thumbs touching before curling up the three fingers and then extending her pinkies—"it would be unacceptable." I close my eyes as she laughs at the ridiculousness of it, and I have to be happy that she sees how much of an idiot he was. "I should have done the same to his dick." The bark of laughter leaves my throat. "I'll grab the plates."

I sit down next to her once the waffles are done and the plates are in front of us. Grabbing my waffles and then some eggs, I pass her the syrup as she puts some on her waffles and then some on her eggs. "Did you have fun last night?" I ask her and she nods her head.

"I did, once I got a little bit of confidence in me," she admits and I chuckle. "People are going to ask you questions." She takes a bite of her waffles.

"They can ask, doesn't mean I have to tell them anything. That's the beauty of all of this. You tell them what you want them to know and keep some things to yourself."

She nods. "Are you okay with meeting my sister?"

"Yeah, why?" I ask her and she shrugs.

"I'm scared," she finally says. "Like, I'm so happy, I'm scared it'll all go away." She looks over at me and gives me a small almost sad smile. "I'm scared this whole thing is going too fast and then it's going to crash and burn." She grabs a piece of strawberry on her fork and then plops it in her mouth. "But it's like I can't stop it."

"I'm scared also," I admit to her, "scared that I am going to be the rebound guy and then you will just up and leave when you realize how strong you are." Her eyes look at me in bewilderment. "But living in fear has never served any of us," I state, and then I don't know why I say it but I do, "I'm falling in love with you, Lexi." I put my fork down. "Pretty much I have fallen in love with you. When I met you the first time, I thought you were the most beautiful woman I had ever seen. Then I saw you with Trent and I was so jealous of him because he had you and he didn't know how good he had it." She puts her fork down and looks at her plate, and I can see her chest rising and falling. "I felt like a total dick feeling what I was feeling for you, knowing you were a married woman. I barely knew you and yet I knew you were one of those people who would come into my life and leave a mark." I put my hand on her leg. "Then I really got to know you, and I just fell deeper and deeper for you."

"Kirby," she says my name and looks at me with tears in her eyes, and all I can do is shake my head side to side.

"You don't have to say anything to me. I'm not telling you so you can say it back to me, or telling you to pressure you into anything. I'm telling you because I've never in my life told another person, who wasn't my sister or my mother, that I loved them." Her breath hitches. "But I wanted you to know, I can be patient with you. With us. With this." My hand moves from her leg to her cheek as my thumb catches the tear. "I'm going to be patient because you are worth it and deserve the time to figure this out too, Lexi."

"I don't know what to say." Her voice quivers.

"You don't have to say anything. I just wanted you to know that you aren't the only one who's scared." I lean to kiss her lips. "We can go as fast or as slow as you want us to go. I don't have to meet your parents this time. Or your sister." I rub her cheekbone. "You've already made such big steps in the last couple of months." I smile. "It's a marathon, not a sprint." I turn and cut another piece of waffle. I can tell she's not ready to finish this conversation, so I change the topic, hoping one day she'll be ready. "I'm off today. Did you want to go and spend the day at your house and take a walk on the beach?"

"Yeah," she says and I can hear her voice quiver, "that would be nice."

"We can invite Kylie over for dinner, if you want?"

"You are okay to stay at my house?" she asks me and I look over at her.

"You are the one always wanting to come here." I point at her.

"It's Ms. Jefferson's fault. I don't want her to be all alone."

"I leave tomorrow," I remind her, "and I'm already back on Friday."

"Who is watching her?" she asks me.

"She has food all the time," I remind her. "She has her own personal water bowl that is hooked up to the bathroom faucet and gives her fresh water. She's fine."

I push away from the counter. "But if you want to come and check in on her, I can give you a key."

"Do you think I can take her to my house?" she asks and I snort. "Probably not, right?" she backpedals. "Okay, I'll come over every night and sit with her so she doesn't get lonely."

"That works," I agree. "I like the fact you'll be in my house."

"Oh yeah," she says, loading the dishwasher and cleaning up, "why is that?"

"I don't know, I just like knowing you'll be here," I tell her. "Go get your hair done and then we can go."

"But you are leaving for five days and you want me to take you away from Jefferson for another day?" She shakes her head. "No can do."

"You know she doesn't even care, right?" I look around. "We've been up for two hours and she hasn't even bothered to come and see if we're okay."

"But she knows we're here," she defends and then I can hear the sound of her bell coming closer to us. "See?" Lexi says, walking to her and picking her up and cradling her. She looks up at Lexi and then looks at me with a glare. "Don't worry, pretty girl, we are going to stay here with you."

THE PLANE TOUCHES down just after noon on Friday and I look out the window at the sun. We usually head home right after we land, but we have a game tomorrow, so we have a late afternoon practice. The bus is waiting for us when we walk off, and I toss my bag under it before heading on and sitting down. Jaxon sits next to me and the two of us don't say a word to each other. I pull my phone out and text Lexi.

Me: Just landed. On our way to practice. Let me know if you are coming over tonight after dinner or not. I missed you.

I put the phone away, looking out the window. Her family started arriving today, and I know she has her big dinner with them. She's nervous about fitting in, which is ridiculous since it's her family and they will do anything for her. Her sister and the kids are staying with her, so I'm not sure if I'm going to see her, which I hate, but it is what it is. She's been at my house all week with Jefferson, even sleeping there one night.

We get to the arena, everyone grabbing their bags and putting it in their respective cars before heading back and changing for practice. I step in and spot some of the other team walking into the visitors' locker room from the ice. "I'll be back," I tell Jaxon who looks at me. "I'm going to go talk to Matty."

"Are you insane?" he asks me. "Why are you doing that?"

"Because it's the right thing to do," I tell him, slapping his chest. "I'll be fine," I assure him and he groans. I walk to the locker room, sticking my head in and not seeing him there. I get a couple of chin-up hellos from some of the players, and I'm about to head to the ice when I see him walking down the corridor.

"Hey," I say to him and he stops walking, and with his

skates on, he has an advantage on me.

"Hey," he replies, unsure.

"I'm Kirby Materson and I thought I should introduce myself," I say, and his face tells me he has no idea what the fuck I'm talking about.

"And why is that?" he asks, taking off his gloves, and I can see the little glimpses of similarity between Lexi and him. She's the one with the clearest eyes out of all three. The one with the darkest hair for sure.

"I'm in love with your sister." *Smooth*, I think to myself, *very fucking smooth.*

"Excuse me?" He turns his head to the side as if he didn't hear me.

"I'm in love with Lexi." Fuck, this is a bad idea. Why didn't I listen to Jaxon?

"She just left her husband!" he hisses out.

"Yeah, and that was a long time coming. Don't you think?" I say and for the second time he's shocked.

"You knew him?" His temper starts to go up.

"I met him over summer break," I tell him. "It was when I got to know Lexi."

"So you fell in love with a married woman?" He snorts out his disgust. "What does that say about you?" He turns and starts to walk away from me.

"I'd do it again in a heartbeat if it led to her leaving him," I announce and he stops moving and turns back around. "That night"—I shake my head—"it got ugly and he said things that hurt her." I don't give him more than that. "I'm sorry she had to hear them."

"What things?" he asks me, his glare deadly.

"You should ask her."

"I'm asking you." He points to me. "You were the one who came to seek me out. So I'm asking you exactly what the fuck happened."

I look to the side, seeing Jaxon leaning against the door to the locker room, far enough away to give us privacy, but close enough if he has to spring into action he can. "Before I tell you, I want to say she never, ever did anything that would have him talk about her the way he did." His eyes are on mine. "In no way, shape, or form did she ever let on or do anything that was inappropriate."

"You don't have to tell me that," he informs me. "I know my sister would never do that. No matter how much…" He trails off.

"I walked outside to get some air and he was there in the corner of the balcony, head bent with a blonde." Matty's head falls back and he looks up to the ceiling. "He saw me and we exchanged words. I asked him how he could disrespect her like that. I just didn't get it. Man, he had the best woman he could ever have and he was fucking around. I didn't know she was there; I would never want her to hear what he said."

"What did he say?" he asks, his jaw clenched and tight. His hands are fisted by his sides.

"That she was a fucking nobody without him," I relay softly and then look around. "She was a nobody when he met her because"—I take a deep breath—"her father is a fucking drug addict." The same gasp I heard that night I now hear again, but this time there is a hiss after it. "She should be thankful that he took pity on her."

"That motherfucking piece of shit," he growls. "If I ever get my hands on him."

"You'll have to get in line," I tell him and he looks at me, "because I'm first in line. Well, maybe second behind Lexi. She may be your sister, but I hear the stories that she tells me. Stories that would make your blood boil. Stories that have impacted her far more than she lets on and that one day I hope she can heal from as we grow together."

"Is that so?" He about smirks at me.

"Yeah." I nod. "So that's why I wanted to introduce myself to you." I hold out my hand. "So again, I'm Kirby." He looks at me and looks at my hand and I don't know what to expect, to be honest. He could turn around and walk away and ignore everything I just said. Or he could accept I love her and semi-accept that I'm in her life. "I know you mean the world to her, so I wanted to do this for her." His eyes go to my hand and back to my eyes, and then I see his hand extended.

"Good to meet you, Kirby," he says, "and it goes without saying that if you hurt her—"

"Yeah." I don't even let him finish. "I know."

"I don't think you do," he starts to explain. "You see, for the past ten years I've seen my sister become a shell of the person I know. I've seen her retreat more and more as the time went by and I felt helpless. Fuck, we all felt helpless. No one knew what to do." His words hit me in the middle of my chest.

"I can't imagine," I tell him. "I had it in my face for weeks and it felt like an eternity, but I can give you this.

I'll treat her with respect because she deserves it. I'll treat her with kindness and care, and I'll take whatever she has to give me. I told her I loved her and I don't know how she feels, but I'll wait for her for eternity." He nods. "It's that kind of love."

"Well, good to meet you. Will you be around this weekend?"

"Probably not this time," I say. "It's time for her to bond with you all. It's not the place for me right now."

"Respect," he states, "you have my respect."

We look at each other and nod, not saying anything to each other as we turn and head to our respective locker rooms.

"Well, good news is you can still play tomorrow," Jaxon teases. "Bad news is he's going to put you through the wringer."

Thirty-Three

LEXI

I PULL UP to the house and jump out of the car and I can hardly contain myself, I'm so excited. I run up the steps to the big brown door and ring the doorbell. I literally feel like I'm bouncing on the tips of my toes as I hear footsteps coming. It swings open and my cousin Gabriella is there wearing a pair of yoga pants and a matching yoga bra. "Oh my God. You're here!" she says to me with the biggest smile on her face. When I step in and hug her, I can't help but feel the stinging in my eyes.

I close them as we rock side to side and I hear more voices coming from the back. "Is it her?" my cousin Zoey yells from somewhere in this mansion, and it is a mansion. Gabriella married one of the up-and-comers from Hollywood when he was just starting out. I mean, his parents are Hollywood royalty, but Romeo wanted to be behind the camera instead of in front of it. The night he won an Oscar, he surprised them with their wedding. It was the last wedding I went to.

"It's her!" Gabriella shouts over her shoulder and then I hear footsteps running toward me, and I see my sister. I don't know why but the tears just run down my face.

I hug her as if I've never hugged her, as if I've been locked away in a tower for the last ten years and I haven't seen her. It's a hug I didn't know I'd been missing. Like someone in the desert wanting to drink that sip of water and then finally getting it. I can't help the sob that escapes me as I shake in her arms.

"Hey," she says softly.

"I'm…" I start to say, but I have to stop, the lump in my throat gets bigger. "I'm so happy you're here." I let her go and smile through the tears, and when I look around, I see all of them crying. Sofia is holding Jagger while Zoey is side-hugging Ariella. "Well, this is awkward," I try to make a joke and we laugh, but my hands come up to hold her face. "I missed you." I roll my lips together and sniffle. "So, so much." She takes me in another hug as I look at everyone. "I've missed everyone so much."

"But she missed me the most," Zara gloats when she turns in my arms and my arm is draped around her shoulders.

"Come on, let's go sit and talk," Gabriella suggests, coming on the other side of me and slipping her hand in mine. It's a little extra strength I didn't know I needed as we walk into the house. The kitchen is filled with people cooking. "Romeo is still trying to make a good impression on you guys, so he's hired all these people to cook for us. Plus, he called that one over there." She points to Sofia, who is one of the best event planners in the South, holding Jagger. "And it's like an event is happening. Wait until you guys see what he did to the backyard. I drew the line at him getting a DJ for the night." I laugh as we step into the family room, away from the noise of the kitchen.

Jagger's toys are in the middle of the room, and when I get close enough to him, he lunges for me. "How is my little man?" I take him from Sofia and giving her a side hug. "Thanks for coming."

"Of course." She rubs my back before walking over to the couch, where she must have been sitting before I got here, glasses of wine are in the middle of the coffee table.

"Where are all the kids?" I look around and listen if I can hear the yelling and screaming they do once they are together.

"Ah," Zara says, "the grandparents took all the kids to some activity so we can have a mini girls' day. I stopped listening, to be honest. I don't know where they are but if no one called me yet, I'm sure everyone is fine."

"That one had to stay with me since I'm his feeding source," Ariella jokes. "But so far we've been handing him off to each other, so he's content."

Gabriella walks over to the couch and then grabs another wineglass. "Okay, I'm going to say it," she starts as she holds up the glass for me. "You look fantastic."

"Doesn't she?" Zoey agrees. "I was going to say something when she walked in but I was like, I hate it when people see me and are like 'you look fantastic' and in my head I'm thinking, '*Wow, did I look like shit before?*'"

"The answer obviously is yes," Zara teases, "but in your case"—she slips her arm in mine—"you did look like shit."

I can't help but laugh and it startles Jagger, who pouts and reaches for his mother. "It's okay," I soothe, walking with Zara to the couch. "I felt like shit, so I probably looked like it too."

"I mean, you looked always put together," Zoey restates, sitting, grabbing her wineglass and tucking her feet under her. "But you looked like you needed a cheeseburger or two."

I sit with Zara next to me and I don't want to let her go. She must sense it too because she sits back and pulls me with her. "Well, I'm eating carbs and—"

"Dick," Zara interjects, laughing. "That will do it."

I can't help but laugh and shake my head. "I want to hear all about everything," Gabriella says, "but I want you to start at the beginning."

I inhale and look over at Zara, who grabs her glass of wine and then hands it to me. "Liquid courage," she urges me and I finish it in two gulps. "Welcome back, Lexi." She winks at me as Gabriella hands me another glass, and I tell them just about everything. From Trent cheating on me, to the embarrassing moment he gave me an STI. Which took Zoey and Gabriella to the edge of their seats as then their legs went up and down with nerves. I wasn't sure if they were going to get up and fly to Phoenix or smash something in Gabriella's house.

"He's a motherfucker." Sofia is the one to say what everyone is thinking. "A small-dicked motherfucker."

Zara grabs my head and puts it on her shoulder as she kisses the top of it. "Anyway, now I have my lawyer blowing up my phone, telling me to take the twenty million dollars for the NDA. It started at twelve and for the past two weeks they've increased it." Zoey stands up and I watch her. "What are you doing?"

"I'm calling fucking Ryleigh," she hisses out, mentioning Romeo's sister, "I know you don't want to get her involved and you want to handle it yourself, but you need the best, and well, she's a pit bull," she declares and then puts the phone on speaker, and I can hear it ringing.

"If you are calling me to gloat about your impromptu girls' day drinking," she hisses, "I'm going to stop sending you pictures of the kids."

Zoey laughs. "No, it's not that. We're here but we're calling because Lexi needs your help."

"Uh-oh," she says. "Should I start the Bat chain?" She mentions the phone chain our family has. It's sort of the emergency phone network that people use. "Does she need bail?"

"NO!" I gasp. "I'm here." I then look at the women around me, who are here to catch me if I fall. "But I might need your help."

"Tell me," she says, and by the end of it, she is pissed.

"I am going to make this guy wish he'd never met you," she grinds out. "He's going to literally sit down on his little stool and think he should've walked away from you when he saw you all those years ago." Zoey snickers. "One, you aren't taking that NDA settlement because chances are he's going to try and hide shit from you. Two, you aren't taking that settlement because he's a piece of shit and I said no, and three, you aren't taking it because you are not going to be fucking silenced. You know if you took that and you even mentioned his name, he could sue you for all of it back." I can hear the hatred in her voice. "Fire your lawyer and send me a dollar."

"What?" I ask her, looking around and Gabriella is already on her phone.

"Sent." I look at her. "We have to pay her a dollar so whatever we say to her goes under client-lawyer privilege. Even though she's my sister-in-law and it's a conflict of interest."

"Send me his lawyer's name," she says and then laughs. "The last time I had this much fun was when I took Charlie's sister-in-law"—she mentions Sofia's cousin—"Harmony's ex to the cleaners." She snickers. "That was a fun, fun day."

"Send her the name," Zara urges from beside me. "You got this." I pull up my phone and send her all the information.

"Just got it," she confirms. "Okay, I'm off to make a couple of phone calls. Oh, and it's Friday and it's almost five. I love ruining people's weekends. I have to go now. Lexi, I'll call on Monday unless something comes up before."

"Okay," I tell her. "Thank you again. I didn't want to bother you."

"Hey, you're family." I nod, not able to say anything.

"Okay, now that that is over," Zoey prods, "tell us about the hot hockey player you are sleeping with." She claps her hands. "We might have stalked him on social media before you got here." She looks at the girls in the room. "But it was for research purposes only."

I can't help but smile when I talk about Kirby. I tell them everything, including how he saw right through me, how he helped me without even knowing, and how his note was the one that gave me the strength to make the phone call.

"I love him," Zara states. "He got you to smile like that"—she points to me—"and to wear jeans. He's got my vote." I laugh at her and I don't say another thing because the front door opens and chaos erupts. The kids come running into the room, and I'm surrounded by my family. I hug the twins, who take me off my feet, and I look up to see my parents watching with tears in their eyes.

I'm shuffled from person to person, getting all the hugs and kisses, talking to each and every one of them. I look around and the only thing that is truly missing from all of this, who I want by my side, is Kirby. My phone is in my hand with the last text he sent me and I never got a chance to answer him. Except, he's not pressing me to answer him. I know if I don't answer him, he's not going to belittle me about it. Not make me feel guilty for not taking the time to answer him. It's going to be the opposite. He's going to want to hear all about how my day with my family was and he's going to do it holding my hand. He won't have to say a word, all he'll have to do is hold my hand, and I know it'll be okay.

I hear commotion again and look over when Matty walks in, wearing his tracksuit. He goes to Sofia first and then kisses his kids before going to my parents. He finally finds me at the end and gives me the biggest hug.

"Hi, my sister," he greets softly in my ear, and like with Zara, I bury myself in his hug and softly cry. "Hey," he says and walks with me to the side, "you're okay."

I let go of him and wipe away the tears from my face. "I know, it's just." I take a deep inhale. "It's so good to see you."

"It's good to see you too." He looks around to see if we are alone. "Met your guy today."

"My guy," I say anxiously but then the feeling leaves, and I just feel proud that he is my guy.

"Kirby." That's all he has to say and the smile on my face just gets even broader and my heart feels like it's getting even bigger inside my chest. "He's a good guy."

"Yeah, I know." I nod, wanting to say that he's more than a good guy.

"But how did you know about him?" I ask him, knowing the girls would not have shared that with him.

"He came to see me. Introduced himself to me." He snickers. "Got to say, he's got balls." I look down, trying not to giggle. "Told me something that burned me to my soul." His words go low and my head whips up to look at him.

"What?" I ask, the back of my neck starts to fill with heat.

"Doesn't matter what," he says, lifting his big hand to my cheek. "What matters is that you know you were too good for Trent. You were and always will be," he says. "Also, if I ever see him, I'm going to break his face." I can't help but snort out laughing at the end. "I mean, I'm sure there is a line I have to get into but…" He shrugs. "Just so you know."

"Thank you. I think I have to make a phone call." His eyebrows shoot up. "Yeah, excuse me." I turn and walk away from him, going into the house and toward the front where the formal living room is.

I pull up his phone number, and he answers on the second ring. "Hey," he says softly, "I wasn't expecting to hear from you."

"I know. What are you doing?"

"Sitting on the couch, watching television," he returns and I turn my head toward the sound of my family.

"Can you come over?" I ask him. "It's literally three minutes from you."

"Are you sure?" he asks me.

"Yeah, something is missing, and it's you."

"Okay, baby. Drop me a pin and I'll come right over."

"Text me when you get here," I tell him, dropping him the pin. "I'll meet you outside."

"Okay," he says, hanging up.

"There you are." I look over and see my father coming into the room. "Was looking around for you and didn't see you."

"I'm here," I say, turning to him. "I was just on the phone." I hold it up.

"Everything okay?" he asks me and I nod my head. "You look different."

I'm about to answer him when my mother comes into the room. "Hey, you two," she says, smiling at us and walking over to my father and wrapping her arms around his waist. "They are bringing out the desserts."

"I don't think I can eat another bite," I state and my phone vibrates with a text.

Kirby: I'm here.

"Can you guys stay here?" I ask them, not giving them anything else before I walk out the door and I see him walking up the driveway. He's wearing jeans and a white T-shirt. I haven't seen him in five days and I practically run to him. He wraps his arms around me and his mouth finds mine.

His tongue slides into my mouth as my front is pressed to his. "Hi," he says when he lets go of my mouth, but not of me, his hand coming up to touch my face, "missed you."

"I missed you." I put my hand to his throat. "Did you get my notes?" While I was there this week, I left him little notes about missing him, all through the house. One in the kitchen, another one on his side table, and another one in the bathroom. I even left one on the garage door.

He laughs. "I liked the one that said I ate cereal leaning over the counter and no one tried to do me." I rub my finger over his lips as we laugh together.

"It was shocking," I retort as he turns me in his arms and we walk to the front door. "I ate the whole bowl and the only one I had to worry about was Jefferson trying to get the milk."

We walk up the steps and head into the house, my parents waiting where I left them. My father's shoulders go back, as he takes in the way I'm holding on to Kirby while my mother's eyes look like they are going to fall out of her sockets. "Hey," I say to them, my arm falling from around his waist and then slipping into his hand. "I would like you guys to meet Kirby"—I look up at him—"my boyfriend." Kirby's eyes look into mine and his eyebrows go up like, "Oh, we're doing this."

"Boyfriend," my father says, his voice tight. "What?"

"It's a pleasure to meet you, Mr. Petrov." He extends his hand and my father just looks at it.

"Viktor," my mother hisses, "shake his hand."

He extends his hand reluctantly. "Lexi," he says my name and I hold up my hand.

"I know it's not what you think I should do." I cut through all the tension. "Jumping from one man to the other isn't a smart thing. That I should take time to find myself. Be by myself. Get to know myself." I take a deep inhale. "But he's helped me through all of that and gives me the space to still figure it all out. Sometimes we find someone we needed all along, and it's hard to walk away from them."

"Are you trying to convince us or yourself?" My father folds his arms over his chest.

"I've been in therapy since I left Trent. I've taken the steps I needed to take, and I'm working on trusting myself and my decisions." I stare at him. "I know you must be doubting me right now because you had to rescue me not too long ago. I've doubted myself for the last ten years, and I've lived in almost a fear of who I wanted to be and who I was. I'm not living like that anymore. I'm me and this is who I want." I look up at him, wrapping my arm around his waist and then rubbing his back. "I love him."

Thirty-Four

KIRBY

I STAND BESIDE her, not saying a word, as she talks to her father. Her mother's eyes go to her and then come to me and then back to her daughter, her hand firmly in her husband's. "I love him." My head turns to look back down at her. This is the first time she's said she loves me. I thought for sure she liked me a lot, but she never told me she loves me. My face fills with a smile and I feel like my heart is going to literally come out of my chest, and I can't stop myself from leaning down and kissing her.

"I love you," I say softly and she shakes her head.

"Not now," she says before turning back to look at her parents. "He's a wonderful man and he treats me with respect and kindness and, most importantly, he makes me feel good about myself. He makes me feel like I'm worthy of my life and the happiness I'm working toward. He makes me feel like, even though I fucked up my life for the last ten years, that it's okay, it was just a bump in the road that was all leading to this new chapter."

"That's not true." I hold up my hand. "I just like to know what she thinks before telling her what I—" She side-eyes me. "I'll stop talking now."

"Oh my God," her mother gasps, "you—" She points to me and I don't know if it's a good point or a bad point. "You're the K." She looks at Lexi. "That frame in your house. The dare." She puts both hands on her mouth. "He's the one."

"He is," Lexi confirms. "He's the reason I—"

"No," I cut her off, "that's not true. You are the reason you made that phone call. You are the reason you got out of the situation. It was you and your strength; it had nothing to do with me. Do not sell yourself short."

"Oh my," her mother says.

Lexi looks up at me. "I dare you to shut up right now." She chuckles before turning back to her parents. "By the way, that's my mother, Zoe," she says, "no Y."

I extend a hand to her. "It's a pleasure to meet you, Mrs. Petrov."

She immediately extends her hand to mine. "Kirby," she says my name, "the pleasure is all mine."

I'm about to say something when Matty comes into the room, followed by Matthew Grant and Max Horton, who to this day is still a beast. "Oh fuck," Matty swears, "did not think I would see you here."

"Got a call"—I look down at Lexi—"and an invitation I couldn't refuse."

"That's nice," Matty says, and I can tell by his tone he's not interested in small talk. "Mom, Lexi, I need to have a word with Dad and this guy." He motions with his chin toward me.

"Okay, wait a second." Lexi moves to stand in between us. "Let's not—"

"Relax," Matty assures her, "I'm not going to hurt him." He smirks. "I'll save that for the game tomorrow."

I chuckle. "It's fine," I tell Lexi. "I'm fine."

She points at all the guys. "If you hurt him, I will not be happy."

"He'll be fine," Zoe says, putting her hand in her daughter's, "or else." She looks at the guys and they slowly make their way out of the room. Lexi looks back over her shoulder at me, and I try to reassure her that it's fine.

"What is all of this?" Matthew now asks. "And who is this guy?"

"This," Viktor replies, "is her boyfriend."

"Her boyfriend," Max now adds, "since when?"

"Okay, this is all fun, and if I had more time, I would let him swing out here," Matty says, "but I have to head back to the hotel for curfew." All the guys look at him, including me. "Now it's come to my attention"—he side-eyes me—"that Trent is a piece of shit even more than we thought."

"What?" Viktor says.

"You heard about the NDA?" I ask Matty and now all eyes are on me and this should have been my sign to shut up. I should have just said forget it and looked away. I should have, but I didn't. "I didn't say anything."

"Oh, yes, you fucking did," Viktor snaps.

"Okay." I put up my hands. "She's going to be pissed

about this."

"She'll survive," Matty says. "Now, spit it out."

"Okay, well, Trent offered her twelve million for her to sign an NDA."

"Oh no, he didn't," Matthew seethes, taking out his phone.

"It gets a bit worse."

"Does it?" Max asks, his stance widening as he glares at me and he folds his arms over his chest. "I don't think so."

"She turned it down. He came back with fifteen and she turned that down, and then he came back yesterday with twenty million."

"What does her lawyer say?" Matty asks me.

"She's pushing her to sign it, but she doesn't want to."

"Why isn't Ryleigh handling this?" Matthew asks. "Until she calls her—"

"She called her today," Viktor tells the group. "She sent me a text, telling me she was going to take care of it."

"Good. I don't think her lawyer was looking out for her."

"I'm going to call Casey." Matthew makes a mention of someone he probably knows. "He's going to get me everything we are going to need to bury him." He walks out of the room.

"I don't want to know what that even means," I tell the men, who just look at me. "I'm going to have to go into that room, and she's going to ask me what all this was about."

"So what, don't tell her," Matty advises, his eyebrows pinched together.

"She was just with a man who lied to her for ten years, and you think I'm going to fuck myself over by lying to her too?" I shake my head. "No fucking way am I going to lose her to keep this a secret."

"Jesus," Matty groans.

"Yeah," I agree. "I'm going to go find her before I hear something else and I have to tell her. I don't know you guys, but from the tone it's not something you guys are going to want her to hear." I take a step to walk out of the room.

"I'm watching you," Viktor warns. "I'll be watching you like a hawk."

I nod at him, but Matty is the one who laughs. "What is it with you and the guys your daughters bring home? You just hate them all."

"I don't hate Gabriel," he retorts and now everyone laughs. "What? He took her away to live on a farm."

"She ran to him," Matty goads and Viktor glares, "willingly."

"When your daughters bring home a man to you"—now Matty glares—"we'll circle back to this conversation."

I walk into the house and follow the noise to outside. I see they have a tent set up outside, with round tables filling the backyard. Kids run around chasing after each other, and then I hear a shriek. I look over to see Lexi sitting there looking at me and shaking her head. I walk toward the table of women. "Oh my Lord," one of them says, and then Lexi gets up and comes to me. She's wearing another pair of jeans and a one-shoulder cream shirt. My hands comes up to rub her arms when she stands in front of me.

She lifts both of my arms to the sides and then looks behind me and then comes back to the front. "No battle scars." She laughs and I pull her closer to me.

"I haven't told you that you look beautiful today," I say, looking into her eyes, seeing them clear and carefree, "and I missed you."

She steps closer to me. "Yeah, is that so?"

I nod my head. "Yeah, baby, that is so."

"I sort of missed you too," she admits, looking up at me and one of my hands goes to her neck.

"Keep that thought in mind," I tell her. "You'll have to show me how much you sort of missed me." I kiss her lips.

"What was all that guys meeting about?" she asks me.

"Can we talk about it later?" She nods her head.

"Ready to meet the girls?" I don't know if she's asking me or telling me. "Because they are ready to meet you."

"Is that so?" I smile at her and can't help but kiss her again.

"He looks at her as if there is no one else in the room," one of them says, and Lexi laughs under my kiss.

"That's my aunt Zara," she mumbles. "My mother's twin."

"Oh, there are two of them?" I deadpan. "Fun." She laughs as she spins around and slips her hand in mine as she turns and heads toward the table.

"Ladies," she sings and I have never met this Lexi. I suddenly hate Trent even more for suppressing her. "I'd like for you guys to meet my boyfriend," she says, giggling.

"Whoa," Zara says, getting up and coming to me, "he's got a title, people." She smirks. "Hey, Kirby." I'm expecting for her to extend her hand but she comes in for a quick hug. "I mean, Lexi's boyfriend."

"I like the sound of that." I look back at Lexi, who lifts one of her shoulders and bats her eyes.

"It's nice to meet you." A woman holds up her hand. "I'm Zoey"—I look at Zoe—"with a y, named after the best one at the table."

"Oh please," Zara groans, and I know it's Zara because Zoe puts her hand in the air like she's raising the roof. The two of them are identical and it'll take some time to get to know which one is which. "It's nice to meet you," she says to me and I nod my head.

"Likewise," I reply.

"Let's sit," Zara suggests, leading me to the table, with me looking back at Lexi, who just giggles. I'll make sure I do whatever I need to do for the rest of my life to hear that giggle.

I sit at the table and look around it. "Okay, ladies." I look over and hold out my hand for Lexi, who comes to stand next to my chair. I take her hand in mine, kissing the top of it before I let it go. She wraps her arm around my shoulders and I hold her around her waist, pulling her to my side. "Fire away, I am an open book."

"I have one," Zoey says. "Are you close to your

parents?"

"No. My father passed away when I was very young, and my mother remarried someone who was not a nice man. He died and is probably rotting in hell, and then my mother passed not too long after him."

"Well, that's a buzzkill," the girl with black hair states. "I'm Gabriella, by the way. Welcome to my home."

"Thanks for having me." I nod at her. "But I do have a sister and we are very close."

"She's amazing," Lexi praises. "You'll meet her tomorrow at the game."

"I have a question." Zoe holds up her hand. "Why Lexi?"

"Oh, good one," her twin, Zara, says.

"Well, that's an easy one." I look up at her. "Besides the fact that she's drop-dead gorgeous." I smile. "She's kind, she's compassionate, she puts everyone else before herself. She's resilient and fiercely loyal. She's funny. She literally lights up the room with the way she smiles. She is also one of the strongest women I've ever met." She bends to kiss my lips. "And those are just a couple of reasons off the top of my head."

"Good answer," Zoe and Zara say at the same time. I don't know how long it goes on, but I answer every single question until Lexi holds up her hand.

"Okay, okay, enough grilling Kirby, it's time to go," she says and I get up, following her lead. It takes another thirty minutes to say goodbye to everyone, and I even offer them my suite for the hockey game tomorrow.

We walk out and she puts her hand in mine. "I have

my SUV," she mentions, and I shake my head.

"I took a cab here," I tell her and she walks over to her SUV and I open the passenger door.

"Wow, are you doing the whole 'you can't drive because I'm here and I'm a man' thing, Kirby?" She cocks her hip to the side.

"No, I'm doing the whole you can't drive because I think you drank an entire bottle of wine, Lexi," I toss back and she giggles.

"Oh, yeah." She hands me the keys. "Good call." She kisses my neck and gets into the SUV, and I shut the door before walking around and getting in.

"Are you coming back to my house?" I ask her and she looks over at me.

"I need a couple of things from home," she says and I pull out of the driveway and head toward her house.

"So…you love me?" I say as I drive us to her house, my heart beating loudly in my chest.

"I do. I think I've known for a while now. You've supported me and given me strength throughout these last few months even when you didn't know it. You've been patient with me and let me keep my light while making it shine brighter."

"I never knew I could be this happy. This carefree. I think I'd even go through the past ten years again if only for this feeling. Only for love." She puts her hand on my shoulder and then slips it to the back of my head as she plays with my hair. "I had fun tonight," she admits when I pull into her garage, "like a lot of fun." She opens the car door and jumps down. "I don't think I've ever had that much fun before."

I get out and wait for her at the front of the SUV and she slides her hand in mine as we walk into her house. The lights are on low in the kitchen as she walks toward her bedroom and I follow her. I go over to her bed, lying down on it, as she walks over to the chair in the corner and grabs her overnight bag. She comes over, putting it on the bed before walking to her closet and taking out a pair of jeans. "Why don't you pack a couple of outfits and leave them at my house?" I suggest to her and she looks up at me. "So you aren't, like, coming back and forth."

"But—" she says.

I smirk at her and put my hands on my stomach. "Or you can move in with me already."

"That's so romantic." She puts her hands over her heart. "Be still my heart."

I can't help but chuckle. "But seriously—"

"I'm still married." She shakes her head.

"So what, it's just a paper. You are still married to him on paper."

"It's a big paper."

"It's not that big of a paper or you wouldn't have had sex with me before you got divorced." I wink at her and she gasps.

"It's not right." She turns to grab a couple more pants.

"Says who?"

"I don't know!" Her voice shrieks. "Society?"

"This isn't the fifties, baby," I point out to her. "It's the twenty-first century. People are even living together without being married." She rolls her eyes at me.

"You were perfect in your marriage to a dickhead, so you might have missed a couple of things," I mumble.

"Nothing was ever perfect." She looks into my eyes. "It was just an illusion."

I smile so big my face hurts when I say the next words. "You, Lexi"—I get up and walk over to her—"you are perfect." I grab her face. "Now if you aren't finished packing in three seconds, we're going to end up sleeping here and only going back to my house in the morning."

"But Jefferson, believe it or not, doesn't like to be alone."

"I don't believe it." I move my hand from her cheek to her jawline. "I was home for an hour and a half and I never even saw her."

She gasps. "Oh my God! Did she get out?"

"No." I shake my head. "I think she was doing her own shit."

"We have to go and make sure she's there," she urges and I bend to kiss her neck.

"She's home. I saw her when I was leaving. She came out to drink water and then went back into the bedroom." I lick her collarbone. "Now, it's been five days without you, so we either fuck here or we fuck at my house. You decide, but make it fast."

Her hands grip my shirt. "How about we fuck here and then go to your house?"

"No can do," I deny, my hands roaming to her ass. "I plan to fuck you so hard you pass out."

"Ugh, I can't focus when you are touching me."

"This wouldn't happen if we lived together." I move my tongue lower and push her top down, her strapless bra covering her nipples. "See? More benefits to us living together." I chuckle before taking her nipple in my mouth and she pushes me away.

"I can't concentrate when I'm worried about Jefferson. So you are going to have to hold your horse there for a bit."

"My horse? You mean my bull. A bull is bigger than a horse."

"You men and your dicks." She rolls her eyes, moving past me and rushing around the room, pulling up her shirt. It takes her a full three minutes before she packs what needs to be packed and we are walking out of her house and toward the garage.

The drive to my house is the longest drive of my life, but that's only because she keeps rubbing her hand on my leg, unaware that it is driving me crazy. We pull up to my house, and when I grab her bag and follow her inside, I smile when she says, "Jefferson, we're home."

Thirty-Five

LEXI

I'M IN THE middle of composing an email when the phone rings beside me. I look over to see it's Ryleigh and my blood turns cold. My stomach lurches and my palms get sweaty. I hate every fucking second of it. Picking it up, I put it to my ear instead of putting it on speakerphone.

"Hey," I answer with a smile and a shaky tone.

"Hey," she returns, her voice is filled with a sort of glee. "So," she starts and then stops, and I close my eyes. "I just got off the phone with Trent's lawyer." I lean back in my chair. "He was so happy to hear from me." She laughs and that makes me laugh. "Anyway, told him to take the twenty million and shove it up his client's ass sideways, no lube, obviously." I silently laugh because I can just imagine Trent's face at being told no. "They want to meet with us face-to-face."

"Why?" I ask, surprised, but not that surprised. This is Trent's MO. Get them in the room and then try to strong-arm them. I sit up in my chair, looking out the window, trying to press down the way my heart is beating erratically.

"So he can fuck with you." Ryleigh already knows his games.

"What if I say no?" I tap the desk with my index finger.

"Then he stalls," she replies reluctantly.

"So he wins," I groan, "again."

"No," she snaps. "You see, showing him you're not under his thumb anymore and how unbothered you are by him and his money will push him to another level. Trust me, I've known guys like him my whole life living in Hollywood."

"I don't know," I waffle, my voice trailing.

"They gave us two dates to work with."

"Fuck no," I snap. "If I do this, and apparently, I have to do this, I'm going to do it on my own time. I'm going to decide the date, not him."

"That's what I'm talking about," she cheers. "Figure out when it's good for you, and then I'll call them back."

"Okay, let me check my calendar," I tell her, "and I'll text you dates tonight, and you see on your end if they work. Then we will send them the acceptable dates."

"Sounds good," she says. "Lexi, you've got this."

"Yeah." I exhale. "Yeah, I do."

"A little bit more convincing next time." She laughs. "Got to run," she says and disconnects.

I sit at my desk for longer than I need to and then close up. I'm walking out to my car when the phone rings and

I look down to see it's Kirby. "Hello."

"Hey," he says softly. "Where are you?"

"Just leaving work," I tell him, opening my SUV door and getting in.

"It's after six. Is everything okay?" I sit in the seat and put my head back on the headrest. I'm literally twenty minutes late and he's calling to check up on me.

"Yeah, just had a call with Ryleigh," I huff out.

"Want me to come and get you?" he asks me and I can't help but smile.

"No, I'll be okay," I assure him. "Have you decided what you want to eat?"

"Why don't you come home and let me worry about that?" he suggests. "I'll see you soon."

"Okay."

"Lexi," he calls my name before I hang up, "drive safe, yeah?"

"I will."

"Love you," he replies, right before he hangs up and I pull out of the parking lot, headed over to his house.

I don't know why I'm surprised that he's outside waiting for me when I get there. He pulls open the driver's side door. "I was tracking you like you were my food delivery." He laughs, and when I step out, he takes me in his arms. "Hi, baby," he says, right before his lips kiss mine. "Let's get you inside."

I nod at him as he grabs my bag with one hand while holding my hand with the other. It's been two weeks since the big game. Since I introduced him as my boyfriend and since he asked me to move in with him. Two weeks since he beat Matty in the hockey game and two weeks of hurling insults back and forth about which team is better.

Living life with Kirby has been so blissful, it's almost as if he was made for me. He has not once walked into the room when I was on the phone with whoever I was on the phone with and told me to end it. He would come in, kiss my head, say hello, and then walk out, giving me privacy. It made me fall deeper and deeper in love with him than I already was.

"So," he starts when he sits next to me at dinner, "what has my baby frowning?" I fill him in with what Ryleigh said. "I want to be there."

"I don't think you can be there."

"I don't mean I want to be in the room, but I want to be there before and after," he restates. "I can give you my schedule and we can work around it. We'll fly in in the morning and out the same day."

"I want to get this over with as soon as possible."

"I agree. That way you can move in with me." He winks at me as I roll my eyes. "Now eat, so we can go for a walk on the beach."

It's something we started doing after dinner, walking on the beach and talking about our day. Then it would change to what we wanted to do in the next week, then the next month. It is easy with Kirby and I have to wonder if this is what a relationship is really supposed to be like. Effortless. The answer is always yes.

Two weeks later, I'm sitting in the back seat of a car

with Ryleigh next to me. She's been texting since we got into the car. I've been back in Phoenix for a whole twenty-five minutes, and I feel like my skin is about to crawl off my bones. I swallow down the bile that is threatening to come up.

"Relax," Ryleigh says from beside me, not even looking at me, "or at least get it all out now. I don't want them to know how bothered you are by him."

"I'm not bothered by him." I look over at her. "I'm bothered by being here," I say, annoyed that she saw right through me.

"Then be annoyed he made you come here." She smirks at me, putting her phone down and then she looks out the window. "We need to make a quick pit stop."

"Good. I'd like a shot of tequila."

Ryleigh laughs as we pull into a parking lot, and I spot a big black Cadillac Escalade. The door in the back is open and I see one foot coming out, a cowboy boot on his foot before I see the man stepping out. He's wearing jeans and a blue knit sweater. Aviator glasses cover his eyes as he watches the car approach him. My eyes go to the side when I see more movement, and I gasp when I see my uncles Matthew and Max there, also in jeans, but in sneakers. They also have aviator glasses.

"What in the world?" I ask, opening my door and stepping out.

"Hey, sweetheart," Matthew says. "I would like for you to meet Gabriel's great-uncle. Don't let the word great fool you." He mumbles out the last part.

"Casey," I say his name and he smiles at me, "it's so

nice to finally meet you."

"Pleasure is all mine," he replies.

"Okay, we don't have much time. Do you have it?" Ryleigh steps up to him as if the two of them are business partners.

"Right here," he confirms, handing her the brown envelope. "Have fun."

"You know I will," she assures him, then looks over to Matthew and Max. "You couldn't let him do this without showing up?"

Matthew pffts out, "This is my family."

"You showed up when it was his family." Ryleigh points to Casey.

"That's because you went, and you're my family," he counters and Ryleigh just shakes her head.

"Go and get 'em," Max says with a smirk. "See you later." He slaps Matthew on the arm before turning and walking back to the SUV.

"Do I want to know?" I ask Ryleigh, walking back to the waiting car, looking over my shoulder one last time.

"It's better if you don't." She gets in and her smirk is scary looking. I take out my phone, texting Kirby.

Me: My uncles Matthew and Max are here.

Kirby: I know. They are coming to my house after. Your father just got here.

"My parents are here?" I look over at Ryleigh.

"I'm not in charge of their travel schedule," she states and the car comes to a stop, and I look up at the office building. "Let's do this."

I grab my purse, step out of the car, and start to walk

toward the office. "Bury the nerves," she advises and then stops. "This motherfucker tried to get you to never talk about him again after making you miserable for the past ten years." I bite down. "He has fucked with you for the last time." I grip the handle of my purse even tighter. "Now, let's go in there and make him pay through his asshole."

I snort before walking in and heading toward the elevator. We step in, and when we walk out, we are faced with a receptionist. Ryleigh walks over to her while the other door pings open. The doors part and I see him— Trent. My eyes go big when I get a good look at him. His eyes have a purple-blue tint to them and the top of his nose is bandaged with a little strip.

He takes one look at me and gives me the whole up and down. "You look trashy," is the first thing he says and I laugh at him. I'm wearing a white linen skirt that reaches to my mid-thigh and a white, long-sleeved button-down shirt with blue flowers all over it. When Kirby saw my outfit, he picked me up and fucked me on the counter.

"Thanks." I smile at him. "That's the look I was going for." The bigger my smile is, the more he glares and hisses. "You look…" I take him in, his hair perfect, outfit perfect, but his face looks a bit battered. "Well, you look like shit."

"I was conveniently mugged," he hisses at me. "Probably your thug family."

I laugh. "There is no way it would be my family."

"Yeah, right." He shakes his head.

"If it was my family," I state calmly, "you'd be

drinking out of a straw, and you would have to be wheeled in here because they would make sure to break every single bone in your body." His eyes pop out of his head. "Maybe it's one of your fuck buddies' husbands who got wind of whatever it is you do with them." I shrug, not giving a shit and Ryleigh is right, fuck him. "Either way, I don't really care."

"Lexi," Ryleigh says my name and I look over at her, and she motions with her head, not even taking Trent into her eyesight. I walk to her. "You good?" she mumbles as we are being led down to the end of the hallway.

"Oh yeah," I confirm, "more than good."

"That's what I'm talking about," she praises as we are ushered in a conference room. A brown table is in the middle of the room with three chairs on each side, facing each other.

She pulls out the chair in the middle, putting her briefcase on the chair next to her, while I sit on the other side of her. "What happened to his face?" she asks, reaching into her bag and pulling out the envelope and a folder.

"He got mugged." I sit down, trying not to laugh. "He tried to blame my family. I told him if it was, he'd be in worse shape."

She snorts. "If it was us, no one would be able to find him," she mumbles. "I love when the bad guys get fucked." She stops talking when the door opens, and a gentleman dressed in a three-piece suit comes in. His white hair is thinning on the top, but healthy on the sides. He is followed by Trent, who just sneers at us. Ryleigh crosses her hands in front of her. "Gentlemen," she says, not getting up to extend her hand, "shall we get started?" She looks at her Rolex. "You are four minutes late."

"Have you given any more thought to our offer?" the man asks once he's sitting.

"Are you going to sign the NDA?" Trent snaps out.

"Not a chance in hell." I smile at him.

"Greedy bitch," he mumbles and Ryleigh cuts him off.

"If you don't control your client, this meeting will be cut very short and, trust me, you guys don't want that to happen," she warns. "Now, shall we get started?" She opens the folder. "My client is looking to get both houses, the marital one and the one that's, well"—she looks down at the papers—"his fuck pad." She grimaces. "And she would also want alimony."

"Fuck that," Trent spits, "she gets nothing. She came into this marriage with nothing, she leaves with nothing."

"I was hoping you would say that. First of all, you never asked her to sign a prenup, therefore, she is entitled to alimony. Either your attorney didn't explain that to you or you're not as smart as you think you are." His face turns beet red and he looks like he has steam coming out of his ears. "Second, this just goes to show how little you know about Lexi's family because if you did, then you would know they are wealthier and more powerful than you are. She actually came into this marriage with more money than you. However, it doesn't matter if she had zero money or if she was a billionaire when you got married, this marriage is over. She's entitled to alimony and it's time for you to pay up. And trust me, you will," Ryleigh says, smiling, opening the envelope Casey gave her. "Here are pictures of Mr. Yoder." She hands them the first paper of him with other women. She adds, "All taken from their Ring cam." I look over at her, trying not to gasp. "Many of them are married. The one who is a constant is Joyce." I can't help but laugh.

"You fucked your best friend's wife?" I shake my head. "How desperate do you have to be?"

"So what, he had affairs," his lawyer replies. "There is nothing illegal about that."

"You're right, there isn't." She looks at me. "That was just for fun. This"—she pulls out the paper—"Mr. Yoder started a nonprofit organization under shell companies in an effort to get the governor elected. Which as you know, Counselor, is highly illegal. If this gets out, Mr. Yoder—"

Trent interrupts her, "It's Dr. Yoder to you! I am the chief of neurosurgery at the hospital and you will respect me."

I lean back in my chair looking over at Ryleigh who chuckles. "It's funny that you're demanding respect when you gave none to my client. As I was saying, if this gets out, Trent." She doesn't even use his last name now, which I know must be killing him and I have to bite the inside of my cheek to stop from smiling in his face. "Well, let's just say that orange is going to be your new black. I'm sure the inmates will give you all the 'respect' you deserve." She pushes away from the table and I look up at her, not sure if I'm supposed to stand with her. We march out in unison, but I can see the smirk on her face as she walks over to the trash can in the corner and brings it back, putting it on the table, pushing it toward where Trent and his lawyer sit. "You can put the NDA in here where it belongs."

"That's blackmail!" Trent shouts and his lawyer just looks down.

"No, it's not. It's called a scorned wife whose husband was unfaithful for their whole marriage. Who brought women into their home and used to fuck them in her bed for fun just because he could," Ryleigh hisses. I want to say it bothers me, but the only thing I feel is the need to shower. "Who brought home an STI. Can you imagine what would happen if she actually said what she really wanted to say? To tell everyone what you've done in your marriage?" Ryleigh shakes her head. "The spiffy image that Dr. Yoder has would be tainted, to say the least. I mean, it's a running joke that he gets to fuck all the new nurses and then keeps them on rotation. Dangling their jobs in front of them. I also have a list of names we can call if we need to."

"After everything I put up with"—I shake my head—"this is the least you can do."

The lawyer looks at him. "She wants both houses. She also wants alimony"—she looks at them—"even if she gets remarried."

"So I'm going to have to pay for her and that creep who is worth nothing?" I snort, because if only he knew Kirby was Richie Rich rich.

"We'll give you twenty-four hours to think about it."

She puts away her papers. "After that, the deal is off the table." She looks at me as she pushes away from the table.

"I don't want her using my name," Trent blurts and now I can't help the snort that comes out.

"I haven't used that name since I left you," I inform him. "I'm a Petrov." I tilt my head to the side. "Something you tried to take away from me. Time's a ticking, Trent." I look at him glaring at me. "Also, get better." I point at him. "You are looking a little puffy. You should lay off the salt."

"Have a great day," Ryleigh adds in as we walk out of the room. Only when we get into the elevator and the door closes do I hold my hands up in the air. "How did that feel?"

"Better than you will ever know," I reply, composing myself as we step out and stopping when I see Kirby there in the lobby. He is walking back and forth and I look over at Ryleigh, who just smiles. "What are you doing here?"

"Came to make sure you were okay," he answers, and I step into his space, putting my hands on his chest.

"I'm okay." I look over at Ryleigh and I nod. "I'm more than okay." I turn back to him. "But I dare you to ask me what you asked me two weeks ago."

He smirks and bends to kiss my lips. "I dare you to move in with me, Lexi." He rubs his nose against mine.

I roll my eyes, trying to fake that I'm annoyed. "Okay." I finally smile big. "I'll move in with you."

Thirty-Six

KIRBY

"WHAT TIME DID you say your parents are going to be here?" I ask her as I take down the frames on top of her bed. It's been two weeks since her meeting with Trent. He called by the time we touched down in LA, four hours after the meeting, to accept her terms. Forty minutes ago, she signed the documents and she is officially divorced. Something we celebrated by me dragging her to bed, before she stripped the sheets and threw them in the wash.

"They should be here any second." She comes into the room wearing a pair of cutoff shorts and a white tank top. "Hey, I have to ask you something."

"Yeah," I say, taking down the second frame and placing it in the box.

"Every year my family has this big family vacation," she explains, leaning against the doorjamb. "It's usually in the summer when everyone is off." I nod, going to the third frame. "This year they are going to Turks."

"Oh fun." I stop taking the frame off and look at her. "What's going on?"

"I want to go," she says and I laugh.

"Okay," I say, not understanding.

"I didn't go for ten years," she starts to explain and I can feel her nervousness in the house.

"Baby." She looks up at me finally. "Do you want to go without me? Either way, it's fine."

"No," she refutes quickly, stepping into the bedroom. "That's the thing, I want to go and I want you to come."

"So we'll go," I state and then I laugh. "Is that what you're nervous about? Me going on your family vacation?"

"Well, I didn't know if you wanted to go or not, and I didn't want to go by myself."

"Lexi," I say, going for the third frame, "if there are get-togethers and I can go too, great. But if there are things I can't go to and you can still go to them, I want you to go to them." I look over at her. "If I can't go because of a game, I wouldn't want you to be stopped from going."

"Really?" she asks and then the doorbell rings.

"Really." I put the frame down and she turns to walk out of the room and toward the front door.

I step out into the living room at the same time her father lets her go and we share a nod before he comes into the living room. I take a step to him and extend my hand. "Good to see you, Mr. Petrov," I say and he looks at me, not saying a word and then looks around the room.

Zoe steps in. "Kirby," she says my name with a smile

on her face and comes to give me a hug.

"What is going on here?" Viktor snaps, looking at the packing boxes.

"Well," Lexi starts, coming to stand next to me, "that is why we asked you to come over here. Can I get you anything to drink?" She tries to keep it casual, looking at her mother, who is waiting for Viktor to say something.

"No," Viktor snaps. "What is all this?"

"I'm moving out," she tells them as she puts her hand in mine. "I signed the divorce papers today, so I'm officially Lexi Petrov."

"You were always Lexi Petrov." Viktor glares at her.

"I was, but then I had a mental judgment lapse and then I was that other name." She laughs. "But now I'm officially a Petrov again. Legally." She looks up at me. "And Kirby asked me to move in with him."

"And you said yes," Viktor surmises and I inhale, trying to keep my cool, since he is her father. "Is that"—he looks at his wife—"wise?"

Lexi wraps her arm around my waist. "Well, I love him and he loves me, so it was either that or get married."

"What?" I yelp out. "No." I look at her father. "That was not how it went."

"So, you don't want to marry my daughter?"

"Well, yeah," I backpedal, "of course, but I'm not sure—"

"That she is the one?" Viktor keeps putting words in my mouth.

"No." I hold up my hand. "I love your daughter, more than anything." I look at her. "And when I feel the time is right, I will ask her to be my wife. Honestly, I would take her now." She gasps. "But I know she's not ready for that, so we'll have to settle with her living with me because that's what she is willing to give me."

"Did you hear him?" Zoe asks Viktor who turns to her. "The whole time he spoke, it wasn't about him; it was about Lexi and what she wanted." She turns to smile at me. "You're a good one, Kirby."

"Pfft." Viktor rolls his eyes. "A good one would have asked her father if it was okay."

"Didn't Zara get pregnant with the twins and you hadn't even met Gabriel?" she mentions her sister.

"We met him," Viktor retorts. "Besides, we are not talking about your sister right now." He looks at Lexi. "We are talking about you and your choices." His voice goes higher.

"Okay." I hold up my hands. "Respectfully," I say to him, "let's bring the tone down a bit."

I'm expecting Lexi to tell me not to talk to her father like that. "Yeah, respectfully," she repeats.

"Watch your tone," Zoe says to him. "Now, sit down because our daughter obviously has something she wants to tell us, or she wouldn't have invited us here."

She starts to move to the couch and then stops. "Oh my God, are you pregnant?" She looks at Lexi.

"No," she says at the same time I mumble, "I wish.

"What?" I say, throwing my hands up. "How cool would that be, us having a baby?" I ask her and she bites down and her jaw gets tight. I've thought about it each and every single time I've seen her with Jagger. I lean in and whisper in her ear, "Seeing you pregnant with my baby turns me on like never before." I move away from her ear seeing her cheeks getting pink. "Not now, but if it happens," I say loudly.

"Can we move in with each other first?" Lexi says to me, walking over to the couch. "Anyway, that is not why I called you here, and I didn't call you here to discuss where I'm going to live either. The reason I called you here is because I signed my divorce papers officially today." She sits and her mother claps her hands together in celebration. "And with that, I got the house I hate and the apartment he used to have affairs in." Viktor looks to the ceiling and I'm sure he is holding on by a string, especially when he was told he wasn't allowed to go there and break his neck. "Anyway," she continues and he looks back at her. "I've obviously decided to sell both of those, along with my wedding ring and engagement ring. And with the profits, I'm going to use half of the money to open a women's shelter for battered and abused women in Arizona." She stuns us all. "The other half will go to the children's cancer unit. Since Kirby and I will be living there in the off-season and then once he retires. It made the most sense."

"Wait a second." I hold up my hand. "Who says we are going to be living there? You hate it there."

"I don't hate it there. I hated being there because it felt like it was my prison, but you have your house there and Kylie says you love it there." She shrugs. "So I want to go back there, with you."

"We don't have to do that." I put my hand on her

knee. "We can do that anywhere. As long as you're there, I don't care where we live."

"Good," she says. "I feel the same. I spoke with Cheryl, who is going to help run the shelter for me when I'm not there, and then I'm hoping to take a more active role once big man over here hangs up his skates."

"Shouldn't you keep some of that money for you, just in case?" Zoe asks and she shakes her head.

"I have everything I need. I'm going to keep this house and rent it out," she tells them. "Plus, I get alimony, which I plan to use to start building my real estate portfolio." Which again shocks me since she never spoke to me about it. She gets up. "Now, I have to continue packing since the movers will be here tomorrow morning, and we have a dinner thing tonight with Kirby and a couple of his teammates."

"Well, what can we do to help?" Zoe asks, getting up, and the four of us work side by side to pack up her house. It doesn't take long since she is only bringing her clothes and a few special mementos.

When we walk out of her house, she hugs her parents and we make plans to get dinner tomorrow after my game. I pull into the garage and look over at her smiling. "Welcome home, officially." I kiss her lips and then slip my hand in hers and pull her into the house. The lights are off, and then when she walks into the living room, I hear the roar of "Surprise!" fill the house.

She takes a step back, not sure what is going on, and I step in behind her. "Surprise, baby," I whisper in her ear and look around to see that Sofia did not fuck around.

"What is this?" She has her hands over her mouth as she looks around.

"It's your divorce party." Kylie rushes up to her first. "The brute over here"—she points to me—"had me write the words 'not' on the 'single and ready to mingle' napkins." She moves out of the way as her aunt Zara and uncle Evan come up to her to give her a hug. Matthew and Max are next, with their wives, Karrie and Allison.

Then she sees her sister, Zara, and she bends her knees and looks like she's going to sit on the floor. "You didn't think I'd miss this party, did you?" She picks her up from the floor. "Come on, let's get you changed."

"I need a hug," she hears from the side, and when she turns her head, she sees Matty there, and that is the straw that breaks the camel's back. She literally sobs in his arms as he whispers something in her ear and she nods her head. "I'm here until eleven and then I have to get on a flight to head back home."

"You came," she croaks out when she lets him go, "all this way for me."

"Lexi." He looks at her. "I would scale Everest for you." Then he looks at me. "After him, that is."

"Let's get her changed," Zara urges, pulling her toward our bedroom. I watch her go and then turn to look at everyone. Zara comes out a couple minutes later. "You can go and get changed also," she tells me. "I think she's still in shock."

I walk to the bedroom and open the door and stick my head in. She's sitting on the bench in front of our bed. "You okay?" I ask her, walking into the room and she looks up at me with tears running down her face. "Baby." I squat down in front of her.

"You planned that party?" she asks me and I look at her. "Like, you called Sofia."

"Well, I couldn't exactly plan a party like this without help." I smile at her and put my hand on her cheek.

"But you called her—"

"Your mother gave me her number," I cut in.

"You called my mother?" she asks, sobbing.

"Baby," I say. "Lexi." I kiss the top of her head as she cries.

"Do you know how big that was?" she asks me, wiping away her tears with the back of her hand.

"No." I laugh. "I just figured it would be a nice thing to do."

"No, Kirby." She finally stops and smiles through her tears. "For ten years I can count on one hand how many times he spoke to my family." I look down at the floor. "For ten years I've had birthdays that he would sometimes forget, and then other times make a big deal about it just in front of people. But never…" She shakes her head. "Never did he reach out to my family to invite them to one." Her bottom lip quivers. "So you have given me in one day what he never gave me." She leans forward and kisses my lips. "You accept them, craziness and all, and never, ever back down."

"Baby, they make you happy," I finally say. "They are a part of you, of course I accept them. They may not like me half the time, but it's not about me, it's about you. It's about making you smile. It's all about you, baby."

"I really want to do dirty things to you right now." She gets up and I shake my head. "But my whole family is in your house."

"Our house," I remind her. "It's our house."

"That whole sentence, and that is the only thing that bothered you about it." She shakes her head. "My whole family is here."

"Almost," I tell her. "Couple couldn't come because they were playing, like Dylan and Michael. But they said they are going to help celebrate you this summer."

"Kirby Materson," she says my full name, "I love you so much. You are too good for me."

"Oh please. Go get changed. They are waiting for you."

She nods her head as she rushes to the bathroom, where I know her aunt Zara hung up the dress she bought her. She is in and out of the shower by the time I head back in there. I've showered and I'm sliding on my black dress pants when she walks into the room. "Can you zip me?" She holds the dress to her chest, and I kiss her shoulder before zipping her up. She turns and I take her in. Her hair is parted down the middle, very much like the first time I met her. The dress is strapless and black and hugs her every single curve. It looks like it dips in the front, showing off just a touch of skin. It goes until her mid-calf, but there is a slit on her left side that goes all the way to the middle of her thigh. Silver beading starts at the left hip and moves all the way up diagonally and then forms a flower that takes over the whole right side where her breast is. She has diamond earrings that hang down to her shoulders, and she is wearing her black strappy heels that I love. "How do I look?" she asks me and I slip my jacket on and smile at her.

"More beautiful than I've ever seen you look," I answer her honestly. "You have a lightness in your eyes now that radiates all over your face, and I plan on spending my days making sure that the look never goes away." I grab her hand in mine and kiss the top of it. "Now let's get out there, shall we?"

"I'm so excited," she chatters when we walk out of our bedroom and she is giddy like a kid in a candy store.

I get to the steps that lead to the party and I whistle so I can get everyone's attention. All eyes come my way when I say, "I present to you the newly divorced but still not single"—I wink at her, holding up the hand I'm holding—"Lexi Petrov."

Epilogue One

LEXI

Seven months later

"SO, AS OF Monday they will start painting the walls," Cheryl says, her voice is filled with excitement and amazement. "It's so pretty and it was such a cool idea to do the shelter in one of the abandoned churches with an attached school."

Once the divorce papers were signed, the first thing I did was put the apartment up for sale, and it sold in three days, going over asking price. I smiled the whole time. As soon as I put the house on the market, my realtor told me about a space that had just become available. It was built to be a church, but they ran out of funding. Which meant that I went in with a lowball offer, and it was approved the very same day. It was as if it was meant to be.

The minute I got the keys, I flew down there to do a walk-through with a construction team and hired a project manager to oversee it since I wasn't going to be living there. He was a dream come true, and Cheryl has been the biggest help of all.

"I figured we can even do an after-school program for the children in the area," I fill her in with another section I plan to add once we get up and running, "but for now it'll be a safe haven for those who need it."

"I've reached out to the shelters that are in the area and told them about what we are doing. They were floored we are so advanced already. They said they were turning away up to fifty people a week."

"That's a lot of beds," I tell her. "The good news is we can now help out and bring in some more resources."

"It's the talk of the town," she starts to say. "You should also know that Trent—" She stops. "Well, I don't know if you care or not."

"I mean, when it has to do with him, there really is not much I care about, but for shits and giggles, what has he done now?"

"One of his old receptionists has just sued him for sexual harassment." I look at the ceiling. "She has a lot of evidence against him, including a couple of pictures of certain parts of his body that, as a boss, he should not be sending to someone who works for him."

"Well, I've seen it and it's probably not a big picture," I deadpan and she bursts out laughing. "Frankly, I'm surprised it took this long."

"Well, the best part is it's Dr. Visabell's granddaughter, and to say he's pissed is an understatement."

"Sadly, he might be a douchebag but he's good at his

job, so he'll always be in demand."

"That is the sad part," she agrees, "but Joyce, who left Bernie to be with him, is now trying to win Bernie back, but he's already moved on."

"Well, the grass isn't always greener on the other side of the fence. Sometimes it's just covering the layer of shit that is under it." I smile.

"You should know that Dr. Visabell asked about you the other day, after he heard about what you were doing. He said he is going to reach out to you."

"I'll let you know when he does," I assure her.

"Okay, I'll keep you posted on the progress of the construction timeframe," she states, "but only if there is something that needs your attention. Enjoy the time with your family, and I'll see you in three weeks."

"Thank you, Cheryl," I reply, smiling when I think about the family trip we leave for tomorrow. "I couldn't do this without you."

"I look forward to having you with us for the summer," she says before she disconnects and my phone beeps with incoming texts, one after another.

I smile when I see the group chat they created for the family vacation.

Zara: I can't wait to be lounging on the beach, without a care in the world. I don't want to see my kids for the whole time we are there.

I snort because she says that now, but three hours later she'll be searching for them.

Zoey: Sign me up, please. I'll have a cocktail right now.

Gabriella: We get in two days after you guys, sadly. Romeo and his stupid movie.

Ryleigh: Sucks to be you. I have a whole month off and I plan to do nothing but drink and have sex. At least for two weeks, the other two weeks will be recovery mode. I'm not twenty anymore.

Zoey: Eeww, that's my brother.

Zara: Eewww, no one wants to know that.

Ryleigh: Just keeping it real. Everyone knows I fell in love with Stone's dick before I fell in love with him.

Zoey: If you bring up my brother and his dick one more time, I'm kicking you out of this group chat.

Zara: When are we doing a girls' spa day?

Zoey: Every day.

I laugh and add on to the text messages.

Me: I am almost packed and ready to go. I can't wait.

I put the phone down when I hear the front door open and then shut. "Lexi." I hear Kirby call out my name.

"In the office." I lean back in my chair and then watch the office doorway, waiting for him to walk through it. He surprised me one day by converting one of the bedrooms into a home office so I can have all my things in one place. He obviously called Ariella and let her design it and she was spot-on. The light-brown desk is in the middle of the room on top of a plush white carpet. The wood floors are bleached, so it makes the carpet pop more. He had built-in shelves installed behind me and they are filled with pictures of my family. Two big, cushioned chairs are in front of the desk.

My eyes go to the wall facing the desk, where the

seven frames he gave me for my house are hanging on the wall that face my desk, right above the big couch. A reminder of everything I've been through to get to this point. A coffee table is in between the two chairs and the couch and has a vase filled with colored flowers. Something he gets me every other week, after he heard the story about how Trent made me throw away the pink flowers.

I hear the bell on Jefferson's collar alongside Kirby's steps walking down the hall. "Are you following me," he asks her and the smile on my face gets even bigger, "or are you going to your favorite hangout?"

I will say that Jefferson spends most of her days on the couch, where I've bought her a nice blanket for her to lie on. She, of course, lies there with her back to you, and if you get on the couch next to her, she looks at you with dragon eyes, and I think secretly plots your murder.

"Hey," he greets, walking into the room, holding Jefferson in his arms, cuddled like a baby. The minute he gets to the couch, he drops her on her blanket.

"Hey." I watch him walk around the desk and come to me, bending and kissing me on the lips—one, twice, three times. "How was your day?"

"Good." He takes off his baseball hat and tosses it in one of the chairs in front of my desk. The chair also has the hat he was wearing two days ago still sitting in it. "How are you doing? Are you packed?"

"Almost." I lean forward on my desk. "I have a couple of things to throw in there and then I'll be good to go." I look at him and he flops down in one of the chairs. "You have yet to pack," I remind him.

"I don't pack to go to Arizona," he tells me, "so I just have to pack for Turks."

"You don't take any stuff from here to Arizona?" I ask him and he shakes his head. After Turks, we are going straight to Arizona.

"I have all my stuff there. Whatever you take there this time should just stay there. Or don't take anything and just go shopping once you get there."

"Oh, just like that? Get a new wardrobe," I say as if it's nothing.

"Um yeah." He nods. "Take Kylie with you. She knows where my card is." Kylie is also going to be coming to Arizona with us for a couple of weeks, at least after the vacation.

"I'm not spending your money," I huff out, getting up and walking around the desk, and he opens his arms for me to sit on his lap. "It's enough you won't let me pay for rent or anything in this house."

"Lexi," he mumbles my name as I wrap my arm around his neck and cuddle closer into him. "I want to be the one who takes care of you. We know that you can take care of yourself. You've proved that, but with this, I'm taking care of you." He gets up with me in his arms. "Now come with me and pack." He carries me to our bedroom that I've added stuff to. Next to my side of the bed is a picture of us from my divorce party, and on his side of the bed, he's opted with a picture of just me from that night. I'm looking directly at the camera, a champagne glass in my hand and a huge smile on my face. My other hand is pointed at the camera, the smile on my face goes from ear to ear. Then behind that one is the picture of me in the stands at a game, standing with his jersey on, celebrating one of his goals. The last picture on his table is of me and Jefferson.

"How long are we going to be in Turks?" he asks me, setting me on my feet. "Two weeks, right?"

"Yes," I reply, walking over to his closet and picking out six T-shirts. "The house has a washing machine."

"It does." He comes over and grabs a handful more, not even counting as he dumps them on one side of the open suitcase that he set up while I was choosing the ones I wanted. "But we're on vacation."

"Do you know how much laundry we are going to have if you don't wash for fourteen days?"

"Nope." He shakes his head, going to one of the drawers that holds his shorts. "But I know I will have nothing but time and a good dry cleaner who can wash them for me once we get back."

I roll my eyes. "Kirby, seriously," I chide and he looks at me like I have two heads.

"Baby, you have your work to keep you busy and I have a couple of golf games to play. I have off-ice training and a couple on-ice training sessions, but usually it's very relaxed during the summer," he scoffs. "Ask Kylie."

"I'm so happy she's coming with us," I mention, grabbing a couple of linen shirts for him. "She's going to have such a good time." I grab two pairs of dress pants. "I'm going to miss her," I admit to him. "We'll be gone for almost four months."

"Lexi," he says my name, "you know she can come and visit us when she wants."

"But will she?" I ask him and he just shrugs. "I'm going to go and call her."

"Use my phone." He pulls his phone out of his pocket and hands it to me. The picture of us that is on my nightstand is on the locked screen on his phone. I see he has five missed calls from Jaxon.

"Kirby, Jaxon has called you five times," I tell him and his eyebrows pinch together, as I hand him back the phone.

"He sent me five texts also," he says and I see his eyes looking at his phone and then hear him gasp. "Oh, man." He looks up at me. "Knox just found his wife in bed with his brother-in-law."

ONLY FOR HIM

KYLIE

Fling with an emotionally unavailable single dad?

Shouldn't have been a problem.

He only had time for hockey and his kids.

It was safe to fall into bed with him because no way would I fall for him.

I didn't want anything real.

He wasn't going to love me.

Except sometimes our hearts don't give us a say.

KNOX

Knox

I thought I had it all.

I was playing pro hockey.

Three beautiful kids and a wife who loved me.

Until I walked in on her in bed with my brother-in-law.

Everything I thought I had was a lie.

But Kylie became my truth.

She was everything I thought I didn't want, and when I least expected it.

I just hope when I finally figure it out, I haven't lost her for good.

Epilogue Two

KIRBY

Ten days later

"KIRBY," I HEAR her call my name and I look up from the sun chair and see her wearing one of her bikinis as she walks to me, "will you come in the water with me?" She dusts off the sand she has on her bottom from sitting in it not too long ago with her cousins.

"For you"—I raise my aviator glasses to look at her before getting off the daybed I was just lying in while I watch her laugh—"anything." I slide my hand in hers as we walk down the soft sand toward the water. The warm water runs over our feet once it hits the sand as we walk into the water.

"It's so warm," she says to me as we get to our waist and then walk in a bit more before I duck down to my knees and pull her to me. She wraps her legs around my waist and then wraps her arms around my shoulders. "This is the best part of my day." She kisses my neck.

"I love you," I declare as she moves her arms to the sides so I can see her face. She has little freckles that started coming out once she got in the sun. For the past ten days, she's been spending most of her time with the girls. Making sure she gets her fill of them, while I sat back and watched her flourish day by day.

When we got here, she was a bit unsure of how she would fit in, since everyone had been going to this family trip for the last ten years. But Zara made sure she never felt left out. The two of them stuck together like glue and it was as if she had been on this trip every year for the past ten years. "Did you have fun at the spa?"

"So much fun." She smiles. "It's been the best time and in four days it's over." Her voice trails off.

"Baby, why don't you invite them to come and stay with us in Arizona?"

She shrugs. "They all have busy lives."

"So, then, we'll take off on weekends and go visit them," I tell her. "Gabriel said we can stay at one of his properties, and he'll let me hang with him so you and Zara can do your own thing."

"You would do that?" she asks me and I laugh.

"Don't you get it already? I'll do whatever it is you want to do."

"You are too good to me." She puts her hands on my shoulders. "And for that, I shall give you a special present tonight." I lift my eyebrows and she just laughs.

"Are you guys banging in there?" Matty shouts from the sand. "Some of the kids want to come in."

"Are you insane?" Lexi shouts back. "You were the

one caught in the bushes the other day."

"My wife fell into them while she was trying to walk, thinking she was a Victoria's Secret fashion model!" he shouts back. "I was pulling her out of them."

"I knew you guys had a big family," I tell her, "but I didn't know that it was so big." I look over at the beach and see it's packed. There are about fifty daybeds all scattered around the private beach. There are two man-made bars that are also set up and five people walking around filling drinks. The nighttime dinner is complete chaos, with kids running everywhere, a couple of them crying, overtired, and some just giving up and falling asleep where they are. But it's the best type of chaos I've ever seen.

"Auntie Lexi!" Colson shouts her name. "Zara is looking for you; she said it's shots o'clock." Lexi laughs as she lets her legs go from around my waist and we walk out of the water, hand in hand.

"After this, I want to go back to the house and rest before dinner," she tells me and I nod at her as she gets on her tippy-toes and kisses my jaw before going over to Zara, who holds a tray of shots. The men in the background groan, telling them no more shots.

I wait for her to take the shot before she walks over to me, grabbing her flip-flops from the daybed that we lay on most of the day when she wasn't with her family members. I spot Kylie in the water with a couple of the girls and lift my hand, telling her we are heading to the house. She holds up her hand and then turns to continue her conversation, fitting in with Lexi's family perfectly.

"Hey," I say. "I'm going to go and get a couple of bottles of water from the restaurant. They didn't restock the fridge yet," I tell her as I stick my head into the bathroom. She's getting out and wrapping herself in a towel. "Do you want anything?"

"I have some water by the bed," she informs me and I look over to see a whole bottle of water there.

"I want a beer," I lie to her. "I'll go get one and come back."

"Are you okay?" she asks me. "You're acting weird."

"I'm fine. I'll just be back in a little bit."

"Okay, bring me back a snack." I inwardly moan because now I'm really going to have to go to the restaurant and get her a bag of chips.

"Got it." I rush out before she asks me something else and stop when I see Kylie walking in with two bags of chips. "Hey, can I borrow one?" I ask her and she looks at me weird. I just take a bag and rush out and head down the pathway to Viktor's house.

I walk up the steps and hear laughing coming from somewhere, but my hands are sweaty and it has nothing to do with the hot weather. I knock on the door and then look down at my feet when I hear footsteps coming to the door. My stomach feels like I'm going to throw up. The door is pulled open and Viktor stands there in a pair of golf shorts and a golf shirt. "What do you want?" he mumbles.

"I was wondering if I can talk to you," I tell him. "I

just need five minutes of your time.”

“No,” he snaps, and he’s going to shut the door in my face when Zoe comes into the room wearing a long silk kimono.

“Who is it?”

“No one,” Viktor clips and Zoe tilts her head to the side.

“Kirby,” she calls my name, coming to me, “is everything all right?”

“Yeah,” I reply. “I was just wondering if I could have a couple minutes of your time.”

“Of course,” she says, while Viktor snaps out, “No,” behind her. She laughs, pushing him out of the way and opening the door for me to step in.

“Do you want something to drink?” she asks me as she puts her arm in mine and takes me to the couch.

“I’m good, thanks,” I assure her, sitting down and seeing Viktor sit down on the couch in front of me and Zoe sits next to him. “Wow.” I laugh out nervously while rubbing my hands on the front of my pants. “This is a bit harder than I thought it would be.”

“So perhaps you shouldn’t say anything.” Viktor glares at me. “Just get up and leave.”

“Oh, would you shush?” Zoe slaps his leg. “Give him a chance, he’s nervous.” She smiles at me. “Whatever it is, you don’t have to be nervous.”

“Mr. and Mrs. Petrov,” I start off, “I hope it comes as no surprise that I’m in love with your daughter.”

“It’s not,” Zoe says with a smile.

“I did doubt it a couple of times,” Viktor states,

leaning back on the couch and putting one of his legs on the other, "more often than not, to be honest."

That makes me laugh because I know he's lying to my face. "I love your daughter." I look him in the eyes. "I would be honored to ask for your daughter's hand in marriage," I say, and Zoe gasps and puts a hand to her mouth.

"No," Viktor says, shaking his head. "Absolutely not."

"Okay," I say, somehow knowing this would be coming, "here is the thing. I love her more than I love anything in this world."

"That is good to know," Viktor says. "Thank you for telling us. If that is all"—he starts to get up—"I'm going to shower."

"I respect you to the highest degree, and I know having her family back in her life is a dream come true for her."

"You saying something?" he asks me, tilting his head to the side.

"I'm going to ask her to marry me tonight, regardless of what you say."

"So why come all this way and ask us for our blessing if you are just going to do it anyway?"

I don't answer him because the front door opens and Matty comes in. "Mom!" he shouts, "Sofia." He stops talking when he sees us. "What's going on in here?"

"Kirby is asking us for your sister's hand in marriage," Zoe says with a smile and tears.

"We told him no," Viktor retorts, "and he's going to

do it anyway."

"Good," Matty declares. "Why would you even say no to him?"

"Because it's too fucking soon," Viktor barks. "She just got divorced."

"Seven months ago," I point out.

"You should be thanking him"—Matty puts his hands on his hips—"for bringing your daughter back to you." I watch the father-and-son showdown. "This time last year we sat down at the beach and what did you tell me?" he asks his father. "You said I'd give anything in the world to have her back." Viktor rolls his eyes. "You would look at everyone with a smile and then you would get that faraway look, like a part of you was missing. I saw it, Mom saw it. Zara saw it. Fuck, everyone saw it."

"This isn't about me." Viktor stands up. "It's about my daughter and—"

"The man who loves her," Zoe puts in for him.

"You know he's part of the reason she's back, right?" Matty says, motioning to me with his head. "You know if it wasn't for his friendship, she would probably still be with Trent. That if it wasn't for him"—he points to me—"getting in his face and making him say shit that I will never fucking repeat, she would probably still be with him and you wouldn't have your whole family together under one roof."

"I might not be the one you would choose for her"—I stand up—"but I vow to spend the rest of my life making her happy."

"We couldn't be happier," Zoe says, coming to me

and giving me a hug.

"Who is we?" Viktor asks.

"Why would you even tell him no?" Matty snorts. "Like, what was the reason?"

"He said no to Gabriel also," Zoe reminds him, "but that was also because he got Zara pregnant after a couple of weeks of dating."

Matty claps his hands, laughing. "They weren't even dating. She had just broken off her engagement and she got knocked up."

"Matty," Zoe warns him.

"I'm just saying." He holds his hands up.

"Why don't you stop saying and mind your business?" Viktor snaps.

"Love you, Dad," he says to him. "You are my hero forever, but even you know there is no one else who is better for her than him. Fuck, the other one didn't even ask you to marry her, he just eloped with her and refused for you guys to throw them a celebration."

"Let's not talk ill of the dead," Zoe hisses.

"He isn't dead." Matty chuckles.

"He is to us." Zoe glares at him. "Now, you have our blessing," she says to me and then turns to Viktor. "Tell him." Viktor just looks at her. "Viktor, if you tell him no and he tells her, how do you think she is going to feel?"

"Bad," Matty says for him. "She's going to feel bad because she finally has a guy who wants to be around her family. Fuck, this whole vacation you've said maybe two words to him. He goes to the beach and watches her the whole time to make sure she's okay." He turns to me.

"It's a little creepy, but I get it."

"She was nervous," I finally say and then stop myself when Viktor snaps.

"What do you mean she was nervous? We're her family," he asks softly.

"She was afraid she wouldn't fit in since it had been so long," I fill them in. "So I was watching to make sure she was okay." I put my hands on my hips. "Now I have to get back to her because she thinks I went to get a beer."

"You don't drink beer." Matty laughs at me.

"I know, but my first excuse was shot down, so I had to think on my feet."

"Well, you suck at it," Viktor retorts. "If you hurt her," he warns and I shake my head.

"Trust me." I hold up my hands. "If that happens, you can do whatever it is you want to me."

"Then fine," he grumbles, "but the second you make her sad."

"When are you doing it?" Zoe asks me and I smile.

"As soon as I get back," I confide to her. "It's been ten days I've been lugging the ring around."

"Let me see it," Zoe says and I pull the ring out of my pocket and open it to show it to her. "Oh my God."

"That's ridiculous," Matty states. "How big is that?"

"Ten carats," I answer. "The last one was five. I had to double that up."

He nods at me like "oh yeah, true." "Go," Zoe urges, "and we shall celebrate tonight, and tomorrow we will throw you guys an engagement party."

"She didn't say yes yet," Viktor interjects. "Until she

says yes, we don't celebrate anything."

I laugh and nod, walking out of the room while Matty tells him that he's ridiculous. I make it back to the house at the same time she's walking out of our bedroom. She's wearing a dress that is crocheted and goes off her shoulder, but it looks like it's hanging in the front. A white slip is under the bottom until her mid-thigh and then it's all bare leg. "You look beautiful."

"Thank you," she replies. "Now, what's up with you?"

"Nothing. Why?" I ask her and my mouth gets dry.

"Well, number one, you don't drink beer." She holds up her hand and I turn my hand around.

"Come for a walk with me?" I ask her softly, and she comes to me and slips her hand in mine. We step out of the house and go to the deserted beach, not one person in sight.

"So are you going to tell me where you went?" she asks softly as the gentle waves hit the sand.

"I went to talk to your dad," I tell her and she looks up at me.

"For what?"

"Well," I start to say, "I had to ask him something."

"Was it for the foundation?" she asks me and I shake my head.

"It was for something bigger," I admit to her and stop walking, "something way bigger."

"Kirby," she says my name, and I let go of her hand and get down on one knee in front of her. The moonlight is shining on us as if I planned it.

"Lexi," I say her name, "the first day I met you, I

thought you were the most beautiful woman in the world." I smile at her. "Then I got to know you and I found out you were beautiful inside and out. Every single day I fall more and more in love with you. Your kindness, your laughter, your empathy, your loyalty are just a few reasons as to why. I promise you; no one will work harder to make you happy or cherish you more than me. You are the love of my life and I can't imagine my future without you in it." I pull out the box and open the top, happy that it comes with a little light for her to see the ring. "Will you do me the honor of becoming my wife"—I smirk—"and Jefferson's mom?"

She sobs in her hands and all she can do is nod her head. I slip the ring on her finger and she doesn't even look at it. Instead, she jumps into my arms and I catch her just like she knows I'm going to catch her for the rest of my life.

She puts her hand on my face. "I'm going to make sure you never go to bed without knowing how much I love you," she declares. "For the rest of my life, I'm going to make our home a happy one. For the rest of my life, our family, our kids, will know what true love is because living with you by my side is as easy as breathing." I smile. "Thank you for giving me back life and for breathing for me, even when I didn't know you were doing it." She kisses me. "I can't believe you asked my father." She laughs.

"He said no," I tell her and she laughs even more.

"He didn't mean it," she says, getting back on her feet. "He likes you."

"Oh yeah, I'm sure he does," I mumble as she laughs and then looks at the ring. "Come on," I urge, "your mother wants to be the first one to see it on your finger."

"She said that?" she asks me.

"Not in so many words," I tell her as we walk back to the houses.

We take a step into the clearing and then I see them. I don't know how they all got there so fast, but the roar of cheers goes up and Lexi jumps up and squeals, "I'm getting married!"